PENGUIN CLASSICS

THE MISER AND OTHER PLAYS

MOLIÈRE was the stage name of Jean Baptiste Poquelin, the son of a wealthy merchant upholsterer. He was born in Paris in 1622. At the age of twenty-one he resigned the office at Court purchased for him by his father and threw in his lot with a company of actors, to found the so-styled 'Illustre Théâtre'. The nucleus of the company was drawn from one family, Béjarts. Armande, the youngest daughter, was to become his wife.

Failing to establish themselves in Paris, the company took to the Provinces for twelve years. When in 1658 they returned to the capital it was with Molière as their leader and a number of the farces he had devised as their principal stock in trade. Invited to perform before Louis XIV, Molière secured his staunch patronage. In 1659 *Les Précieuses ridicules* achieved a great success, which was confirmed by *L'École des femmes* three years later. With *Tartuffe*, however, Molière encountered trouble; it outraged contemporary religious opinion and was forbidden public performance for several years. *Don Juan* also had a controversial history. *Le Misanthrope*, first played in 1666, is generally accorded to be the peak of Molière's achievement. Among plays that followed were *L'Avare*, *Le Médecin malgré lui*, *Les Femmes savantes*, *Amphitryon*, and *Le Bourgeois Gentilhomme*, one of the comedy-ballets to which Lully contributed the music.

By 1665 the company had become *La Troupe du Roi*, playing at the Palais-Royal. While taking the part of Argan in *Le Malade Imaginaire*, Molière was taken ill, and he died the same evening. The Troupe survived, however, to become one of the forerunners of the *Comédie-Française*.

•

JOHN WOOD was born in 1900 and went to Manchester University. After some years in teaching and adult education he spent his working life in educational administration. Concern with the relevance of the arts in education, combined with personal predilection, led to involvement with theatre and with the work of Molière in particular, as producer and translator. He also translated *The Misanthrope and Other Plays* and Beaumarchais' *The Barber of Seville* and *The Marriage of Figaro* for the Penguin Classics.

Molière

*

THE WOULD-BE GENTLEMAN
THAT SCOUNDREL SCAPIN
THE MISER
LOVE'S THE BEST DOCTOR
DON JUAN

Translated with an Introduction by

JOHN WOOD

PENGUIN BOOKS

PENGUIN BOOKS

Published by the Penguin Group
Penguin Books Ltd, 27 Wrights Lane, London W8 5TZ, England
Penguin Books USA Inc., 375 Hudson Street, New York, New York 10014, USA
Penguin Books Australia Ltd, Ringwood, Victoria, Australia
Penguin Books Canada Ltd, 10 Alcorn Avenue, Toronto, Ontario, Canada M4V 3B2
Penguin Books (NZ) Ltd, 182–190 Wairau Road, Auckland 10, New Zealand

Penguin Books Ltd, Registered Offices: Harmondsworth, Middlesex, England

This translation first published as *Five Plays* 1935
Reprinted as *The Miser and Other Plays* 1962
23 25 27 29 30 28 26 24 22

Printed in England by Clays Ltd, St Ives plc
Set in Monotype Garamond

The terms for the performance of these plays may be obtained
from the League of Dramatists
84 Drayton Gardens, London SW10 9SD
to whom all applications for permission
should be addressed

To

JOHN STEUART ERSKINE

*

Contents

Introduction

MOLIÈRE was born in Paris in 1622 and died there in 1673. His father, Jean Poquelin, was a merchant upholsterer and a man of some substance. He had purchased an office at court and in 1637 secured the reversion to his son. Meanwhile young Poquelin (the name Molière was assumed later) was receiving, as a pupil of the Jesuits, the best education the age afforded. Afterwards he appears to have studied law at a university, but where is not known for certain.

At the age of 21, on the threshold of the career that was planned for him, he resigned his rights in the office at court, compounded for his share of his deceased mother's estate, and threw in his lot with a company of actors. What motives there were, if any, beyond the irresistible attraction of the theatre we do not know. One thing is certain, that the choice was final and decisive. Thereafter through all the vicissitudes of thirty years on the stage his passion for acting burned unabated to his death.

The nucleus of the company to which Molière attached himself was provided by members of one family, the Béjarts. Three daughters, Madeleine, Geneviève, and Armande, and two sons, Joseph and Louis, were at various times members of the troupe and, once enrolled, never left it. Madeleine, it has always been assumed, was at one time Molière's mistress; that she was his comrade and colleague until her death the year before his own is beyond question; Armande, younger by twenty years, was to become his wife.

The project of establishing a new theatre in competition with the two companies then playing permanently in Paris did not meet with success. Molière was imprisoned for debt and released on the intervention of his father. In 1646 he and his companions forsook the capital for the provinces and, for the next twelve years, led the life of itinerant players. They have been traced in various provincial towns mainly in the South, but little is known of their adventures. It is clear, however, that it was in this school that Molière learned his trade: when in 1658 the company came back to Paris, they were an experienced team of actors, he had become their acknowledged leader, and their repertory included, with many of the well-known plays of the time, a number of short farces of his own devising which had already proved popular with provincial audiences. A further turning-point in Molière's career came when his company, having established a precarious foothold in Paris, secured an invitation to perform before the young King, Louis XIV. The play chosen was a tragedy of Corneille, but it was followed by Molière's short farce, now lost, *Le Docteur amoureux*. The King was amused and the way to patronage and success was opened. The company had already come under the protection of the King's brother; they now established themselves in the hall of the Petit-Bourbon which they shared with the Italian company of the great farcical actor Fiorelli, the creator of Scaramouche. Each company took certain fixed days of the week. Molière now played *L'Étourdi* and *Le Dépit amoureux*, and in 1659 achieved a resounding success with *Les Précieuses ridicules*, a high-spirited and farcical treatment of contemporary literary enthusiasms. This success was surpassed and consolidated by *L'École des femmes*, a full-length comedy in verse which made its author the talk of the town. It also provoked the jealousy of rival companies and authors, but the box office throve on controversy and in the war of the theatres Molière proved well able to look after himself. He showed in this play a new range of comic invention, a growing sureness of touch and, at the same time, a tendency to cut deeper than the conventional surface of things and provoke reactions other than laughter which was to make him one of the most controversial figures of his time. If *L'École des femmes* put the strongholds of convention on the alert, *Le Tartuffe*, the first of the great comedies of human obsession, went on to outrage them. It is concerned with religion and religious hypocrisy and, in Tartuffe himself, Molière created an unforgettable character. The play is a major achievement, as strong theatrically as challenging in its implications; but it hit the age hard on a sensitive spot and the reaction was immediate and violent. Despite the known support of the King, the author was attacked, execrated, anathematized and not only by those whom he chose to regard as the professional and organized forces of hypocrisy but by many of the truly devout. To this day there are those, not all among his detractors, who feel that in this play and its successor Molière attacked not religiosity but the foundations of religion itself. The King was driven to temporize. The play was forbidden public performance. Even when reshaped and probably toned down, in the form that we know, it was not allowed to be played for nearly five years. For Molière the setback was serious and the disappointment acute, but his output did not slacken – with the limited play-going public of Paris of that day new plays were a constant necessity. Nevertheless his attitude hardens. He is no longer content to assert that the test of a play lies in its ability to please. The function of comedy is now to castigate folly and vice and when in an attempt, as it would seem, to cut a way out of his difficulties, he chose for his new play one of the most popular themes of the day, the story of Don Juan, where the known plot required that religion should triumph and unbelief be confounded, he produced one of the most enigmatic and powerful of his comedies, a masterpiece, in the circumstances, of artistic intransigence! It provoked a fierce renewal of polemics against him, but it was played to full houses. Between 15 February and 20 March 1665 the play was performed fifteen times, a considerable run for those days, but thereafter never again in Molière's lifetime and not for nearly two centuries after his death in the form in which he wrote it. It was not printed until 1682 and then in a bowdlerized version. In what form the interdict fell is not known, but the effect was conclusive.

Meanwhile Molière had been at work for some time on *Le Misanthrope*. First played in 1666, it enjoyed only a moderate success, but discerning contemporaries acclaimed the masterpiece which posterity has recognized it to be, a consummate revelation of character and human relationships within the terms of pure comedy. If, after *Le Misanthrope*, the peak of artistic achievement was past, Molière's verve and creative energy were undiminished. Spectacular plays for the court, *Amphitryon, Psyché, Les Amants magnifiques*, jostle with plays for the town, *L'Avare, Le Médecin malgré lui, Scapin*, and plays which pleased court and town alike, *Le Bourgeois Gentilhomme, Monsieur de Pourceaugnac, La Comtesse d'Escarbagnas, Les Femmes savantes*. In these years he exploited increasingly the comedy-ballet, seeking the ideal union of acting, music, and dancing.

He had experimented with this form much earlier in *Les Fâcheux* and turned to it again, after the tumults of *Tartuffe* and *Dom Juan*, in *L'Amour médecin*. Molière was himself musical and came, on his mother's side, of a family of musicians; the King was at that time passionately fond of music and dancing; the court adored ballet and spectacle, and, in Lully, Molière found a collaborator of genius, whose music lent a charm to the most hurriedly extemporized of plays and diversions. The conception of comedy-ballet was most completely realized in *Le Bourgeois Gentilhomme* and *Le Malade imaginaire*. The former, first played in 1670, exemplifies the mood of these later years at its happiest.

Favoured by the King – he had resumed the office of Groom of the Bedchamber on the death of his brother in 1667 and his company had become *La Troupe du Roi* in 1665 – playing now in the Palais-Royal, once the private theatre of Richelieu, the ban on *Tartuffe* finally lifted in 1669, enjoying the friendship of many of the great men of his day, Molière knew success in full measure, but his personal life was unhappy. His two sons died in infancy. His relationship with his young wife, Armande, was such that for a time they lived apart. His health, which gave trouble as early as 1665, grew worse. His relations with Lully deteriorated as the Italian exploited the royal favour increasingly to his own advantage. His friends advised him to give up acting and enjoy a more leisurely life, but in vain. The road he had taken in 1643 he followed to the end. In February 1673 he produced *Le Malade imaginaire*, playing himself the role of Argan, the invalid more fortunate on the stage than his creator in life. At the third performance Molière was taken ill and died shortly afterwards. His fame did not save him from the penalty of an outcast profession and the malice of his enemies. Only the appeal of his widow to the King in person secured him burial in consecrated ground.

Molière's company, which had stood by him in good times and bad, held together and was playing again within a week of his death: it survived to unite eventually with its old rivals of the theatres of the Hôtel de Bourgogne and Le Marais, and maintain, as the *Comédie-Française*, the tradition of French acting from the theatre of Molière to that of our own day.

The bare facts of Molière's life are well known, but the man himself eludes us. Contemporary descriptions are fragmentary: the most complete are done by his enemies with intent to malign him. His manner in company was said to have been reserved. Boileau called him 'Le Contemplateur'. As he depicts himself in *L'Impromptu de Versailles* rehearsing his cast, he is quick, highly strung, and irascible, immersed in the immediate task of dealing with those most difficult of creatures, actors and actresses. His portraits show a man with fine eyes and wide mouth. The daughter of his colleague Du Croisy, speaking of him long afterwards as she remembered seeing him in her youth, said he was of medium build, imposing carriage, grave in manner with a large nose, wide mouth and full lips, dark of complexion, with eyebrows black and strongly marked which he could move in a way which gave his whole face a most comical expression.

Molière's relations with his father seem to have been close in spite of their early divergence of purpose. He had the loyalty and respect of his company over many years, no common thing in the theatre. With the King his relations seem to have been consistently fortunate. Louis may have found it necessary at times to set bounds to his impetuosity, but on critical occasions he gave his support with deliberate discrimination. When the attacks on *L'École des femmes* were being pressed hard he made his own position clear by the award of a pension and *L'Impromptu de Versailles* in which Molière replied to his enemies seems to have been a royal commission; at a time when personal attacks on Molière and his wife exceeded all bounds the King stood godfather to their first child: at the most critical stage of his fortunes, when *Le Tartuffe* was under interdict and the position of the company precarious, the King increased his annual subvention and conferred on them the title of *Troupe du Roi*. That such a relationship was possible attests the enlightenment of the monarch and the discretion of the subject. In dedications of the plays and the petitions he addressed to the King, Molière shows that he could play the courtier to achieve his own purposes: life at court must have made great demands on his physical strength and perhaps on his integrity but only a man of great inward serenity and courage could, after the storms of *Tartuffe* and *Dom Juan* and what we assume to have been the partial disappointment of *Le Misanthrope*, have retained such zest and love of life as found expression in the later comedies and comedy-ballets. Yet he was under no illusion. 'Among all human weaknesses' – says Filerin in *L'Amour médecin* – ' love of living is the most powerful.' If it was not himself he put on the stage as Argan, the dupe of the doctors, it was his own dilemma. He who turned so many others to comic account did not except himself.

MOLIÈRE'S ACHIEVEMENT

It is a measure of Molière's achievement that he has so often been judged not as poet, playwright, maker of acting tradition, but in terms of ideas and morals as if he were a teacher, philosopher, or metaphysician. Generations of critics, scholars, and fellow artists have commented and explained, discussed and disputed what he thought and intended – and the process goes on. One thing is beyond question, that comedy, which immediately before his time was confined to farce, vulgar and vigorous with stock situations and recognized characters or, in its more respectable forms, to plays of contrivance and artifice, he raised in a space of less than twenty years to the pitch of great art, placed it alongside tragedy – the tragedy of Corneille and Racine – in the esteem of his countrymen and set standards by which comedy and comic acting have ever since and everywhere in the western world been judged. The plays remain a source of delight, a commentary on life which men still find valid, an expression of the comic spirit which has not lost its piquancy. Delight one puts first because Molière did so himself. First and last he was a man of the theatre to whom the touchstone of success was the pleasure of the audience. No doubt, like the Dancing Master in *Le Bourgeois Gentilhomme*, he preferred discerning applause, but he was at pains to make clear that he respected all sections of his audiences. The laughter which his plays excite expresses delight not derision. There is little bitterness and no condescension in Molière and, notwithstanding the stormy history of some of his plays, and the power they still have to disturb, his work as a whole is essentially happy and humane. The idea of laughter which sweeps away care, restores health and proportion, is one from which he never strays far or for long.

> *Who'er would drive away*
> *The cares of every day,*
> *The sorrows, grief and pain,*
> *The troubles that can kill,*
> *Should shun the doctors' skill*
> *And come to us again.*

Thus sing Comedy, Music, and Ballet in *L'Amour médecin* and one cannot doubt that for Molière this expressed essential values. His joyousness is not of the surface, not a product of high spirits, wit, or buffoonery, though all these have their place in his plays. It is a part of his attitude towards his characters and to life. He laughs at his people, or has us do so, but he has for the least likeable of them – Harpagon, Tartuffe, Don Juan – an understanding which approaches compassion.

His own views on life he reveals by implication, not by assertion. He makes no protest against the nature of the world or the state of society. The heroic virtues – courage, constancy, fortitude – are not found in his plays. Such words as fate, fortune, existence occur only in joke. Love, death, and partings are objects of fun. There is no belief in perfection or perfectibility, in progress, individual or social. What his people are at the beginning of a play they are still at the end. For the great deformities of man's nature he offers no cure. Harpagon returns to his '*cassette*', Jourdain is left to his folly, Don Juan goes to the fate his character made inescapable. He shows men through their foibles, vain, gullible, self-obsessed, and it is his achievement that under the impact of laughter, by the solvent of comedy, we experience the moment of truth, feel the compulsion of reason, share his compassion for common humanity. If he does not assert a system of virtues he identifies the reverse of them, pretentiousness, insincerity, hypocrisy; finds amusement in the contrasts between what men are and what they think themselves, what they endeavour to do and what is in their nature to be: he reveals the things which deform men, separate them from their fellows, and magnify their differences. Certain recurrent relationships form both the material and mechanics of his plays – master and man, old husband and young wife, father and son, expert and layman, rascal and dupe – all potentially comic, and part of the immemorial material of farce which he took to himself and transformed. The achievement lies in the degree in which he used a medium previously earth bound and limited as a commentary on character and human relationships, a revelation of man's nature.

Molière accepts the rationality and sufficiency of the world and man's place in it. His is an art of deliberate limitation, and in the practice of it he is representative of his age and his country. He was French in the great age of France and his work has become part of French culture. 'Every Frenchman', it has been said, 'is born to a Molièresque constitution.' His ideas, his characters, his very words have passed into French life and come to be an accepted expression of the French genius.

Molière has no ambition to explore the ultimate reaches of human feelings – Harpagon and Alceste are not Lear or Hamlet. He does not even seek to be original or inventive. His plots, his characters, his stage business, the very words which sound most apt to their purpose he has culled from all sorts of sources, classical and contemporary, borrowing from others and from himself, using and re-using to the lengths, at times, of tiresomeness and banality. But his limited world is a real one, the parts fit together, the characters take life from the inspiration of genius, are warmed by the author's own abounding vitality and, because he is a master of his craft, they take the stage with conviction, endowed with a verisimilitude which the centuries have scarcely diminished.

MOLIÈRE ON THE STAGE

'Everyone knows that plays are written to be acted.' There are few plays to which Molière's words can be more justly applied than his own. They read well for the most part: they are the work of a poet, a man of letters familiar with classical and contemporary literature and philosophy. Nevertheless, their essential qualities are less literary than dramatic and to assess them on the basis of reading alone may well be to misjudge them. 'On one thing there was general agreement', says Jouvet of his own production of *Dom Juan*, 'that reading of the play gave no indication of what came out in performance.' Another case in point is *Le Bourgeois Gentilhomme*, often regarded as consisting of three acts of comedy, among the finest Molière wrote, and two of only half-relevant buffoonery. That is a literary judgement. On the stage the music and dances which round off each act integrate the action, heighten the effect of hilarious abandon and sweep the play along to a triumphant conclusion where the reader may see only weak anticlimax, a petering out of the original theme. *L'Avare*, a play with many loose ends and discrepancies, has in reading an episodic quality, as if too many disparate elements had been only partially resolved, but it has great strength on the stage because of the dramatic effectiveness of so many of the scenes and the dominance of the central character which gives unity to the theme. *Scapin*, which Boileau deplored as unworthy of the author of *Le Misanthrope*, is dramatically foolproof. Molière was an actor, first and last, however much he was more than that, and his text is always closely related to practical dramatic possibilities. He wrote not for an ideal stage but for particular ones, for himself and his own group of actors, for audiences whose tastes he knew well and had to consider. Every phrase of his dialogue has its implicit movement or gesture: every dramatic effect is calculated and virtue is made even of necessities – his own cough and his brother-in-law's limp in *L'Avare*, Mlle Beauval's gift for infectious laughter in the part of Nicole, the permanent sets of the Italians which he had to make the best of when he shared their theatre with them.

The precise forms in which he saw dramatic effectiveness were determined by his peculiar genius, but also, and to a very considerable degree, by the physical conditions of the theatre for which he wrote and the traditions in which, as a man of the theatre, he had grown up. In its material shape the French theatre of the mid seventeenth century was still in the stage of improvisation. Such companies as

Molière's *Illustre Théâtre*, which he founded with the Béjarts, played in tennis courts, inn-yards, or the halls of great houses with little specialized setting and, originally, no proscenium curtain. The audience stood before the stage in the *parterre* or pit (not around it as in Elizabethan England) or sat in tiers on three sides of the room. The young men of fashion sat on the stage. With the development of spectacular plays the proscenium curtain came into general use to withhold the surprise of the setting, cover scene changes, and mask the *machines* which enabled gods to fly, nymphs to emerge from their fountains, and villains to go to their last account as in *Dom Juan*. The influence of a stage without front curtain is seen in Molière's openings – with individuals walking and conversing – and in his endings which so often become processions or dances. The elaborations seen at Versailles were much modified elsewhere and the contemporary inventories show how simple were stage furniture and properties. For *L'Avare*, a table, a chair, an inkstand, paper, a cash-box, a broom, a stick, overalls, spectacles, two candles on the table in the fifth act; for *Le Bourgeois Gentilhomme*, chairs, table for the meal and one for the buffet, accessories for the Turkish ceremony; for *Dom Juan*, a trap, incense (to make smoke), two chairs, and a stool. Costumes, on the other hand, were rich, varied, and stylized according to character. The audience could recognize characters by their dress and deportment immediately they entered, master and man, mistress and maid, soldier, doctor, pedant, ruffian, poor, rich, old, young, comic, serious. There are relatively few references in the plays to the setting, but allusions to costume and personal appearance are abundant and indicative of character – as Don Juan's flame-coloured ribbons, Cléante's fashionable attire in *L'Avare*, and Jourdain's finery. Costume was used to concentrate attention on the actor, and the stage was the unencumbered space where he must create his illusion by voice, movement, and gesture in patterns of colour and sound.

The main traditions of acting to which Molière succeeded were twofold. In tragedy, speech was declamatory; the lines were intoned rather than spoken, and in gesture the emphasis was on dignity and a theatrical impressiveness. Molière attempted to introduce a more natural manner, but his ideas seem to have gained little acceptance and his practice of them may account for the contemporary view that he was not seen to advantage in tragedy. The other tradition, from which in a large degree Molière developed his conceptions of comedy and comic acting, was that of the farce. Native farce had a long history in France, but it would seem that it was the Italians, long favourites of Parisian audiences, who had the greatest influence upon him. Theirs was predominantly an art of gesture and mime. Plots and characters were conventional, familiar to the audience, a framework of improvisation. Dialogue was largely extemporized, according to the inspiration of the moment and the reaction of the audience, and interspersed with stock passages of repartee which could be introduced to fit recurrent situations. The actors were commonly masked and the effect of the mask was to increase the significance of movement and gesture and at the same time to stylize it. A mask is most effective when seen in full face. Thus it was the outline, the shape of the gesture as seen from the front, which was significant and the movement had the effect of figures on a frieze. Gestures were clear cut, emphatic. The elements of such a convention are clearly to be seen in Molière's work.

Many of the earlier plays are little more than farcical scenes strung together with only the slightest intrinsic connexion or plot. Development and structural logic were never a strong point with Molière. Don Juan, Harpagon, Jourdain are revealed in loose sequences of scenes wherein the main character is the link and plot of no great significance. Characters too are taken directly from or have close affinities with the stock figures of farce. What Molière did was to deepen and enlarge their significance, to clothe them afresh with new comic traits, and to widen the range, effect, and appeal. Scenes of pure farce abound in the plays and a technique of acting derived from farce is implicit throughout, even though the form may be widened and refined. In Act III of *Le Bourgeois Gentilhomme*, for example, where master and man (Cléonte and Covielle) meet mistress and maid (Lucile and Nicole) the short sharp exchanges of speech cut down at times to single words and exclamations are the notation of a series of formalized movements, a development and counter-development indicated by only the slightest of stage directions. In effect the scene is a dance. Its charm is almost wholly visual, its relevance to the plot of the slightest.

In *Dom Juan* the methods of farce are used to achieve a deeper significance, as in the first encounter of Don Juan and Elvira. The scene, so far as the principal characters are concerned, is not obviously comic – certainly not in the common sense of the word, but Sganarelle is present throughout and his interventions or rather the occasions when he is brought into the dialogue are revealing. To Elvira's inquiry as to why Don Juan had abandoned her the answer is 'Sganarelle here knows why I came away'. Now, the reader may forget Sganarelle until he is recalled by the dialogue, but on the stage, in actual production, he has to be accounted for; he must play his part all the time. If it is assumed – and there is no alternative – that Sganarelle has mimed throughout the preceding speeches his commentary upon what has been passing and, that the culmination was a mute gesture of appeal to his master in sympathy with Elvira, then the sudden ironic resort to him falls dramatically into place. Here, as throughout the play, Sganarelle, the farcical character, or the most completely farcical among the main characters, upholds not as contemporaries suggested, religion in the character of a fool, but, confused, contradictory, foolish as he may be, the cause of common humanity. Jourdain in *Le Bourgeois Gentilhomme* appeals to us in the same way, through a kind of lyricism of folly.

Molière's language in the prose plays shows a singular range and variety suited to rank and character of the speakers. It extends, within the same play, from the heroic and the precious to the most colloquial and direct or, as in *Dom Juan*, to naturalistic stage dialect. The influence of farce is seen in the stock exchanges, some of which occur with little change in different plays, in comic situations, to express rage, surprise, and frustration – for example, those between Géronte and Scapin, Harpagon and La Flèche, where the character relationship is wholly farcical. Such passages are there primarily because the actors knew them and found them convenient. On the whole, however, Molière's prose is direct and aimed at the immediate target. There is a drift of preciosity, there are interludes of fine talk and eloquence like the superb speeches of Scapin or the self-communings of Don Juan, but these are in character. In the speeches of Don Luis and the brothers in *Dom Juan* the rhythm is sufficiently rhetorical to remind one that Molière was the contemporary of Corneille and Racine. Here, as in some of the speeches in *L'Avare*, one feels, beneath the cadence of prose, 'the ground swell of the Alexandrine'. Molière is rarely witty, unless aptness to purpose be wit. There are few applied decorations. His prose is, in general, a language to be heard in the theatre, direct, unadorned. Where his sayings have passed into the common speech of his countrymen it is by virtue of aptness to character or to situations of common and recurrent experience.

One thing which apparently impressed contemporaries as new in Molière's company was the ease and precision of their acting. 'Never was comedy so well performed', said de Visé of *L'École des femmes*, 'or with so much art. Every actor knows how many steps he has to take and his every glance is counted.' La Grange, writing of his former colleague, notes the same quality. After referring to Molière's inimitable acting in his own plays he describes the precision of the acting as a whole where 'every glance, every step, every gesture was controlled'. The methods of achieving such a reconciliation of art and nature can still be studied in *L'Impromptu de Versailles*. By ironic praise of the contrary methods Molière indicates his own intention of holding the mirror to nature, suiting the action to the word and avoiding bombast and ranting. The parallel with Hamlet's advice to the players is so close as to suggest that it is perhaps not accidental.

MOLIÈRE'S ACTORS

The successes of Molière's company and its enduring influence on the acting of comedy in France seem to have been due not so much to outstanding personality among the players, Molière

himself excepted, as to his teaching and, as indicated above, to
team work and precision.

Madeleine Béjart had made some reputation as an actress
before the foundation of the *Illustre Théâtre*. She was a capable
actress, particularly in tragedy. Her younger sister Geneviève
left no particular mark but, under her stage name of Mlle
Hervé, she fitted unobtrusively into the team. Armande,
Molière's wife, young enough to be schooled in her husband's
ideas, appears to have been a charming and versatile actress.
She was Célimène in *Le Misanthrope*, Lucile in *Le Bourgeois
Gentilhomme*, and, probably, Charlotte in *Dom Juan*. After
Molière's death she provided the financial support and, with
La Grange, kept the company together. Joseph and Louis
Béjart were competent actors. Joseph played the lovers' parts
in spite of a stammer, Louis the comic valets. He was the
original La Flèche and apparently a favourite of Parisian audiences. Among other members of long standing was La Grange
who took the young lovers' parts after the death of Joseph
Béjart. He was the original Don Juan, and Cléonte in *Le
Bourgeois Gentilhomme*. He succeeded Molière as the orator of
the company, the man who made the announcements and kept
the audience in order. He kept the records of the company and
his *Registre* is the main source for its history. Of similar standing was Du Croisy, fat, cheerful, and handsome, the original
Tartuffe. He played Géronte in *Les Fourberies de Scapin*. La
Grange and Du Croisy were married, and their wives were
members of the company but of no particular distinction.
Quite the reverse was the case with the Du Parc and de Brie.
The husbands were useful actors – Du Parc, called Gros René,
played the buffoons in the earlier comedies and de Brie the
ruffians and soldiers (he was Silvestre in *Scapin*) – but the wives
played great parts in the company's history. Mlle Du Parc was
a beauty. Molière, Corneille, La Fontaine, and Racine were all
said to have been in love with her. Under Racine's influence
she deserted the company for their rivals of the Hôtel de
Bourgogne, taking her husband with her. Less imperious in
temperament but also accounted beautiful was Mlle de Brie.
She played Marianne in *L'Avare* and Dorimène in *Le Bourgeois
Gentilhomme*. Other members of the company who enjoyed

particular reputations were Hubert, long a favourite in the parts of old women (he was the first Madame Jourdain), and Mlle Beauval, an uneducated woman whose country accent is implied in the part of Nicole. She specialized in maids' parts and it was for her that Molière wrote the part of Toinette in *Le Malade imaginaire*. Among younger members was Baron, the son of an actor and actress, befriended by Molière and destined to become, under his tutelage, and by his own talents, one of the great names of the French theatre. He made a great success of Domitien in Corneille's *Bérénice*, playing opposite Molière's wife. He was Cupide in *Psyché*, Octavio in *Scapin*. After Molière's death he played Alceste in *Le Misanthrope* and Jupiter in *Amphitryon*. In him we see one of the representative figures of French acting, one of the great line which continues from Molière's day to our own, through whom much of the original business of the plays has been preserved, in whom the inspiration of a great tradition has survived for nearly three centuries.

THE MUSIC OF MOLIÈRE'S PLAYS

The music written by Lully for several of the *Comédies-Ballets* is, in part, extant in the form of manuscript scores written down by Philidor the Elder, Keeper of the King's Music. There is no orchestral score in the modern sense: for the songs there is a simple bass accompaniment for a harpsichord: music for the dances is scored for five-stringed instruments with occasional additions – as in the case of *Le Bourgeois Gentilhomme* – for flutes, oboes, and bassoons. When the plays were performed at court there was an orchestra of twenty or more. For other occasions Molière retained both singers and dancers but on a more modest scale. Lully succeeded in obtaining a Royal Ordinance in 1672 reducing the number of musicians Molière could employ to six singers and twelve instrumentalists, and later to two singers and six instrumentalists. Molière, his wife, and other acting members of the company also sang on occasion. A piano arrangement of Lully's music for *Le Bourgeois Gentilhomme* was made by Wekerlin in 1878 and published by

Durand and Schoenewerke. Lully's music for other plays in so far as it is extant is included in the edition of the *Œuvres de Molière* published by Payot in 1925. Charpentier's music for *Le Malade imaginaire* edited by Saint-Saëns is published by Durand except that for the first intermission which was collected by Tiersot and published by Heugel in 1925. Music for *Le Sicilien*, Lully's fragments rearranged by Sauzay, was published by Firmin-Didot in 1881.

MOLIÈRE IN ENGLISH

Molière's fame was established abroad within his lifetime and by the end of the century the major plays were known in translation and adaptation in most European languages. In no country was his influence more apparent than in England. The political circumstances which caused many Englishmen to sojourn in France during the Commonwealth and to form in that country their standards of pleasure and taste opened the way for a great revival of French influence at the Restoration and in the theatre particularly. Puritan prejudice had created a breach in tradition, a vacuum filled in the first instance largely from France, but even allowing for these favourable circumstances Molière's influence was remarkable and it lasted for over a century. The following examples confined to names well known in English theatrical history serve to illustrate the extent of direct borrowing only: Dryden adapted *L'Étourdi* as *Sir Martin Marall* and made a version of *Amphitryon* with music by Purcell. Shadwell adapted *L'Avare*, *Dom Juan*, and *Psyché* and drew on *Les Fâcheux* in *The Sullen Lovers*. Wycherley based *The Plain Dealer* on *Le Misanthrope* and owes something to *L'École des femmes* in *The Country Wife*. Vanbrugh made of *Le Dépit amoureux* *The Amorous Mistake* and, with Congreve, adapted *Monsieur Pourceaugnac* as *Squire Trelooby*. *George Dandin* is the basis of Betterton's *The Amorous Widow*. Otway kept close to the original in form and in title in *The Cheats of Scapin*. Cibber in the next century gained his greatest success with *The Non Juror*, which is *Tartuffe* adapted to English prejudices and turned against the Roman Catholics. David Garrick followed

Dryden with a version of *Amphitryon* which appeared as *The Two Sosias*. Fielding did a new version of *The Miser* following a success with *The Mock Doctor*, a play which occurs in several English disguises. Sheridan embodies vestigial Molière in *St Patrick's Day* and in *A Trip to Scarborough* (at second hand by way of Vanbrugh). Not all borrowers were as ungracious as Shadwell – 'The foundations of this play I took from one of Molière's called *L'Avare* ... and I think I may say without vanity that Molière's play has not suffered in my hands. Nor did I ever know French comedy made by the worst of our poets which was not bettered by 'em. 'Tis not poverty or wit nor invention which makes us borrow from the French but laziness.' Whatever the motive the practice was widely followed. Molière's influence can be traced, diminishing but unmistakable, to the end of the eighteenth century, but with the triumph of Romanticism it seems to disappear entirely. The theatre in the eighteenth century had gone over to sentiment and Molière was never sentimental; in the nineteenth century romance and sentiment were supreme, and Molière was relegated to the school and the study. The recorded professional performances in English between 1850 and 1900 can be counted on the fingers of two hands. As the earlier adaptations became outmoded they fell into oblivion and were not replaced, and it was not until the rise of a new comic genius at the end of the century that the shadow of Molière again fell across the English stage.

Modern adaptations of Molière have been made by Lady Gregory – the *Kiltartan Molière* – F. H. Anstey, and, more recently, Mr Malleson, but none covers a full range of the plays. Of translations that of Baker and Miller (1739) is familiar to English readers because it was used by the Everyman Edition, but the English is now much out of date and does not follow the best original text. Other translations are those of Heron Wall (1876), Waller (1926), and the American Curtis Hidden Page (1913). Biographies and critical studies are innumerable. The following are perhaps outstanding among modern works in English: Chapman, *The Spirit of Molière, an Interpretation* (Princeton University Press); Turnell, *The Classical Moment*, studies of Corneille, Molière, and Racine (Hamish

Hamilton); and Moore, *Molière, a Critical Study* (Oxford University Press).

Performances, apart from those given by visiting French companies and in recent years the indefatigable *Troupe Française*, are few and far between. William Poel produced *Dom Juan* in 1899 among the revivals of his Elizabethan Stage Society, but the critics were not enthusiastic. 'It was a foggy night', says *The Times* account, 'and some of the fog seemed to have got into the hall.' Nigel Playfair made a success of *Le Bourgeois Gentilhomme* in a free adaptation at Hammersmith in the twenties and Mr Malleson has shown recently that the old spell still holds.

THE PRESENT TRANSLATION

A translation which begins by omitting the verse plays avoids the difficulty of finding an acceptable English equivalent to Molière's graceful and dramatically effective verse, but it need hardly be said that a selection which does not include *Le Tartuffe* and *Le Misanthrope* cannot claim to be representative. On the other hand, of the seven or eight greatest plays of Molière, four are in prose and, of those, three are here, and the five plays chosen may, it is hoped, be found to present at least an indication of the power and variety of Molière's genius.

In general the translation seeks to keep close to the original wherever the equivalent word or phrase can be found. Where it cannot, the aim has been to give an equivalent effect, and to keep within the bounds of dramatic effectiveness. Thus subtleties of the original inevitably give way at times to directness. The excuse one might claim is that Molière himself was on the whole direct – so much so that often the nearest modern equivalents are found in slang and Americanisms which give in English, however, an effect that is not in the original. Molière could at times outrage the purists but in general his characters speak a classical French.

Strict adherence to the text is most difficult in passages where not only the speech but the convention itself is outmoded. Thus the '*jargon amoureux*' – the language of lovers which Élise and Cléante use in the opening scenes of *L'Avare* –

will not pass now as it stands. One suspects that by Molière's time the coinage was already debased and the scenes are not among the most dramatically effective he wrote. Then again there is throughout the plays a whole vocabulary of terms of derogation and abuse which have now lost their freshness or lack modern equivalents and one is driven to ring the changes on scoundrel, knave, villain, rascal, fool, idiot, dog, traitor, slut, hussy, and creature. Similarly with oaths and imprecations, one is handicapped by the inroads of the 'tushery' school and all the debasing ingenuity of centuries of euphemism which have together made 'ods bodikins', ''sdeath', ''slife', and many another expression unusuable now though they are what is required. In the second act of *Dom Juan* there is the formidable *patois* of the peasants, a remarkable deformation of French for which a synthetic west country alternative is offered with suitable diffidence. An excuse, if it is needed, is that Molière's original seems also to have been a stage version.

Money is a minor but intractable difficulty. The only solution seems to be to abandon literal forms and use what is dramatically effective. Thus in Jourdain's scene with Dorante, and where Scapin is taking toll of the fathers, and the sums must add up, *écus, pistoles, livres, louis d'or* have been reduced to our still familiar pounds and guineas. Elsewhere pounds and crowns have been used as the nearest equivalents, and when the exact original savour was needed, francs and even louis d'or retained as sufficiently self-explanatory.

Clothing has been treated similarly, keeping original terms or using modern ones or something recognizably equivalent, according to dramatic necessity.

In *Le Bourgeois Gentilhomme* there is the difficulty of the Philosopher's lesson on the pronunciation of vowels. It seemed better on the whole to stick to the French values than alter the text to suit English ones. The only serious complication arises with I and E and a producer can alter, if he thinks fit, for the stage.

The Turkish interlude is a second problem in this play. Molière was obviously amused by the Mediterranean polyglot which he used here and several times elsewhere. It is quite untranslatable. Pidgin English seemed to give the right farcical flavour. In *Scapin* there are the difficult assumed accents when

Scapin is beset by imaginary enemies. In the original they are Gascon and Swiss. The alternatives offered are not very satisfactory, but here much depends on the actor and one may perhaps leave it at that.

In Act III of *Dom Juan* there is the insoluble case of *Le Moine Bourru*. Here it is dramatically important that after God and the Devil, as objects of scepticism, there should be a farcical alternative which everyone believes in. *Le Moine Bourru* requires explanation now to a Frenchman. On the whole 'Bogey Man' seems better than anything else. In an age when superstition no longer takes that form there can be no effective equivalent.

Then there is the question of scene divisions. The plays are still printed in French and English with scene divisions of the period, i.e. a new scene is taken to begin whenever a principal character enters or goes out. This is distracting to a modern reader and meaningless from the point of view of the producer. The divisions have, therefore, been omitted and the plays fall naturally into conventional acts without scene divisions except in one case, the fourth act of *Dom Juan*. Change of scene is indicated here and the act has, therefore, been subdivided into two scenes.

The text used is that of the *Œuvres complètes de Molière* prepared by Michaut and published in 1947 by the Imprimerie Nationale. It is rather more sparing of stage directions than some well-known editions which in general follow the collected edition of 1682. In a few cases a stage direction has been inserted where the sense appeared to require one.

I am indebted to many people for help in the course of this translation, in particular to Dr E. V. Rieu, whose example and precept set the standards to which I have striven to attain; to Dr W. T. Gairdner of Sedbergh School for criticisms which have delivered me from many an error and for improvements beyond computation, to Monsieur René Varin of the French Embassy in London for unfailing help and encouragement, and to Mr S. G. Beagley, County Librarian of the North Riding of Yorkshire, for every assistance which a library can offer to a student *in partibus infidelium*.

J.W.

Osmotherley, Yorkshire
1952

The Would-be Gentleman

LE BOURGEOIS GENTILHOMME

A Comedy-Ballet

CHARACTERS IN THE PLAY

MR JOURDAIN
MRS JOURDAIN, his wife
LUCILE, their daughter
NICOLE, a maidservant
CLÉONTE, in love with Lucile
COVIELLE, valet to Cléonte
DORANTE, a nobleman
DORIMÈNE, a lady
MUSIC MASTER
MUSIC MASTER'S PUPIL
DANCING MASTER
FENCING MASTER
PHILOSOPHER
MASTER TAILOR
TAILOR'S APPRENTICES
TWO LACKEYS
SINGERS AND DANCERS, MUSICIANS, COOKS
THE MUFTI, TURKS, AND DERVISHES

*The scene is a room in the house of
Mr Jourdain in Paris*

Act One

The overture is played by a great assemblage of instruments and the music pupil is discovered composing the air which MR JOURDAIN *has commissioned for his concert. As the song ends the* MUSIC MASTER *and the* DANCING MASTER *enter with their attendant musicians, singers, and dancers.*

MUSIC MASTER [*to musicians*]. Come in here and wait until he comes.

DANCING MASTER [*to dancers*]. And you can stay on this side.

MUSIC MASTER [*to his pupil*]. Well, is it finished?

MUSIC PUPIL. Yes.

MUSIC MASTER [*taking manuscript*]. Let me see. . . . Very good!

DANCING MASTER. Is it something new?

MUSIC MASTER. It is an air for a serenade I set him to compose while we were waiting for our friend to awake.

DANCING MASTER. May one see what it is?

MUSIC MASTER. You will hear it when he comes. He can't be long now.

DANCING MASTER. We are both being kept pretty busy at present.

MUSIC MASTER. Yes. We have found here the very man we both needed. This fellow Jourdain with the fantastic notions of gentility and gallantry he has got into his head means quite a nice thing for us. I only wish, both for my music and your dancing, that there were more people like him.

DANCING MASTER. I can't altogether agree. For his own sake I would like him to have a little more understanding of the things we provide for him.

MUSIC MASTER. It's true that he understands little – but he pays well, and, after all, that's the great need in our line of business just now.

DANCING MASTER. Yes – though for my own part I must confess that what I long for most is applause; it is appreciation I live for. To my way of thinking there is no fate more distressing for an artist than to have to show himself off before fools, to see his work exposed to the criticism of the vulgar and ignorant. You can say what you like but there *is*

3

no joy like that of working for people who have a feeling for the fine points of one's art, who can appreciate the beauties of a work and repay all one's trouble by praise which is really discerning. There is no reward so delightful, no pleasure so exquisite, as having one's work known and acclaimed by those whose applause confers honour.

MUSIC MASTER. I agree. My feelings exactly. There is nothing more pleasing than the recognition you speak of, but you can't live on applause. Praise alone doesn't keep a man going. One needs something more substantial than that, and, to my mind, there's no praise to beat the sort you can put in your pocket. It's true that this fellow here has no great share of enlightenment: he usually gets hold of the wrong end of the stick and applauds all the wrong things, but his money makes up for his lack of discernment. His praise has cash value. Vulgar and ignorant he may be but he's more use to us, you know, than your fine cultured gentleman who put us in touch with him.

DANCING MASTER. There's something in what you say, but I still think you set too much value on money. Cultivated people should be superior to any consideration so sordid as a mercenary interest.

MUSIC MASTER. All the same you don't refuse to take our friend's pay.

DANCING MASTER. Of course not. But I don't find that it entirely contents me. I still wish that with all his great wealth he had a little more taste.

MUSIC MASTER. So do I, and isn't that just where we are both trying to help him – so far as we can? In any case, he is giving us a chance to make a name in the world and he will make up for the others by paying while they do the praising.

DANCING MASTER. Hush! Here he comes.

Enter MR JOURDAIN *in dressing-gown and night-cap attended by two lackeys.*

MR JOURDAIN. Well, gentlemen, what is it to be to-day? Are you going to show me your bit of tomfoolery?

DANCING MASTER. Tomfoolery? What bit of tomfoolery?

MR JOURDAIN. You know – your what ye may call it – your

4

prologue or dialogue or whatever it is – your singing and dancing.

DANCING MASTER. Oh! That's what you mean!

MUSIC MASTER. You find us quite ready.

MR JOURDAIN. I had to keep you waiting a while because I'm getting dressed up to-day like one of the quality and my tailor had sent me a pair of silk stockings so tight I thought I should never get into them.

MUSIC MASTER. We are entirely at your disposal, sir.

MR JOURDAIN. I don't want you to go, either of you, until they've brought me my suit. I want you to see how I look in it.

DANCING MASTER. Whatever you please.

MR JOURDAIN. You'll see me turned out in style – head to foot, everything just as it should be.

MUSIC MASTER. We don't doubt that at all.

MR JOURDAIN [*showing his dressing-gown*]. I had this Indian stuff made up for me specially.

DANCING MASTER. Very fine indeed.

MR JOURDAIN. My tailor tells me the quality wear this sort of thing on a morning.

MUSIC MASTER. It suits you splendidly.

MR JOURDAIN. Lackey! Hello there! Both my lackeys!

FIRST LACKEY. Your wishes, sir?

MR JOURDAIN. Nothing. I just wanted to be sure you could hear me. [*To the others*] What d'ye think of my liveries, eh?

DANCING MASTER. Magnificent.

MR JOURDAIN *opens his dressing-gown and shows his tight breeches of red velvet and his green velvet jacket.*

MR JOURDAIN. This is a little rig-out to do my morning exercises in.

DANCING MASTER. Most elegant.

MR JOURDAIN. Lackey!

LACKEY. Sir!

MR JOURDAIN. T'other lackey!

SECOND LACKEY. Sir!

MR JOURDAIN. Take my dressing-gown. [*To the others*] What d'ye think of me now?

DANCING MASTER. Excellent. Nothing could be finer.

MR JOURDAIN. Right then. Let us have a look at your show.

MUSIC MASTER. I would like you to hear first an air which this young man [*indicating the pupil*] has just composed for the serenade that you asked for. He is a pupil of mine who has quite a gift for this kind of thing.

MR JOURDAIN. Very well – but it shouldn't have been left to a pupil. You shouldn't have been above doing this job yourself.

MUSIC MASTER. Ah, don't be misled, sir, by my use of the word 'pupil'. Pupils like him know as much as the great masters, and the air itself couldn't be bettered. Do but listen.

MR JOURDAIN. Here. [*As the singer is about to begin*] Give me my dressing-gown so that I can listen better. Stop – I think perhaps I shall do better without it. No – give it me back. I can do best with it on.

SINGER. I languish night and day and sad must be my lay,
Till consenting to their sway I give your eyes their way,
If thus you treat your friends – fair Iris,
If thus you treat your friends,
Alas! Alas! How will you treat,
How will you treat your enemies?

MR JOURDAIN. It sounds a bit dismal to me. It makes me feel sleepy. Can't you liven it up a bit here and there?

MUSIC MASTER. But the tune must suit the words, sir!

MR JOURDAIN. I learned a song once – a really pretty one it was – wait a minute – la – la la – how does it go?

DANCING MASTER. I've not the remotest idea.

MR JOURDAIN. It had something about sheep in it.

DANCING MASTER. Sheep?

MR JOURDAIN. Yes – or lambs. Now I've got it!
[*Singing*] I thought my Janey dear
As sweet as she was pretty, oh!
I thought my Janey dear as gentle as a baa-lamb, oh!
Alas, alas! She is a thousand times more cruel
Than any savage tiger – oh!
Isn't that nice?

MUSIC MASTER. Very nice indeed.

DANCING MASTER. And you sing it very well.

MR JOURDAIN. And yet I never learned music.

MUSIC MASTER You ought to learn, sir, just as you are learning to dance. The two arts are closely allied.

6

DANCING MASTER. And develop one's appreciation of beauty.

MR JOURDAIN. What do the quality do? Do they learn music as well?

MUSIC MASTER. Of course.

MR JOURDAIN. Then I'll learn it. But I don't know how I'm to find time. I already have a fencing master giving me lessons and now I've taken on a teacher of philosophy and he's supposed to be making a start this morning.

MUSIC MASTER. Well, there is something in philosophy, but music, sir, music –

DANCING MASTER. And dancing, music and dancing, what more can one need?

MUSIC MASTER. There's nothing so valuable in the life of the nation as music.

DANCING MASTER. And nothing so necessary to mankind as dancing.

MUSIC MASTER. Without music – the country couldn't go on.

DANCING MASTER. Without dancing – one can achieve nothing at all.

MUSIC MASTER. All the disorders, all the wars, that we see in the world to-day, come from not learning music.

DANCING MASTER. All the troubles of mankind, all the miseries which make up history, the blunders of politicians, the failures of great captains – they all come from not having learned dancing.

MR JOURDAIN. How d'ye make that out?

MUSIC MASTER. What is war but discord among nations?

MR JOURDAIN. True.

MUSIC MASTER. If all men studied music wouldn't it be a means of bringing them to harmony and universal peace?

MR JOURDAIN. That seems sound enough.

DANCING MASTER. And what do we say when a man has committed some mistake in his private life or in public affairs? Don't we say he made a false step?

MR JOURDAIN. We certainly do.

DANCING MASTER. And making a false step – doesn't that come from not knowing how to dance?

MR JOURDAIN. True enough. You are both in the right.

DANCING MASTER. We want to make you realize the

importance, the usefulness of music and dancing.

MR JOURDAIN. Yes. I quite see that now.

MUSIC MASTER. Would you like to see our performances?

MR JOURDAIN. Yes.

MUSIC MASTER. As I have told you already, the first is a little exercise I devised a short time ago in the expression of various emotions through music.

MR JOURDAIN. Very good.

MUSIC MASTER [*to singers*]. Come forward. [*To* MR JOUR-DAIN] You must imagine them dressed as shepherds.

MR JOURDAIN. But why shepherds again? It always seems to be shepherds.

MUSIC MASTER. Because, if you are to have people discoursing in song, you must for verisimilitude conform to the pastoral convention. Singing has always been associated with shepherds. It would not seem natural for princes or ordinary folk for that matter, to be indulging their passions in song.

MR JOURDAIN. Very well. Let's hear them.

TRIO

FIRST SINGER [*woman*]. Who gives her heart in loving
To a thousand cares is bound;
Men speak of love and wooing
As one continual round
Of rapture. – Not for me!
No, not for me!
I keep my fancy free,
I keep my fancy free.

SECOND SINGER [*man*]. Could I succeed in proving
The ardour of my heart,
Could I succeed in moving
You to that better part –
Surrender – then for me,
Oh then for me,
How happy life would be,
How happy life would be!

THIRD SINGER [*man*]. If one could find in loving
But one true faithful heart,
Could one succeed in proving
Faith were the better part
Of woman's heart – alas for me!

Alas for me!
None such there be,
None such there be!

SECOND SINGER. Oh rarest rapture.

FIRST SINGER. Would I could capture!

THIRD SINGER. Deceivers ever.

SECOND SINGER. Love, leave me never.

FIRST SINGER. Happy surrender –

THIRD SINGER. Faithless pretender –

SECOND SINGER. Change, change to love that scorn disdainful!

FIRST SINGER. Behold, behold, one lover faithful!

THIRD SINGER. Alas! where can one such a lover find?

FIRST SINGER. To vindicate my sex's part
I offer you – I offer you my heart.

SECOND SINGER. Oh, shepherdess how can I trust –
My heart you'll ne'er deceive?

FIRST SINGER. That time shall prove,
Ah, time shall prove
Who truest loves – who truest loves.

ALL THREE SINGERS. To love's tender ardours
Our hearts then we plight,
For whate'er can compare
With love's tender delights?
With love's tender delights?
Whate'er can compare with love's tender delights?

MR JOURDAIN. Is that all?

MUSIC MASTER. It is.

MR JOURDAIN. Well I thought it was very nicely worked out and there were some quite pretty sayings in it.

DANCING MASTER. Well now, in my show you will see a small demonstration of the most beautiful movements and attitudes which the dance can exemplify.

MR JOURDAIN. They aren't going to be shepherds again?

DANCING MASTER. They are whatever you please. [*To the dancers*] Come along!

The dancers at the command of the DANCING MASTER perform successively minuet, saraband, coranto, galliard, and canaries. The dance forms the First Interlude.

Act Two

MR JOURDAIN. Well that wasn't too bad. Those fellows can certainly shake a leg.

DANCING MASTER. When the dancing and music are fully co-ordinated it will be still more effective and you will find that the little ballet we have arranged for you is a very pretty thing indeed.

MR JOURDAIN. Yes, but that's for later, when the lady I am doing all this for is going to do me the honour of dining here.

DANCING MASTER. Everything is arranged.

MUSIC MASTER. There is just one other thing, sir. A gentleman like you, sir, living in style, with a taste for fine things, ought to have a little musical at-home, say every Wednesday or Thursday.

MR JOURDAIN. Is that what the quality do?

MUSIC MASTER. It is, sir.

MR JOURDAIN. Then I'll do it too. Will it be really fine?

MUSIC MASTER. Beyond question! You will need three singers, a treble, a counter tenor, and a bass accompanied by a bass viol, a theorbo, a harpsichord for the thorough-bass, and two violins for the ritornellos.

MR JOURDAIN. I'd like a marine trumpet* as well. It's an instrument I'm fond of, It's really harmonious.

MUSIC MASTER. Leave these things in our hands.

MR JOURDAIN. Well, don't forget to arrange for people to sing during the meal.

MUSIC MASTER. You shall have everything as it should be.

MR JOURDAIN. And above all make sure that the ballet is really fine.

MUSIC MASTER. You will be pleased with it, particularly with some of the minuets.

MR JOURDAIN. Ah! Minuets! The minuet is my dance. You must see me dance a minuet. Come along, Mr Dancing Master.

* Not a trumpet but a one-stringed instrument.

DANCING MASTER. A hat, sir if you please. [MR JOURDAIN
takes the LACKEY'S *hat and puts it on over his night-cap. The*
DANCING MASTER *takes his hand and makes him dance to the*
tune which he sings.] La, la, la la la la la etc. . . . once again . . .
keep time if you ple-ease . . . la-la lala – now the right leg . . .
la la . . . don't move . . . your shoulders so much . . . la la la . . .
la la . . . your arms . . . are hanging too limply . . . la la la . . .
up with your head, point your toes outward . . . point your
toes out-ward . . . la la la . . . keep your body . . . e . . . rect.

MR JOURDAIN. Phew! What about that?

MUSIC MASTER. Well done! Well done!

MR JOURDAIN. And that reminds me. Just show me how to
make a bow to a countess. I shall need to know that before
long.

DANCING MASTER. How to make a bow to a countess?

MR JOURDAIN. Yes. A countess called Dorimène.

DANCING MASTER. Give me your hand.

MR JOURDAIN. No. Just do it yourself. I shall remember.

DANCING MASTER. If you wish to show great respect you
must make your bow first stepping backwards and then
advance towards her bowing three times, the third time
going down right to the level of her knee.

MR JOURDAIN. Let me see you do it. Good!

LACKEY. Sir, your fencing master is here.

MR JOURDAIN. Tell him to come in and give me my lesson
here. [*To the* MUSIC MASTER *and* DANCING MASTER] Don't
go! I'd like you to see me perform.

Enter FENCING MASTER *with* LACKEY *carrying the foils.*

FENCING MASTER [*after presenting a foil to* MR JOURDAIN].
Come, sir, your salute! Hold yourself straight. Take the
weight of your body a little on your left thigh. Legs not so
far apart. Feet more in line. Wrist in line with your hip.
Point of the foil level with your shoulder. Arm not quite so
far extended. Left hand level with your eye. Left shoulder
squared a little more. Head up. Firm glance. Advance! Keep
your body steady. Engage my point in quart and lunge. One,
two. As you were. Once again, repeat! Do keep your feet
firm. One, two, and recover! When you make a pass, sir, it is
important that the foil should be withdrawn first – so –

keeping the body well covered. One, two. Come along.
Engage my foil in tierce and hold it. Advance! Keep your
body steady. Advance and lunge from there! One, two, and
recover. As you were. Once again. One, two. Back you go.
Parry, sir, parry! [*The* FENCING MASTER *scores two or three
hits crying as he does so, Parry! Parry!*]

MR JOURDAIN. Phew!

MUSIC MASTER. You do splendidly.

FENCING MASTER. I have told you before that the whole art
of sword-play lies in two things only – in giving and not receiving. And, as I showed you the other day by logical demonstration, it is impossible for you to receive a hit if you
know how to turn your opponent's sword from the line of
your body, for which all that is needed is the slighest turn of
the wrist – inward or outward.

MR JOURDAIN. At that rate, then, a fellow can be sure of
killing his man and not being killed himself – without need
of courage.

FENCING MASTER. Exactly! Didn't you follow my demonstration?

MR JOURDAIN. Oh yes.

FENCING MASTER. Well then, you see what respect should
be paid to men of my profession and how much more important is skill in arms than such futile pursuits as dancing
and music –

DANCING MASTER. Go easy, Mr Scabbard Scraper. Mind
what you say about dancing.

MUSIC MASTER. And try to treat music with a little more
respect if you please.

FENCING MASTER. A fine lot of jokers you are, to think of
comparing your professions with mine.

MUSIC MASTER. Just listen who's talking.

DANCING MASTER. The ridiculous creature, with his leather
upholstered belly!

FENCING MASTER. My little dancing master, I could make
you skip if I had a mind to, and as for you, Mr Music Master,
I could make you sing to some tune!

DANCING MASTER. Mr Sabre-rattler, I shall have to teach
you your trade.

MR JOURDAIN [*to* DANCING MASTER]. You must be mad to quarrel with a man who knows all about tierce and quart and can kill a man by logical demonstration.

DANCING MASTER. I don't give a rap for his logical demonstration, his tierce, or his quart.

MR JOURDAIN [*to* DANCING MASTER]. Do be careful I tell you.

FENCING MASTER [*to* DANCING MASTER]. You impertinent jackanapes!

MR JOURDAIN. Oh, Mr Fencing Master!

DANCING MASTER. You great cart horse!

MR JOURDAIN. Oh, Mr Dancing Master!

FENCING MASTER. If I once set about you –

MR JOURDAIN [*to* DANCING MASTER]. Gently there – gently!

DANCING MASTER. If I once get my hands on you –

MR JOURDAIN. Easy now! Easy!

FENCING MASTER. I'll let a little daylight into you.

MR JOURDAIN [*to* FENCING MASTER]. Please – please – if – you please.

DANCING MASTER. I'll give you such a drubbing.

MR JOURDAIN [*to* DANCING MASTER]. I ask you – 1 –

MUSIC MASTER. Just give us a chance and we'll teach him how to talk to –

MR JOURDAIN [*to* MUSIC MASTER]. Do for goodness sake – stop!

Enter the PHILOSOPHER

MR JOURDAIN. Ah, Mr Philosopher. You've arrived in the nick of time with your philosophy. Come and make peace between these fellows.

PHILOSOPHER. What is it? What is it all about, gentlemen?

MR JOURDAIN. They've got so worked up about which of their professions is the most important that they've started slanging each other and very nearly come to blows.

PHILOSOPHER. Come, come, gentlemen! Why let yourselves be carried away like this? Have you not read Seneca *On Anger*? Believe me there is nothing so base and contemptible as a passion which reduces men to the level of animals! Surely, surely, reason should control all our actions!

DANCING MASTER. But, my good sir, he's just been black-guarding the pair of us and disparaging music, which is this gentleman's profession, and dancing which is mine.

PHILOSOPHER. A wise man is superior to any insults which can be put upon him, and the best reply to unseemly behaviour is patience and moderation.

FENCING MASTER. They had the impudence to compare their professions with mine.

PHILOSOPHER. Well, friend, why should that move you? We should never compete in vainglory or precedence. What really distinguishes men one from another is wisdom and virtue.

DANCING MASTER. I maintain that dancing is a form of skill, a science, to which sufficient honour can never be paid.

MUSIC MASTER. And I that music has been held in foremost esteem all down the ages.

FENCING MASTER. And I still stick to my point against the pair of them that skill in arms is the finest and most necessary of all the sciences.

PHILOSOPHER. In that case where does philosophy come in? I consider you are all three presumptuous to speak with such assurance before me and impudently give the title of sciences to a set of mere accomplishments which don't even deserve the name of arts and can only be adequately described under their wretched trades of gladiator, ballad singer, and mountebank!

FENCING MASTER. Oh get out! You dog of a philosopher!

MUSIC MASTER. Get out! You miserable pedant!

DANCING MASTER. Get out! You beggarly usher!

PHILOSOPHER. What! Rascals like you dare to – [*He hurls himself upon them and all three set about him.*]

MR JOURDAIN. Mr Philosopher!

PHILOSOPHER. Scoundrels, rogues, insolent –

MR JOURDAIN. Mr Philosopher!

FENCING MASTER. Confound the brute!

MR JOURDAIN. Gentlemen!

PHILOSOPHER. Insolent scoundrels!

MR JOURDAIN. Oh, Mr Philosopher!

DANCING MASTER. The devil take the ignorant blockhead!

MR JOURDAIN. Gentlemen!

PHILOSOPHER. Villains!

MR JOURDAIN. Mr Philosopher!

MUSIC MASTER. Down with him!

MR JOURDAIN. Gentlemen!

PHILOSOPHER. Rogues! Traitors! Impostors! Mountebanks!

MR JOURDAIN. Mr Philosopher, Gentlemen, Mr Philosopher, Gentlemen, Mr Philosopher, Gentlemen.

They rush out still fighting.

MR JOURDAIN. Go on then! Knock yourselves about as much as you like. I can do nothing about it and I'm not going to spoil my new dressing-gown in trying to separate you! I should look a fool shoving in among them and getting knocked about myself for my pains!

MR PHILOSOPHER *returns, straightening his neck-band.*

PHILOSOPHER. Let us come to our lesson.

MR JOURDAIN. Oh, Mr Philosopher, I'm sorry they've hurt you.

PHILOSOPHER. It is nothing. A philosopher learns how to take things as they come and I will get my own back on them with a satire in the manner of Juvenal. I'll fairly tear them to pieces. Let us think no more of it. What would you like to learn?

MR JOURDAIN. Whatever I can, for I want, above all things, to become a scholar. I blame my father and mother that they never made me go in for learning when I was young.

PHILOSOPHER. A very proper sentiment! *Nam sine doctrina vita est quasi mortis imago.* You know Latin I suppose?

MR JOURDAIN. Yes, but just go on as if I didn't. Tell me what it means.

PHILOSOPHER. It means that without knowledge, life is no more than the shadow of death.

MR JOURDAIN. Ay. Your Latin has hit the nail on the head there.

PHILOSOPHER. Have you not mastered the first principles, the rudiments of the Sciences?

MR JOURDAIN. Oh yes, I can read and write.

PHILOSOPHER. Well, where would you like to begin? Shall I teach you logic?

MR JOURDAIN. Yes, but what is it?

PHILOSOPHER. Logic instructs us in the three processes of reasoning.

MR JOURDAIN. And what are they, these three processes of reasoning?

PHILOSOPHER. The first, the second, and the third. The first is the comprehension of affinities, the second discrimination by means of categories, the third deduction by means of syllogisms. *Barbara, celarent, Darii, Ferio, Baralipton.*

MR JOURDAIN. No. They sound horrible words. Logic doesn't appeal to me. Let me learn something nicer.

PHILOSOPHER. Would you like to study moral philosophy?

MR JOURDAIN. Moral philosophy?

PHILOSOPHER. Yes.

MR JOURDAIN. And what's moral philosophy about?

PHILOSOPHER. It is concerned with the good life and teaches men how to moderate their passions.

MR JOURDAIN. No, we'll leave that out. I'm as hot-tempered as they make 'em and whatever moral philosophy may say I'll be as angry as I want whenever I feel like it.

PHILOSOPHER. Well, do you wish to study physics – the natural sciences?

MR JOURDAIN. The natural sciences? What have they to say for themselves?

PHILOSOPHER. Natural science explains the principles of natural phenomena, and the properties of matter; it is concerned with the nature of the elements, metals, minerals, precious stones, plants, and animals, and teaches us the causes of meteors, rainbows, will-o'-the-wisp, comets, lightning, thunder and thunderbolts, rain, snow, hail, tempests, and whirlwinds.

MR JOURDAIN. This is too much of a hullabaloo for me, too much of a rigmarole altogether.

PHILOSOPHER. Then what am I to teach you?

MR JOURDAIN. Teach me to spell.

PHILOSOPHER. Willingly.

MR JOURDAIN. And then you can teach me the almanac so that I shall know if there's a moon or not.

PHILOSOPHER. Very well. Now, to meet your wishes and at the same time treat the matter philosophically one must begin, according to the proper order of these things, with the precise recognition of the nature of the letters of the alphabet and the different ways of pronouncing them, and, in this connexion, I must explain that the letters are divided into vowels, so called because they express the various sounds, and consonants, so named because they are pronounced 'con', or with, the vowels and serve only to differentiate the various articulations of the voice. There are five vowels, A, E, I, O, U.*

MR JOURDAIN. I understand all that.

PHILOSOPHER. The vowel A is pronounced with the mouth open wide. So – A, Ah, Ah.

MR JOURDAIN. Ah, Ah. Yes.

PHILOSOPHER. The vowel E is pronounced by bringing the jaws near together. So, A, E – Ah, Eh.

MR JOURDAIN. A, E. Ah, Eh, now that's fine.

PHILOSOPHER. For the vowel I, bring the jaws still nearer together and stretch the mouth corners towards the ears, so – A, E, I. Ah, Eh, EEE.

MR JOURDAIN. A, E, I. Ah, Eh, EEE – It's quite right. Oh! what a wonderful thing is knowledge!

PHILOSOPHER. To pronounce the vowel O you must open the mouth again and round the lips so – O.

MR JOURDAIN. O, O. You are right again. A, E, I, O, splendid. I, O. I, O.

PHILOSOPHER. The opening of the mouth is exactly the shape of the letter – O.

MR JOURDAIN. O, O. You are right. O. How wonderful to know such things!

PHILOSOPHER. The vowel U is pronounced by bringing the teeth close together but without quite meeting and pushing the lips out so – U, U, as if you were making a face – so if you happen to show that you don't think much of a person you only need say U!

MR JOURDAIN. U, U. It's perfectly true. Oh why didn't I learn all this earlier.

* The Philosopher's instructions refer to the French vowels.

PHILOSOPHER. To-morrow we will take the other letters, the consonants.

MR JOURDAIN. Are they as interesting as those we have done?

PHILOSOPHER. Undoubtedly. The consonant D, for example, is pronounced by pressing the tip of the tongue against the upper teeth so – D, D. Da.

MR JOURDAIN. Da! Da! Splendid! Splendid!

PHILOSOPHER. F by bringing the upper teeth against the lower lip. Fa!

MR JOURDAIN. Fa, Fa. It's quite true. Oh, fa-father and mother, why didn't you teach me this –

PHILOSOPHER. And R by placing the tip of the tongue against the palate so that, alternately resisting and yielding to the force of the air coming out, it makes a little trilling R, R, R.

MR JOURDAIN. R, R, Ra. R, R, R, Ra. It's true. Ah what a clever man you are and how I've been wasting my time. R, R, Ra.

PHILOSOPHER. I will explain all these fascinating things for you.

MR JOURDAIN. Do please. And now I must tell you a secret. I'm in love with a lady of quality and I want you to help me to write her a little note I can let fall at her feet.

PHILOSOPHER. Very well.

MR JOURDAIN. That's the correct thing to do, isn't it?

PHILOSOPHER. Certainly. You want it in verse no doubt?

MR JOURDAIN. No. No. None of your verse for me.

PHILOSOPHER. You want it in prose then?

MR JOURDAIN. No. I don't want it in either.

PHILOSOPHER. But it must be one or the other.

MR JOURDAIN. Why?

PHILOSOPHER. Because, my dear sir, if you want to express yourself at all there's only verse or prose for it.

MR JOURDAIN. Only verse or prose for it?

PHILOSOPHER. That's all, sir. Whatever isn't prose is verse and anything that isn't verse is prose.

MR JOURDAIN. And talking, as I am now, which is that?

PHILOSOPHER. That is prose.

MR JOURDAIN. You mean to say that when I say 'Nicole, fetch me my slippers' or 'Give me my night-cap' that's prose?

PHILOSOPHER. Certainly, sir.

MR JOURDAIN. Well, my goodness! Here I've been talking prose for forty years and never known it, and mighty grateful I am to you for telling me! Now, what I want to say in the letter is, 'Fair Countess, I am dying for love of your beautiful eyes!' but I want it put elegantly, so that it sounds genteel.

PHILOSOPHER. Then say that the ardour of her glances has reduced your heart to ashes and that you endure night and day –

MR JOURDAIN. No. No. No! I don't want that at all. All I want is what I told you. 'Fair Countess, I am dying for love of your beautiful eyes.'

PHILOSOPHER. But it must surely be elaborated a little.

MR JOURDAIN. No, I tell you I don't want anything in the letter but those very words, but I want them to be stylish and properly arranged. Just tell me some of the different ways of putting them so that I can see which I want.

PHILOSOPHER. Well, you can put them as you have done, 'Fair Countess, I am dying for love of your beautiful eyes', or perhaps 'For love, fair Countess, of your beautiful eyes I am dying', or again 'For love of your beautiful eyes, fair Countess, dying I am', or yet again 'Your beautiful eyes, fair Countess, for love of, dying am I', or even 'Dying, fair Countess, for love of your beautiful eyes, I am'.

MR JOURDAIN. But which of these is the best?

PHILOSOPHER. The one you used yourself, 'Fair Countess, I am dying for love of your beautiful eyes'.

MR JOURDAIN. Although I've never done any study I get it right first time. Thank you with all my heart. Please come in good time to-morrow.

PHILOSOPHER. You may rely upon me, sir. [*He goes out.*]

MR JOURDAIN. Hasn't my suit arrived yet?

LACKEY. Not yet, sir.

MR JOURDAIN. That confounded tailor has kept me waiting a whole day, and just when I'm so busy too. I'm getting really annoyed. Confound him! I'm sick to death of him! If only I had him here now, the detestable scoundrel, the rascally dog, I'd – I'd . . . Ah, there you are! I was beginning to get quite annoyed with you.

The TAILOR *has come in, followed by his apprentice carrying the suit.*

TAILOR. I couldn't get here any earlier. I've had a score of my men at work on your suit.

MR JOURDAIN. The silk stockings you sent me were so tight I could hardly get them on. I've already torn two ladders in them.

TAILOR. They'll stretch all right, by and by.

MR JOURDAIN. Yes, if I tear them enough! Then, the shoes that you made for me pinch me most dreadfully.

TAILOR. Not at all, sir.

MR JOURDAIN. How d'ye mean 'not at all'?

TAILOR. They don't pinch you at all.

MR JOURDAIN. But I tell you they do!

TAILOR. No, you imagine it.

MR JOURDAIN. I imagine it? If I imagine it, it's because I can feel it. Isn't that a good enough reason?

TAILOR. Tch! Tch! The coat I have here is as fine as any at the court, most beautifully designed. It's a work of art to have made a suit which looks dignified without using black. You won't find another anywhere to touch it.

MR JOURDAIN. But what's this? You've put the sprigs up-side down.

TAILOR. You didn't say you wanted them the other way up.

MR JOURDAIN. Ought I to have told you?

TAILOR. Certainly. All gentlemen of quality wear them this way up.

MR JOURDAIN. Gentlemen of quality wear the sprigs upside down?

TAILOR. Undoubtedly.

MR JOURDAIN. Well, that's all right then.

TAILOR. You can have them the other way up if you want.

MR JOURDAIN. No. No. No.

TAILOR. You've only to say so.

MR JOURDAIN. No, you've done very well. Do you think it will fit me?

TAILOR. What a question! If I'd drawn you on paper I couldn't have got nearer your fit. I have a man who is a genius at cutting out breeches and another who hasn't an equal at fitting a doublet.

MR JOURDAIN. Are my wig and hat all they should be?

TAILOR. Everything is excellent.

MR JOURDAIN [*looking at the* TAILOR'S *suit*]. Ha ha! Master Tailor! Isn't that some of the stuff I got for the last suit you made me? I am sure that I recognize it.

TAILOR. Yes, the fact is I liked the material so much I felt I must have a suit cut from it myself.

MR JOURDAIN. That's all very well but it shouldn't have come out of my stuff.

TAILOR. Are you going to try your suit on?

MR JOURDAIN. Yes, hand it here.

TAILOR. Wait a moment! That is not the way things are done. I have brought my men with me to dress you to music. Suits like these must be put on with ceremony. Hello there! Come in! *Enter four tailor boys dancing.*

TAILOR. Put on the gentleman's suit in a manner befitting a gentleman of quality!

Four tailor boys dance up to MR JOURDAIN. *Two take off the breeches in which he did his exercises: the others remove his jacket, after which they dress him in his new suit.* MR JOURDAIN *struts round to be admired in time with the music.*

FIRST TAILOR BOY. Now, kind gentleman, please give something to these fellows to drink your health.

MR JOURDAIN. What did you call me?

TAILOR BOY. 'Kind gentleman.'

MR JOURDAIN. 'Kind gentleman.' What it is to be got up as one of the quality! Go on dressing as an ordinary person and nobody will ever call you a gentleman. Here! That's for your 'kind gentleman'.

TAILOR BOY. My lord! We are infinitely obliged to you.

MR JOURDAIN. 'My lord!' Oh my goodness! 'My lord.' Wait a minute, my lad. 'My lord' is worth something more. 'My lord' is something like! Here, that's what 'My lord' brings you [*gives more money*].

TAILOR BOY. My lord, we will all drink to your Grace's good health.

MR JOURDAIN. 'Your Grace!' Oh. Oh wait! Don't go away. Come here. 'Your Grace!' [*Aside*] If he goes as far as Your Highness he'll get the whole purse. Take this for your 'Your Grace'.

TAILOR BOY. My lord, we thank your Lordship for your Grace's liberality.

MR JOURDAIN. Just as well he stopped. I nearly gave him the lot.

The four tailor boys show their satisfaction by a dance which forms the Second Interlude.

Act Three

MR JOURDAIN *and* LACKEYS.

MR JOURDAIN. Follow me! I'm going out to show off my clothes in the town. Mind you keep close behind me so that people know you belong to me.

LACKEYS. Very good, sir.

MR JOURDAIN. Wait! Call Nicole for me. I want to tell her what she has to do. No, wait a minute. She's coming.

Enter NICOLE.

MR JOURDAIN. Nicole!

NICOLE. Yes sir, what is it?

MR JOURDAIN. Listen.

NICOLE [*laughing*]. Ha ha ha! Ha ha ha!

MR JOURDAIN. What are you laughing at?

NICOLE. Ha ha ha! Ha ha ha!

MR JOURDAIN. What's wrong with the hussy?

NICOLE. Ha ha ha! Ha ha ha! Fancy you got up like that! Ha ha ha!

MR JOURDAIN. Whatever d'ye mean?

NICOLE. Oh, my goodness! Ha ha ha! Ha ha ha!

MR JOURDAIN. Silly creature! Are you laughing at me?

NICOLE. No master. I should hate to do that. Oh ho ho! Ho ho ho! Ha ha ha! Ha ha ha!

MR JOURDAIN. I'll box your ears if you laugh any more.

NICOLE. Ha ha ha! Ha ha ha! I can't help it, master [*laughs again*].

MR JOURDAIN. Are you never going to stop?

NICOLE. I'm sorry, master, but you look so funny I just can't help laughing [*laughs again*].

MR JOURDAIN. Oh! the impudence!

NICOLE. But you look so – so funny like that [*laughs again*].

MR JOURDAIN. I'll –

NICOLE. Forgive me, I – [*laughs again*].

MR JOURDAIN. Look here! If you laugh any more I'll give you such a smack across the face as you've never had in your life.

NICOLE. All right, master, I've finished! I shan't laugh any more.

MR JOURDAIN. Well take care you don't. You must clean up the hall ready for –

NICOLE. Ha ha ha!

MR JOURDAIN. You must clean it up properly or –

NICOLE. Ha ha ha!

MR JOURDAIN. What! Again?

NICOLE. Look here, master, wallop me afterwards but let me have my laugh out first. It'll do me more good – ha ha ha!

MR JOURDAIN. I'm losing my temper –

NICOLE. Oh master, please, let me laugh – ha ha ha!

MR JOURDAIN. If I once start to –

NICOLE. I shall die if you don't let me laugh – ha ha ha!

MR JOURDAIN. Was there ever such a good-for-nothing! She laughs in my face instead of listening to what I'm telling her.

NICOLE. What – what is it you want me to do, sir?

MR JOURDAIN. What do you think, you slut? Get the house ready for the company I'm expecting here shortly.

NICOLE. My goodness. That stops my laughing. Those visitors of yours make such an upset that the very word company puts me out.

MR JOURDAIN. And am I to shut my door on my visitors to please you?

NICOLE. You ought to shut it on some of them.

Enter MRS JOURDAIN

MRS JOURDAIN. What new nonsense is it this time? What are you doing in that get-up, man? Whatever are you thinking about to get yourself rigged out like that! Do you want to have everybody laughing at you?

MR JOURDAIN. My good woman, only the fools will laugh at me.

MRS JOURDAIN. Well, it isn't as if folk have not done it

before! Your goings on have long been a laughing-stock for most people.

MR JOURDAIN. What sort of people may I ask?

MRS JOURDAIN. People with more sense than you have. I'm disgusted with the life you are leading. I can't call the house my own any more. It's like a carnival-time all day and every day with fiddling and bawling enough to rouse the whole neighbourhood.

NICOLE. The mistress is right. I can't keep the place clean because of the good-for-nothing pack you bring into the house. They pick up mud all over the town and cart it in here. Poor Frances is wearing her knees out polishing the floors for your fine gentlemen to come and muck them up again every day.

MR JOURDAIN. Now, now, our Nicole! For a country lass you've a pretty sharp tongue.

MRS JOURDAIN. Nicole is quite right. She has more sense than you have. I'd like to know what you think you want with a dancing master at your time of life.

NICOLE. Or with that great lump of a fencing master that comes stamping in, upsetting the house and loosening the very tiles in the floor.

MR JOURDAIN. Be quiet, both of you!

MRS JOURDAIN. Are you learning dancing against the time when you'll be too feeble to walk?

NICOLE. Is it because you want to murder somebody that you are learning fencing?

MR JOURDAIN. Shut up, I tell you! You are just ignorant, both of you. You don't understand the significance of these things.

MRS JOURDAIN. You'd do much better to think about getting your daughter married now that she's of an age to be pro-vided with a husband.

MR JOURDAIN. I'll think about getting my daughter married when a suitable husband comes along. In the meantime I want to give my mind to learning and study.

NICOLE. I've just heard tell, madam, that, to crown all, he's taken on a philosophy master to-day.

MR JOURDAIN. Well, why not? I tell you I want to improve

my mind and learn to hold my own among civilized people.

MRS JOURDAIN. Then why don't you go back to school one of these days and get yourself soundly whipped?

MR JOURDAIN. Why not? I wish to goodness I could be whipped here and now and never mind who saw me if it would help me to learn what they teach them in schools.

NICOLE. My goodness! A lot of good that would do you!

MR JOURDAIN. Of course it would.

MRS JOURDAIN. No doubt it's all very useful for carrying on your household affairs.

MR JOURDAIN. Of course it is. You are both talking nonsense. I'm ashamed of your ignorance. For example, do you know what you are doing – what you are talking at this very moment?

MRS JOURDAIN. I'm talking plain common sense – you ought to be mending your ways.

MR JOURDAIN. That's not what I mean. What I'm asking is what sort of speech are you using?

MRS JOURDAIN. Speech. I'm not making a speech. But what I'm saying makes sense and that's more than can be said for your goings on.

MR JOURDAIN. I'm not talking about that. I'm asking what I am talking now. The words I am using – what are they?

MRS JOURDAIN. Stuff and nonsense!

MR JOURDAIN. Not at all! The words we are both using. What are they?

MRS JOURDAIN. Well, what on earth *are* they?

MR JOURDAIN. What are they called?

MRS JOURDAIN. Call them what you like.

MR JOURDAIN. They are prose, you ignorant creature!

MRS JOURDAIN. Prose?

MR JOURDAIN. Yes, prose! Everything that's prose isn't verse and everything that isn't verse is prose. Now you see what it is to be a scholar! And you [*to* NICOLE], do you know what you have to do to say 'U'?

NICOLE. Eh?

MR JOURDAIN. What do you have to do to say 'U'?

NICOLE. What?

MR JOURDAIN. Say 'U' and see!

NICOLE. All right then – 'U'.

MR JOURDAIN. Well what did you do?

NICOLE. I said 'U'.

MR JOURDAIN. Yes, but when you said 'U' what did you do?

NICOLE. I did what you told me to.

MR JOURDAIN. Oh! What it is to have to deal with stupidity! You push your lips out and bring your lower jaw up to your upper one and – 'U' – you see? I make a face like this – 'U-U-U'.

NICOLE. Yes, that's grand I must say!

MRS JOURDAIN. Really remarkable!

MR JOURDAIN. Yes, but that's only one thing. You should have heard 'O' and 'Da' and 'Fa'.

MRS JOURDAIN. What on earth is all this rigmarole?

NICOLE. And what good is it going to be to anybody?

MR JOURDAIN. It exasperates me to see how ignorant women can be!

MRS JOURDAIN. Oh get off with you! You ought to send all these fellows packing with their ridiculous tomfoolery.

NICOLE. And especially that great lump of a fencing master who fills my kitchen with dust.

MR JOURDAIN. Fencing master again! You've got him on the brain. I can see I shall have to teach you your manners. [*Calls for the foils and hands one to* NICOLE.] There, take it! Now for a logical demonstration! The line of the body! When you lunge in quart you do – so, and when you lunge in tierce you do – so! If you only do like that you can be sure that you'll never be killed. It's a grand thing to know that you are safe when you are fighting. There now – have at me. Let's see what you can do.

NICOLE. Very well, what about that? [*She thrusts at him several times.*]

MR JOURDAIN. Steady on! Steady on! Confound the silly creature!

NICOLE. Well you told me to do it.

MR JOURDAIN. Yes, but you led in tierce before you led in quart and you never gave me time to parry.

MRS JOURDAIN. You are mad, my lad! All this nonsense has

gone to your head. It all comes of hanging round the gentry.

MR JOURDAIN. If I hang round the gentry I show my good taste. It's better than hanging round your shopkeeping crowd.

MRS JOURDAIN. Oh yes, I've no doubt! A lot of good you'll get out of hanging round the gentry, especially this fine gentleman you are so struck on.

MR JOURDAIN. Be quiet and mind what you say. You don't know what you are talking about. He's a much more important person than you think. He's a nobleman in high favour at court. He talks to the king just as I'm talking to you. Isn't that something to be proud of – that folks should see him coming to my house and that a man of his rank should be calling me his friend and treating me as an equal? You've no idea how good he is to me! I am quite embarrassed by the kindness he shows me, and quite openly too.

MRS JOURDAIN. Ay, he'll show you kindness, no doubt, and then borrow your money.

MR JOURDAIN. And isn't it a privilege to lend money to a gentleman like that? Can I do less for a nobleman who calls me his dear friend?

MRS JOURDAIN. And what does he do for you, this nobleman?

MR JOURDAIN. Things that would surprise you if you only knew.

MRS JOURDAIN. Such as?

MR JOURDAIN. Never you mind. I'm not going to explain. It's enough that, if I've lent him money, he'll pay it back before long.

MRS JOURDAIN. Do you really expect him to?

MR JOURDAIN. Of course! Has he not given me his promise?

MRS JOURDAIN. Yes, and I don't doubt he'll go back on it.

MR JOURDAIN. He's given me his word as a gentleman.

MRS JOURDAIN. Oh fiddlesticks!

MR JOURDAIN. You are very obstinate, my dear. You can take it from me he will stand by his word. I'm sure of it.

MRS JOURDAIN. And I'm sure he won't, and that all his kindness is just to get round you.

MR JOURDAIN. Be quiet! Here he comes.

MRS JOURDAIN. That's the last straw. I expect he's come to

borrow again. I am fed up at the very sight of him.

MR JOURDAIN. Oh be quiet, I tell you.

Enter DORANTE.

DORANTE. Ah Jourdain, my friend, how do you do?

MR JOURDAIN. I am very well, sir, at your service.

DORANTE. And Mrs Jourdain, how is she?

MRS JOURDAIN. Mrs Jourdain is as well as can be expected.

DORANTE. Well, Jourdain, you look very smart.

MR JOURDAIN. Do you think so?

DORANTE. Oh yes! You look very handsome indeed in this coat. We have no young men at court better turned out than you are.

MR JOURDAIN. He he!

MRS JOURDAIN [*aside*]. That's scratching him where it itches.

DORANTE. Turn around. Most elegant.

MRS JOURDAIN [*aside*]. Yes, he looks as silly behind as in front.

DORANTE. Upon my word, Jourdain, I have been looking forward to seeing you. You know I have the greatest regard for you. I was talking about you only this morning in the Royal Presence.

MR JOURDAIN. You do me great honour, sir. [*Aside to* MRS JOURDAIN] In the Royal Presence!

DORANTE. Come, put on your hat!

MR JOURDAIN. Sir, I know the respect I owe to you.

DORANTE. Please, put on your hat. No ceremony between us, I beg you.

MR JOURDAIN. Sir –

DORANTE. Do put on your hat, Mr Jourdain. You are my friend.

MR JOURDAIN. Sir, I'm your very humble servant.

DORANTE. But I cannot put on my own hat unless you put on yours.

MR JOURDAIN [*putting on his hat*]. I'll forgo my manners rather than be a nuisance.

DORANTE. As you know, I am your debtor.

MRS JOURDAIN [*aside*]. We know that all right.

DORANTE. You have very kindly lent me money on various occasions in a most obliging and considerate fashion.

MR JOURDAIN. Sir, you don't mean it!

DORANTE. No no! I know how to repay what I owe and how to acknowledge a kindness.

MR JOURDAIN. Sir, I don't doubt it at all.

DORANTE. I would like to settle up with you. I came along so that we might reckon up our accounts together.

MR JOURDAIN [*to* MRS JOURDAIN – *aside*]. You see! What have you to say now, woman?

DORANTE. I am a man who likes to meet his obligations as promptly as possible.

MR JOURDAIN [*to* MRS JOURDAIN *as before*]. What did I tell you?

DORANTE. Shall we see what I owe you?

MR JOURDAIN [*again as before*]. You and your silly suspicions!

DORANTE. You can recollect, I assume, all the amounts you have lent me?

MR JOURDAIN. Yes, I think so. I have kept a note of them. Here we are – the first time I let you have two hundred guineas.

DORANTE. Agreed.

MR JOURDAIN. Next time, a hundred and twenty.

DORANTE. Yes.

MR JOURDAIN. Third time, a hundred and forty.

DORANTE. Correct.

MR JOURDAIN. That makes four hundred and sixty guineas, say four hundred and eighty-three pounds.

DORANTE. Yes, the amount is correct, four hundred and eighty-three pounds.

MR JOURDAIN. Then there was a further ninety-six pounds paid to your plume-maker.

DORANTE. Right.

MR JOURDAIN. One hundred and ninety to your tailor.

DORANTE. Good.

MR JOURDAIN. Two hundred and eighteen pounds, twelve shillings and eightpence to another of your tradesmen –

DORANTE. Twelve shillings and eightpence. That's exactly right.

MR JOURDAIN. Add eighty-seven pounds, seven shillings and fourpence paid to your saddler.

DORANTE. And what does all that come to?

MR JOURDAIN. Total – one thousand and seventy-five pounds exactly.

DORANTE. Agreed. One thousand and seventy-five pounds exactly. Now – add on another two hundred and twenty-five pounds, that you are going to let me have, and that will make thirteen hundred pounds that I will repay you at the earliest possible opportunity.

MRS JOURDAIN [*to* MR JOURDAIN *aside*]. Ha ha! Didn't I guess as much.

MR JOURDAIN [*aside*]. Shut up!

DORANTE. Are you sure it won't inconvenience you to let me have that amount?

MR JOURDAIN. Not at all.

MRS JOURDAIN [*to* MR JOURDAIN *aside*]. This fellow is making a milch cow of you!

MR JOURDAIN [*aside*]. Oh! Do be quiet!

DORANTE. If it isn't convenient I can go somewhere else.

MR JOURDAIN. No no, sir.

MRS JOURDAIN [*as before*]. He'll never be satisfied until he's brought you to ruin.

MR JOURDAIN [*aside*]. Be quiet, will you!

DORANTE. If it's any trouble – you've only to say so.

MR JOURDAIN. It's no trouble at all.

MRS JOURDAIN [*as before*]. He's a real wheedler, he is!

MR JOURDAIN [*aside*]. Be quiet, I tell you!

MRS JOURDAIN [*aside*]. He'll drain your last farthing.

MR JOURDAIN [*aside*]. Will you be quiet?

DORANTE. There are plenty of people who would lend me money with pleasure, but as you are my dearest friend I thought you would be offended if I asked anyone else.

MR JOURDAIN. I'm only too glad to oblige you, sir. I'll go and fetch what you want.

MRS JOURDAIN [*aside as before*]. What! You aren't going to let him have more!

MR JOURDAIN [*going*]. What can I do? Would you have me refuse a man of his position – a man who was talking about me only this morning in the Royal Presence!

MRS JOURDAIN [*as before*]. Oh, go on with you! You are a real mug, you are!

MR JOURDAIN goes out.

DORANTE. You look troubled, Mrs Jourdain. What is the matter?

MRS JOURDAIN. I've got a head on my shoulders.

DORANTE. And your daughter, where is she? I don't see her to-day.

MRS JOURDAIN. My daughter's all right where she is.

DORANTE. And how is she getting on?

MRS JOURDAIN. On her two legs, I suppose.

DORANTE. Would you care to bring her along one day to see the ballet and the plays at the court?

MRS JOURDAIN. Yes, why not? We like a good laugh, we do that!

DORANTE. I imagine, Mrs Jourdain, you must have had many admirers in your young days – charming and attractive as you no doubt were then.

MRS JOURDAIN. Really! Mrs Jourdain is as old and doddery as all that, is she?

DORANTE. Forgive me, Mrs Jourdain! I was forgetting how young you still are – I am quite absent-minded. Please pardon my foolishness.

Re-enter MR JOURDAIN.

MR JOURDAIN. Here we are. Two hundred and twenty-five pounds exactly.

DORANTE. Remember, Mr Jourdain, I am entirely at your disposal. If I can render you any service at court – I shall be only too pleased.

MR JOURDAIN. You are really too kind.

DORANTE. If Mrs Jourdain would care to see one of the Royal Entertainments, I could arrange for her to have one of the very best seats.

MRS JOURDAIN. Mrs Jourdain says no, thank you very much.

DORANTE [*to* MR JOURDAIN]. As I told you in my note, our fair countess will be here soon to dine with us and see the ballet. I persuaded her in the end to accept your invitation.

MR JOURDAIN [*aside to* DORANTE]. Let us move a little further away. You understand the reason why.

DORANTE. It is a week since I saw you, so I haven't told you about the diamond you entrusted me to give to her. I had the very greatest difficulty in overcoming her scruples and the fact is she only agreed to accept it to-day.

MR JOURDAIN. And how did she like it?

DORANTE. Very much indeed! I shall be surprised if the diamond doesn't make her look much more kindly upon you.

MR JOURDAIN. Ah! If only it would!

MRS JOURDAIN [*to* NICOLE]. Once this fellow is with him, there's no getting him away.

DORANTE. I have impressed upon her both the value of your present and the ardour of your affection for her.

MR JOURDAIN. You overwhelm me with kindness, sir. I'm only concerned that a gentleman of your rank should demean himself so on my account.

DORANTE. Don't mention it! What are things like that between friends? Wouldn't you do as much for me if you had the chance?

MR JOURDAIN. Of course! With all my heart.

MRS JOURDAIN [*aside*]. I can't bear the sight of him.

DORANTE. I never spare myself if I can be of service to a friend, and when you confided in me your love for this charming lady, as I happened to know her, I offered my help at once on your behalf, as you know.

MR JOURDAIN. That's true, and I can't thank you enough for your kindness.

MRS JOURDAIN [*to* NICOLE]. Is he never going to go?

NICOLE [*to* MRS JOURDAIN]. Thick as thieves, they are!

DORANTE. You have gone the right way to win her affection. Women love nothing so much as having money spent on them. Your serenades and repeated presents of flowers, the superb firework display on the lake, the diamond you sent her, and the entertainment you are now preparing are bound to influence her in your favour more than anything you could say for yourself.

MR JOURDAIN. I would go to any expense if only it would open the way to her heart. I would give anything in the world to win the love of a lady of quality.

MRS JOURDAIN [*to* NICOLE]. What on earth are they talking

about for so long? Just steal up and listen.

DORANTE. You will soon enjoy the pleasure of seeing her and be able to feast your eyes on her to your heart's content.

MR JOURDAIN. To avoid any complications, I've arranged for my wife to dine at my sister's and stay there after dinner.

DORANTE. That was very prudent. Your wife might have been in the way. I have given the necessary instructions to the cook on your behalf and made all arrangements for the ballet. Everything is just what I should have chosen myself, and, provided it comes up to my hopes, I a m sure that –

MR JOURDAIN [*noticing that* NICOLE *is eavesdropping, gives her a slap.*] The impudence! [*To* DORANTE] Let us go. [*They go out.*]

NICOLE *and* MRS JOURDAIN *come down stage.*

NICOLE. That's what I get for being inquisitive! But I'm sure there is something fishy going on, and it's something they aren't going to let you have a hand in.

MRS JOURDAIN. It's not the first time, Nicole, that I've had suspicions of my husband. Unless I'm much mistaken, he is involved in a love affair, and I'm going to get to the bottom of it. But let us think about my daughter first. You know Cléonte is in love with her. He's a man after my own heart and I mean to help him to marry Lucile if I can.

NICOLE. Well, madam, I'm delighted to hear you say so, for if you fancy the master for her, I fancy the man for myself, and I hope our marriage can be arranged along with theirs.

MRS JOURDAIN. Go and have a word with him and ask him to come along to see me. Then we can tackle my husband together. [*She goes out.*]

NICOLE. I'll run along at once. Nothing could give me more pleasure. [*Alone*] That ought to please these fellows, I should think.

Enter CLÉONTE *and* COVIELLE.

NICOLE. Ah, there you are, sir! Just at the right moment! I'm the bringer of good news and . . .

CLÉONTE. Get out, you deceitful hussy! Don't try to bamboozle me with your lies.

NICOLE. Is that how you receive –

CLÉONTE. Go, I tell you, and let your false mistress know that she'll never again make a fool of her too trusting Cléonte.

NICOLE. Whatever can have upset him? My dear Covielle, do tell me what it all means!

COVIELLE. Your dear Covielle! You little minx! Get out of my sight and never trouble me any more!

NICOLE. So you turn on me too!

COVIELLE. Get out of my sight! Never speak to me again!

NICOLE. Well, I never! What's bitten them? I must go tell the mistress about this. [*She goes out.*]

CLÉONTE. What a way of treating a lover! And a lover as sincere and devoted as I am –

COVIELLE. Yes, it's too bad – too bad for the pair of us.

CLÉONTE. I show her every imaginable affection and tenderness. She's the only thing in the world that I care for. I haven't a thought for anyone else. I think of her, dream of her, long for her, live for her – for her and her only! And what do I get in return? I go two days without seeing her, two days that seem like two centuries. I meet her by accident. I'm overwhelmed with the joy of it. Radiant with happiness, I fly towards her and – what happens? The perfidious creature turns away from me and passes me by as if she'd never seen me before in her life!

COVIELLE. That all goes for me too.

CLÉONTE. Did you ever, Covielle, see the like of this ungrateful Lucile?

COVIELLE. Or you, sir, of this wicked Nicole?

CLÉONTE. After all I have done for her, the sighs – the devotion that I have paid to her charms.

COVIELLE. After all my constant attentions, all the service I've done in the kitchen.

CLÉONTE. The tears I have shed at her feet!

COVIELLE. All the buckets I've drawn from the well.

CLÉONTE. The ardour I have shown for her – loving her more than myself.

COVIELLE. The heat that I've suffered – turning the spit for her.

CLÉONTE. And now she passes me by in disdain.

COVIELLE. And mine just turns her back on me.

CLÉONTE. Such perfidy deserves to be punished severely.

COVIELLE. What mine needs is a box on the ear.

CLÉONTE. Don't dare mention her name to me any more.

COVIELLE. I, sir? Heaven forbid!

CLÉONTE. Never come and try to excuse her.

COVIELLE. Never fear!

CLÉONTE. Try as you will to defend her – it won't make any difference.

COVIELLE. I have no such intention.

CLÉONTE. I'll nurse my resentment and have no more to do with her.

COVIELLE. I'm all for that too.

CLÉONTE. That nobleman who comes to the house has perhaps taken her fancy. Clearly she is letting herself be dazzled by rank and position. For my own self-respect I must break it off first and forestall her inconstancy. She shan't have the satisfaction of jilting me first.

COVIELLE. Quite right! I am with you entirely.

CLÉONTE. Hold me to my resentment. Support my resolve against any last, lingering vestige of love that may plead for her. Tell me all the harsh things you can think of her. Describe her in terms that will make me despise her. Bring out all her faults so that I may come to dislike her.

COVIELLE. Well, what is she, anyhow? She's an empty-headed piece of affectation for anyone to be so much in love with! I never could see what there was in her. You could find a hundred girls more worthy of you. In the first place – her eyes are too small.

CLÉONTE. Yes. They are small. But how full of fire, how sparkling, how lively, how tender!

COVIELLE. Her mouth is too large.

CLÉONTE. True, but there's no other like it – so enticing – so tempting – just made for kissing.

COVIELLE. She's not very tall.

CLÉONTE. No – but how slender and graceful.

COVIELLE. She affects a casual manner of speech and behaviour.

CLÉONTE. But how well it suits her! Her ways are quite irresistible.

COVIELLE. As for wit –

CLÉONTE. Ah, come, Covielle! She has the most delicate wit in the world – so subtle – so –

COVIELLE. Her conversation –

CLÉONTE. Her conversation's delightful.

COVIELLE. She tends to be serious –

CLÉONTE. Ah! You prefer jocularity, everlasting high spirits! Don't you find something tiresome in women who giggle at everything?

COVIELLE. Finally, she's the most capricious of women.

CLÉONTE. Capricious. Yes. I agree, capricious she is, but then, how her caprices become her!

COVIELLE. Well, there you are! It's obvious that you are determined to love her whatever may happen.

CLÉONTE. Me? I'd sooner die first! I intend to hate her now as much as I once used to love her.

COVIELLE. But how can you, when you think she's perfection?

CLÉONTE. That's how I shall get my revenge and show my strength of purpose the better – by hating her, despising her, giving her up, beautiful, charming, lovable though I know her to be! Here she comes.

Enter LUCILE *with* NICOLE.

NICOLE. Really shocking, I call it!

LUCILE. It can only be what I told you, Nicole. But here he is!

CLÉONTE. I won't even speak to her.

COVIELLE. Neither will I.

LUCILE. Is there something wrong, Cléonte?

NICOLE. What ails you, Covielle?

LUCILE. Has something annoyed you?

NICOLE. Did you get out of bed the wrong side this morning?

LUCILE. Can you not answer, Cléonte?

NICOLE. Have you lost your tongue, Covielle?

CLÉONTE. It's shameful!

COVIELLE. A regular Jezebel.

LUCILE. I suppose our meeting a little while ago has upset you.

CLÉONTE. It seems they know what they've done.

NICOLE. The way we passed you this morning has got your goat, has it?

COVIELLE. They've guessed what the trouble is.

LUCILE. Is that not it, Cléonte? Is that not why you are angry?

CLÉONTE. Yes, faithless creature, since we must speak, it is. And let me tell you that you shan't have the satisfaction of jilting me, as you think, for I mean to break with you first. I shall find it hard to forget my love for you. I shall grieve. I shall suffer for a while but I shall get over it eventually, and I'd die rather than be so weak as to come back to you.

COVIELLE. That goes for me too.

LUCILE. What a fuss about nothing. Do let me tell you, Cléonte, why I avoided you this morning.

CLÉONTE. No, I won't listen.

NICOLE. Let me tell you, Covielle, why we were in such a hurry.

COVIELLE. No, I don't want to hear.

LUCILE. When we met you this morning –

CLÉONTE. No, I say –

NICOLE. Let me tell you that –

COVIELLE. No, no! You traitress –

LUCILE. Listen –

CLÉONTE. Not a word!

NICOLE. Just let me say –

COVIELLE. I'm deaf. I can't hear.

LUCILE. Cléonte!

CLÉONTE. No.

NICOLE. Covielle!

COVIELLE. Never.

LUCILE. Do stay one moment –

CLÉONTE. Oh! Fiddlesticks!

NICOLE. Listen to me –

COVIELLE. Nonsense!

LUCILE. One moment.

CLÉONTE. Not an instant.

NICOLE. Just be patient a minute!

COVIELLE. Fiddle de dee!

LUCILE. Just one word.

CLÉONTE. It's over and done with.

NICOLE. One word in your ear.

COVIELLE. Not even a syllable.

LUCILE. Very well, then, since you won't listen, you can think what you like and do as you please.

NICOLE. If that's how you behave, take it which way you choose.

CLÉONTE. Well then, let us hear why you behaved so charmingly.

LUCILE. I don't feel like telling you now.

COVIELLE. Tell us what happened.

NICOLE. No! I won't tell you either!

CLÉONTE. Do please say –

LUCILE. No, I don't choose to tell.

COVIELLE. Come, won't you tell me?

NICOLE. No, I won't tell you anything.

CLÉONTE. Please.

LUCILE. No, I say –

COVIELLE. Oh come, have a heart!

NICOLE. No. Nothing doing.

CLÉONTE. Please, I beg you –

LUCILE. Do leave me alone.

COVIELLE. I implore you.

NICOLE. Get out of here.

CLÉONTE. Lucile!

LUCILE. No.

COVIELLE. Nicole.

NICOLE. Never!

CLÉONTE. For heaven's sake!

LUCILE. No, I won't.

COVIELLE. Speak to me.

NICOLE. Not I!

CLÉONTE. Please clear up my doubts.

LUCILE. I shall do no such thing.

COVIELLE. Put me out of my misery.

NICOLE. No, I don't want to.

CLÉONTE. Very well. Since you don't care to relieve my anxiety, since you refuse to explain your heartless behaviour to me – look on me for the last time, ungrateful girl! I'm going far away to perish of grief and love.

COVIELLE. And I'm going to follow in his footsteps.

LUCILE. Cléonte!

CLÉONTE. Eh?

NICOLE. Covielle!

COVIELLE. Did you say something?

LUCILE. Where are you going?

CLÉONTE. Where I told you.

COVIELLE. We are going to our death.

LUCILE. *You* aren't going to die, Cléonte?

CLÉONTE. Yes, cruel girl. Since that is your wish.

LUCILE. What, I wish you to die?

CLÉONTE. Yes you wish me to die.

LUCILE. Who told you that?

CLÉONTE. You must wish it since you won't clear up my doubts.

LUCILE. Is it my fault? If you would only have listened I would have told you that the whole trouble you complain of arose because my old aunt was with us this morning, and she firmly believes that no young girl should ever so much as let a man come anywhere near her. She is for ever lecturing us on the subject. According to her, men are all devils, and we must shun their advances.

NICOLE. And that's all there is in it.

CLÉONTE. You are not deceiving me, Lucile?

COVIELLE. Nicole, you're not taking me in?

LUCILE. That is the truth, the whole truth –

NICOLE. And nothing but the truth.

COVIELLE. Is this where we give in?

CLÉONTE. Ah, Lucile, how well you know the way to allay all my troubles with one single word from your lips. How easily one can be reassured by those whom one loves.

COVIELLE. How easily one can be led by the nose you mean – by these – confounded creatures!

Enter MRS JOURDAIN.

MRS JOURDAIN. Ah, I am delighted to see you, Cléonte. You have come just at the right moment. My husband is coming in, so take your chance quickly and ask him to let you marry Lucile.

CLÉONTE. Ah, madam, no command could be nearer to my desires, or more gracious, more acceptable to me.

Enter MR JOURDAIN.

CLÉONTE. Sir, I wanted to put to you myself, rather than through a third person, a request I have long been considering, so, without further preliminary, may I ask you to accord me the honour and the privilege of becoming your son-in-law?

MR JOURDAIN. Before giving you a reply, sir, I must ask you to answer one question. Are you a gentleman?

CLÉONTE. Most men would have little hesitation, sir, in answering that question. Such a matter is quickly decided. The title is easy enough to assume, and custom to-day appears to sanction the appropriation. I myself am a little more scrupulous. I believe that any form of deception is unworthy of an honourable man and that it is wrong to disguise the estate to which it has pleased Heaven to call one, to appear in the eyes of the world under an assumed title, to pretend to be what one is not. I was born, sir, of honourable parentage. I have served for six years in the army and with some credit, and have, I believe, means sufficient to maintain a pretty fair position in the world. Nevertheless, I make no pretence to a title which others in my place might very well consider themselves entitled to assume. I, therefore, tell you frankly that I am not, as you put it, a gentleman.

MR JOURDAIN. That settles it, then. My daughter is not for you.

CLÉONTE. What!

MR JOURDAIN. If you aren't a gentleman, you can't have my daughter.

MRS JOURDAIN. What are you talking about? You and your gentleman! Do you reckon we are of the blood of St Louis?

MR JOURDAIN. Be quiet! I know what you are getting at.

MRS JOURDAIN. What are we, either of us, but plain, decent folk?

MR JOURDAIN. What a way to be talking!

MRS JOURDAIN. Wasn't your father a tradesman, the same as mine?

MR JOURDAIN. Oh, confound the woman! She never fails to bring that up! If your father was a tradesman, so much the worse for him – but as for mine, people who make such a statement don't know what they are talking about. And what I do say is that I insist on having a gentleman for my son-in-law.

MRS JOURDAIN. And I say that our daughter should marry someone of her own sort. Far better a decent man, good-looking and comfortably off, than a beggarly gentleman who is neither use nor ornament.

NICOLE. The mistress is right. The squire's son in our village is the most awkward good-for-nothing lout you ever saw.

MR JOURDAIN. Be quiet, Miss Impertinence! You are always putting your oar in. I can afford to see that my daughter goes up in the world, and I mean to make her a marchioness.

MRS JOURDAIN. A marchioness!

MR JOURDAIN. Yes! A marchioness!

MRS JOURDAIN. Heaven forbid!

MR JOURDAIN. I've made up my mind on it.

MRS JOURDAIN. Yes, and I've made up mine too, and I'll never consent. Marrying above one's station always brings trouble. I don't want a son-in-law who'll look down on my daughter because of her parentage, and I don't want her children to be ashamed to call me their grandmother neither, nor to have her coming to see me in style and perhaps forgetting to say 'How d'ye do' to one of the neighbours. Folk wouldn't fail to say all sorts of ill-natured things. 'See the grand lady with her high and mighty airs,' they would say, 'it's old Jourdain's daughter. She was glad enough to play at being ladies with us when she was a child. She's gone up in the world since then, but both her grandparents sold cloth in the market by Holy Innocents' Gate: they scraped money together for their children and they must be paying pretty dear for it now in the next world, for you don't get as rich as that by remaining honest.' No, I don't want that sort of gossip. I want a man who will be grateful to me for my daughter so that I shall be able to say to him, 'Sit down and have dinner with us, lad.'

MR JOURDAIN. That all shows what a little mind you have – not to want to rise in the world. It's no use arguing. I shall make my daughter a marchioness if all the world is against me, and if you provoke me any further I'll make her a duchess! [*He goes out.*]

MRS JOURDAIN. Don't lose heart yet, Cléonte. Come with me Lucile and tell your father firmly that if you can't have

Cléonte you won't marry anyone [*They go out.*]

COVIELLE [*to* CLÉONTE]. A nice mess you've made of it now with your high-sounding sentiments.

CLÉONTE. What else could I do? To me it's a matter of principle.

COVIELLE. Why take the man seriously? Can't you see that he's mad? Couldn't you have humoured his fancies?

CLÉONTE. You may be right, but I never thought I should need to offer proofs of nobility to become old Jourdain's son-in-law.

COVIELLE. Ha ha ha!

CLÉONTE. What are you laughing at?

COVIELLE. Just an idea that occurred to me. A way we could take the old fellow in and get what you want at the same time.

CLÉONTE. Well?

COVIELLE. It's quite an amusing idea.

CLÉONTE. Well then, what is it?

COVIELLE. An idea I got from a play I saw some time ago. It would make a lovely practical joke to play on the old blockhead. It's really quite farcical, but I imagine we can risk almost anything with him without worrying unduly. He fits the part to perfection and he'll swallow any nonsensical story we see fit to tell him. I have actors and costumes ready. Just leave it to me.

CLÉONTE. But tell me what it's about.

COVIELLE. I'll tell you all in good time. Let's be off now, for he's coming.

Enter MR JOURDAIN.

MR JOURDAIN. I don't see what the deuce the fuss is about. The only thing they have to reproach me about is my respect for the quality. Yet there is nothing to compare, in my opinion, with genteel society. There's no true honour and dignity except among the nobility. I would give my right hand to have been born a count or a marquis.

LACKEY. Sir! Here is my lord and a lady with him.

JOURDAIN. Oh! Heavens! And I still have some instructions to give. Tell them I'll be here in a minute. [*He goes out.*]

Enter DORIMÈNE *and* DORANTE.

LACKEY. The master says that he will be with you in a moment.

DORANTE. Very good.

DORIMÈNE. I don't know, Dorante. I feel it is very strange behaviour on my part to allow you to bring me to a house where I don't know a soul.

DORANTE. Where then, madam, would you wish me to entertain you, since, to avoid scandal, you rule out both your own house and mine?

DORIMÈNE. But you do not mention how I am becoming insensibly more and more committed every day to accepting these extravagant tokens of your affection. And it is no use my objecting. You wear down my resistance. Your suave insistence is reducing me gradually to doing whatever you wish. The process began with your assiduity in calling upon me, passed in due course to protestations of love, then to serenades, entertainments, and, finally, to-day's celebrations. I set my face against all these things, but you will not take no for an answer, and step by step you undermine my resolve until I can no longer answer for anything and I believe that in the end you will persuade me into a marriage contrary to all I intended.

DORANTE. Upon my word, madam, a very good thing too. You are a widow and your own mistress. I am independent and love you more than life itself. What is to prevent your making me happy this very day?

DORIMÈNE. Heavens, Dorante! Many good qualities are needed, on both sides, if people are to live happily together, and even the most reasonable people in the world often find it hard to make a success of it.

DORANTE. But why imagine such difficulties, madam? Your experience of one marriage proves nothing about others.

DORIMÈNE. Still, I come back to my point. These expenses which I see you incurring on my behalf cause me concern for two reasons: firstly, they commit me further than I would wish, and secondly I feel sure, if I may say so, that you are spending more than you can afford – and that I don't in the least want.

DORANTE. Madam, these things are mere trifles, and on that score –

DORIMÈNE. No. I know what I am talking about. For example, the diamond you have obliged me to accept is so valuable that –

DORANTE. Ah, madam, please don't exaggerate the value of a thing which I feel is quite unworthy of you. Allow me to – ah, here comes the master of the house.

Enter MR JOURDAIN *and* LACKEY.

MR JOURDAIN [*after making two bows and finding himself too close to* DORIMÈNE]. A bit further back, madam.

DORIMÈNE. Whatever – ?

MR JOURDAIN. Another step more, if you please.

DORIMÈNE. What is all this about?

MR JOURDAIN. You must go back a bit, for the third one.

DORANTE. Mr Jourdain knows how to behave in society, madam.

MR JOURDAIN. Madam, I am greatly honoured in having the good fortune to be favoured with your condescension in deigning to accord me the favour – of your presence and if I should also have the merit to merit a merit such as yours and had heaven – envying my good fortune – accorded me the advantage of being worthy –

DORANTE. That's enough, Mr Jourdain. My lady has no liking for fine compliments. She knows very well that you are a man of the world. [*Aside to* DORIMÈNE] He's a worthy merchant, but, as you see, rather foolish in his ways.

DORIMÈNE. It is not difficult to see that.

DORANTE. Madam, Mr Jourdain is one of my dearest friends –

MR JOURDAIN. Ah, sir, you do me too much honour.

DORANTE. A gentleman of parts.

DORIMÈNE. I am honoured to make his acquaintance.

MR JOURDAIN. Madam, your condescension is quite undeserved.

DORANTE [*aside to* JOURDAIN]. Whatever you do, be careful not to mention the diamond you gave her.

MR JOURDAIN [*aside to* DORANTE]. Can't I even inquire how she likes it?

DORANTE [*as before*]. Not on any account. That would be most vulgar behaviour. If you wish to act as a gentleman should, you must behave as if it were not you who gave her the present. [*To* DORIMÈNE] Mr Jourdain is just saying, madam, how delighted he is to see you in his house.

DORIMÈNE. I am greatly honoured.

MR JOURDAIN [*aside to* DORANTE]. I am most grateful to you, sir, for putting in a word for me.

DORANTE [*aside to* MR JOURDAIN]. I had the greatest trouble in the world to get her to come.

MR JOURDAIN [*aside to* DORANTE]. I don't know how to thank you.

DORANTE [*to* DORIMÈNE]. Mr Jourdain is just saying, madam, how charming he finds you.

DORIMÈNE. That is extremely kind of him!

MR JOURDAIN. Ah, madam, it is you who are kind –

DORANTE. Let us think about supper.

LACKEY [*to* MR JOURDAIN]. Everything is ready, sir!

DORANTE. Come, then, let us take our places. Have the musicians summoned.

Six cooks dance together and bring in a table laden with viands, which forms the Third Interlude.

Act Four

DORIMÈNE, DORANTE, MR JOURDAIN, SINGERS, *and* LACKEYS.

DORIMÈNE. Why, Dorante, this is a magnificent repast.

MR JOURDAIN. You are not serious, madam. I only wish it were more worthy of you. [*All take their seats at the table*.]

DORANTE. What Mr Jourdain has said is quite true, madam. I am indebted to him for receiving you so hospitably in his own house, but I agree with him that the meal is not worthy of you. I made the arrangements myself but I lack the inspiration of some of our friends in such matters. Thus the meal may, I fear, be found wanting if judged by the most critical standards: you may find there are gastronomic incongruities, certain crudities of taste. If Damis had had the ordering of it, everything would have been according to rule, all elegance and erudition. He would not have omitted to commend to you each dish as it came forward, and dazzle you with his knowledge of all that pertains to good eating; he would have expatiated on the virtues of newly baked bread, golden crusted, crisp and crunchy all over; on the qualities of the wine, its smoothness, its body, its precise degree of sharpness or mellowness; on saddle of mutton, garnished with parsley, loin of Normandy veal, as long as my arm, white and delicately flavoured, melting in the mouth like almond paste; partridges cooked to preserve the flavour to perfection, and his crowning masterpiece, a plump turkey in a pearly broth flanked with young pigeons and wreathed in onions and endive. For my own part, I confess I cannot aspire to such heights, so I can only join with Mr Jourdain in wishing the meal were more worthy of you.

DORIMÈNE. My reply to these compliments is to eat as heartily as you see I am doing.

MR JOURDAIN. Ah! And what lovely hands!

DORIMÈNE. The hands are but so so, Mr Jourdain, but no doubt you are referring to the diamond, which is really magnificent.

MR JOURDAIN. I, madam! Heaven forbid that I should say a word about it. That would be shockingly vulgar behaviour, unworthy of a gentleman – the diamond is a mere bagatelle.

DORIMÈNE. You are very fastidious.

MR JOURDAIN. You are too kind –

DORANTE. Come! Wine for Mr Jourdain and for these gentlemen who are going to be good enough to give us a song.

DORIMÈNE. Nothing adds to the delights of good cheer more than music. We are most admirably entertained.

MR JOURDAIN. Madam, it isn't –

DORANTE. Mr Jourdain. Let us give silence for these gentlemen. They will entertain us better than we can ourselves.

The singers take their glasses and sing, supported by the instrumentalists.

First Drinking Song

A health to you, Phyllis – we begin thus our round.
In a glass and your eyes our best pleasures are found:
You and wine, wine and you, combine in disarming

Our care – and we ne'er
Find you other than charming!
So we swear, so we swear,
To love and to wine, ever faithful to be;
Ever faithful to wine, ever constant to thee!

Touch the glass with your lips and give wine a new relish
The wine in its turn doth those bright eyes embellish.
You and wine, wine and you, together combining,
For a lass and a glass set us ever repining.
So we clink, as we drink,
To love and to wine, ever faithful we'll be;
Ever faithful to wine, ever faithful to thee!

Second Drinking Song

Drink, let us drink, for time is fleeting!
Drink while we may, for brief our meeting!
Once love and life have passed us by,
Too long we lie.
Drink, then, to-day and while we may –
We may not drink to-morrow!

Drink, let us drink, leave fools to reason;
Short is this life and brief our season.
Wealth, fame, and glory all pass by –
Too long we lie.
Let care away, drink while we may!
We may not drink to-morrow.
Fill up the glass, let it go round,
We may not drink to-morrow!

DORIMÈNE. That could not have been better sung. It was really charming.

MR JOURDAIN. But I can see something here even more charming – madam.

DORIMÈNE. Dear me! Mr Jourdain is more gallant than I thought.

DORANTE. Why, madam, what do you take Mr Jourdain for?

MR JOURDAIN. I know what I'd like her to take me for –

DORIMÈNE. What again!

DORANTE. Ah, you don't know him yet.

MR JOURDAIN. She shall know me all in good time.

DORIMÈNE. Oh, I give it up.

DORANTE. He is a gentleman who always has an answer ready. Have you noticed, madam, that he eats the pieces you have touched and put aside?

DORIMÈNE. Mr Jourdain is charming!

MR JOURDAIN. If only I could really charm you I should be –

Enter MRS JOURDAIN.

MRS JOURDAIN. Ah! Here's a nice company, I must say. It's easy to see I'm not expected. So this is why you were so anxious that I should dine at my sister's! There's a theatre downstairs and a feast fit for a wedding up here. This is where your money is going – in entertaining your lady friends and providing them with music and play-acting, while I'm sent off to amuse myself elsewhere!

DORANTE. Whatever are you talking about, Mrs Jourdain? Where did you get the idea that this was your husband's festivity? Let me inform you that I am entertaining this lady and that Mr Jourdain is merely permitting me the use of his house. You should take a little more care of what you say.

MR JOURDAIN. Yes, you impudent creature! My lord is providing all this for her ladyship, and she, I would have you know, is a lady of quality. My lord does me the honour of using my house and has invited me to dine with him.

MRS JOURDAIN. Fiddlesticks! I wasn't born yesterday.

DORANTE. Allow me to tell you, madam –

MRS JOURDAIN. I don't need any telling. I can see for myself. I've known for some time there was something afoot. I'm not a fool. And it's downright wicked of a fine gentleman like you to encourage my husband's tomfoolery. As for you, madam, it ill becomes a fine lady to be causing trouble in a decent family and letting my husband think he's in love with you.

DORIMÈNE. How dare you say such things! Come, Dorante! What are you thinking of, to expose me to the ridiculous suspicions of this outrageous creature [*She goes out.*]

DORANTE. Stay, madam, where are you going?

MR JOURDAIN. Madam – my lord – give her my apologies and try to bring her back. [*They are gone.*] As for you and your meddling, see what a fine mess you've made now. You come and insult me before company and drive people of quality out of the house –

MRS JOURDAIN. I don't give a rap for their quality!

MR JOURDAIN. I don't know how I keep myself from smashing the pots over your head, you old hag!

Lackeys remove the table.

MRS JOURDAIN [*going*]. I don't care what you do. I stand for my rights, and every wife will be on my side.

MR JOURDAIN. You'd better keep out of my way, that's all! [*Alone*] She couldn't have come at a worse time. I was just in the mood for saying all sorts of pretty things. I never felt so lively in my life. But whatever's this?

Enter COVIELLE *disguised.*

COVIELLE. Sir, I don't think I have the honour of being known to you.

MR JOURDAIN. No, sir.

COVIELLE. But I knew you when you were only so high [*indicating with his hand*].

MR JOURDAIN. Me?

COVIELLE. Yes. You were the prettiest child I ever saw. All the ladies were for ever picking you up and cuddling you.

MR JOURDAIN. Cuddling me?

COVIELLE. Yes. You see I was a great friend of the late gentleman, your father.

MR JOURDAIN. The late gentleman my father.

COVIELLE. Yes – a very worthy gentleman he was too.

MR JOURDAIN. What's that you say?

COVIELLE. I said a very worthy gentleman he was too.

MR JOURDAIN. My father?

COVIELLE. Of course.

MR JOURDAIN. Did you know him well?

COVIELLE. Certainly.

MR JOURDAIN. And you knew him to be a gentleman?

COVIELLE. Undoubtedly.

MR JOURDAIN. I don't understand what people mean, then.

COVIELLE. What is your trouble?

MR JOURDAIN. There are foolish people about who will have it that my father was in trade.

COVIELLE. In trade! Sheer slander! Never in his life! It was just that he was obliging, anxious to be helpful, and as he knew all about cloth he would go round and select samples, have them brought to his house and give them to his friends – for a consideration.

MR JOURDAIN. I'm delighted to know you. You'll be able to testify that my father was a gentleman.

COVIELLE. I'll maintain it before everybody.

MR JOURDAIN. I shall be eternally grateful to you. But what brings you here?

COVIELLE. Since the time when, as I was saying, I knew the late gentleman, your father, I have been travelling all round the world.

MR JOURDAIN. All round the world!

COVIELLE. Yes.

MR JOURDAIN. That must be a tidy long way.

COVIELLE. It is. I only returned from my travels four days ago and I've hurried along here because of my concern for your interests, to bring you some most exciting news.

MR JOURDAIN. And what's that?

COVIELLE. Have you heard that the Grand Turk's son is here?

MR JOURDAIN. No, I didn't know.

COVIELLE. Why! He has a splendid retinue of attendants, and everybody is running round to get a look at him. He is being received here as a personage of the greatest distinction.

MR JOURDAIN. Upon my word! I didn't know that.

COVIELLE. What is so fortunate for you is that he has fallen in love with your daughter.

MR JOURDAIN. The son of the Grand Turk?

COVIELLE. Yes, and he won't be happy until he's your son-in-law.

MR JOURDAIN. My son-in-law. The Grand Turk's son?

COVIELLE. That's it. The son of the Grand Turk – your son-in-law. I have been to see him and, knowing the language, of course, had quite a chat. In the course of the conversation he said, 'Acciam croc soler onch alla moustaph gidelum amanahem varahini oussere carbulath', meaning, 'Have you ever come across a very beautiful young lady, the daughter of Mr Jourdain, a gentleman of Paris?'

MR JOURDAIN. The Grand Turk's son said that about me?

COVIELLE. He did. And when I told him that I knew you personally and had met your daughter, he said, 'Marababa Sahem', which means, 'Ah, how I love her!'

MR JOURDAIN. 'Marababa Sahem' means 'Ah, how I love her!'

COVIELLE. That's it.

MR JOURDAIN. My goodness, I am glad you told me. I should never have thought that 'Marababa Sahem' meant 'Ah, how I love her!' What a wonderful language Turkish is!

COVIELLE. You'd be surprised. Do you know what 'cacaracamouchen' means?

MR JOURDAIN. 'Cacaracamouchen'? No.

COVIELLE. It means 'Dear Heart!'

MR JOURDAIN. 'Cacaracamouchen' means 'Dear Heart'?

COVIELLE. Yes.

MR JOURDAIN. Well, isn't that wonderful! 'Cacaracamouchen' – 'Dear Heart'. Who would ever have thought it! It's amazing.

COVIELLE. But to conclude my mission. He's on his way here to ask to marry your daughter and in order that his father-in-law may be worthy of him he wants to make you a Mamamouchi, a title of great rank in his country.

MR JOURDAIN. Mamamouchi?

COVIELLE. Mamamouchi or, as we should say, a Paladin. Paladins are the former . . . paladins. There's no higher rank anywhere in the world. You'll be on an equality with the greatest of noblemen.

MR JOURDAIN. Well, I'm very much obliged to the son of the Grand Turk. Please take me to him so that I can thank him.

COVIELLE. But I told you – he's coming here.

MR JOURDAIN. Coming here!

COVIELLE. Yes, and he's bringing everything needed for the ceremony.

MR JOURDAIN. It's all very sudden.

COVIELLE. His love brooks no delay.

MR JOURDAIN. The only thing that worries me is that my daughter is a most obstinate girl, and she's taken a fancy to a fellow called Cléonte and swears that she'll marry nobody else.

COVIELLE. You'll see she'll change her mind when she sees the Grand Turk's son. By a most remarkable coincidence he is very like Cléonte, whom I've had pointed out to me, and her love for the one can easily be transferred to the other – but I hear him coming. Here he is.

Enter CLÉONTE *in Turkish dress. Three pages bear his train.*

CLÉONTE. Ambousahim oqui boraf, Jordina! Salamalequi!

COVIELLE [*to* MR JOURDAIN]. Which is, being interpreted, Mr Jourdain, may your heart be all the year like a rose tree in flower. These are the usual forms of polite greeting in his country.

MR JOURDAIN. I am his Turkish Highness's most humble servant.

COVIELLE. Carigar camboto oustin moraf.

CLÉONTE. Oustin yoc catamalequi basum base alla moran.

COVIELLE. He prays that Heaven may endow you with the strength of lions and the wisdom of serpents.

MR JOURDAIN. His Turkish Highness is too kind. Say I wish him every prosperity.

COVIELLE. Ossa binamin sadoc babally oracaf ouram.

CLÉONTE. Bel men.

COVIELLE. He requests that you go with him at once to prepare for the ceremony, so that he may then meet your daughter and conclude the marriage.

MR JOURDAIN. All that in two words?

COVIELLE. Yes. That's what the Turkish language is like. You can say a great deal in few words. Follow where he wants you to go.

MR JOURDAIN follows CLÉONTE *and his pages.*

COVIELLE [*alone*]. Oh, oh, oh! My goodness, what a lark! And what a fool! If he had learned his part by rote he couldn't play it better.

Enter DORANTE.

COVIELLE. Ha ha! I hope, sir, that we can count on your help in a little affair we have in hand here.

DORANTE. Why, Covielle! Who would have known you! What a get-up!

COVIELLE. Yes, isn't it! Ha ha!

DORANTE. What are you laughing at?

COVIELLE. Something very amusing.

DORANTE. Well?

COVIELLE. You would never guess the trick we are playing on Mr Jourdain. It's intended to persuade him to let his daughter marry my master.

DORANTE. I don't know what the trick is, but I've no doubt it's a good one since you have a hand in it.

COVIELLE. I see that you know me, sir.

DORANTE. Tell me what it is.

COVIELLE. Be good enough to come a little further away and watch what I see coming in. You'll be able to see something of the story and I can tell you the rest.

The Turkish ceremony with dancing and music forms the Fourth Interlude.

Six Turks enter gravely, two by two, to the strains of the Turkish March. They carry carpets which they wave as they dance. Enter next Turkish singers and dancers who pass beneath the carpets held on high. They are followed by four Dervishes who escort THE MUFTI. *As the music ends, the Turks lower their carpets to the ground and kneel upon them,* THE MUFTI *remaining standing in the centre. He makes a comic invocation, raising his eyes to Heaven, moving his hands like wings at each side of his head. The Turks prostrate themselves, singing, 'Allah!' as they alternately rise on their knees and prostrate themselves. They rise to their feet on the words 'Allah Eckbar!' The Dervishes now carry on* MR JOURDAIN *dressed as a Turk but without wig, turban, or sabre.* THE MUFTI *sings the following song:*

THE MUFTI [*singing to* MR JOURDAIN]. If him compree him say yum yum!

If no compree him keepee mum.

Me am Mufti what am he?

Him no compree?

CHORUS OF TURKS. No compree! No compree! No compree!

Two Dervishes menace MR JOURDAIN, *who retreats a step on each 'No compree'.*

THE MUFTI [*chanting*]. Speakee quickly, what am he?
Him no heathen? Him no Jew?

CHORUS. No, no, no! No, no, no!

THE MUFTI [*chanting*]. Him no Buddhist? No Hindu?

CHORUS. No, no no! No, no, no!

THE MUFTI. Him no Coffite? Puritan?

CHORUS. No, no, no! No, no, no!

THE MUFTI [*as before*]. Him no Hussite? Lutheran?

CHORUS. No, no, no! No, no, no!

THE MUFTI [*as before*]. What am he? Mohametan?

CHORUS [*as before*]. We swear it. We swear it.

THE MUFTI. Him called how? How him called?

CHORUS. Him called Jourdain, Jourdain, Jourdina.

THE MUFTI [*singing and dancing*]. We pray for Mr Jourdain
To Mahomet night and morn'n',
Going to make a Paladina
Of Jourdina, of Jourdina.
Give him sabre, give him turban.
Give him sabre, give him turban.
Give him galley, brigantina
Him go fight for Palestina
Good Mahometan! Jourdina!

THE MUFTI. Him be good Turk Jourdina?

TURKS. Hey Valla! Hey Valla!

THE MUFTI [*singing and dancing*]. Ha la ba, ba la ba, ba la da!

TURKS [*joining in dance*]. Ha la ba, ba la chou, ba la ba, ba la da!

General dance of Turks and Dervishes, during which THE MUFTI
retires.

Re-enter THE MUFTI *in his great ceremonial turban, which is an
outsize in turbans, decorated with lighted candles in several rows.
With him enter two Dervishes bearing the Koran. Two more Dervishes bring forward* JOURDAIN, *who is quite overcome by the
ceremony, and they make him go on his knees with his hands touching the ground before him. They set the Koran on his back.* THE
MUFTI *makes a second invocation, pretending to read, turning
the pages rapidly, finally crying in a loud voice, 'Hou!'*

The TURKS *meanwhile bow and raise themselves alternately, chanting 'Hou! Hou! Hou!'*

MR JOURDAIN [*when they take the Koran off his back*]. Ouf!

THE MUFTI [*chanting*]. Him no scoundrel, him no knave?
TURKS. No, no, no.
THE MUFTI [*as before*]. Him no coward, him be brave?
TURKS. Him be brave! Him be brave!
   Give him turban! Give him turban!
Enter Turkish dancers who put the turban on JOURDAIN'S *head.*
THE MUFTI [*giving him sabre*]. No be scoundrel? No be
   knave?
   Take then, take then scimitar.
   Dance, during which the dancers give JOURDAIN *slaps seriatim
   with their scimitars.*
THE MUFTI [*singing*]. Give him, give him Bastonnade,
Thus am Jourdain Muslim made.
Repeat.
                 Dance and slaps with scimitar.
THE MUFTI [*singing*]. Be not offended! All is ended.
TURKS [*singing*]. Be not offended! All is ended.
THE MUFTI *makes a last invocation, the Turks holding up his
   arms, after which the Turks dance and* MR JOURDAIN *and*
   THE MUFTI *are carried off in triumph. Thus ends the Fourth
   Interlude.*

Act Five

MR JOURDAIN *and* MRS JOURDAIN.

MR JOURDAIN *is making obeisances and singing Turkish phrases as
   she enters.*
MRS JOURDAIN. Oh Lord have mercy on us! Whatever is he
   up to now? What a sight! Are you going mumming? Is this
   a time to be in fancy dress? What's it all about? Who on
   earth has togged you up like this?
MR JOURDAIN. The impertinence of the woman! How dare
   you talk like that to a Mamamouchi?
MRS JOURDAIN. A what?
MR JOURDAIN. You'll have to be more respectful now that
   I've been made a Mamamouchi.

MRS JOURDAIN. What on earth is the man talking about, with his Mamamouchi?

MR JOURDAIN. I tell you I am a Mamamouchi.

MRS JOURDAIN. And whatever sort of creature is that?

MR JOURDAIN. A Mamamouchi is what we should call a – Paladin.

MRS JOURDAIN. You ought to know better than go a-ballading at your age.

MR JOURDAIN. The ignorance! Paladin is a dignity that has just been conferred upon me. I come straight from the ceremony.

MRS JOURDAIN. What sort of ceremony?

MR JOURDAIN [*singing and dancing*]. Good Mahometan Jourdina!

MRS JOURDAIN. And what does that mean?

MR JOURDAIN. Jourdina means Jourdain.

MRS JOURDAIN. And what about Jourdain?

MR JOURDAIN [*sings*]. Going to make a Paladina – of Jourdina, of Jourdina.

MRS JOURDAIN. Eh?

MR JOURDAIN [*sings*]. Give him galley, brigantina!

MRS JOURDAIN. I don't understand a word of it!

MR JOURDAIN [*sings*]. Him go fight for Palestina.

MRS JOURDAIN. What on earth –

MR JOURDAIN [*as before*]. Give him, give him Bastonnade!

MRS JOURDAIN. Whatever is this nonsense?

MR JOURDAIN [*as before*]. Be not offended – all is ended!

MRS JOURDAIN. What on earth!

MR JOURDAIN [*dancing and clapping his hands*]. Ba la ba, ba la chou, ba la ba, ba la da! [*He tumbles over.*]

MRS JOURDAIN. Oh my goodness! He's off his head.

MR JOURDAIN [*as he picks himself up and goes off*]. Silence! Show more respect to a Mamamouchi! [*He goes out.*]

MRS JOURDAIN [*alone*]. He's off his head! I must run and stop him going out. [*Sees* DORANTE *and* DORIMÈNE *coming.*] Oh, it only needed that! I can see nothing but troubles everywhere. [*She goes out.*]

DORANTE [*laughing*]. Really, madam, you have never seen anything so amusing. I would not have believed anyone could be such a fool! All the same we must try to further Cléonte's affairs and keep up the masquerade. Cléonte is a good fellow and deserves our support.

DORIMÈNE. Yes, I esteem him highly. He deserves to be fortunate.

DORANTE. There is still a ballet for us to see, and then perhaps we may find whether a certain hope of mine is realized.

DORIMÈNE. Yes, I have seen how lavish the preparations are, Dorante, and I cannot permit this sort of thing any longer. I am determined to stem the flood of your extravagance on my account, and so I have decided to marry you at once. That seems to be the only solution. Marriage puts an end to such things, as you know.

DORANTE. Ah, madam, can you really have come to the decision I have so much desired?

DORIMÈNE. Only to prevent you from ruining yourself. I can quite see that if I didn't you would soon be without a penny to your name.

DORANTE. I am most grateful for your consideration for my fortune, but it is entirely yours, and my heart along with it, to dispose of as you wish.

DORIMÈNE. I shall make demands upon both. But here comes our friend, and what a wonderful sight he is!

Enter MR JOURDAIN *still in his Turkish costume.*

DORANTE. We have come to celebrate your new dignity, sir, and to join in the rejoicing on the occasion of the marriage of your daughter to the son of the Grand Turk.

MR JOURDAIN [*bowing in Turkish fashion*]. Sir, I wish you the strength of serpents and the wisdom of lions.

DORIMÈNE. I am very pleased to be among the first with my felicitations on your newly acquired honours.

MR JOURDAIN. Madam, I hope that your rose-tree may blossom all the year. I am infinitely obliged to you for coming to share in the honours which have befallen me, and I'm the more delighted to see you here because it allows me to make my humble apologies for the ill-behaviour of my wife.

DORIMÈNE. That was of no consequence. One can make allowance for her feelings. She must value your affections and it is not surprising that she shows concern lest she may lose any part of them.

MR JOURDAIN. My affections, madam, are entirely in your keeping.

DORANTE. You observe, madam, that Mr Jourdain is not one of those people whom good fortune makes forgetful. Even in his new-found greatness he remembers his friends.

DORIMÈNE. Yes, it is the mark of a truly noble mind.

DORANTE. But where is his Turkish Highness? We should like, as your friends, to pay him our respects.

MR JOURDAIN. He's coming now and I've sent for my daughter to give him her hand.

Enter CLÉONTE *in Turkish costume.*

DORANTE [*to* CLÉONTE]. We have come to pay our respects to Your Highness and to offer our humble services to you as friends of your father-in-law to be.

MR JOURDAIN. Where is the interpreter so that I can tell him who you are and make him understand what you are saying? You'll see he'll reply to you in Turkish. He speaks it wonderfully well. Hello! Where the deuce has he gone to? Strouf, strif, strof, straf. This gentleman is a grand signor, grand signor, grand signor – and the lady is a grand dama – dama – damnation! Ah! [*To* CLÉONTE *and pointing to* DORANTE] Gentleman – him French Mamamouchi – lady, she French Mamamouchess. That's as plain as I can put it. Ah, good! Here's the interpreter!

Enter COVIELLE.

MR JOURDAIN. Where have you been? We can't exchange a word without you. Just tell him that they are people of great consequence who have come as my friends to pay their respects and offer their services to him. [*To* DORANTE *and* DORIMÈNE] You'll see how he can talk back!

COVIELLE. Alabala crociam acci borem alabamen.

CLÉONTE. Catalequi tubal ourin soter amalouchen.

MR JOURDAIN. There, you see!

COVIELLE. He says that he hopes that a rain of prosperity may ever water the gardens of your family.

MR JOURDAIN. Didn't I tell you he would speak Turkish?

DORANTE. It's wonderful!

Act Five

MR JOURDAIN. Come on, my girl! Come along and give your hand to this gentleman, who has done you the honour of asking to marry you.

LUCILE. Really, father! Whatever are you dressed like that for? Is this supposed to be a play?

MR JOURDAIN. No play about it. It's a most serious matter and a mighty lucky one for you. This is the gentleman I have arranged for you to marry.

LUCILE. Me – marry him, father?

MR JOURDAIN. Yes. You marry him. Come on, give him your hand and thank Heaven for your good fortune.

LUCILE. But I don't want to marry.

MR JOURDAIN. But I do want you to, and I'm your father.

LUCILE. Well, I shan't, that's all!

MR JOURDAIN. Oh, what a fuss! Come along, I tell you. Give him your hand.

LUCILE. No, father, I've told you no power on earth will make me marry anyone but Cléonte, and I'll go to any lengths rather than – [*Recognizing* CLÉONTE] But, as you say, you are my father and it is my duty to obey you, and it is for you to decide these things.

MR JOURDAIN. I'm delighted to see you remember your duty so quickly. What a pleasure it is to have an obedient daughter!

Enter MRS JOURDAIN.

MRS JOURDAIN. Now, then! What's all this? They tell me you are giving your daughter to a mummer.

MR JOURDAIN. Oh, will you be quiet, you tiresome woman! You are always butting in with your silly ideas. There seems to be no teaching you sense.

MRS JOURDAIN. It's you who need teaching sense. You go from one mad idea to another. What is all this collection here for?

MR JOURDAIN. I intend to marry my daughter to the son of the Grand Turk.

MRS JOURDAIN. To the son of the Grand Turk!

MR JOURDAIN. That's right. Make your compliments to him through the interpreter here.

MRS JOURDAIN. I need no interpreter. I'll tell him to his face that he shall never have my daughter.

MR JOURDAIN. Once again, will you be quiet!

DORANTE. How can you refuse such an honour, Mrs Jourdain. Surely you don't decline to have his Turkish Highness as your son-in-law?

MRS JOURDAIN. My goodness! Why can't you look after your own affairs?

DORIMÈNE. You can't refuse a great honour like this.

MRS JOURDAIN. I'd be glad, madam, if you also would not meddle with things which don't concern you.

DORANTE. It's because of our friendly feeling towards you that we wish to be helpful.

MRS JOURDAIN. I can manage without your friendly feelings, thank you.

DORANTE. But your daughter herself is willing to fall in with her father's wishes.

MRS JOURDAIN. My daughter consents to marry a Turk?

DORANTE. Beyond question.

MRS JOURDAIN. She can forget Cléonte?

DORANTE. What won't a woman do to become a great lady!

MRS JOURDAIN. I'd strangle her with my own hands if she did a thing like that.

MR JOURDAIN. Enough of your cackle. I say she shall marry him.

MRS JOURDAIN. And I say she shan't! Never! Never! Never!

MR JOURDAIN. Oh, what a row!

LUCILE. Mother, dear –

MRS JOURDAIN. Go along with you, you're a hussy!

MR JOURDAIN. What! You abuse her merely because she does as I want her to!

MRS JOURDAIN. She's my daughter as well as yours.

COVIELLE [to MRS JOURDAIN]. Mistress.

MRS JOURDAIN. What have you got to say!

COVIELLE. One word!

MRS JOURDAIN. I don't want your one word.

COVIELLE [to MR JOURDAIN]. Master! If she'll only give me one word in private I can promise I'll get her to agree to what you want.

MRS JOURDAIN. I shall never agree.

COVIELLE. Do listen to me.

MRS JOURDAIN. No.

MR JOURDAIN. Just listen to him.

MRS JOURDAIN. I won't listen.

MR JOURDAIN. He'll tell you –

MRS JOURDAIN. He shan't tell me anything.

MR JOURDAIN. The obstinacy of women! What harm will it do you to listen?

COVIELLE. Just listen a moment; you can do as you please afterwards.

MRS JOURDAIN. Go on, then! What is it?

COVIELLE [*aside to* MRS JOURDAIN]. We have been trying to tip you the wink for the past hour! Don't you realize that we are just playing up to your husband's fantastic ideas, that we are taking him in with all this paraphernalia and that the Grand Turk's son is none other than Cléonte himself?

MRS JOURDAIN [*aside to* COVIELLE]. Oh!

COVIELLE [*as before*]. And that the interpreter is nobody but me – Covielle?

MRS JOURDAIN [*as before*]. In that case I give in.

COVIELLE [*as before*]. Don't let on!

MRS JOURDAIN. Yes, that settles it, I consent to the marriage.

MR JOURDAIN. Well, now – we all see reason at last! [*To* MRS JOURDAIN] You wouldn't listen. I knew he'd explain to you all about the Grand Turk.

MRS JOURDAIN. He has explained everything very nicely and I'm entirely satisfied. Send for a notary.

DORANTE. Well said. And finally, to set your fears at rest, Mrs Jourdain, to clear your mind of any jealousy about your husband, let me say that this lady and I intend to be married at the same time.

MRS JOURDAIN. I don't object to that either.

MR JOURDAIN [*aside to* DORANTE]. Is that to make her believe that –

DORANTE [*aside to* MR JOURDAIN]. Yes, we must keep up the pretence to her.

MR JOURDAIN. Good! [*To the others*] Send for the notary, then.

DORANTE. While the contracts are being drawn up, let us have the ballet to entertain his Turkish Highness.

MR JOURDAIN. Excellent idea! Come, let us take our places!

MRS JOURDAIN. But what about Nicole? Isn't she to be married?

MR JOURDAIN. I give her to the interpreter – and my wife to anyone who will have her.

COVIELLE. Thank you, sir! [*Aside*] If there's a bigger fool than this anywhere, I'd like to meet him!

Enter ballet and singers to end the play.

That Scoundrel Scapin

LES FOURBERIES DE SCAPIN

A Farce

PERSONS OF THE PLAY

ARGANTE, father of Octavio and Zerbinetta
GÉRONTE, father of Leander and Hyacintha
OCTAVIO, son of Argante, in love with Hyacintha
LEANDER, son of Géronte, in love with Zerbinetta
ZERBINETTA, believed to be a gipsy girl, but really
    the daughter of Argante, beloved of Leander
HYACINTHA, daughter of Géronte, beloved of
    Octavio
SCAPIN, valet to Leander, a rascal
SILVESTER, valet to Octavio
NÉRINE, nurse to Hyacintha
CARLO, a rascal
TWO PORTERS

The scene is Naples

Act One

OCTAVIO. Poor sort of news for a lover, I must say! I'm already at my wit's end, Silvester, and now you tell me you've heard down at the harbour that my father's coming back.

SILVESTER. That's it.

OCTAVIO. And that he's arriving this very morning?

SILVESTER. This very morning.

OCTAVIO. And he's coming home with the intention of getting me married!

SILVESTER. Of getting you married.

OCTAVIO. To Signor Géronte's daughter?

SILVESTER. To Signor Géronte's daughter.

OCTAVIO. And the girl is being sent over specially from Taranto?

SILVESTER. That's it. Specially from Taranto.

OCTAVIO. And you had this news from my uncle?

SILVESTER. From your uncle.

OCTAVIO. My father has told him it all in a letter?

SILVESTER. In a letter.

OCTAVIO. And you say that my uncle knows all we have been up to?

SILVESTER. All we've been up to.

OCTAVIO. Oh! Can't you say something yourself instead of taking the words out of my mouth?

SILVESTER. What more can I say? You have it off pat.

OCTAVIO. Well, at least give me your advice. Tell me what I'm to do in a desperate situation like this.

SILVESTER. Confound it! I'm as much in the cart as you are. I could do with advice myself.

OCTAVIO. It has done for me completely – his coming back just now.

SILVESTER. It's just as bad for me.

OCTAVIO. I foresee a storm of reproaches when my father finds out how things are.

SILVESTER. Reproaches? Reproaches are nothing! I only wish

I could get off as easily! I can see myself paying dearly for your follies. I foresee a storm too – but it will break on my back!

OCTAVIO. Oh Lord, I wish I knew how to get out of this mess!

SILVESTER. You should have thought of that before you got into it.

OCTAVIO. Oh, you make me tired! What's the use of lecturing me now?

SILVESTER. You are not as tired as I am of your stupid goings on.

OCTAVIO. What am I to do? How am I to get out of it?

Enter SCAPIN.

SCAPIN. What's the matter, Signor Octavio? What's wrong with you? What's the trouble? What's it all about? Something seems to be worrying you.

OCTAVIO. My dear Scapin, I'm in despair. I'm done for. I'm the unluckiest dog alive.

SCAPIN. How do you make that out?

OCTAVIO. Haven't you heard about me?

SCAPIN. No.

OCTAVIO. My father is on his way back, with Signor Géronte, and they intend to get me married.

SCAPIN. And what is there so dreadful in that?

OCTAVIO. Ah, you little know the extent of the trouble!

SCAPIN. Well, you have only to tell me. I'm the man to console you. I'm always ready to take an interest in young folks' affairs.

OCTAVIO. Ah, Scapin, if you can think of a solution or contrive some means of getting me out of this mess I'll be eternally grateful to you.

SCAPIN. Well, to tell the truth, there isn't much I can't manage when I'm put to it. There's no doubt about it. I've quite a gift for smart ideas and ingenious little dodges. Of course, those who can't appreciate them call 'em shady, but, boasting apart, there are not many fellows to equal yours truly when it comes down to scheming or something that needs a little manipulation. I had built up a pretty good reputation for that sort of thing, but it's like everything else to-day –

66

credit goes to anyone but those who have earned it! I got
into trouble over a certain little matter, and since then I've
sworn I'll give it all up.

OCTAVIO. What trouble was that?

SCAPIN. Just a case where the law and I didn't see eye to eye.

OCTAVIO. The law, was it?

SCAPIN. We had a bit of a difference.

OCTAVIO. You and the law?

SCAPIN. Yes, they treated me badly. I was so disgusted with
the way things are done nowadays, I made up my mind I'd
do no more for anyone. But there, go on with your story.

OCTAVIO. Well, you know that two months ago Signor
Géronte and my father set out on a voyage together in connexion with some business they are interested in.

SCAPIN. I know.

OCTAVIO. They left us behind. Silvester was to look after me
and you were to be responsible for Leander.

SCAPIN. Yes, I've done my job, all right.

OCTAVIO. Some time afterwards Leander met a young gipsy
girl and fell in love with her.

SCAPIN. I know something of that.

OCTAVIO. Well, we are great friends so he at once takes me
into his confidence and we go round to see her. I must admit
she wasn't bad looking, though not quite what he had made
her out to be. He could talk about nothing else all day long
but her looks and her brains, her grace, her charm, and
her manners, and he must needs repeat to me every blessed
word she uttered. To hear him talk, there never was such a
girl! Every now and again he would take me to task because
I wasn't sufficiently impressed by what he was telling me and
get annoyed because I wouldn't rave about her as he did.

SCAPIN. I don't quite see where all this is getting us.

OCTAVIO. One day when we were on our way to visit her we
heard sounds of sobbing and crying in a little house down a
side-street. We asked what the trouble was, and a woman
told us that there were two foreign women there in a pitiable
condition – it couldn't fail to move anyone with any feelings
at all.

SCAPIN. And where does all this take us?

OCTAVIO. Out of curiosity I made Leander come and see
what was happening. We went into a room and there was an
old woman dying, a servant woman pouring out lamenta-
tions, and a young girl in tears. It was beautiful – the most
touching sight I ever saw.

SCAPIN. Ha ha!

OCTAVIO. Most girls would have looked dreadful in the circumstances, for she was wearing nothing but a miserable
little petticoat and a sort of bed-jacket of some coarse
material. On her head she had a yellow bonnet which
allowed her hair to fall in disorder on to her shoulders, but,
believe me, even dressed like that she looked wonderful –
positively charming!

SCAPIN. Yes, I see we are coming to it now!

OCTAVIO. Ah, if only you'd seen her, Scapin, *you* would have
thought she was wonderful.

SCAPIN. I don't doubt it. Even without seeing her I can imagine how charming she was.

OCTAVIO. You know, even her tears were becoming. They
didn't spoil her at all. No, there was something so graceful,
so beautiful, so affecting in the way that her tears . . .

SCAPIN. Yes, I quite see how it was.

OCTAVIO. She threw herself down beside the dying woman
and called her mother. It brought tears to everyone's eyes.
No one could help being moved by such a display of affection.

SCAPIN. No, it must have been – very moving – indeed. And
I suppose that this – display of affection – made you display
your affection?

OCTAVIO. Ah, Scapin, anyone would have loved her!

SCAPIN. Of course, who could have helped it?

OCTAVIO. I tried to offer a few words of consolation and then
we left the house. When I asked Leander what he thought of
her he answered that he thought her quite passable looking.
I was so offended by such indifference that I couldn't bring
myself to let him see what an impression she had made on
me –

SILVESTER. If you don't cut it short we shall be here till to-
morrow. I can finish it for you in a few words. He falls

madly in love with her from the very first moment. He's never happy unless he is consoling her until the servant who had taken charge when her mother died forbids him the house. Picture of a young man in despair! He argues, begs, and beseeches. Nothing doing! It seems that though the girl is penniless and friendless she comes of a decent family, so it's a case of marriage or nothing. But love thrives on difficulties! He racks his brains, argues, reasons, ponders, and finally comes up to scratch, and there he is – married three days ago!

SCAPIN. I see.

SILVESTER. Add to this his father's return when he isn't expected for another two months, his uncle's disclosure of the marriage, and the news that his father means to marry him off to Signor Géronte's daughter, his daughter by a second wife he is said to have married at Taranto.

OCTAVIO. And worst of all, the girl I've married is living in poverty and I haven't a penny to help her.

SCAPIN. Is that all? Well, you both seem mightily upset about very little. What is there to be so worried about? You should be ashamed, Silvester, to be stumped by a problem like this. What the devil! You are big enough to be both father and mother to him and yet you can't think up some dodge, some little scheme for setting things right. Tcha! You are a blockhead! I only wish I'd had the chance to lead these old chaps by the nose when I was younger. I'd have made rings round them. I'd already shown my mettle on a hundred occasions before I was that high.

SILVESTER. I admit that I never was up to your standards. I haven't the brains – to get myself involved with the law.

OCTAVIO. Hear comes my dear Hyacintha.

Enter HYACINTHA.

HYACINTHA. Ah, Octavio, is it true, as Silvester has just told Nérine, that your father is back and intends you to marry someone else?

OCTAVIO. It is, my dear Hyacintha, and a dreadful shock it is to me too. But you are not crying? Surely you don't think I'm untrue to you? You don't doubt my love?

HYACINTHA. Oh, I don't doubt your love for me now,

Octavio, but will you always love me? That's what I'm not
sure about.

OCTAVIO. How could anyone love you once and not love you
always?

HYACINTHA. I have heard, Octavio, that men are less constant than women; that a man can fall out of love as easily as
he falls in.

OCTAVIO. Ah, my dearest Hyacintha, I'm not like that. My
love will endure as long as life itself.

HYACINTHA. I want to believe that you mean what you say. I
don't doubt your sincerity but I fear another influence on
you – one that is opposed to your love for me. You depend
on your father and he wants you to marry someone else. If
that should happen it would kill me.

OCTAVIO. No, dear Hyacintha, no father on earth shall make
me give you up. I will renounce my country, my life itself,
rather than be parted from you. I have never set eyes on this
girl he intends me to marry but I hate her already. I wish the
sea would swallow her up. Don't cry, dear Hyacintha, I can't
bear to see you in tears.

HYACINTHA. Well, to please you I will dry my tears and
await as bravely as I can whatever fate may have in store
for me.

OCTAVIO. Fortune will favour us.

HYACINTHA. If you remain constant, nothing can harm me.

OCTAVIO. I shall, you may be certain.

HYACINTHA. Then how happy I shall be!

SCAPIN [*aside*]. Upon my word, she's not such a fool and quite
passable to look at.

OCTAVIO. Here's a man who could be a wonderful help to us,
if he would.

SCAPIN. I have sworn that I'd never meddle any more in other
folks' business, but if you both ask me very nicely – perhaps –

OCTAVIO. Ah, if it's only a question of asking, then I implore
you to take us under your wing.

SCAPIN [*to* HYACINTHA]. And you, have you nothing to say
to me?

HYACINTHA. Yes, I also beseech you, by everything dear to
you, to help us.

SCAPIN. Well, I can see I must let myself be persuaded. Go on – I will do what I can for you.

OCTAVIO. Then you can be sure –

SCAPIN [*to* OCTAVIO]. Hush! [*To* HYACINTHA] Run along and don't worry.

Exit HYACINTHA.

SCAPIN. What *you* have to do now is to prepare to stand up to meeting your father.

OCTAVIO. I must admit that the idea makes me tremble already. I have a sort of natural diffidence I just can't get over.

SCAPIN. Well, unless you stand firm from the outset he'll take advantage of that natural diffidence to treat you like a child. Come, try to pull yourself together. Make up your mind to answer him firmly whatever he says to you.

OCTAVIO. I'll do what I can.

SCAPIN. We had better practise a little to get you used to the idea. We'll put you through your part and see how you get on. Come now, a resolute air, head up, firm glance.

OCTAVIO. Like this?

SCAPIN. A bit more yet.

OCTAVIO. That it?

SCAPIN. Right. Now imagine I am your father coming in. Answer me boldly as if I were he. 'Now, you scoundrelly good for nothing! You disgrace to a decent father! How dare you come near me after what you have done while I have been away? Is this what I get for all I've done for you, you dog! Is this the way you obey me? Is this how you show your respect for me?' – Come on, now – 'You have the audacity, you rascal, to tie yourself up without your father's consent and contract a clandestine marriage? Answer me, you rogue, answer me! Let's hear what you have to say for yourself?' What the devil – you seem completely nonplussed!

OCTAVIO. Yes – you sound so much like my father.

SCAPIN. Well, that's the very reason why you mustn't stand there like an idiot. . . .

OCTAVIO. I'll be more determined this time. I'll put a bold face on it.

SCAPIN. Sure?

OCTAVIO. Certain.

SCAPIN. That's good then, for here comes your father!

OCTAVIO. Heavens! I'm done for! [*Runs off.*]

SCAPIN. Hey, Octavio! Stop, Octavio! There – he's gone!
What a miserable specimen he is! Well, we had better wait
for the old man all the same.

SILVESTER. What shall I tell him?

SCAPIN. Leave the talking to me – just back me up.

Enter ARGANTE.

ARGANTE. Who ever heard of such a thing.

SCAPIN [*aside to* SILVESTER]. He's already heard about it! It's
so much on his mind that he's talking to himself.

ARGANTE. Such a rash thing to do!

SCAPIN [*to* SILVESTER]. Let's listen for a moment.

ARGANTE [*still talking to himself*]. I'd like to know what
they'll find to say about this confounded marriage.

SCAPIN [*aside*]. We have been considering that.

ARGANTE. Will they try to deny it?

SCAPIN [*aside*]. No, we aren't going to do that.

ARGANTE. Or will they try to excuse it?

SCAPIN [*aside*]. That might be done.

ARGANTE. Or fob me off with some fanciful story?

SCAPIN [*aside*]. Maybe we shall!

ARGANTE. They can tell what tale they like. It will have no
effect.

SCAPIN [*aside*]. We shall see about that!

ARGANTE. They won't take me in.

SCAPIN [*aside*]. Don't be too sure!

ARGANTE. I'll find means to put my rascally son in safe
custody.

SCAPIN [*aside*]. We'll look to that!

ARGANTE. As for that scoundrel Silvester, I'll have the hide
off him.

SILVESTER [*aside*]. I might have known he wouldn't leave me
out.

ARGANTE. Ah, there you are! You're a fine fellow to leave in
charge of a family, a fine example to the young.

SCAPIN. Sir, I'm delighted to see you back again.

ARGANTE 'Morning, Scapin! [*To* SILVESTER] You *have*

carried out my orders nicely, haven't you! My son *has*
behaved well in my absence – hasn't he?

SCAPIN. You seem very well.

ARGANTE. Tolerably well, thank ye. [*To* SILVESTER] You
don't say a word, you rascal, not a word!

SCAPIN. Have you had a pleasant journey?

ARGANTE. Yes, a very pleasant journey! Do let me work off
my temper in peace.

SCAPIN. Work off your temper?

ARGANTE. Yes, work off my temper!

SCAPIN. On whom, sir?

ARGANTE. On that scoundrel there!

SCAPIN. But why?

ARGANTE. Haven't you heard what has happened while I
have been away?

SCAPIN. I did hear some trivial thing or other.

ARGANTE. Trivial! You call that sort of thing trivial!

SCAPIN. Well, perhaps not from your point of view.

ARGANTE. Such a piece of effrontery!

SCAPIN. True, true enough!

ARGANTE. For a son to marry without his father's consent!

SCAPIN. Yes, there's something to be said against that, but
you shouldn't make a fuss about it, that's my opinion.

ARGANTE. Well, it's not mine! I'll make as much fuss as I
like. What! Don't you agree that I've every reason to be
angry?

SCAPIN. Yes, I do. I was angry myself at first, until I heard the
whole story. I went so far as to give your son a good talking
to on your behalf. He'll tell you what a fine dressing down I
gave him. I reminded him of the respect he owed to his
father – how he ought to worship the very ground you trod
on. You couldn't have told him the tale better yourself, but
then I came to the conclusion that on the whole he wasn't
so much at fault as one might have thought.

ARGANTE. What are you trying to put over me? What could
be worse than to go and get himself wed to a nobody?

SCAPIN. What would you have him do? He had to do it. It
was his destiny.

ARGANTE. Now that *is* a fine reason! You can commit all the crimes in the calendar, lie, rob, murder, and claim as an excuse that it was your destiny. You had to do it!

SCAPIN. Oh, my goodness, how you do take me up! I mean he found himself involved in this affair without a chance of escape.

ARGANTE. And why was he involved?

SCAPIN. Do you expect him to be as wise as you are? Youth will be served, you know – we can't always be prudent and reasonable. For example, there's my Leander here, who, in spite of all my teaching, in the teeth of all my remonstrances, has gone and done something much worse than your boy. And you – weren't you young once? Didn't you sow your wild oats like the rest of 'em? I've heard that you were fond of the ladies yourself, once upon a time, and had your fun with the best of them, and weren't to be denied neither!

ARGANTE. That's true enough. I admit it. But I never let myself in for a wedding. No – I never tied myself up as he has done.

SCAPIN. But what would you have him do? He sees this young lady who takes a liking to him – for he takes after you, he's a favourite with the ladies – he finds her charming, goes to see her, whispers sweet nothings, sighs, plays the devoted lover and she responds to his advances. He makes the best of his good fortune – and then one day he is taken by surprise by her kinsmen and obliged – by main force – to promise to marry her.

SILVESTER [*aside*]. What a cunning rascal he is!

SCAPIN. Would you have had him let them kill him? After all, better be married than dead.

ARGANTE. I never heard that was how it happened.

SCAPIN. Ask *him* – he'll tell you the same.

ARGANTE. So he was married under duress?

SILVESTER. Yes, master.

SCAPIN. Why should I lie to you?

ARGANTE. He ought to have gone to a magistrate and laid information at once.

SCAPIN. He didn't want to do that.

ARGANTE. It would have made it easier for me to get the marriage dissolved.

SCAPIN. Get the marriage dissolved?

ARGANTE. Yes.

SCAPIN. You'll never dissolve it.

ARGANTE. I shall never dissolve it?

SCAPIN. No.

ARGANTE. What! Haven't I the rights of a father and the justification that they used violence against my son?

SCAPIN. He'll never admit it.

ARGANTE. Never admit it?

SCAPIN. No.

ARGANTE. My son?

SCAPIN. Your son. Would you have him admit that he was afraid, that he let himself be forced into it? He can't admit that – he would disgrace himself and show himself unworthy of his father.

ARGANTE. I care nothing about that.

SCAPIN. He must, for his own reputation and yours, tell people that he married her of his own free will.

ARGANTE. Well, I'm determined, for my reputation and his, that he shall tell them the opposite.

SCAPIN. No. I'm sure he won't do it.

ARGANTE. I'll make him.

SCAPIN. I repeat, he won't do it.

ARGANTE. He will – or I'll disinherit him!

SCAPIN. You?

ARGANTE. Yes, me!

SCAPIN. That's a good one!

ARGANTE. How do you mean, 'that's a good one'?

SCAPIN. You'll not disinherit him.

ARGANTE. I'll not disinherit him?

SCAPIN. No.

ARGANTE. No?

SCAPIN. No.

ARGANTE. Well – this is a joke! I won't disinherit my own son if I want to?

SCAPIN. No.

ARGANTE. Who's going to stop me?

SCAPIN. You, yourself.

ARGANTE. Me?

SCAPIN. Yes. You won't have the heart to do it.

ARGANTE. Won't I?

SCAPIN. You are joking.

ARGANTE. No. I'm not joking.

SCAPIN. You are too fond of him.

ARGANTE. Not I!

SCAPIN. Oh, yes you are.

ARGANTE. I tell you, I am not.

SCAPIN. Fiddlesticks!

ARGANTE. It's no use saying fiddlesticks to me!

SCAPIN. My goodness, as if I don't know you – you are far too good-natured.

ARGANTE. I'm not a bit good-natured – I can be as ill-natured as anyone when I like! I've had enough of this conversation – it's only getting me annoyed. [*To* SILVESTER] Get out, you blackguard – go and find my rascal of a son, while I go and see Signor Géronte and tell him of the misfortune that's befallen me.

SCAPIN. Sir, if I can be of any help to you in any way I am at your service.

ARGANTE. Thank you! Ah, why had he to be my only son? Why could Heaven not have spared me my daughter – so that I could have left my money to her? [*He goes out.*]

SILVESTER. I admit you are a great man, and you are doing splendidly – but, on the other hand, money is getting tight: there are people simply shouting for their money on all sides.

SCAPIN. Leave it to me. The plot is laid. I'm just trying to think of a reliable man to play a part I need. Wait – stop a minute – stick your hat at an angle and look like a blackguard! Limp a bit with one leg! Hand to your side! Scowl! Strut like a tragedy king! Good. Follow me! I can show you how to disguise your face and your voice.

SILVESTER. Whatever you do, I implore you not to get me involved with the law!

SCAPIN. Go on! We'll share the risks like brothers. What are three years or so in the galleys to a man of spirit?

Act Two

GÉRONTE. Yes, beyond question, with this wind we shall have our people here to-day. A sailor from Taranto told me he saw my man ready to embark, but my daughter's arrival is going to come at an awkward time for our plans, and what you have just told me about your son seems to upset our arrangements altogether.

ARGANTE. Don't worry. I undertake to get over the difficulty. I'll go and deal with it straight away.

GÉRONTE. I'll tell you what, Signor Argante, one takes something on when one begins to bring up a family!

ARGANTE. That's true – but what have you particularly in mind?

GÉRONTE. I had in mind that unsatisfactory behaviour in young men is usually the result of bad upbringing.

ARGANTE. Sometimes. But what are you getting at?

GÉRONTE. What am I getting at?

ARGANTE. Yes.

GÉRONTE. Well, if you had brought your son up properly, he would never have played you the trick that he has.

ARGANTE. Good. And I suppose you have brought yours up better?

GÉRONTE. Of course – I should be very upset if *he* had done anything of the sort.

ARGANTE. And what if this precious son of yours, whom you have brought up so well, has done something even worse than mine, eh?

GÉRONTE. What are you talking about?

ARGANTE. What am I talking about?

GÉRONTE. Yes. What do you mean?

ARGANTE. What I mean, Signor Géronte, is that one shouldn't be quite so ready to criticize other people. In fact, people who live in glass houses shouldn't throw stones.

GÉRONTE. Oh! I can't make head or tail of this.

ARGANTE. Then I shall have to explain.

GÉRONTE. Can you have heard something about *my* son?

ARGANTE. Maybe – it's just possible.

GÉRONTE. Out with it, then!

ARGANTE. Your man, Scapin, only managed to give me the outline, I was so vexed – but you can get the details from him. I'm off to my lawyer myself to find out what line I'm to take. [*He goes.*] I'll be seeing you.

GÉRONTE [*alone*]. What can it be? – worse than his! I can't see how it could be! To marry without his father's consent – that's beyond anything I can imagine!

Enter LEANDER.

GÉRONTE. Ah, there you are!

LEANDER [*coming forward to embrace his father*]. Father! How nice to see you back again!

GÉRONTE [*repulsing him*]. Steady on! We've something to talk about first.

LEANDER. But allow me to embrace you –

GÉRONTE [*again repulsing him*]. Go easy, I tell you.

LEANDER. You won't allow me to welcome you, father?

GÉRONTE. We've got something to straighten out first.

LEANDER. What is it?

GÉRONTE. Hold on, let me look at you.

LEANDER. What on earth –

GÉRONTE. Look me in the eyes!

LEANDER. Well?

GÉRONTE. What has been going on here?

LEANDER. What has been going on?

GÉRONTE. Yes – what have you been doing while I've been away?

LEANDER. What did you expect me to do, father?

GÉRONTE. It's not a question of what I expected you to be doing but of finding out what you *have* done.

LEANDER. I've done nothing you have any cause to complain of.

GÉRONTE. Nothing?

LEANDER. No.

GÉRONTE. You seem very certain.

LEANDER. Because I know that I'm innocent.

GÉRONTE. But Scapin has told me the truth.

LEANDER. Scapin?

GÉRONTE. That makes you blush!

LEANDER. He has told you something about me?

GÉRONTE. We can't settle it here. We must go into it elsewhere. Get off home! I'll be there directly. Ah, you traitor,
if you really have disgraced me, I'll disown you and you can
make up your mind to clear out for good. [*He goes out.*]

LEANDER. Fancy giving me away like that! A rascal who, for
a score of reasons, ought to be the last to reveal what I
have confided to him. Yet he is the first to give me away to
my father. Heaven's my witness, he shall pay for this!

Enter OCTAVIO *and* SCAPIN.

OCTAVIO. My dear Scapin, I am most grateful for the trouble
you've taken! You are a splendid fellow! How lucky it was
I got you to help me!

LEANDER. So there you are! I'm delighted to see you –
Master Twister!

SCAPIN. At your service, sir. You are too kind.

LEANDER [*hand on his sword*]. You think you'll make a joke of
it, do you? I'll teach you.

SCAPIN [*on his knees*]. Master –

OCTAVIO [*coming between them*]. Leander!

LEANDER. No, Octavio, don't interfere, please.

SCAPIN [*to* LEANDER]. But, master –

OCTAVIO [*holding* LEANDER *back*]. Please!

LEANDER [*threatening to strike* SCAPIN]. Just let me get my
own back on him!

OCTAVIO. For my sake, Leander, don't hurt him.

SCAPIN. But, master, what have I done to you?

LEANDER. What have you done? Traitor! [*Tries to strike him
again.*]

OCTAVIO [*holding* LEANDER *back*]. Steady – steady.

LEANDER. No, Octavio. I'll make him confess to me here and
now. Yes, you scoundrel, I know what tricks you've been
up to. I've just heard. I expect you thought I shouldn't find
out. But I'll have the confession from your own lips, or I'll
run my sword through your guts.

SCAPIN. Oh, master, you wouldn't have the heart to do that?

LEANDER. Out with it, then.

SCAPIN. Something I've done, master?

LEANDER. Yes, you villain, and your conscience should tell you only too well what it is.

SCAPIN. I assure you I can't think of anything.

LEANDER [*threatens to strike him*]. You can't think of anything?

OCTAVIO [*holds him back*]. Leander!

SCAPIN. Well then, master, since you will have it, I confess that I and a few friends drank that small quartern cask of Spanish wine someone gave you a few days ago. It was I who made a hole in the cask and poured water on the floor to make you think the wine had run out.

LEANDER. So that was you, you dog! You drank my Spanish wine, and were the cause of my abusing the servant girl, thinking she was to blame?

SCAPIN. Yes, master – I ask your forgiveness.

LEANDER. I'm glad to know about that – but it's not what I'm after.

SCAPIN. Isn't that it, master?

LEANDER. No. It's something much more serious than that, and I'm going to have it out of you.

SCAPIN. I can't think of anything else, master.

LEANDER [*threatening to strike him*]. So you won't admit it?

SCAPIN. Ow!

OCTAVIO [*holding him back*]. Gently!

SCAPIN. Yes, master, I confess that one evening about three weeks ago you sent me with a watch to the young gipsy girl you are in love with and I came home with my clothes torn and my face covered with blood and I told you I'd been beaten and robbed. It was me, master – I'd kept the watch for myself!

LEANDER. You kept my watch for yourself?

SCAPIN. That's it, master – to tell the time by!

LEANDER. We *are* finding things out. A fine faithful servant I have, I must say. But that still isn't what I want.

SCAPIN. That isn't it?

LEANDER. No, you scoundrel – there's something else yet you have to own up to.

SCAPIN. The devil there is!

LEANDER. Quickly! I'm in a hurry.

SCAPIN. Master. That's absolutely everything.

LEANDER [*about to strike*]. Absolutely everything, is it?

OCTAVIO [*getting in front of* LEANDER]. Hey!

SCAPIN. All right, then, master. You remember the apparition you met one night, about six months ago, that beat you up and nearly made you break your neck running away and falling into a cellar. . . .

LEANDER. Well –

SCAPIN. That was me, master. I was the apparition.

LEANDER. You were the apparition, were you, you scoundrel!

SCAPIN. Yes, sir, just to give you a bit of a scare and to cure you of having us running round after you every night as you used to.

LEANDER. I'll bear in mind all you've told me at the proper time and place, but I'll have you come to the point and own up to what you've been saying to my father.

SCAPIN. Your father?

LEANDER. Yes, rascal, to my father!

SCAPIN. I've never as much as seen him since his return.

LEANDER. You haven't seen him?

SCAPIN. No.

LEANDER. Are you sure?

SCAPIN. Certain. He'll tell you as much.

LEANDER. But I have it from his own lips.

SCAPIN. Well, pardon my saying so, he's not spoken the truth.

Enter CARLO.

CARLO. Bad news for you, master.

LEANDER. What?

CARLO. The gipsies are on the point of carrying off your Zerbinetta. She implored me with tears in her eyes to come at once and tell you that unless you can bring the money within two hours you will lose her for ever.

LEANDER. Two hours?

CARLO. Two hours!

Exit CARLO.

LEANDER. Ah, my dear Scapin, help me, I beg you.

SCAPIN [*gets up and walks proudly past* LEANDER]. My dear Scapin! So I'm your dear Scapin now that you need me!

LEANDER. Come on! I forgive all that you've done – ay, and worse things, if you've done them.

SCAPIN. No, no! Don't forgive me anything. Run your sword through my guts. I should be very glad if you would kill me.

LEANDER. No, I implore you, save my life instead, by helping me!

SCAPIN. No, no, no! You'd do much better to kill me.

LEANDER. No! I'm much too fond of you. Do please use your wonderful abilities and find a way out of my difficulty!

SCAPIN. No! Kill me off, please.

LEANDER. Oh, for goodness' sake think no more of that and give your mind to helping me.

OCTAVIO. Scapin! You must do what you can for him.

SCAPIN. How can I, after the way he insulted me?

LEANDER. I implore you to overlook my hasty temper and give me your assistance.

OCTAVIO. I join my petition to his.

SCAPIN. The insult still rankles.

OCTAVIO. You must let him off.

LEANDER. Surely you wouldn't leave me, Scapin, in this cruel extremity?

SCAPIN. To insult me like that without provocation!

LEANDER. I was wrong. I admit it.

SCAPIN. To call me a rogue, a villain, a scoundrel!

LEANDER. I can't say how sorry I am.

SCAPIN. To talk of running a sword through my guts!

LEANDER. I beg your pardon, with all my heart. I'll go down on my knees if you like [does so]. Scapin, I implore you once more not to leave me without your help.

OCTAVIO. Come on, Scapin, you must give way now.

SCAPIN. Well, get up. Only another time, don't be so hasty.

LEANDER. Promise you'll help me!

SCAPIN. I promise to think about it.

LEANDER. But you know how little time there is.

SCAPIN. Don't worry. How much is it you need?

LEANDER. Five hundred guineas.

SCAPIN. And you?

OCTAVIO. Two hundred pounds.

SCAPIN. I'll get this out of your fathers. [*To* OCTAVIO] For yours, the plot is already laid. [*To* LEANDER] As for yours, old miser though he is, it will be even easier. He isn't very sharp-witted, thank goodness! I think he'll believe pretty well anything that we want him to. Don't look offended. You aren't a bit like him – you know what the general opinion is, that he's your father only in name.

LEANDER. That's enough, Scapin.

SCAPIN. Well, well, that's nothing to worry about. But I see your father coming, Master Octavio. We'll start with him since he's here. Off you go, both of you. [*To* OCTAVIO] Tell Silvester to come quickly. I need him to play his part.

Exeunt LEANDER *and* OCTAVIO. *Enter* ARGANTE.

SCAPIN [*aside*]. Here he comes – chewing it over!

ARGANTE. Such inconsiderate behaviour! To go rushing headlong into a commitment like that. Ah, the folly of youth!

SCAPIN. Your servant, sir.

ARGANTE. Good day t'ye, Scapin.

SCAPIN. You are thinking about this business of your son?

ARGANTE. I must admit it annoys me beyond all bearing.

SCAPIN. Well, you know, sir, life is full of disappointments. It's well to be prepared for them. I remember hearing once a saying of one of the philosophers that has always stuck in my mind.

ARGANTE. What was that?

SCAPIN. That when a father of a family has been away from home, however short the time may be, he ought to turn over in his mind all the dreadful things that might await him on his return – imagine his house burned down, his money stolen, his wife dead, his son crippled, his daughter gone to the dogs, and thank his lucky stars for whatever hasn't happened! I've always followed his advice myself, in my own little way, and I've never come home but I've been prepared to face rows, bad temper, insults, kicks and beatings from my masters, and for whatever I don't receive may the Lord make me truly thankful!

ARGANTE. That's all very well, but this foolish marriage has upset all my plans. It is more than I can stand, and I've just taken legal opinion about getting it dissolved.

SCAPIN. My goodness, if you take my advice, you'll try to settle it some other way. You know what a lawsuit is in this country – you are going to land yourself into a fine predicament, I must say.

ARGANTE. You are right, I know, but what other way out is there?

SCAPIN. I think I've got one. I was so concerned at seeing you in difficulty that I kept turning over in my mind the possible means of helping you. I don't like to see decent fathers upset by their sons, and of course I've always had a very special concern for you.

ARGANTE. I'm very grateful to you.

SCAPIN. I've just been to see the brother of the girl your son has married. He's a professional blackguard, one of these fellows who are free with their swords, talk of nothing but cutting people to pieces, and think no more of killing a man than tossing off a glass of wine. I led him on to the question of this marriage, and I made him see how easy it would be to get it dissolved on a plea of violence and your strong position as a father and the influence you would bring to bear in a court of law by reason of the justice of your cause, your money, and your friends. Eventually, I influenced him to the extent that he began to listen to the possibility of settling it for a sum of money, and he's prepared now for the marriage to be dissolved, provided you will make it worth his while.

ARGANTE. And how much was he asking?

SCAPIN. Oh, fabulous sums to begin with!

ARGANTE. Such as?

SCAPIN. Out of all reason.

ARGANTE. Go on!

SCAPIN. He wouldn't talk of less than five or six hundred pounds.

ARGANTE. Five or six hundred devils! What sort of a fool

does he think he has to deal with?

SCAPIN. That's what I said. I wouldn't hear of such a proposition. I told him that you weren't a fellow he could ask
five or six hundred pounds from. Well, after a lot of argument, this is what it boils down to. 'Very soon', he said, 'I
shall have to rejoin the army; I am busy getting my equip-
ment together – it's only because I need money that I am
prepared to agree, all against my inclination, to what you
propose. I must have a horse, and I can't get one at all suitable under sixty pounds.'

ARGANTE. Well, if it's a matter of sixty pounds, I'll stand that.

SCAPIN. Then he says, 'I shall need the harness and a set of
pistols. That'll probably run me into another twenty pounds.'

ARGANTE. Sixty and twenty, that'll be eighty.

SCAPIN. Correct.

ARGANTE. It's a lot, but go on – I agree to it.

SCAPIN. Then he says, 'I shall need a horse for my man –
that'll cost another thirty pounds.'

ARGANTE. What the devil! Be off with him – he'll get no
more out of me.

SCAPIN. Oh, sir!

ARGANTE. No, he's a rogue!

SCAPIN. Must his man go on foot then?

ARGANTE. Let him go as he pleases, and his master as well.

SCAPIN. But surely, sir, you aren't going to jib at a trifle like
that? I do beseech you not to go to law! Give him what he
asks rather than get yourself into the courts!

ARGANTE. Very well. Go on. I'll agree to give him another
thirty pounds.

SCAPIN. 'Then', he says, 'I shall need a mule to carry –'

ARGANTE. The devil take him and his mule! That's enough
of it. I'll go to court.

SCAPIN. Sir – please –

ARGANTE. No, I'll have no more to do with it!

SCAPIN. Sir – just a little mule!

ARGANTE. No. Not even a donkey.

SCAPIN. But consider –

ARGANTE. No, I'll go to law.

SCAPIN. Oh, sir – what are you talking about? Think what

you are doing! Think of the devious ways of the law, the appeals to higher courts, the wearisome procedure, the swarms of rapacious creatures who'll get their claws into you – serjeants, attorneys, counsellors, substitutes and re-membrancers, judges and clerks! Any of these gentry is capable of knocking the bottom out of the best case in the world, for the merest trifle. A bailiff can serve a forged writ and you'll be sunk without knowing a word about it. Your attorney may come to terms with the other side, and sell you out for ready money. Your counsel may be bribed so that he's not there when he's wanted, or if he is there, he may get up and blather and never come to the point. The registrar may issue writs against you for contumacy. The recorder's clerk may purloin your documents, or the re-corder himself refuse to record what he ought to record. And if you use every possible precaution and get by all this, you'll find the judges have been got at and turned against you by bigots or women. Oh, my good sir, if you can at all, keep out of that sort of purgatory! It's hell on earth to be mixed up with the law – the very idea of a lawsuit would make me pack up and fly to the ends of the earth.

ARGANTE. How much does he reckon his little mule brings it to?

SCAPIN. Well, sir, for the mule and his horse and another for his man, harness, pistols, and settlement of a little account with the woman he lodges with, he asks in all for two hundred pounds.

ARGANTE. Two hundred pounds?

SCAPIN. Yes.

ARGANTE [*walking across the stage in a rage*]. Come on! I'll go to court.

SCAPIN. Do think –

ARGANTE. I'll go to court!

SCAPIN. Don't go get yourself into a –

ARGANTE. I'll go to court!

SCAPIN. But going to court will mean money. Money for the summons, money for the writs, money for registration, power of attorney, rights of presentation and solicitors' fees, consultations in chambers and pleadings of counsel, with-drawal of briefs and engrossing of documents. Money!

Money for reports of substitutes, money for the judges, registrars' emoluments, provisional decrees, rolls, signatures, and messengers' expenses, all this, without mention of palm-greasing here, there, and everywhere. Give the money to this fellow and you are quit of the whole business.

ARGANTE. But, two hundred pounds!

SCAPIN. Yes. And you'll save on it. I've totted it up roughly in my head – the legal costs, that is, and I reckon that by giving this fellow two hundred pounds you'll save a clear hundred and fifty, without counting all the trouble and annoyance you'll spare yourself. If it were only to avoid being the butt of counsel's witticisms in public, I'd prefer to pay three hundred rather than go to court.

ARGANTE. I don't care a rap for all that! I defy any lawyer to make fun of me!

SCAPIN. Well, you'll do as you like, but if I were you, I would avoid a lawsuit.

ARGANTE. I'm giving no two hundred pounds!

SCAPIN. Here's the very man we are talking about!

Enter SILVESTER, *disguised as an assassin.*

SILVESTER. Scapin! Show me this fellow, Argante, Octavio's father!

SCAPIN. Why, sir?

SILVESTER. I've just heard he's going to bring a lawsuit against me, and get my sister's marriage dissolved.

SCAPIN. I don't know if he's going to do that, but he certainly won't agree to the two hundred pounds you are asking. He says it's too much!

SILVESTER. Death and damnation! If I catch him I'll cut him to pieces, if I swing for it.

ARGANTE *hides behind* SCAPIN.

SCAPIN. But, sir, Octavio's father is a man of spirit – he probably won't be frightened of you in the least.

SILVESTER. Won't he! Hell and damnation! If he were here I'd run my sword through him this very minute. [*Sees* ARGANTE] Who's this fellow?

SCAPIN. This isn't him, sir, this isn't him!

SILVESTER. Not one of his friends even?

SCAPIN. No, sir, on the contrary – his deadly enemy!

SILVESTER. His deadly enemy?

SCAPIN. That's it.

SILVESTER. Ah! I'm delighted to meet you! You are the enemy of that scoundrel Argante, eh?

SCAPIN. Yes – I'll answer for him.

SILVESTER [*shaking hands roughly*]. Give me your hand! Give me your hand! I give you my word, I swear on my honour, by the sword that I bear and by every oath I know, that before the day is out I'll rid you of that miserable rogue, that scoundrel, Argante! Rely upon me!

SCAPIN. But, sir, violence is illegal in this country.

SILVESTER. What do I care? I've nothing to lose!

SCAPIN. He'll be on his guard, you may depend. He has relations, friends, servants to protect him against you.

SILVESTER. That's just what I want! That's just what I want! Hell and damnation. [*Draws sword.*] If only I had him here with all his supporters. Let him bring a score of them with him! Let them all come armed to the teeth! [*Takes his guard.*] Come on! You blackguards – so you have the insolence to come at me, have you? Come on then, slay and no quarter! [*Hitting out on all sides.*] At them! Stand your ground. Have at you! A stout sword and a trusty hand! Come on, you villains, you rapscallions, you asked for it! I'll give you a bellyful! Stand to it, you blackguards, come on! Hey there, have at you! [*Lunges at* SCAPIN *and* ARGANTE.] Have at you! What! You are flinching! Come on! Confound you, stand your ground!

SCAPIN. Eh, eh! Steady on, mister. We are on your side!

SILVESTER. That'll teach you to play tricks on me!

Exit SILVESTER.

SCAPIN. Well, there you are! You see how many people can be killed for the sake of two hundred pounds! I'll wish you good luck!

ARGANTE [*trembling*]. Scapin. . . .

SCAPIN. Yes?

ARGANTE. I'm ready to go to two hundred.

SCAPIN. For your own sake, I'm delighted to hear it.

ARGANTE. Let us go find him! I have the money with me.

SCAPIN. You can give it to me! You can't very well meet him

88

when you have just passed as someone else. What's more, if you made yourself known, he might take it into his head to ask for more.

ARGANTE. Yes, but I like to know what I am doing with my money.

SCAPIN. Don't you trust me?

ARGANTE. Yes, only –

SCAPIN. Confound you, sir, either I'm a rogue or an honest man, one or the other! Why should I want to deceive you? What interest have I in all this except yours and my master's? If you don't trust me, I'll have no more to do with it, and you can find someone else to look after your business for you.

ARGANTE. Take it, then.

SCAPIN. No, don't trust me with your money! I shall be glad enough for you to get somebody else.

ARGANTE. For Heaven's sake, take it!

SCAPIN. No. I tell you, don't entrust it to me! Who knows I shan't run off with it?

ARGANTE. Take it, I tell you! Don't keep me arguing. But take care to get some sort of security from him.

SCAPIN. Leave it to me. He'll not find me a fool to deal with.

ARGANTE. I'll wait for you at my house.

Exit ARGANTE.

SCAPIN. You can rely on me to come. [*Aside*] That's one dealt with! Now for the other. When the luck's in they come straight to the net.

Enter GÉRONTE.

SCAPIN [*pretending not to see him*]. Oh, Lord, what an unexpected misfortune. Unhappy father. Poor Géronte, whatever will you do.

GÉRONTE. [*aside*]. What's this he's saying about me? What is he looking so miserable for?

SCAPIN. Can nobody tell me where Signor Géronte is?

GÉRONTE. What's the matter, Scapin?

SCAPIN [*searches round the stage pretending not to see* GÉRONTE]. Where shall I find him? I must tell him of this disaster.

GÉRONTE. Whatever is it?

SCAPIN. I'm looking everywhere and can't find him.

GÉRONTE. But here I am!

SCAPIN. He must have hidden himself where nobody can see him.

GÉRONTE [*stopping him*]. Hey! Are you blind, that you can't see me?

SCAPIN. Ah, master, is there no means of finding you?

GÉRONTE. I've been standing in front of you this half-hour past. Whatever's the matter?

SCAPIN. Master!

GÉRONTE. What is it?

SCAPIN. Your son, master.

GÉRONTE. Well then, my son?

SCAPIN. He's met with the strangest misfortune.

GÉRONTE. What is it?

SCAPIN. I found him a little while ago, terribly upset because of something or other you had said to him, and, by the way, you had brought me into it when I'd nothing to do with it. I tried to console him by walking down by the harbour and there we noticed a smart Turkish galley. Up comes a pleasant-looking young Turk, and invites us aboard. We go on board and he receives us most hospitably – entertains us to a meal with dessert and wines of the best. . . .

GÉRONTE. And what harm did that do you?

SCAPIN. Listen, master! Here we are on board. While we are having the meal, the galley puts out to sea, and as soon as we are well off shore he dumps me into a skiff and sends me to you to say that unless he gets five hundred guineas right away, he'll ship your son off to Algiers!

GÉRONTE. The devil! Five hundred guineas!

SCAPIN. That's it, sir, and what's more, he's given me only two hours to get it.

GÉRONTE. The scoundrelly Turk! He'll be the death of me!

SCAPIN. What you have to do, sir, is to think quickly of some way to save your dear son from slavery.

GÉRONTE. But what the deuce did he go in the galley for?

SCAPIN. He never thought of this happening.

GÉRONTE. Off you go, Scapin, and tell this Turk that I'll set the police after him.

SCAPIN. The police on the open sea! What are you thinking about?

GÉRONTE. But what the deuce did he go in the galley for?

SCAPIN. Some people are fated to get into trouble.

GÉRONTE. Well then, Scapin, you must do your duty as a faithful servant.

SCAPIN. What's that, sir?

GÉRONTE. Go tell the Turk to send my son back, and say that you'll take his place till I scrape together the money.

SCAPIN. Oh, master, you don't know what you are talking about! Do you think this Turk has no more sense than to accept a poor wretch like me in place of your son?

GÉRONTE. But what the deuce did he go in the galley for?

SCAPIN. He never foresaw this trouble. Remember, master, we've only got two hours!

GÉRONTE. How much did you say he wanted?

SCAPIN. Five hundred guineas.

GÉRONTE. Five hundred guineas! Has he no conscience?

SCAPIN. Yes, a Turkish conscience!

GÉRONTE. Does he know what five hundred guineas are?

SCAPIN. He knows well enough!

GÉRONTE. And does the scoundrel think that five hundred guineas can be picked up in the gutter?

SCAPIN. Fellows like that don't know what's reasonable.

GÉRONTE. Oh! What the deuce did he go in the galley for?

SCAPIN. Very true, but you can't foresee everything. Do be quick, master!

GÉRONTE. Here – here's the key of my cupboard.

SCAPIN. Good.

GÉRONTE. Open it!

SCAPIN. Very good.

GÉRONTE. You'll find a big key on the left-hand side which unlocks my attic.

SCAPIN. Yes.

GÉRONTE. Go take all the old clothes that are in the big hamper, and sell them to the brokers to redeem my son.

SCAPIN [*giving him the key back*]. You must be dreaming, sir. You wouldn't get five pounds for the lot, and, moreover, think how little time we've got.

GÉRONTE. Oh! what the deuce did he go in the galley for?

SCAPIN. Oh, what's the use of talking like that? Forget the

galley, remember time is passing and that you run the risk of losing your son. Alas, my poor young master! I may never see you again! At this very moment they may be carrying you off to Algiers. But Heaven knows I've done what I can, and if you aren't ransomed it will be because your father just didn't care.

GÉRONTE. Wait a minute, Scapin. I'll go and get the money myself.

SCAPIN. Then do be quick, sir! I'm trembling lest we hear the clock strike.

GÉRONTE. Four hundred guineas, you said?

SCAPIN. Five hundred.

GÉRONTE. Five hundred.

SCAPIN. That's it.

GÉRONTE. Oh, what the deuce did he go in the galley for?

SCAPIN. Quite – but hurry up.

GÉRONTE. Couldn't he have gone for a walk somewhere else?

SCAPIN. Very likely – but don't waste time.

GÉRONTE. Confound the galley!

SCAPIN [*aside*]. The galley seems to stick in his gullet.

GÉRONTE. Here, Scapin. It hadn't occurred to me – I've just had that sum paid to me in gold – I never dreamt that I'd have to part with it so soon. [*Takes the purse from his pocket and offers it to* SCAPIN.] Take it! Off you go and ransom my son.

SCAPIN [*holding his hand out*]. Very good, sir.

GÉRONTE [*keeping his purse, though making as if to give it to* SCAPIN]. And tell that Turk he's a scoundrel!

SCAPIN [*still holding his hand out*]. Right.

GÉRONTE [*same gesture as before*]. A villain!

SCAPIN [*still holding his hand out*]. Yes.

GÉRONTE [*as before*]. A robber!

SCAPIN. You leave it to me.

GÉRONTE. Say that he's simply getting five hundred guineas out of me without the slightest right or justice!

SCAPIN. Yes.

GÉRONTE. That I'll make him account for them, dead or alive!

SCAPIN. Very good.

GÉRONTE. And that if I ever catch him, I'll have my revenge on him!

SCAPIN. Right.

GÉRONTE [*putting the purse back in his pocket and moving off*]. And now go get my son back!

SCAPIN [*running after him*]. Heh, master!

GÉRONTE. Well?

SCAPIN. Where's the money?

GÉRONTE. Didn't I give you it?

SCAPIN. You put it back in your pocket.

GÉRONTE. Ah! It's grief that makes me do that! I don't know what I'm doing.

SCAPIN. So I see.

GÉRONTE. What the deuce did he go in the galley for! Confound the galley! Treacherous dog of a Turk – the devil take him!   *Exit* GÉRONTE.

SCAPIN [*aside*]. He can't get over the five hundred guineas I've got out of him, but we aren't quits yet. He's still to be paid out for the tale he told his son about me.

Enter OCTAVIO *and* LEANDER.

OCTAVIO. Well, Scapin, any success?

LEANDER. Have you managed to do anything for me?

SCAPIN [*to* OCTAVIO]. Here are two hundred pounds I've got out of your father.

OCTAVIO. Ah, that cheers me up!

SCAPIN [*to* LEANDER]. I've not managed to do anything for you.

LEANDER [*making as if to go*]. Then I'm done for. I have nothing to live for if I lose Zerbinetta.

SCAPIN. Here! Steady on! Where the devil are you hurrying off to?

LEANDER. What else is there for me to do?

SCAPIN. Go on! I've got your share here.

LEANDER. Ah! You put new life into me.

SCAPIN. On condition that you give me leave to get my own back on your father for the way he has treated me.

LEANDER. Do anything you like!

SCAPIN. Promised before witnesses?

LEANDER. Yes.

SCAPIN. There you are then, five hundred guineas.

LEANDER. Now we'll go and ransom my loved one.

Act Three

SILVESTER. Yes. Your young men have decided that you should be together and we are carrying out their orders.

HYACINTHA [*to* ZERBINETTA]. The orders suit me very well. I am happy to have you as my companion, and it won't be my fault if the friendship between those we love doesn't unite us too.

ZERBINETTA. I agree. I am not one to refuse an offer of friendship.

SCAPIN. And an offer of love?

ZERBINETTA. Love is another matter. There is more at stake and I am less venturesome.

SCAPIN. You are set against my master, but what he has just done for you should surely encourage you to look more kindly on his love.

ZERBINETTA. I don't yet trust him beyond the limits of friendship, and what he has just done does not reassure me completely. I may be light-hearted but there are some things I am serious about, and your master makes a mistake if he thinks because he has put down money for my freedom he can assume I am his entirely. He must be prepared to surrender something more than money, and before I return his passion as he wishes he must plight me his faith and confirm it with the customary ceremony.

SCAPIN. That's what he means to do. His intentions are entirely honourable and sincere. I shouldn't be helping him if it were otherwise!

ZERBINETTA. I will believe it, since you say so, but I foresee trouble with his father.

SCAPIN. Oh, we'll find means of dealing with that.

HYACINTHA. The similarity of our strange adventures ought to strengthen the ties of friendship between us. We share the same fears and are exposed to the same misfortune.

ZERBINETTA. But you have at least the advantage of knowing who your parents are. You can hope to find them again and expect them to ensure your happiness by giving their approval to the match you have already made. But I can hope for nothing from learning who I am and there is little enough in my present condition to commend me to a father who has eyes for nothing but money.

HYACINTHA. But you have this in your favour, that your lover is under no temptation to marry anyone else!

ZERBINETTA. There is one thing even more to be feared than that one's lover may change his mind – one can hope to rely on one's own powers to retain *his* affections – what I dread above all is the power of a father. In comparison with that, one's virtues count for nothing.

HYACINTHA. Oh dear, why does the path of true love never run smooth! How happy we lovers should be if there were no hindrance to the union of our hearts!

SCAPIN. That's just where you are wrong. When love's path runs smoothly it makes life as dull as can be. Happiness undiluted soon cloys. We need ups and downs to make us know when we are well off.

HYACINTHA. Come, tell us the story, Scapin – they say it is most amusing – of how you got the money out of the old skinflint. You know I always repay a good story by the pleasure I get from it.

SCAPIN. Silvester here can tell it as well as I can. I am trying to think out a little revenge I mean to enjoy.

SILVESTER. But why go out of your way to get yourself into trouble?

SCAPIN. It amuses me to tackle things where there is a little risk involved.

SILVESTER. Well, if you take notice of me you'll give it up.

SCAPIN. Yes, but I don't take notice of you.

SILVESTER. Why the deuce should you trouble?

SCAPIN. Why the deuce need you worry?

SILVESTER. Because I don't like to see you get yourself a hiding unnecessarily.

SCAPIN. It will be my hiding, not yours.

SILVESTER. True. Your blood's on your own head.

SCAPIN. I have never been put off by risks. I reckon nothing of fellows who are so frightened of what may happen that they never tackle anything at all.

ZERBINETTA [*to* SCAPIN]. But we shall be needing your help.

SCAPIN. Off you go! I shall be with you in no time. [*Exeunt all but* SCAPIN.] It shall never be said that anyone knew me give a secret away – not with impunity.

Enter GÉRONTE.

GÉRONTE. Well, Scapin, how have you got on about my son?

SCAPIN. Your son, sir, is safe, but you yourself are now in very serious danger. I would give a good deal to see you safe in your own house.

GÉRONTE. But why?

SCAPIN. At this very minute there are people seeking you everywhere – to kill you.

GÉRONTE. Me?

SCAPIN. Yes.

GÉRONTE. Who is it?

SCAPIN. The brother of the girl Octavio has married. He has the idea that you want to get the marriage dissolved in order to have your daughter take his sister's place. He has sworn to have your blood! He's determined to make you pay for his honour with your life. He and his friends – all desperadoes like himself – are looking for you everywhere. I have seen some of his gang; they are questioning everyone they meet and have set guards on all the ways to your house so that you can't go home or move a step from here without falling into their hands.

GÉRONTE. But what am I to do, my dear Scapin?

SCAPIN. I don't know, sir. It's a very bad business. I am worried to death about you. Hey! Stop a moment. [*He goes to the wings and makes as if to listen.*]

GÉRONTE [*trembling*]. Eh!

SCAPIN [*returning*]. No, it's nothing.

GÉRONTE. Can't you think of some way of getting me out of this?

SCAPIN. I can think of one way, but I should run the risk of getting beaten myself.

GÉRONTE. Scapin, show yourself a faithful servant! Don't desert me, I beg you!

SCAPIN. I will do what I can. I am too fond of you to leave you defenceless.

GÉRONTE. I will see that you are well repaid, I assure you.
You shall have this suit of clothes – when I have worn it a
bit longer.

SCAPIN. Wait, here's the very thing to save you! You must
get into this sack.

GÉRONTE [*thinking he sees someone*]. Ah –

SCAPIN. No – there's nobody there. You must get into this
sack and take care not to make the least movement! I'll
carry you on my back like a sack of – something or other –
take you past your enemies and get you right home. Once
there we can at least barricade ourselves in and send for
assistance.

GÉRONTE. That's a marvellous idea.

SCAPIN. It will do splendidly. You'll see. [*Aside*] I'll pay you
out now for the trick you played on me.

GÉRONTE. Eh?

SCAPIN. I was saying that we shall get you out and trick them
all right. Get right in! Take care not to show yourself, and
don't stir, whatever happens!

GÉRONTE. Rely on me – I'll keep still.

SCAPIN. Hide yourself now! Here's one of the blackguards
who are after you.
[*In a feigned voice*] 'Vat? I not have de chance to kill dis
Geronta? Vill nobody be goot enough to tell me vere he is?'
[*To* GÉRONTE] Keep still.
[*Feigned voice*] 'Indeed yes, I vill find him if it is in de
middle of de earth dat he hide-a.'
[*To* GÉRONTE] Don't show yourself.
[*Feigned voice*] 'You man with de sack-a!'
Sir?
'I vill give you vone pound if you vill tell me vere is Mr
Geronta.'
Looking for Mr Géronte, are you?
'My gootness yes, I vill seek him!'
On what business, sir?
'On vat business?'
Yes.
'To beat him to death – my gootness yes!'
Oh, my good sir, you can't do things like that to a gentleman

like Mr Géronte – you can't treat him that way.

'Vat, not dat fool, dat rascal, dat scoundrel?'

Mr Géronte is not a fool, nor a rascal, nor a scoundrel neither – you'll be good enough, please, not to talk of him like that.

'Vat! – you vill talk to me like dat, you impudence – you –'

I defend a gentleman when l hear him insulted. It's my duty to do so.

'Vat, are you friend of Geronta?'

I am that, sir!

'You vone of his friends, eh? [SCAPIN *beats the sack.*] You take dat for him, den!'

[SCAPIN *cries out as if he were receiving the blows.*] Ow! Ow! Steady on, sir! Steady! Ah, ah! Easy!

'Take him those from me. So long-a!'

Oh the devil take the rascal!

GÉRONTE [*putting his head out of the sack*]. Oh, Scapin, I can't bear any more.

SCAPIN. Oh, sir, I'm beaten black and blue. My shoulders are raw.

GÉRONTE. But how d'ye make that out? It was my shoulders he was beating.

SCAPIN. No, no, you only got the thin end of the stick.

GÉRONTE. Well, why didn't you move away to save me from –

SCAPIN. Look out! Here's another of 'em. He looks like a foreigner.

[*Pretending again.*] 'Ronning round all day like a hare till I'm tired after dis confounded Géronte I am.'

[*In his own voice*] Keep well in!

[*Feigned voice again*] 'You, sir, you dell me, yes, if you know vere is dis fellow Géronte?'

No, sir, I don't know where he is.

'Com' – you tell me der truth now – I have only vone leetle bit business mit him – just vone few blows mit der stick, and vone few thrusts mit der sword through der chest!'

I assure you, sir, I have no idea where he is.

'I t'ink I see somet'ing move in dat sack dere.'

Excuse me, you are mistaken.

'Yes, somet'ing dere is in dat sack.'

No, sir, nothing at all.

'I just vant my sword through dat sack once to stick.'

Steady, sir, steady.

'Ah – vell, den, you show me vat in dat sack is?'

Steady, sir.

'Steady?'

You have no right to be looking into what I'm carrying.

'But I vant into vat you carry to look.'

Well you shan't! See!

'Ah, vat nonsense!'

It's just a bundle of clothes.

'Vell, den, you show me!'

Never!

'You von't never do?'

No.

'I vill dis stick about your back lay! Ha!'

I don't care.

'You make joke mit me, eh?'

[SCAPIN *strikes and calls out as before*] Oh, oh, sir! Oh, eh, oh!

'Till ve again meet, eh? Dat teach you to be impudent no more ah!'

Oh, confound him and his jabber – oh!

GÉRONTE [*peeping out of sack*]. I'm nearly beaten to death.

SCAPIN. I'm dead already!

GÉRONTE. But why the devil should he beat *me*?

SCAPIN [*shoving his head in*]. Look out! Here come half a dozen altogether.

[*He imitates several people*] 'We gotta find Géronte!'

'We must search everywhere!'

'Spare nothing, scour the town! Search every corner here, there – yes – no! Try in here! No, not here! To the left there – over on the right! No, no!'

[*To* GÉRONTE] Keep well in.

'Ah! This is his servant! Now, you rascal, where's your master?'

Don't hurt me, masters!

'Speak up! Quick! We are in hurry – look slippy.'
Now! Ah, gentlemen, go easy. [GÉRONTE, *peeping out, sees the trick.*]

'Tell us where your master is or we'll beat you black and blue!'
You can do what you like, but I'll never give my master away.

'We'll do you in if you don't!'
Do as you will!

'So you are determined to have a hiding, are you?'
I'll never betray my master!

'Right, then – look out – take what's coming to you.'
[GÉRONTE *gets out, and* SCAPIN *runs away.*]

GÉRONTE. Oh, infamous! The traitor! The fraud! The scoundrel – that's how you treat me!

Enter ZERBINETTA.

ZERBINETTA [*laughing, without seeing* GÉRONTE]. I'll take a breath of air.

GÉRONTE [*aside*]. I swear you shall pay for this.

ZERBINETTA [*still without seeing* GÉRONTE]. Ah! ha, ha! What an amusing story! What a fool the old fellow was!

GÉRONTE. It's nothing to laugh at. There's no call for you to laugh, anyway.

ZERBINETTA. Why, whatever do you mean, sir?

GÉRONTE. You've no business to make fun of me.

ZERBINETTA. Of you?

GÉRONTE. Yes.

ZERBINETTA. But whoever thought of making fun of you?

GÉRONTE. Well, why do you come laughing in my face?

ZERBINETTA. It's nothing to do with you. I'm laughing to myself over a story I've just heard. It's really very funny. I don't know if it's because I have a personal interest, but it's the funniest thing I've ever heard. It's a trick which a young man played on his father to get money out of him.

GÉRONTE. On his father to get money out of him?

ZERBINETTA. If you like, I'll tell you the whole tale. I'm itching to tell someone.

GÉRONTE. All right then, tell me!

ZERBINETTA. There is no harm in telling you, because it's sure to get out before long. It so happened that I was with a band of gipsies who wander up and down the country, telling fortunes and doing various other things too, when we arrived in this town and a young man saw me and fell in love with me. From that moment he followed me everywhere, and, like all young men, he thought he had merely to say the word and I would fall into his arms; but he found he had to change his ideas a little. He told the gipsies he was in love with me and found they were willing to give me up, but they wanted a large sum of money. Unfortunately, the young man was in the usual state of young men, he hadn't a penny. His father, though rich, was as mean as could be, a horrible man! Let me see, what was his name? Oh dear, help me – can't you tell me the name of the meanest man in the town? Don't you know him?

GÉRONTE. No.

ZERBINETTA. Oh, his name is something like Ronte, Oronte, no – Géronte, that's it, Géronte! That's got it! That's the old skinflint! He's the old miser I was talking about! But to return to the story. The gipsies wanted to leave the town to-day, and the young man would have lost me for want of the money if a servant of his hadn't got it out of his father. Now I do know the servant's name. He is called Scapin. He's a wonderful fellow. No word is too good for him.

GÉRONTE [*aside*]. Yes, the wretch.

ZERBINETTA. Listen to the trick he played on the old man! Ah ha ha! I can't think of it without laughing. Ah ha ha! He went to this old miser – oh ha ha ha! and told him that when he was walking with his son near the harbour they saw a Turkish galley, and were invited on board. And that a young Turk gave them a meal, and while they were eating he put to sea and sent him ashore in a skiff to tell his father that his son would be carried off to Algiers unless he brought him five hundred guineas immediately. Ah ha ha! There was the skinflint, the miser, suffering agonies – love of his son struggling with love of his gold. Five hundred guineas were like five hundred daggers in his heart. Ah ha ha! He just couldn't bring himself to part with the money and he thought of all sorts of absurd ways of getting his son back. He was for sending the police after the galley and then he wanted the servant to take his son's place until he got together the money that he wasn't willing to pay – then he was for parting with a few old suits not worth five pounds let alone five hundred! Ah ha! The servant showed him how silly each idea was, and all the time he kept repeating, 'What the deuce did he go in the galley for? Oh, the confounded galley. The rascally Turk!' After much groaning and sighing, he – but you don't seem to be laughing? What do you think of the story?

GÉRONTE. I think that the young man is a scoundrel, a good-for-nothing, and his father will punish him for the trick he played. As for the gipsy girl, she is a brazen-faced impertinent hussy, to come insulting an honourable man, and he will see that she gets what she deserves for coming here to lead young men astray. As for the servant, he is an infamous scoundrel, and Géronte will have him on the gallows before another day passes.

Exit.   Enter. SILVESTER

SILVESTER. Where are you running off to? Don't you know that the man you were speaking to is Leander's father?

ZERBINETTA. I was just beginning to wonder, and there, I have gone and told him his own story without knowing it!

SILVESTER. How do you mean, his own story?

ZERBINETTA. I was full of it and dying to tell someone! But what does it matter? So much the worse for him! I don't think things can be any worse for me, anyway.

SILVESTER. I suppose you have to talk! You'd think people could keep quiet about their own affairs.

ZERBINETTA. Well, he would have heard it all from somebody, wouldn't he?

ARGANTE [*offstage*]. Silvester!

SILVESTER. Go inside. It's my master calling.

ARGANTE. So you had it all arranged, you scoundrels, you and Scapin and my son – you had it all arranged to deceive me, had you? And you thought that I'd stand for it, eh?

SILVESTER. My goodness, master, if Scapin has deceived you I wash my hands of it entirely. I assure you I've nothing to do with it.

ARGANTE. We shall see about that, you rascal. We shall see about that. Don't think you can hoodwink me!

Enter GÉRONTE.

GÉRONTE. Ah, Argante, you find me bowed down by trouble.

ARGANTE. I'm bowed down too.

GÉRONTE. That scoundrel, Scapin, has got five hundred guineas out of me.

ARGANTE. And he's got two hundred pounds out of me.

GÉRONTE. Not content with getting five hundred guineas out of me, he treated me in a way I just can't bring myself to describe, but I'll pay him out.

ARGANTE. Yes, and I'll make him answer for what he's done to me too!

GÉRONTE. I'll make an example of him.

SILVESTER [*aside*]. I only hope I can keep out of all this!

GÉRONTE. I've not told you everything, Argante. Troubles never come singly. I was looking forward to-day to welcoming my daughter I thought the world of. I've just heard that she left Taranto a considerable time ago, and it looks as if she has perished with the ship she was sailing in.

ARGANTE. But why did you leave her at Taranto instead of having her with you?

GÉRONTE. I had any reasons; certain family interests obliged me to keep my second marriage secret. But what's this?

Enter NÉRINE.

GÉRONTE. It's never you, nurse?

NÉRINE [*throwing herself at* GÉRONTE's *feet*]. Ah Signor Pandolphe!

GÉRONTE. Call me Géronte. The reasons which forced me to take another name at Taranto no longer apply.

NÉRINE. Alas! What troubles that change of name has given me in trying to find you!

GÉRONTE. Where are my daughter and her mother?

NÉRINE. Your daughter, sir, is close at hand, but before you see her, I must ask your pardon for having allowed her to marry during the period when we despaired of ever seeing you again.

GÉRONTE. My daughter is married?

NÉRINE. Yes, sir.

GÉRONTE. To whom?

NÉRINE. To a young man named Octavio, son of a gentleman called Argante.

GÉRONTE. Heavens!

ARGANTE. What a coincidence!

GÉRONTE. Take us to her at once.

NÉRINE. You need only step into this house.

GÉRONTE. Go ahead, follow me, Signor Argante!

SILVESTER, *left alone.*

SILVESTER. Well here's a pretty how d'ye do!

Enter SCAPIN.

SCAPIN. Well, Silvester, how are things going?

SILVESTER. I have two things to tell you. First, Octavio's affair is all settled. Our little Hyacintha turns out to be Signor Géronte's daughter, and chance has achieved what the parents intended. The second thing is that the two old fellows are full of the most horrible threats against you, especially Signor Géronte.

SCAPIN. That's nothing. Threats never broke any bones. Mere passing clouds.

SILVESTER. You had better look out. The sons may very well make it up with their fathers and leave you in the cart!

SCAPIN. You leave it to me. I'll find means of smoothing them down.

SILVESTER. Look out, they're coming.

Exit SCAPIN. *Enter* GÉRONTE, ARGANTE, HYACINTHA, ZERBINETTA, *and* NÉRINE.

GÉRONTE. Come, my dear, come to my house. My happiness would have been complete if only I had been able to welcome your mother too.

ARGANTE. Here comes Octavio, just at the right moment.

Enter OCTAVIO.

ARGANTE. Come, my son, and celebrate your happy marriage! Heaven –

OCTAVIO. No, father, your plans for my marriage are futile.

I must be open with you – you have learned, I believe, of my marriage?

ARGANTE. Yes, all I need to know.

OCTAVIO. I want to tell you that Signor Géronte's daughter can never be anything to me.

ARGANTE. But she is the very person that I –

OCTAVIO. No, sir. I ask you to forgive me, but I have made up my mind.

SILVESTER. Listen –

OCTAVIO. Be quiet! I won't listen to anything –

ARGANTE. Your wife –

OCTAVIO. No, father. I'll die rather than give up my dear Hyacintha. [*Crosses stage and stands beside her.*] Yes, you can do what you like, but I have plighted my faith to her – and I mean to have her and no woman else.

ARGANTE. Good. She is the wife I want you to have. How obstinate you are! You will stick to your point!

HYACINTHA. Octavio – this is my father whom I have found again, so all our troubles are over.

GÉRONTE. Come to my house! We can talk more comfortably at home.

HYACINTHA. Father, I ask not to be separated from this dear friend. You have only to know her to love and esteem her.

GÉRONTE. What! You would have me take into my house the girl your brother is entangled with, after she has insulted me to my face?

ZERBINETTA. Sir, please forgive me. I would not have spoken as I did, had I known who you were. I only knew you by reputation.

GÉRONTE. By reputation – what ever do you mean?

HYACINTHA. Father, Leander's love for her is wholly honourable, and her virtue I will answer for.

GÉRONTE. That's all very well. Would you have me marry my son to a girl nobody knows anything about – a girl from the streets?

Enter LEANDER.

LEANDER. Father, you don't need to complain any more that I love an unknown girl with neither means nor family. The people from whom I ransomed her have just revealed that she belongs to this very city, and to a good family, from whom they stole her when she was only four years old. Here is a bracelet they have handed over, which may help us to trace her parentage.

ARGANTE. Heavens! This bracelet shows that she is my own daughter, whom I lost at that very age.

GÉRONTE. Your daughter!

ARGANTE. Yes, and I see from her features she is indeed my daughter. My dear –

HYACINTHA. Heavens! How wonderful!

Enter CARLO.

CARLO. Gentlemen, a dreadful thing has happened.

GÉRONTE. Ah!

CARLO. Poor Scapin –

GÉRONTE. I'm going to see that rascal hanged!

CARLO. Oh, sir, you won't need to trouble. He was passing a building when a mason's hammer fell on his head and laid his skull right open. He's dying, and has begged them to bring him here so that he can speak to you before he passes away.

ARGANTE. Where is he?

CARLO. Here he comes.

Enter SCAPIN, *carried by two men, his head in bandages.*

SCAPIN. Oh, oh, gentlemen! You see what a sad state I have come to, but I couldn't die without asking forgiveness of those I have offended. Oh, oh, gentlemen! before I breathe my last, I implore you to forgive me all I've done – expecially you, Signor Argante, and you, Signor Géronte. Oh!

ARGANTE. For my part I forgive you. Die in peace.

SCAPIN [*to* GÉRONTE]. It's you, sir, that I have offended most with the beating which I –

GÉRONTE. Say no more. I also forgive you.

SCAPIN. It was a terrible liberty on my part to beat –

GÉRONTE. We'll forget it.

SCAPIN. I'm troubled in my dying moments because of that beating –

GÉRONTE. For goodness' sake be quiet!

SCAPIN. That unfortunate beating that I –

GÉRONTE. Say no more, I tell you. I forgive you everything.

SCAPIN. Ah, what kindness! But do you really forgive with all your heart for the beating –

GÉRONTE. Yes, yes. Let's say no more about it – I forgive you everything. That's the end of it.

SCAPIN. Ah, sir. I feel better already for hearing that.

GÉRONTE. Yes, but I only forgive you on condition that you die.

SCAPIN. How d'ye mean, sir?

GÉRONTE. If you get better, I withdraw my forgiveness.

SCAPIN. Oh, oh – I'm feeling worse again.

ARGANTE. Signor Géronte – to celebrate the happy occasion I ask you to pardon him unconditionally.

GÉRONTE. All right, then.

ARGANTE. Come, let us go to supper together and celebrate our happiness.

SCAPIN. As for me, carry me to the foot of the table and I'll wait there till death comes to claim me.

THE END

The Miser

L'AVARE

PERSONS OF THE PLAY

HARPAGON, father of Cléante and Élise,
    suitor for the hand of Marianne
CLÉANTE, his son, in love with Marianne
ÉLISE, his daughter, in love with Valère
VALÈRE, son of Anselme and in love with
    Élise
MARIANNE, in love with Cléante and courted
    by Harpagon
ANSELME, father of Valère and Marianne
FROSINE, an adventuress
MASTER SIMON, an intermediary
MASTER JACQUES, cook and coachman to
    Harpagon
BRINDAVOINE ⎫
LA MERLUCHE ⎬ servants to Harpagon
DAME CLAUDE ⎭
LA FLÈCHE, valet to Cléante
OFFICER
OFFICER'S CLERK

The scene is in Paris

Act One

VALÈRE. Come, my dear Élise, surely you are not feeling sad, after giving me such generous assurance of your love? Here am I, the happiest of men, and I find you sighing! Is it because you regret having made me happy? Do you repent the promise which my ardour has won from you?

ÉLISE. No, Valère. I could never regret anything I did for you. I cannot even bring myself to wish things were other than as they are, though I must confess I am concerned about the outcome and more than a little afraid that I may love you more dearly than I ought.

VALÈRE. But what can you possibly have to fear from loving me, Élise?

ÉLISE. Alas! A hundred and one things: my father's anger, the reproaches of my family, what people may say about me, but most of all, Valère, a change in your affection for me. I dread the cruel indifference with which men so often requite an innocent love too ardently offered them.

VALÈRE. Ah! Do not be so unjust as to judge me by other men. Believe me capable of anything, Élise, rather than of failure in my duty to you. I love you too dearly, and mine is a love which will last as long as life itself.

ÉLISE. Ah, Valère, you all talk like that. Men are all alike in their promises. It is only in their deeds that they differ.

VALÈRE. If deeds alone show what we are, then at least wait and judge my love by mine. Do not look for faults which only exist in your own fond forebodings. I implore you not to let such wounding and unjust suspicions destroy my happiness! Give me time to convince you and you shall have a thousand proofs of the sincerity of my love.

ÉLISE. Ah! How easy it is to let ourselves be persuaded by those we love! I am convinced that you would never deceive me, Valère. I do believe you love me truly and faithfully. I have not the least wish to doubt you, and my only concern is that other people may find cause to blame me.

VALÈRE. And why should that trouble you?

ÉLISE. Ah, if only everyone could see you as I do, I should
have nothing to fear. The qualities I see in you justify everything I do for you. My love is founded on knowledge of
your virtues and sustained by my gratitude, a gratitude which
Heaven itself enjoins. How can I ever forget the dreadful
danger which first brought us together, your noble courage
in risking your life to snatch me from the fury of the waves,
your tender solicitude when you had brought me to the
shore and the unremitting ardour of your love which neither
time nor adversity has diminished, a love for which you neg-
lect your parents and your country, conceal your true rank
and stoop to service in my father's household merely for the
sake of being near me! These are the things which weigh
with me, Valère, and justify, for me, my promises to you,
but the justification may not seem sufficient to others – and
I cannot be certain that they will share my feelings.

VALÈRE. Of all these things you have mentioned, only one
gives me any claim on you, Élise, and that is my love. As for
your scruples, surely your father has done everything he
could to justify you in the eyes of the world! Surely his
avarice and the miserable existence he makes his children
lead, would justify still stranger things! Forgive me, my dear,
for speaking of him in this way, but you know that on this
issue there is nothing good one can say of him. However, if
only I can find my parents again, as I hope I may, we shall
have little difficulty in gaining his consent. I grow impatient
for news of them, and if I do not hear soon I shall set out in
search of them myself.

ÉLISE. Oh no, Valère. Do not go away, I beseech you! Stay
and give your whole attention to gaining my father's confidence.

VALÈRE. Cannot you see how I am endeavouring to do so?
You know what adroitness and subservience I had to show
to get into his service, what a mask of sympathy and con-
formity with his feelings I assumed in order to ingratiate myself with him, how in his presence I am for ever playing a
part with a view to gaining his favour. And am I not, indeed,
making remarkable progress? I find that the best way to win
people's favour is to pretend to agree with them, to fall in

with their precepts, encourage their foibles and applaud whatever they do. One need have no fear of overdoing the subservience. One can play up to them quite openly, for, when it comes to flattery, the most cunning of men are the most easily deceived, and people can be induced to swallow anything, however absurd or ridiculous, provided it is sufficiently seasoned with praise. Such methods may impair one's integrity, but if one has need of people one must accommodate oneself to them, and if there is no other way of gaining their support, well then, the blame lies less with the flatterers than with those who want to be flattered.

ÉLISE. Why don't you try to win my brother's support in case the maidservant should take it into her head to betray us?

VALÈRE. No, I couldn't handle father and son at the same time. They are so utterly different that one could not be in the confidence of both simultaneously. Do what you can with your brother and make use of your mutual affection to win him to our side. He is coming in now. I will withdraw. Take this opportunity of speaking to him, but tell him only so much of our affairs as you think fit.

ÉLISE. I don't know whether I can bring myself to take him into my confidence.

Enter CLÉANTE.

CLÉANTE. I am delighted to find you alone, sister. I have been longing for a talk with you. I want to tell you a secret.

ÉLISE. Well, here I am, ready to listen, Cléante. What have you to tell me?

CLÉANTE. Lots of things, my dear, but – to sum it up in one word – I'm in love.

ÉLISE. *You* are in love?

CLÉANTE. Yes. I'm in love, and let me say before we go any further that I am fully aware that I am dependent on my father, that as a son I must submit to his wishes, that we should never give a promise of marriage without the consent of those who brought us into the world, that Heaven made them the arbiters of our choice, that it is our duty never to bestow our affections except as they may decide, that, not being blinded by passion, they are less likely to be deceived

and better able to see what is good for us than we are ourselves, that it behoves us to trust to the light of their prudence rather than to our own blind desires, and that youthful
impetuosity leads, as often as not, to disaster! I mention all
this, my dear sister, to save you the trouble of saying it.
The fact is that I am too much in love to listen to anything
you have to say and I, therefore, ask you to spare your
remonstrances.

ÉLISE. And have you actually given her your promise?

CLÉANTE. No, but I am determined to do so, and I ask you,
once again, not to try to dissuade me.

ÉLISE. Am I such a strange person as that, Cléante?

CLÉANTE. No, Élise, but you aren't in love. You know nothing of the power of the tender passion over the hearts of us
lovers. I am afraid you may take too prudent a view.

ÉLISE. Oh, don't talk of my prudence! There is no one who is
not imprudent at some time or other, and if I were to reveal
all that is in my own heart you might find I was even less
prudent than you are.

CLÉANTE. Ah, if only you were like me – if only you loved –

ÉLISE. Let us deal with your troubles first. Tell me who she is.

CLÉANTE. A new-comer to our neighbourhood – the most
charming person in the world. I was completely carried away
from the first moment I saw her. Her name is Marianne and
she lives with her invalid mother, to whom she is wonderfully devoted. She cares for and consoles her in her sufferings with the most touching devotion. She lends a charm to
everything she touches and a grace to everything she does.
She is so gentle, so kind, so modest – so adorable. Oh, Élise,
I only wish you had seen her!

ÉLISE. Oh, I can see her very well from your description, and
the fact that you love her tells me sufficiently what sort of
person she is.

CLÉANTE. I have discovered, indirectly, that they are not very
well off, and that, even living modestly, as they do, they are
hard put to make ends meet. Just think, my dear, what a
pleasure it would be if I could restore her fortunes or even
discreetly supplement the modest needs of a virtuous family.
Imagine, on the other hand, my despair at my inability to

enjoy such a pleasure, thanks to my father's avarice, or even to offer a single token of my love.

ÉLISE. Yes, I can see how galling it must be for you.

CLÉANTE. Ah, my dear, it's worse than you could ever imagine. Could anything be more cruel than this rigorous economy he inflicts on us, this unnatural parsimony under which we perforce languish? What use will money be to us if it only comes when we are too old to enjoy it; if, to manage at all in the meantime, I have to run into debt on all sides, and, like you, am constantly reduced to going to tradesmen for help in order to clothe myself decently? I wanted to talk to you and ask you to help me to sound father about what I have in mind. If I find he is opposed to it, I'm determined to run away with my beloved and take whatever fortune Heaven may vouchsafe us. With this end in view I am trying to raise money everywhere. If you are in the same position as I am, my dear sister, and father opposes your wishes too, let us both leave him and free ourselves from the tyranny his intolerable avarice has so long imposed on us.

ÉLISE. He certainly gives us more and more cause every day to regret our dear mother's death.

CLÉANTE. I hear his voice. Let us go and discuss our plans somewhere else and later we can join forces in an attack on his obduracy.

They go out. Enter HARPAGON *and* LA FLÈCHE.

HARPAGON. Get out at once! I'll have no back answers! Go on! Clear out of my house, sworn thief and gallows-bird that you are!

LA FLÈCHE [*aside*]. I never came across such a confounded old scoundrel. I reckon he is possessed of a devil, if you ask me!

HARPAGON. What are you muttering about?

LA FLÈCHE. What are you turning me out for?

HARPAGON. What right have you to ask me my reasons? Get out before I throw you out.

LA FLÈCHE. What have I done to you?

HARPAGON. Enough for me to want to be rid of you.

LA FLÈCHE. Your son – my master – told me to wait for him!

HARPAGON. Go wait in the street, then! Don't let me see you

in the house any more, standing there keeping a watch on everything that goes on, and an eye for anything you can pick up. I want no spy for ever watching my affairs, a sneaking dog with his confounded eyes on everything I do, devouring everything I possess and rummaging everywhere to see if there's anything he can steal.

LA FLÈCHE. And how the deuce do you think anyone is going to steal from you? Is it likely anyone is going to steal from you when you keep everything under lock and key and stand guard day and night?

HARPAGON. I'll lock up what I want and stand guard when I please. I never saw such a pack of prying scoundrels! They've an eye on everything one does! [*Aside*] I'm only afraid he's got wind of my money. [*To* LA FLÈCHE] You are just the man to go spreading it round that I have got money hidden, aren't you?

LA FLÈCHE. You have money hidden?

HARPAGON. No, you rogue – I never said so! [*Aside*] Oh, it infuriates me! [*To* LA FLÈCHE] All I'm asking is that you shan't go spreading malicious rumours that I have!

LA FLÈCHE. What does it matter to us whether you have or you haven't? It's all the same either way.

HARPAGON. So you'll argue, will you! [*Raising his fist*] I'll teach you to argue! Once again, get out of here!

LA FLÈCHE. All right! I'm going.

HARPAGON. Wait! You are not taking anything with you?

LA FLÈCHE. What could I be taking?

HARPAGON. Come here! Let me see! Show me your hands.

LA FLÈCHE. There!

HARPAGON. Now the others.

LA FLÈCHE. The others?

HARPAGON. Yes, the others.

LA FLÈCHE. There you are!

HARPAGON [*pointing to his breeches*]. Have you nothing in there?

LA FLÈCHE. See for yourself!

HARPAGON [*feeling at the bottom of his breeches*]. These wide breeches are the very things for hiding stolen property. They deserve hanging – whoever makes such things.

LA FLÈCHE [*aside*]. A fellow like this deserves to get what he expects. I only wish I could have the pleasure of robbing him.

HARPAGON. Eh?

LA FLÈCHE. What's that?

HARPAGON. What did you say about robbing?

LA FLÈCHE. I said, 'Have a good look and make sure I am not robbing you'.

HARPAGON. That's what I intend to do. [HARPAGON *feels in* LA FLÈCHE's *pockets*.]

LA FLÈCHE [*aside*]. A plague on all misers and their miserly ways.

HARPAGON. What's that? What d'ye say?

LA FLÈCHE. What did I say?

HARPAGON. Yes, what did you say about misers and miserly ways?

LA FLÈCHE. I said a plague on all misers and their miserly ways!

HARPAGON. And who are you referring to?

LA FLÈCHE. Misers, of course.

HARPAGON. And who are they?

LA FLÈCHE. Who are they? Stingy old scoundrels.

HARPAGON. But who d'ye mean by that?

LA FLÈCHE. What are *you* worrying about?

HARPAGON. I am worrying about what I've a right to worry about.

LA FLÈCHE. Did you think I meant you?

HARPAGON. I think what I choose, but I want to know who you were talking to.

LA FLÈCHE. To – to my hat.

HARPAGON. Yes, and I'll talk to your thick skull.

LA FLÈCHE. Can't I say what I like about misers?

HARPAGON. Yes, you can if you like, but I can put a stop to your impudent nonsense! Hold your tongue.

LA FLÈCHE. I mentioned no names.

HARPAGON. If you say a word more, I'll leather you.

LA FLÈCHE. If the cap fits – I say –

HARPAGON. Will you be quiet?

LA FLÈCHE. Yes, if I must!

HARPAGON. Ah! You –

LA FLÈCHE [*shows a pocket in his jerkin*]. Steady on! Here's another pocket! Will that satisfy you?

HARPAGON. Come on! Hand it over without my having to search you!

LA FLÈCHE. Hand over what?

HARPAGON. Whatever it is you've taken from me!

LA FLÈCHE. I've taken nothing from you.

HARPAGON. Sure?

LA FLÈCHE. Certain!

HARPAGON. Be off, then, and go to the devil!

LA FLÈCHE. That's a nice sort of leave taking.

HARPAGON. I leave you to your conscience. [*Alone.*] He's a confounded nuisance, this scoundrelly valet. I hate the sight of the limping cur! It is a terrible worry having a large sum of money in the house. Much better have one's money well invested and keep no more than is needed for current expenses. It's difficult to find a safe hiding-place in the house. I've no confidence in strong boxes. I don't trust 'em. They are just an invitation to thieves, I always think – the first things they go for. All the same I'm not sure I was wise to bury in the garden the ten thousand crowns I was paid yesterday. Ten thousand crowns in gold is a sum which ... [*Enter* ÉLISE *and* CLÉANTE *talking together in low voices.*] Oh Heavens! Have I given myself away? I let myself be carried away by my temper – I do believe I was talking aloud. [*To* CLÉANTE] What is it?

CLÉANTE. Nothing, father.

HARPAGON. Have you been here long?

ÉLISE. No, we have only just come.

HARPAGON. Did you hear – er –

CLÉANTE. Hear what, father?

HARPAGON. Just now –

ÉLISE. What was it?

HARPAGON. What I have just been saying.

CLÉANTE. No.

HARPAGON. Yes, you did, you did! You did!

CLÉANTE. Pardon me, we heard nothing.

HARPAGON. I can see you overheard something. The fact is I was just saying to myself how difficult it is nowadays to get hold of any money and how fortunate anybody is who has ten thousand crowns by him.

CLÉANTE. We hesitated to come near you for fear of interrupting you.

HARPAGON. I'm very glad of the chance to explain to you, in case you got the wrong impression and imagined I was saying that I had ten thousand crowns.

CLÉANTE. We don't concern ourselves with your affairs.

HARPAGON. I only wish I had ten thousand crowns.

CLÉANTE. I don't believe –

HARPAGON. It would be a good thing for me if I had.

ÉLISE. Such things –

HARPAGON. I could well do with a sum like that.

CLÉANTE. I think –

HARPAGON. It would come in very useful.

ÉLISE. You are –

HARPAGON. I should have less cause to complain of hard times than I have.

CLÉANTE. Good Heavens, father! You have no cause to complain. Everybody knows you are well enough off!

HARPAGON. Me? Well off! What a lie! Nothing could be further from the truth! It's scandalous to spread such tales!

ÉLISE. Well, don't be angry.

HARPAGON. It's a queer thing when my own children betray me and turn against me.

CLÉANTE. Is it turning against you to say that you are well off?

HARPAGON. Yes. What with your saying things like that and your extravagant ways someone will be coming and cutting my throat one of these days in the belief that I'm made of money.

CLÉANTE. What extravagant ways have I got?

HARPAGON. What, indeed! What could be more scandalous than the sumptuous apparel you flaunt round the town? Only yesterday I was complaining of your sister – but you are far worse! It's a crying scandal! What you are wearing now, taking you as you stand, would add up to a nice competency. I have told you a score of times already, my lad, I don't like your goings on at all: this aping of the nobility and going about dressed up as you are can only mean that you are robbing me somehow.

CLÉANTE. But how can I be robbing you?

HARPAGON. How should I know? Where do you get the money to live as you do?

CLÉANTE Where do I get the money? From cards. I happen to be lucky and I put my winnings on my back.

HARPAGON. That's no way to go on! No way at all! If you are lucky at cards you should take advantage of it and put your winnings into some sound investment. Then they'll be there when you want 'em. But what I would like to know, never mind anything else, is what's the use of all these ribbons that you are decked out with from head to foot? Wouldn't half a dozen pins do to fasten up your breeches? Why need you spend money on a wig, when you can wear your own hair – which costs nothing? I'm willing to bet that your perukes and ribbons cost you twenty guineas at least, and twenty guineas invested bring in one pound thirteen shillings and elevenpence farthing a year at no more than eight per cent.

CLÉANTE. That's true enough.

HARPAGON. Well now, suppose we leave that and come to something else – Eh? [*Aside*] I believe they are making signs to each other to steal my purse. [*To* CLÉANTE] What do you mean by making signs like that?

ÉLISE. We are just arguing as to who should speak first. We both have something to tell you.

HARPAGON. Yes, and I have something to tell both of you.

CLÉANTE. We want to talk to you about marriage, father.

HARPAGON. Ay, and it's marriage I want to talk to you about.

ÉLISE. Oh, father!

HARPAGON. Why the 'Oh, father'? Is it the word marriage or the idea of getting married yourself you are afraid of, my girl?

CLÉANTE. The word marriage might well alarm both of us. It depends on what you understand by it. We are afraid that what *we* want may not agree with what *you* want.

HARPAGON. Now do be patient. Don't get alarmed. I know what is good for both of you. Neither of you shall have any cause to complain of what I am going to do for you. First of all, do you know a young lady named Marianne who lives not far from here?

CLÉANTE. Yes, father, I do.

HARPAGON [*to* ÉLISE]. And you?

ÉLISE. I have heard of her.

HARPAGON. Well now, my boy, what is your opinion of this young lady?

CLÉANTE. She is a most charming person.

HARPAGON. Her looks?

CLÉANTE. Modest and intelligent.

HARPAGON. Her manner?

CLÉANTE. Admirable, beyond question.

HARPAGON. You think a girl like that is worth serious consideration?

CLÉANTE. I do, father.

HARPAGON. An eligible match, in fact?

CLÉANTE. Most eligible.

HARPAGON. And she looks as if she'd make a good housewife?

CLÉANTE. Without a doubt.

HARPAGON. And whoever marries her can count himself a lucky man, eh?

CLÉANTE. Assuredly.

HARPAGON. There's one little difficulty. I'm afraid she may not bring as much money as one would like.

CLÉANTE. Ah! What does money matter, father, when it is a question of marrying a good woman?

HARPAGON. Oh no, I don't agree with you there! But there *is* this to be said, that if she hasn't as much money as one would wish there may be some other way of making up for it.

CLÉANTE. Of course.

HARPAGON. Well now, I'm very pleased to find you agree with me, because her modest ways and gentle disposition have quite won my heart. Provided that I find she has *some* money – I've made up my mind to marry her.

CLÉANTE. Eh?

HARPAGON. What do you mean by 'Eh'?

CLÉANTE. You have made up your mind to – what did you say?

HARPAGON. Marry Marianne.

CLÉANTE. You mean – you – you yourself?

HARPAGON. Yes. Me! Me! Me myself. What about it?

CLÉANTE. I feel faint. I must get out of here.

HARPAGON. It will pass off. Go into the kitchen and have a good drink – of cold water. [*Exit* CLÉANTE.] There! You see what these effeminate young men are! They haven't the strength of a chicken! Well, there you are, my girl, that is what I've decided for myself. For your brother I have a certain widow in mind. Someone came to talk to me about her this morning. As for you, yourself, I mean to bestow you on Seigneur Anselme.

ÉLISE. Seigneur Anselme!

HARPAGON. Yes, he's a man of ripe experience, prudent and discreet, not more than fifty years of age and reputed to be very rich.

ÉLISE [*curtseying*]. If you please, father, I don't want to marry.

HARPAGON [*imitating her*]. If *you* please, my pet, I want you to marry.

ÉLISE. Excuse me, father –

HARPAGON. Excuse *me*, my dear –

ÉLISE. I am Seigneur Anselme's very humble servant but, if you don't mind, I won't marry him.

HARPAGON. And I am your very humble servant, my dear, but, if you don't mind, you *will* marry him, and this very evening too.

ÉLISE. This evening!

HARPAGON. This evening!

ÉLISE. No, father, I won't.

HARPAGON. Yes, daughter, you will.

ÉLISE. No!

HARPAGON. Yes!

ÉLISE. I tell you I shan't!

HARPAGON. But I say you shall!

ÉLISE. I will never agree to it!

HARPAGON. But I shall make you agree to it!

ÉLISE. I'll kill myself rather than marry such a man.

HARPAGON. You won't kill yourself and you shall marry him. The impertinence! Who ever heard of a daughter talking like this to her father!

ÉLISE. Who ever heard of a father requiring his daughter to make such a marriage!

HARPAGON. It is a most suitable match. I am willing to bet that everyone will approve of my choice.

ÉLISE. And I am willing to bet that no reasonable person would do any such thing.

HARPAGON. Here comes Valère. Will you agree to let him judge between us?

ÉLISE. Yes, I agree.

HARPAGON. You'll accept his decision?

ÉLISE. Yes, I'll abide by whatever he says.

HARPAGON. That's settled, then. Come here, Valère! We want you to decide which of us is in the right – my daughter here, or myself.

VALÈRE. Oh, you sir, beyond question.

HARPAGON. But you don't know what we are talking about!

VALÈRE. No, but you *couldn't* be wrong. You are always in the right.

HARPAGON. I intend to marry her this evening to a man who is both wealthy and wise, and the silly chit tells me to my face that she won't have him at any price. What d'ye say to that?

VALÈRE. What do I say to that?

HARPAGON. Yes.

VALÈRE. Ah well – I –

HARPAGON. Well?

VALÈRE. What I say is that fundamentally I agree with you – for of course you just must be right, but, on the other hand, she isn't altogether in the wrong.

HARPAGON. Why! Seigneur Anselme is an eligible match, well born, quiet, assured, prudent, and very well off and with no surviving children of his first marriage. What more could she want?

VALÈRE. That's true – though she might perhaps contend that it is rather precipitate and that she ought at least to be allowed time to see if she can reconcile herself to . . .

HARPAGON. No! An opportunity like this won't stand delay. What is more, there is a special, a unique advantage. He is willing to take her – without dowry!

VALÈRE. Without dowry?

HARPAGON. Yes.

VALÈRE. Oh! I say no more. There you are! One must agree
– that's absolutely conclusive.

HARPAGON. It means a considerable saving for me.

VALÈRE. Of course, there's no gainsaying that. It is true that
your daughter might contend that marriage is a more serious
matter than people sometimes realize, that a lifetime's happiness or unhappiness may depend upon it and that one
ought not to enter into a commitment for life without giving
it serious consideration.

HARPAGON. But – without dowry!

VALÈRE. Yes, you are right! That's the important thing, of
course – although there are people who would contend that
in a case like this your daughter's own feelings should be
considered, and that where there is such a great disparity of
age, temperament, and opinions there is a risk that the marriage might turn out badly. . . .

HARPAGON. But – without dowry!

VALÈRE. Yes, one must admit there's no answer to that.
There is no arguing against it. Not that there are not
some fathers who would attach more importance to their
daughter's happiness than the money they might have to
part with and refuse to sacrifice it to mercenary considerations. They would rather seek to secure before everything
else that union of mutual affection from which spring happiness, joy, and contentment –

HARPAGON. Without dowry!

VALÈRE. True. It is unanswerable. Without dowry! There's
no countering that!

HARPAGON [*aside – looking offstage*]. Ah, I thought I heard a
dog barking. Can it be someone after my money? [*To
VALÈRE*] Don't go away. I'll be back directly. [*Goes out.*]

ÉLISE. Surely you don't mean what you are saying, Valère?

VALÈRE. If we are to get what we want from him we must
avoid rubbing him the wrong way. It would ruin everything
to oppose him directly. There are some people you can't
deal with except by humouring them. Impatient of opposi-
tion, restive by nature, they never fail to shy at the truth and
won't go about things in a common-sense fashion. The only

way to lead them is to turn them gently in the direction you
want them to go. Pretend to give your consent and you'll
find it's the best way to get what you want.

ÉLISE. But this marriage, Valère?

VALÈRE. We will find some excuse for breaking it off.

ÉLISE. But how – when it is to take place this evening?

VALÈRE. You must pretend to be ill and have it post-
poned.

ÉLISE. But they will discover the truth when they call in the
doctor.

VALÈRE. Not they! What do those fellows know about anything? Have whatever malady you like, they'll explain how
you got it.

HARPAGON[*returning – to himself*]. It's nothing, thank Heaven!

VALÈRE. If the worst comes to the worst we must take refuge
in flight, that is, if you love me well enough, my dear Élise,
to face – [*seeing* HARPAGON] Yes, it's a daughter's duty to
obey her father. It's not for her to worry about what her
husband looks like; when it's a case of – without dowry –
she must take what she's given.

HARPAGON. Good! That's the way to talk.

VALÈRE. Forgive me, sir, for letting my feelings run away
with me and taking the liberty of talking to her in this way.

HARPAGON. Not at all. I am delighted. I give you a free hand
with her. [*To* ÉLISE] It's no use running away. I invest him
with full parental authority over you. You must do whatever he tells you.

VALÈRE [*to* ÉLISE]. Now will you resist my remonstrances!
[*To* HARPAGON] I'll follow her and continue the homily I
was giving her.

HARPAGON. Do. I shall be grateful to you.

VALÈRE. It is as well to keep her on a tight rein.

HARPAGON. True. We must –

VALÈRE. Don't worry. I think I can deal with her.

HARPAGON. Do, by all means! I am just going to take a stroll
in the town. I'll be back before long.

VALÈRE. Yes. Money is the most precious thing in all the
world! You ought to thank Heaven you have such a good
father. He knows the value of things. When a man offers to

take a girl without dowry there's no point in looking any further. That's the only thing that matters. 'Without dowry' – it counts for more than good looks, youth, birth, honour, wisdom, and probity.

They go out together.

HARPAGON. Good lad! Spoken like an oracle! How lucky I am to have such a man in my service.

Act Two

CLÉANTE, LA FLÈCHE.

CLÉANTE. Now, you scoundrel! where have you been hiding yourself? Didn't I tell you to . . .

LA FLÈCHE. Yes, sir, and I came in here with every intention of waiting for you, but your father, who's a most awkward old man to deal with, would chase me out willy-nilly. I very nearly got myself a hiding.

CLÉANTE. How is our affair progressing? Things have become more pressing than ever, and since I last saw you I have found out that my father is my rival in love.

LA FLÈCHE. Your father in love?

CLÉANTE. Yes, and I had the greatest difficulty in the world in preventing him from seeing how upset I was by the discovery.

LA FLÈCHE. Fancy his being in love! What the devil is he thinking about? Is he trying to take a rise out of everybody? What use is love to a fellow like him, anyway?

CLÉANTE. It must be a judgement on me – his getting an idea like this into his head!

LA FLÈCHE. But why do you conceal your own love affair from him?

CLÉANTE. To give him less cause for suspicion, to keep myself in a position to prevent this marriage of his if it comes to the point. What reply did they give you?

LA FLÈCHE. Upon my word, sir, borrowing money is a miserable business. Anyone who has to go through the money-lender's hands, as you have, must put up with some pretty queer things.

CLÉANTE. So nothing will come of it?

LA FLÈCHE. Oh no! Master Simon, the agent they put us in touch with, is a keen business-like fellow, and he's moving Heaven and Earth for you. He assures me he has taken quite a fancy to you.

CLÉANTE. So I shall get the fifteen thousand I'm asking for?

LA FLÈCHE. Yes – subject to a few trifling conditions you'll have to accept if you want it to go through.

CLÉANTE. Has he put you in touch with the actual lender?

LA FLÈCHE. Now really, sir, that isn't the way these things are done! He's even more anxious to conceal his identity than you are. There is more involved in these jobs than you think. They won't give his name and he is to have an opportunity of talking to you to-day at a house hired for the purpose, so that he can learn from your own lips about your means and your family. I have no doubt at all that the mere mention of your father's name will make everything easy.

CLÉANTE. Especially as my mother is dead and they can't stop me getting her money.

LA FLÈCHE. There are a few conditions here which he himself has dictated to our go-between. He wants you to see them before going any further. 'Provided that the lender shall be satisfied as to the securities and that the borrower be of age and of a family with means sufficient, substantial and secure, free and quit of all encumbrance there shall be executed a proper and precise undertaking before a notary, of known probity, who to this end and purpose shall be nominated by the lender inasmuch as he is the more concerned that the instrument be executed in due form.'

CLÉANTE. I have nothing to say against that.

LA FLÈCHE. 'The lender, that his conscience may be free from all reproach, proposes to make his money available at no more than five and a half per cent.'

CLÉANTE. Five and a half per cent! My goodness, but that's very reasonable. There's nothing to complain of there!

LA FLÈCHE. True. 'But – whereas the lender aforesaid has not the sum in question by him and in order to oblige the borrower is himself obliged to borrow elsewhere at the rate of twenty per cent, the aforesaid borrower shall agree to meet this interest without prejudice to the five and a half per cent aforementioned in consideration of the fact that it is only to oblige the aforesaid borrower that the lender aforesaid undertakes to borrow the aforesaid amount.'

CLÉANTE. What the devil! What sort of Jew or Turk have we got hold of? That's more than twenty-five per cent!

LA FLÈCHE. True. That's what I said. You'd better think about it.

CLÉANTE. What's the use of thinking about it. I need the money, so I shall have to agree to everything.

LA FLÈCHE. That's what I told them.

CLÉANTE. Is there anything else?

LA FLÈCHE. Just one small clause. 'Of the fifteen thousand francs which the borrower requires, the lender can only dispose of twelve thousand in cash, and for the other three thousand the borrower shall undertake to take over the effects, clothing, and miscellaneous objects as set out in the following inventory and priced by the aforesaid lender at the most moderate valuation possible.'

CLÉANTE. What does that mean?

LA FLÈCHE. Listen to the inventory. 'Item – one four-poster bed complete with hangings of Hungarian lace, very handsomely worked upon an olive-coloured material, together with six chairs and a counterpane to match, the whole in very good condition and lined in red and blue shot silk; item – one tester bed with hangings of good Aumale serge in old rose with silk fringes and valance.'

CLÉANTE. What does he expect me to do with that?

LA FLÈCHE. Wait. 'Item – one set of hangings in tapestry representing the loves of Gombaut and Macaea; item – one large table in walnut with twelve pedestal or turned legs with draw-out leaf at either end and fitted underneath with six stools.'

CLÉANTE. Confound it! What use is that to me?

LA FLÈCHE. Patience, please. 'Item – three muskets, inlaid in mother-of-pearl, with three assorted rests; item – one brick furnace with two retorts and three flasks, very useful for anyone interested in distilling; item –'

CLÉANTE. Oh! It's infuriating –

LA FLÈCHE. Now, now! 'Item – one Bologna lute complete with strings or nearly so; item – one fox-and-goose board, one draughts-board, one game of mother goose as derived from the ancient Greeks, very useful for passing the time when one has nothing else to do; item – one crocodile skin three feet six inches in length and stuffed with hay, a very attractive curio for suspension from the ceiling – all the aforementioned articles valued at upwards of four thousand five hundred francs and reduced to three thousand at the discretion of the lender.'

CLÉANTE. Confound him and his discretion! The miserable rogue! Did you ever hear of such usury! Not content with charging outrageous interest, he must rook me three thousand francs for his collection of old junk. I shan't get two hundred for the lot, and yet I suppose I must just resign myself to agreeing to whatever he wants! He's in a position to make me put up with it. His dagger's at my throat, the scoundrel!

LA FLÈCHE. It seems to me, master, if you don't mind my saying so, that you are going the same road to ruin as Panurge – drawing your money in advance, buying dear, selling cheap, and eating your corn in the blade.

CLÉANTE. Well, what else can I do? That's what young men are driven to by the cursed niggardliness of their fathers. Can anyone wonder that their sons wish them dead!

LA FLÈCHE. I must admit that your father's behaviour would exasperate the mildest of men. I have no particular fancy for getting myself hanged, thank the Lord, and when I see some of my colleagues involving themselves in transactions of a certain sort I know when to keep out and steer clear of the little amusements which lead one too near the gallows, but I'm bound to say that I think his behaviour is a sheer invitation to robbery. I should even consider it a praiseworthy action to rob him.

CLÉANTE. Give me the inventory a moment, I'll have another look at it.

Enter MASTER SIMON *and* HARPAGON.

MASTER SIMON. Yes, as I was saying, sir, the young man is in need of money. His affairs are such that he needs it urgently, and he will agree to any conditions you like to make.

HARPAGON. And you feel certain, Master Simon, that there's not the least risk? You know your client's name, means, and family?

MASTER SIMON. No, I can't tell you exactly. It was only by chance that he was put in touch with me, but he will tell you it all himself, and his servant assures me that you'll be completely satisfied when you make his acquaintance. All I can tell you is that his family is very wealthy, his mother is dead, and that he'll guarantee, if need be, that his father will die within six months!

HARPAGON. Well, that's something! After all, it's only charitable to assist people when we can, Master Simon.

MASTER SIMON. Of course.

LA FLÈCHE [*to* CLÉANTE *in a whisper*]. What's the meaning of this – our Master Simon talking to your father?

CLÉANTE [*to* LA FLÈCHE *in a whisper*]. Someone must have told him who I was. Could *you* betray me?

MASTER SIMON. You *are* in a hurry! Who told you this was the meeting-place? [*To* HARPAGON] I didn't disclose your name and address to them, sir, but I think there's no great harm done. They are people of discretion and you can discuss things between you here.

HARPAGON. What's this?

MASTER SIMON. This gentleman is the person I was speaking of, sir, who wants to borrow fifteen thousand francs.

HARPAGON. So it's you, is it, you blackguard? You descend to this sort of thing, do you?

CLÉANTE. So it's you, is it, father? You stoop to this kind of trade, do you?

MASTER SIMON *and* LA FLÈCHE *go out*.

HARPAGON. So you are the man who is ruining himself by such outrageous borrowing?

CLÉANTE. And you are the man who is enriching himself by such criminal usury!

HARPAGON. How can you ever dare to face me after this?

CLÉANTE. How will you ever dare to face anyone at all?

HARPAGON. Aren't you ashamed to stoop to such extravagance, to involve yourself in such frightful expense, to squander in this disgraceful fashion the fortune your parents have toiled so hard to accumulate for you?

CLÉANTE. Don't you blush to disgrace your position by transactions of this kind, to sacrifice your honour and reputation to your insatiable lust for piling coin on coin and outdoing anything the most notorious usurers ever invented in the way of scandalous interest!

HARPAGON. Get out of my sight, you scoundrel! Get out of my sight!

CLÉANTE. I ask you, who commits the greater crime, the man who borrows to meet his necessities, or the one who extorts money from people which he doesn't need?

HARPAGON. Go away, I tell you! You make my blood boil. [*Exit* CLÉANTE.] I'm not sorry this has happened! It's a warning to me to keep a closer watch on him than ever.

Enter FROSINE.

FROSINE. Sir –

HARPAGON. Just a minute. I'll come back and talk to you presently. [*Aside*] It's time I had a look at my money!

He goes out. Enter LA FLÈCHE.

LA FLÈCHE [*to himself*]. It's a most peculiar business. He must have a regular furniture store somewhere. We didn't recognize any of the stuff in the inventory.

FROSINE. Ah, it's you, my poor La Flèche. Fancy meeting you!

LA FLÈCHE. Why, Frosine! What are you doing here?

FROSINE. Following my usual occupation – acting as go-between, making myself useful to people and picking up what I can from such small abilities as I possess. You have to live on your wits in this world, you know, and those of us who have no other resources must rely on scheming and hard work.

LA FLÈCHE. Have you some business with the master?

FROSINE. Yes, I'm handling a little transaction for him and hoping for some recompense.

LA FLÈCHE. From him? My goodness! You'll be clever if you get anything out of him! Money is hard to come by in this house I warn you.

FROSINE. But there *are* certain services which are wonderfully effective in opening the purse-strings.

LA FLÈCHE. Well I won't contradict you, but you don't know our Mr Harpagon yet. He just isn't human at all, our Mr Harpagon – he hasn't one scrap of humanity in him! He has the hardest heart and the closest fist of any man living. There's no service of any kind, sort, or description would make him grateful enough to put his hand in his pocket. Praise, compliments, fine words, friendliness, yes, as much as you like, but money – nothing doing! You may win his favour, be in his good graces – but nothing ever comes of it. He has such a dislike of the word 'giving' that he won't even give you 'good morning'.

FROSINE. Good Heavens! As if I don't know how to get round men! Why, I know all there is to be known about stroking them the right way, arousing their sympathy, and finding their soft spots.

LA FLÈCHE. Not the slightest use here. Where money's involved I defy you to make any impression. On that score he's adamant – absolutely past praying for. You could be at death's door but *he* wouldn't budge. He puts money before reputation, honour, or virtue, and the mere sight of anyone asking for money is enough to throw him into a fit. It's like inflicting a mortal wound on him, taking his heart's blood, tearing out his very entrails, and if – but he's coming back. I must be off. . . .

He goes out. Enter HARPAGON.

HARPAGON [*to himself*]. Everything is all right. [*To* FROSINE] Well now, Frosine, what is it?

FROSINE. Goodness me, how well you are looking – the very picture of health.

HARPAGON. Who? Me!

FROSINE. I never saw you looking so fresh and so sprightly.

HARPAGON. Really?

FROSINE. Why, you've never looked so young in your life. I know fellows of twenty-five who are not half as youthful as you are.

HARPAGON. Nevertheless, I'm well over sixty, Frosine.

FROSINE. Well, what's sixty? What of it? It's the very flower of one's age. You are just coming to the prime of life.

HARPAGON. True, but I reckon I should be no worse for being twenty years younger.

FROSINE. What are you talking about! You need wish no such thing. You've the constitution to live to a hundred.

HARPAGON. Do you think so?

FROSINE. I'm certain. You have all the indications. Keep still a moment! Look what a sign of longevity that is – the line between the eyes!

HARPAGON. Is that really so?

FROSINE. Of course. Give me your hand. Heavens! What a line of life!

HARPAGON. What d'ye mean?

FROSINE. You see where that line goes to?

HARPAGON. Well, what does that mean?

FROSINE. Upon my word. Did I say a hundred? You'll live to a hundred and twenty!

HARPAGON. No! Is it possible?

FROSINE. I tell you they'll have to knock you on the head! You'll see your children buried, ay, and your children's children.

HARPAGON. So much the better! And how is our little business getting on?

FROSINE. Need you ask? Did you ever know me start a job and not finish it? I really have a wonderful talent for matchmaking. There's nobody I couldn't pair off, given a little time to arrange things. I really think, if I took it into my head, I could match the Grand Turk and the Venetian Republic! Not that there was anything very difficult about this little business of yours. I am friendly with the two ladies and have talked to them both about you and told the mother of the intentions you have formed in regard to Marianne from seeing her pass along the street and taking the air at her window.

HARPAGON. And her reply?

FROSINE. She was delighted by the proposal, and when I intimated that you would like her daughter to be present this evening at the signing of your own daughter's marriage contract she agreed without hesitation and put her in my charge.

HARPAGON. You see, I am committed to giving a supper for Seigneur Anselme, Frosine, and I shall be very pleased if she will join the party too.

FROSINE. Good. She is to visit your daughter after dinner and then go to the fair, which she wants to do, and return in time for supper.

HARPAGON. Very well. I'll lend them my carriage and they can go down together.

FROSINE. That's the very thing for her!

HARPAGON. Now, have you sounded the mother as to what dowry she can give her daughter, Frosine? Have you told her she must make an effort to contribute something and put herself to some pinching and scraping on an occasion like this? After all, nobody is going to marry a girl unless she brings something with her.

FROSINE. Why, this girl will bring you twelve thousand a year.

HARPAGON. Twelve thousand a year!

FROSINE. Yes. In the first place she's been brought up on a very spare diet. She is a girl who is used to living on salad and milk, apples and cheese, so she'll need no elaborate table, none of your rich broths or eternal barley concoctions, nor any of the delicacies other women would require, and that's no small consideration. It might well amount to three thousand francs a year at least. Moreover, her tastes are simple; she has not any hankering after extravagant dresses, expensive jewellery, or sumptuous furnishings which young women of her age are so fond of – and this item alone means more than four thousand a year. Then, again, she has a very strong objection to playing for money, a most unusual thing in a woman nowadays. I know one woman in our neighbourhood who has lost twenty thousand francs at cards this year. Suppose we reckon only a quarter of that – five thousand a year for cards and four thousand on clothes and jewellery, that's nine thousand, and another three thousand on food – that gives you your twelve thousand a year, doesn't it?

HARPAGON. Yes, it's not bad, but all these calculations don't amount to anything tangible.

FROSINE. Come, come! Do you mean to say that a modest appetite, a sober taste in dress, and a dislike of card playing don't amount to anything tangible? Why, they are a marriage portion and an inheritance rolled into one!

HARPAGON. No. It's just nonsense to try and make a dowry out of the expenses she won't incur. I'll give no credit for anything I don't actually receive. I really must have something I can get my hands on.

FROSINE. Heavens, man! You'll get your hands on plenty. They've mentioned that they have money abroad somewhere. That will come to you.

HARPAGON. Well, we shall have to look into that, but there's another thing worrying me, Frosine. The girl is young, as you know, and young people generally prefer those of their own age and don't fancy other society. I am afraid she may not take to a man as old as I am, and that might lead to certain little domestic complications which wouldn't please me at all.

FROSINE. How little you know her! It's another thing I was going to mention. She can't bear young men at all and keeps all her affection for old ones.

HARPAGON. Does she really?

FROSINE. Yes! I only wish you could have heard her on the subject. She can't bear the sight of a young man. She declares that nothing gives her more pleasure than to see a fine old man with a venerable beard. The older men are the better she likes them, so don't go making yourself look younger than you are. She wants someone in the sixties at least. She was on the point of being married when she suddenly broke it off because the man let it out that he was no more than fifty-six and he didn't put spectacles on to sign the marriage contract.

HARPAGON. That was the only reason?

FROSINE. Yes, she says fifty-six isn't old enough for her, and she likes a nose that wears spectacles.

HARPAGON. Well, that's something entirely new to me!

FROSINE. You wouldn't believe the lengths she goes to. She has a few pictures and engravings in her room, and what do you think they are? Adonis, Cephales, Paris, or Apollo? Not at all! Pictures of Saturn, King Priam, the aged Nestor, and good old father Anchises borne on the shoulders of his son.

HARPAGON. Well, that *is* remarkable! I should never have thought it. I'm delighted to hear that her tastes run that way. I must say if I'd been a woman I should never have fancied young men.

FROSINE. I can well believe you. What poor stuff young men are for anyone to fall in love with – a lot of snotty-nosed infants and fresh-faced country bumpkins. To think of anyone feeling any attraction towards them!

HARPAGON. I can never understand it myself. I don't know how it is that women are so fond of them.

FROSINE. They must be completely mad to find young men attractive. It doesn't make sense! These young fops aren't men. How can anyone take to such creatures?

HARPAGON. That's what I'm always saying. What with their effeminate voices and their two or three wisps of beard turned up like cat's whiskers, their tow wigs, their flowing breeches and unbuttoned coats!

FROSINE. Ay! They make a poor show compared with a man like you. You are something like a man, something worth looking at. You have the sort of figure women fall in love with, and you dress the part too.

HARPAGON. You think I'm attractive?

FROSINE. Why, you are quite irresistible. Your face is a picture. Turn round a little, if you please. What could be more handsome? Let me see you walk. There's a fine figure of a man – as limber and graceful as one could wish to see! Not a thing ails you.

HARPAGON. No, nothing very serious, Heaven be praised, except a bit of catarrh that catches me now and again.

FROSINE. Oh, that's nothing. Your catarrh is not unbecoming. Your cough is quite charming.

HARPAGON. Tell me now, has Marianne ever seen me? Has she not noticed me passing by?

FROSINE. No, but we've talked a lot about you. I've described you to her and I've not failed to sing your praises and tell her how fortunate she would be to have such a husband.

HARPAGON. You've done well. Thank you, Frosine.

FROSINE. I should like to make one small request to you, sir. [HARPAGON *looks grave.*] I'm involved in a lawsuit, and on the point of losing it for lack of a little money. You could easily ensure that I win my case if you were disposed to help me. You've no idea how pleased she will be to see you. [HARPAGON *looks cheerful.*] How delighted she will be with you. How she'll adore that old-fashioned ruff of yours! She will be absolutely charmed with your way of wearing your breeches pinned to your doublet. A lover with pinned-up breeches will be something quite out of the ordinary for her.

HARPAGON. I'm delighted to hear it.

FROSINE. This lawsuit is really a serious matter for me, sir – [HARPAGON *looks grave again.*] If I lose it I'm ruined, but a very little help would retrieve my position. I only wish you could have seen how delighted she was to hear me talking about you. [HARPAGON *looks cheerful again.*] As I recounted your good qualities, her eyes filled with pleasure and in the end I made her quite impatient to have the marriage all settled.

HARPAGON. You have been very kind, Frosine, and I can't say how much obliged I am to you.

FROSINE. I beseech you, sir, grant me the small assistance I'm asking. [HARPAGON *looks grave again.*] It will put me on my feet again and I shall be eternally grateful to you.

HARPAGON. Good-bye. I must finish my letters.

FROSINE. I do assure you, sir, I am in the most urgent need of your help.

HARPAGON. I'll give instructions for my carriage to be got ready to take you to the fair.

FROSINE. I wouldn't trouble you if I weren't absolutely obliged to.

HARPAGON. I'll see that we have supper early so that it won't upset any of you.

FROSINE. Please don't refuse me. You couldn't imagine, sir, how pleased –

HARPAGON. I'm off. There's somebody calling me. Until later – [*He goes.*]

FROSINE. May you rot, you stingy old cur! The skinflint held out against all my attempts. Devil take him! But I won't give it up. I can always count on getting something handsome out of the other party, whatever happens.

Act Three

HARPAGON, CLÉANTE, ÉLISE, VALÈRE, DAME CLAUDE, MASTER JACQUES, BRINDAVOINE, LA MERLUCHE.

HARPAGON. Come along. Let us have you all in here. I want to give you your instructions for this evening and see that everybody has his job. Come here, Dame Claude, we'll start with you. [*She carries a broom.*] Good, I see you are ready for the fray. Your job is to clean up all round, and do be careful not to rub the furniture too hard. I'm afraid of your wearing it out. Then, I'm putting you in charge of the bottles during the supper. If there's a single one missing or if anything is broken I shall hold you responsible and take it out of your wages.

MASTER JACQUES [*aside*]. A shrewd penalty!

HARPAGON [*to* DAME CLAUDE]. Off you go! [*She goes.*] Now you, Brindavoine, and you, La Merluche, I give you the job of rinsing the glasses and serving the wine, but mind, only when people are thirsty. Don't do, as some scoundrelly servants do, egg people on to drink, putting the idea into their heads when they would never have thought of it otherwise. Wait till they have asked several times and always remember to put plenty of water with it.

MASTER JACQUES [*aside*]. Yes, wine without water goes to the head.

LA MERLUCHE. Be we to take off our aprons, master?

HARPAGON. Yes, when you see the guests arriving, but take care not to spoil your clothes.

BRINDAVOINE. You mind, master, that there be a great

blotch of lamp oil on one side of my doublet.

LA MERLUCHE. And my breeches be that torn behind, master, that, saving your presence, they'll see my . . .

HARPAGON. That's enough. See that you keep it against the wall. Face the company all the time – and you – hold your hat in front of you like this when you are serving the guests. [He *shows* BRINDAVOINE *how to keep his hat over his doublet to hide the oil stain.*] As for you, my girl [*to* ÉLISE], you are to keep an eye on what is cleared away from the tables and see that nothing is wasted. That's the proper job for daughters to do. In the meantime get yourself ready to welcome my mistress. She is coming to call on you and take you to the fair. Do you hear what I'm telling you?

ÉLISE. Yes, father.

HARPAGON. And you, my effeminate fop of a son, I'm willing to forgive you for what happened just now, but don't you be giving her any of your black looks either.

CLÉANTE. I give her black looks, father? Whatever for?

HARPAGON. Oh Lord! We know very well how children carry on when their fathers marry again and what the usual attitude towards a stepmother is! If you want me to forget your last escapade, I'd advise you to put on a cheerful face for the young lady and make her as welcome as ever you can.

CLÉANTE. I really can't promise to be glad that she should become my stepmother. I couldn't truthfully say that I am, but I can promise to obey you to the letter in putting on a cheerful face to receive her.

HARPAGON. Well, mind that you do.

CLÉANTE. You will find you have no cause to complain on that score.

HARPAGON. Very well! [CLÉANTE *goes out.*] Valère, I want your help in this. Now then, Master Jacques, come along; I've kept you until last.

MASTER JACQUES. Do you want to speak to your cook or your coachman, sir? I'm both the one and the other.

HARPAGON. I want both.

MASTER JACQUES. But which d'ye want first?

HARPAGON. The cook.

MASTER JACQUES. Just a minute, then, if you don't mind. [*He* takes off his coachman's overcoat and appears dressed as a cook.]

HARPAGON. What the deuce is the meaning of this ceremony?

MASTER JACQUES. At your service now, sir.

HARPAGON. I am committed to giving a supper to-night, Master Jacques –

MASTER JACQUES. Wonders never cease!

HARPAGON. Now tell me, can you give us something good?

MASTER JACQUES. Yes, if you give me plenty of money.

HARPAGON. What the devil! It's always money. It seems to be all they can say. Money! Money! Money! It's the one word they know. Money! They are always talking of money. They can never do anything without money!

VALÈRE. I never heard such a fatuous answer. As if there's anything in providing good food if you have plenty of money. It's the easiest thing in the world. Any fool can do that much. The man who is really good at his job can put on a good meal without spending money.

MASTER JACQUES. Put on a good meal without spending money!

VALÈRE. Yes.

MASTER JACQUES. Upon my word, Mr Steward, I would like you to show how it's done. You had better take on my job as cook since it seems you want to be managing everything.

HARPAGON. Be quiet! Just tell us what we shall need.

MASTER JACQUES. Ask Mr Steward there. He is the man who can put on a meal without spending money.

HARPAGON. Hey! I want an answer from *you*.

MASTER JACQUES. How many will you be at table?

HARPAGON. We shall be eight or ten, but reckon on eight. Provide for eight and there's always plenty for ten.

VALÈRE. Of course.

MASTER JACQUES. Right. You need to provide four sorts of soup and five main courses – soups, entrées –

HARPAGON. The devil! You are not feeding the whole town.

MASTER JACQUES. Roasts –

HARPAGON [*putting his hand over his mouth*]. You scoundrel You'll eat me out of house and home.

MASTER JACQUES. Entremets –

HARPAGON. Still going on?

VALÈRE. Do you want them to burst themselves? Do you think the master is asking people to come and gorge themselves to death? Go study the rules of health! Ask the doctor whether there's anything does people more harm than over-eating.

HARPAGON. How right he is!

VALÈRE. You need to learn, you, and folk like you, Master Jacques, that an overloaded table is a veritable death-trap. Anyone who is really concerned for the well-being of his guests should see that the meal that he offers them is distinguished by frugality. As the ancient philosopher has it, 'One should eat to live and not live to eat'.

HARPAGON. Ah, well said, well said! Come, let me embrace you for that. It is the finest precept I've ever heard – 'One should live to eat and not eat to' – that's not it – how does it go?

VALÈRE. 'One should eat to live and not live to eat.'

HARPAGON. Yes. [*To* MASTER JACQUES] Do you hear that? [*To* VALÈRE] Who was the great man who said that?

VALÈRE. I don't remember his name just now.

HARPAGON. Remember to write the words down for me! I'll have them engraved in letters of gold over the chimney-piece in the dining-room.

VALÈRE. I won't fail to do so. As for the supper, just leave it to me. I will see that everything is as it should be.

HARPAGON. Yes, do.

MASTER JACQUES. So much the better. I shall have the less to worry about.

HARPAGON. We must have things people don't go in for much these days, things which soon fill them up – some good thick stew with dumplings and chestnuts. Have plenty of that.

VALÈRE. You may rely on me.

HARPAGON. And now, Master Jacques, I must have my carriage cleaned.

MASTER JACQUES. Just a minute. This is the coachman's job. [*Puts on his coat again.*] You were saying, sir?

HARPAGON. I must have my carriage cleaned and the horses made ready to go to the fair.

MASTER JACQUES. Your horses, master? Upon my word, they

are in no state for work. I can't say that they are down on
their litter because the poor creatures haven't a scrap, and
that's the truth of it. You keep them on such short commons
that they are no more than ghosts or shadows of horses.

HARPAGON. They are in a bad way, then – but they never do
anything!

MASTER JACQUES. Because they never do anything are they
never to eat anything? It would be far better for them to
work more, poor creatures, if they could only eat in proportion. It fair breaks my heart to see them so thin – for the fact
is, I'm fond of my horses and I suffer along with them. Not
a day passes but I go short myself to feed them. A man must
be very hard-hearted, master, not to have pity for his fellow-
creatures.

HARPAGON. It's no great job to go as far as the fair.

MASTER JACQUES. No, I haven't the heart to drive them,
master, and I should be ashamed to use the whip to them in
the state they are in. How do you expect them to pull the
coach when they can hardly drag themselves along?

VALÈRE. I will arrange for Le Picard next door to drive them,
sir. We shall want his help in preparing the supper, too.

MASTER JACQUES. Right. I'd far rather they died under
someone else's hand than mine.

VALÈRE. You are a great talker, Master Jacques.

MASTER JACQUES. And you are a great meddler, Master
Steward!

HARPAGON. Be quiet!

MASTER JACQUES. I can't stand flatterers, master, and I can
see that everything he does, all his everlasting prying into
the bread and the wine and the wood and the salt and the
candles is nothing but back-scratching, all done to curry
favour with you. That's bad enough, but on top of it all I
have to put up with hearing what folk say about you and,
after all, I have a soft spot for you, in spite of myself. Next
to my horses I think more of you than anybody else.

HARPAGON. Would you mind telling me what people say
about me?

MASTER JACQUES. Yes, master – if I could be sure it
wouldn't annoy you.

HARPAGON. Not in the least.

MASTER JACQUES. Excuse me, but I know very well you'll be angry.

HARPAGON. On the contrary. I shall enjoy it. I like to know what people are saying about me.

MASTER JACQUES. Well, since you will have it, master, I'll tell you straight then – they make a laughing stock of you everywhere; we have scores of jokes thrown at us about you; there's nothing folk like better than running you down and making game of your stinginess. One tale is that you've had special almanacs printed with double the numbers of fast days and vigils so that you can save money by making your household keep additional fasts; another is that you are always ready to pick a quarrel with your servants when they have a present due to them or when they are leaving your service so that you don't have to give them anything; one fellow tells how you had the law on your neighbour's cat for eating the remains of a leg of mutton, another how you were caught one night stealing oats from your own horses and how your coachman, the one before me, gave you a drubbing in the dark and you never said anything about it; in fact, I'll tell you what it is, there's no going anywhere without hearing you pulled to pieces. You are a butt and a byword for everybody, and nobody ever refers to you except as a miser, a skinflint, and a niggardly old usurer.

HARPAGON [*beating him*]. And you are a silly, rascally, scoundrelly, impudent rogue!

MASTER JACQUES. Ah, well! Didn't I guess as much? You wouldn't believe me. I said you'd be angry if I told you the truth.

HARPAGON. I'll teach you to talk like that. [*He goes out.*]

VALÈRE. You seem to have got a poor reward for your frankness, Master Jacques.

MASTER JACQUES. Upon my word, Mr Upstart, you are mighty self-important, but it's no affair of yours. Keep your laughter for your own hidings when you get 'em. Don't come laughing at mine.

VALÈRE. Ah, my dear Master Jacques, please don't be annoyed –

MASTER JACQUES [*aside*]. He's climbing down. I'll put on a bold front and give him a beating if he's fool enough to be frightened. [*To* VALÈRE] *You* may laugh, but I'd have you know that I'm not laughing, and if you get me annoyed I'll make you laugh on the other side of your face. [*Drives him across stage, threatening him.*]

VALÈRE. Go easy!

MASTER JACQUES. How d'ye mean, go easy? Suppose I don't choose to go easy.

VALÈRE. Please –

MASTER JACQUES. You are an impudent fellow!

VALÈRE. My dear Master Jacques –

MASTER JACQUES. I don't care tuppence for your dear Master Jacques. If I once take my stick to you I'll beat you black and blue.

VALÈRE. How d'ye mean, your stick! [VALÈRE *makes him retreat in his turn.*]

MASTER JACQUES. I didn't mean anything.

VALÈRE. Just understand, my dear fat-head, that if anyone's going to feel the stick you are the one!

MASTER JACQUES. I don't doubt it.

VALÈRE. And that you are only a good-for-nothing cook when all's said and done.

MASTER JACQUES. Yes, I know I am.

VALÈRE. And that you don't half know me yet.

MASTER JACQUES. Please forgive me!

VALÈRE. Did you say that you'd beat me?

MASTER JACQUES. It was only a joke.

VALÈRE. Well, I don't like your jokes. [*Beats him.*] Your jokes are in very bad taste. Just understand that. [*He goes out.*]

MASTER JACQUES. So much for sincerity! It's a poor sort of trade. From now on I've done with it. No more telling the truth. I can put up with my master. He's got some right to beat me, but as for this precious steward, I'll have my own back on him if I can.

Enter MARIANNE *and* FROSINE.

FROSINE. Do you know if the master is in, Master Jacques?

MASTER JACQUES. Ay, indeed he is. I know only too well.

FROSINE. Please tell him that we are here. [*He goes out.*]

MARIANNE. What a strange position to be in, Frosine! I must say I am dreading the meeting.

FROSINE. Why? What is there to worry about?

MARIANNE. Oh, dear! How can you ask! Can't you imagine what a girl feels when she is about to confront the fate that's in store for her.

FROSINE. I agree that Harpagon isn't what you would choose if you wanted a pleasant sort of death, and I guess from your expression that your thoughts still turn to the young man you were telling me about.

MARIANNE. Yes, I won't pretend to deny it, Frosine. The respectful manner in which he paid his visits to us made a most favourable impression upon me.

FROSINE. But did you find out who he is?

MARIANNE. No, I don't know in the least, but I do know that he is very attractive, and that if I had my own choice I would as soon have him as another. Indeed he makes me loathe this husband they have chosen for me all the more.

FROSINE. Good Lord, yes! these young sparks are all attractive enough, and can tell a good tale, but most of them are as poor as church mice. You would do much better to take an old husband with plenty of money. I admit it may seem to fly in the face of nature and there may well be some distasteful things to put up with, but then it won't be for long. When he dies you may be sure he'll leave you in a position to choose one you like better, and he'll make up for everything.

MARIANNE. But it doesn't seem right, Frosine, that one should have to look forward to someone else dying before one can be happy. Moreover, death doesn't always fall in with our schemes.

FROSINE. Don't be silly. You only marry him on the strict understanding that he leaves you a widow before very long. That must be put in the contract. It would be most inconsiderate of him if he didn't die within, say, three months! – But here comes the man himself.

MARIANNE. Oh, Frosine! What a face!

HARPAGON. Don't be offended, my dear, if I come to meet you with my spectacles on. I know that your charms are striking enough, sufficiently visible; they need no glasses to discover them, but it is through glass that one observes the stars, you know, and you yourself are a star, I declare, the loveliest one in all the firmament. [*To* FROSINE] Frosine, she doesn't say a word, and from what I can see she doesn't seem at all pleased to see me.

FROSINE. She is a little overcome. Young girls are always shy of showing their feelings at first.

HARPAGON. Perhaps you are right. [*To* MARIANNE] Now my dearie, here is my daughter coming to greet you.

Enter ÉLISE.

MARIANNE. I fear I am late in paying my respects.

ÉLISE. On the contrary, I should have come to you first.

HARPAGON. You see what a big lass she is, but ill weeds do grow fast.

MARIANNE [*aside to* FROSINE]. What a horrible man!

HARPAGON. What did my pretty one say?

FROSINE. She was saying how much she admires you.

HARPAGON. That's very kind of you, my pet.

MARIANNE [*aside*]. Oh, what a creature!

HARPAGON. Very gratifying sentiments indeed!

MARIANNE [*aside*]. I can bear it no longer.

Enter CLÉANTE.

HARPAGON. This is my son. He has come to pay his respects too.

MARIANNE [*aside to* FROSINE]. Ah, Frosine! What an encounter. This is the very young man I was telling you about.

FROSINE [*to* MARIANNE]. How very remarkable!

HARPAGON. I see you are surprised to find I have a grown-up family, but I shall be rid of both of them before long.

CLÉANTE. I must say this is a most unexpected meeting. I was completely taken aback when my father told me of his intentions a little while ago.

MARIANNE. I am in the same position. The meeting is as much a surprise to me as to you. I was quite unprepared for such a coincidence.

CLÉANTE. Truly, madam, my father could have made no better choice, and it is indeed a pleasure to meet you. All the same I cannot bring myself to say that I should welcome your becoming my stepmother. I must admit that the honour is not one I appreciate. Indeed the title, if I may say so, is the last one I should wish you to assume. All this might appear rude to some people, but you, I am sure, will know in what sense to take it, understand how repugnant this marriage must be to me, and how contrary to all my intentions. In short, I am sure you will allow me to say, with my father's kind permission, that if I had my way this marriage would never take place.

HARPAGON. That's a fine way of paying your respects. What a tale to be telling her!

MARIANNE. My answer is that I feel as you do. If you are loath to see me as your stepmother I am no less opposed to having you as a stepson. Please do not think it is by any wish of mine that you are placed in such a dilemma. I should be grieved to cause you distress, and had I any freedom of choice I should never consent to a marriage which would cause you unhappiness.

HARPAGON. She's quite right. Answer a fool according to his folly. I must apologize, my dear, for my son's silliness. He is young and foolish and doesn't yet understand what he is saying.

MARIANNE. I am not the least offended, I assure you. On the contrary, it has been a pleasure to hear your son express his feelings so frankly. I value such an avowal coming from him. Had he spoken otherwise I should not esteem him so highly.

HARPAGON. It's very good of you to overlook his faults. He will get more sense as he grows older, and you'll find that his feelings will change.

CLÉANTE. Never, father! My feelings will not change. I ask the lady to believe that.

HARPAGON. You see what an absurd fellow he is. He gets worse and worse.

CLÉANTE. Would you have me be false to my love?

HARPAGON. Still at it? Kindly try a different tune!

CLÉANTE. Very well, then, since you wish me to speak in a different vein – permit me, madam, to put myself in my father's place and assure you that you are the most charming person I ever met, that the greatest happiness I could imagine would be to win your favour and that I would rather be your husband than the greatest king on earth. Yes, madam, to enjoy your love would be for me the height of good fortune, and that is indeed my only ambition. There is nothing that I would not do to achieve so enviable a purpose, and whatever the obstacles may be –

HARPAGON. Steady on, lad, if you don't mind.

CLÉANTE. I am addressing the lady on your behalf.

HARPAGON. Good Lord! I have a tongue of my own. I don't need you as my advocate. Here, bring some chairs.

FROSINE. No, I think it would be better if we set out for the fair at once, so as to get back earlier and have plenty of time to talk later.

HARPAGON. Have the horses put in the carriage, then. Please forgive me, my dear, for not having thought to provide some refreshment before you go.

CLÉANTE. I have arranged it, father. I told them to bring in a bowl of china oranges, lemons, and sweetmeats. I had them ordered on your behalf.

HARPAGON [*in a whisper*]. Valère!

VALÈRE [*to* HARPAGON]. He's out of his mind!

CLÉANTE. Do you think there is not enough, father? The lady will perhaps excuse any deficiency.

MARIANNE. There was no need to have troubled.

CLÉANTE. Did you ever see a finer diamond, madam, than the one my father has on his finger.

MARIANNE. It *is* very brilliant.

CLÉANTE [*taking it from his father's finger and offering it to* MARIANNE]. You need to look at it from close to.

MARIANNE. It is certainly exquisite, so full of fire.

CLÉANTE [*preventing* MARIANNE *from returning it*]. No, no madam. It is in hands which are worthy of it now. My father has made a present of it to you.

HARPAGON. *I* have?

CLÉANTE. You do wish the lady to keep it for your sake, don't you, father?

HARPAGON [*aside to* CLÉANTE]. What d'ye mean?

CLÉANTE [*aside*]. What a question! [*To* MARIANNE] He means that I am to make you accept it.

MARIANNE. But I don't at all want to –

CLÉANTE. You really can't mean that! He would never hear
of taking it back.

HARPAGON [*aside*]. I can't bear it!

MARIANNE. It would be –

CLÉANTE [*still preventing her from returning it*]. No, I assure
you, he would be offended –

MARIANNE. Please –

CLÉANTE. Not at all!

HARPAGON [*aside*]. Confound the –

CLÉANTE. You see how put out he is at your refusal.

HARPAGON [*aside*]. You traitor!

CLÉANTE. You see! He's losing his patience.

HARPAGON [*whispers to* CLÉANTE, *threatening him*]. You
scoundrel!

CLÉANTE. It's not my fault, father; I'm doing the best I can
to make her keep it, but she's very obstinate.

HARPAGON [*furious, whispers to* CLÉANTE]. You blackguard!

CLÉANTE. You are making my father angry with me, madam.

HARPAGON [*as before*]. You villain!

CLÉANTE. You will make him ill. Madam, please do not refuse any further.

FROSINE. Good Lord, what a fuss! Keep the ring since the
gentleman wants you to.

MARIANNE. Rather than cause further annoyance I will keep
it for the time being, but I will find another occasion to
return it.

Enter BRINDAVOINE.

BRINDAVOINE. There's a man wanting to speak to you, sir.

HARPAGON. Tell him I'm busy. Tell him to come back
another time.

BRINDAVOINE. He says he has some money for you.

HARPAGON. Excuse me. I'll be back presently.

Enter LA MERLUCHE, *running. He knocks* HARPAGON *over*.

LA MERLUCHE. Master!

HARPAGON. Oh! He's killed me.

CLÉANTE. What is it, father? Are you hurt?

HARPAGON. The scoundrel must have been bribed to break
my neck by people who owe me money.

VALÈRE. It's nothing serious.

LA MERLUCHE. Master, I beg your pardon, I thought I was doing right to hurry.

HARPAGON. What did you come for, you scoundrel?

LA MERLUCHE. To tell you that your horses have cast their shoes.

HARPAGON. Have them taken to the smith at once.

CLÉANTE. While they are being shod I will do the honours of the house for you, father, and take the lady into the garden. I will have the refreshments taken out there.

HARPAGON. Valère, keep your eye on that stuff, and do, I implore you, save as much of it as you can so that it can go back to the shop.

VALÈRE. Very good, sir.

HARPAGON [*alone*]. Oh what a scoundrel of a son! He's determined to ruin me!

Act Four

CLÉANTE, MARIANNE, ÉLISE, FROSINE.

CLÉANTE. We'll do better to go in here. There's no one here to worry about, so we can talk openly.

ÉLISE. My brother has told me about his love for you. I know how trying your position must be and I assure you that you have my whole sympathy.

MARIANNE. It is a great comfort to know that one has the support of such a person as yourself, and I do hope you will always maintain the same friendliness for me. It is such a consolation in adversity.

FROSINE. Upon my word, it is most unlucky for both of you that you didn't let me into your secrets a bit earlier. I could have saved you all this trouble. I would never have let matters go the way they have done.

CLÉANTE. What's the use! It's my ill luck! It just had to happen this way. [*To* MARIANNE] What decisions have you come to, my dear?

MARIANNE. Alas! How can I come to any decisions? Dependent as I am on other people, what more can I do than hope for the best?

CLÉANTE. Is that all the help you can offer me? Just to hope for the best? No compassionate support? No helping hand? No positive token of your affection?

MARIANNE. What can I say? Put yourself in my place and tell me what I should do! Advise me! Command me! I will put myself in your hands, and I know that you will not ask more of me than honour and propriety permit.

CLÉANTE. But how can I do anything effective if you expect me to keep within the bounds of rigorous honour and scrupulous propriety?

MARIANNE. But what would you have me do? Even if I could disregard the scruples of my sex I must still consider my mother. She has always shown me the most tender affection. I could never bring myself to give her cause for sorrow. You must persuade her. Use every endeavour to gain her approval. I give you leave to say and do whatever you think necessary, and if the issue should depend on my declaring my love for you I shall be willing to avow to her all that I feel.

CLÉANTE. Frosine, dear Frosine, won't you help us out?

FROSINE. Goodness me! Need you ask? I should like to – with all my heart. I'm really quite kind-hearted, you know! I'm not hard by nature, and when I see people really and truly in love I'm only too willing to help them. The question is, what can we do?

CLÉANTE. Please, do think of something.

MARIANNE. Do make some suggestions.

ÉLISE. Find some way of undoing the mischief you've done.

FROSINE. It isn't so easy. [To MARIANNE] Your mother isn't altogether unreasonable. She might be persuaded to transfer to the son what she intended to bestow on the father. [To CLÉANTE] The real difficulty, as I see it, is that your father's your father!

CLÉANTE. Exactly!

FROSINE. What I mean is that he'll have a grievance if he finds his offer refused, and be in no mood to agree to your marriage. What we really need is that the refusal shall come from him. We must try to find some means of making him take a dislike to you, Marianne.

CLÉANTE. That's the idea.

FROSINE. Yes, I know it's the right idea. That's what we need, but how the deuce can we manage it? Wait a minute. Suppose we could produce someone, an elderly woman, say, with a touch of any sort of talent who could carry off the part of a lady of quality with the help of a few scratch retainers and some fancy title or other – a Marchioness or Viscountess of Lower Britanny, should we say – I might contrive to make your father believe she was a wealthy woman with a hundred thousand crowns in ready money and landed property as well, and that she was head over heels in love with him – so anxious to marry him that she would be willing to hand over all her money under the terms of the marriage contract. I don't doubt he'd listen to that proposition, for though I know he loves you very much [*to* MARIANNE] he loves money better. Once he has swallowed the bait and agreed to all that you want it wouldn't matter that he found out the truth when he came to examine our Marchioness's possessions more closely!

CLÉANTE. It sounds a most ingenious notion.

FROSINE. Leave it to me. I've just remembered a friend of mine who is the very person we want.

CLÉANTE. You can count on my showing my gratitude, Frosine, if you can carry it off. Meanwhile, dear Marianne, let us make a start by winning over your mother. It would be a great deal accomplished if we could only break off the marriage. I do implore you to do all you can. Make use of her affection for you. Employ all your charm, and all the eloquence of looks and of speech that Heaven has endowed you with. Use all your gentle persuasions and tender entreaties, those endearing caresses of yours, and they will, I am sure, prove irresistible.

MARIANNE. I will do all I can. I won't forget anything you tell me.

Enter HARPAGON.

HARPAGON [*aside*]. Ha! My son kissing the hand of his stepmother to be! And the stepmother to be doesn't seem to be offering much objection. Is there more in this than meets the eye?

ÉLISE. Here comes father.

HARPAGON. The carriage is ready. You can set out as soon as you like.

CLÉANTE. I will go with them, father, as you are not going.

HARPAGON. No, you stay here. They will get along very well by themselves, and I need you here.

ÉLISE, MARIANNE, *and* FROSINE *go out.*

HARPAGON. Well now, forget she's your stepmother and let me hear what you think of her?

CLÉANTE. What I think of her?

HARPAGON. Yes, her looks, her manners, her figure, her intelligence?

CLÉANTE. Oh – so so.

HARPAGON. Is that all you can say?

CLÉANTE. Well, frankly, she doesn't come up to what I expected. She's just a coquette – nothing more; her figure is not particularly graceful, her looks are no more than middling, and her intelligence is very ordinary. Don't think I'm trying to put you off, father. As stepmothers go I would as soon have her as anyone else.

HARPAGON. But you were telling her just now that –

CLÉANTE. Merely a few conventional compliments on your behalf, and purely to please you.

HARPAGON. So you wouldn't fancy her for yourself, then?

CLÉANTE. Me? Not in the least!

HARPAGON. I'm sorry about that. It cuts across an idea that was passing through my mind. Looking at her just now I began thinking about my age and the way people would talk about my marrying a girl so young, and I was on the point of giving up the idea, but as I had asked for her hand and pledged my word to her I would have let you have her, had you not taken a dislike to her.

CLÉANTE. You would have given her to me?

HARPAGON. Yes, to you.

CLÉANTE. In marriage?

HARPAGON. In marriage.

CLÉANTE. Listen. It's true that she's not exactly what I should choose, but, to please you, father, I am prepared to marry her if you want me to.

HARPAGON. No, I'm not so unreasonable as you think. I have no wish to make you marry a girl against your will.

CLÉANTE. No, but I'm willing to make the effort out of consideration for you.

HARPAGON. No, no! There's no happiness in marriage without love.

CLÉANTE. Well, perhaps that might come afterwards. They say that love often comes after marriage.

HARPAGON. No. I'm against taking chances where the man is concerned. I don't want to run any risk of things turning out badly. If you'd felt any inclination for her, that would have been fine and I'd have arranged for you to marry her instead of me, but, as it is, I'll stick to my original plan and marry her myself.

CLÉANTE. Very well, father, since that's how things stand I must disclose my real feelings and tell you our secret. The truth is that I have loved her since the first day I saw her. I was intending just now to ask your permission to marry her; it was only when you revealed your own feelings and for fear of displeasing you that I refrained from doing so.

HARPAGON. Have you visited her home?

CLÉANTE. Yes, father.

HARPAGON. Often?

CLÉANTE. Fairly often, considering what time there has been.

HARPAGON. And were you well received?

CLÉANTE. Very well, but without their knowing who I was. That was why Marianne was so surprised when she saw me just now.

HARPAGON. Did you tell her you loved her and that you intended to marry her?

CLÉANTE. Of course. I have even made some approach to her mother.

HARPAGON. And she entertained your proposals on her daughter's behalf?

CLÉANTE. Yes, she was very kind.

HARPAGON. And the daughter returns your affections?

CLÉANTE. If one may judge from appearances, I think she likes me a little.

HARPAGON [*aside*]. I'm very pleased to have found all this out. It is just what I wanted to know. [*To* CLÉANTE] Right, my lad, you want to know what the position is? It's this. You'll just put this fancy of yours out of your head if you don't mind; you'll stop paying attentions to the lady I am intending to marry myself, and marry the woman I've chosen for you – and at once.

CLÉANTE. So that was your game, father! Very well! Since that's what things have come to, let me tell you this – I will never give up my love for Marianne, I will stop at nothing to prevent your having her, and even if you have the mother's consent I may find I have some resources on my side.

HARPAGON. What, you rascal! You have the audacity to trespass on my preserves!

CLÉANTE. It's you who are trespassing on mine. I was there first.

HARPAGON. Am I not your father? Aren't you bound to defer to my wishes?

CLÉANTE. This isn't a case where a son needs defer to his father. Love is no respecter of persons.

HARPAGON. I'll make *you* respect *me* – with a stick!

CLÉANTE. You will do no good with threats.

HARPAGON. You shall give up Marianne.

CLÉANTE. Never!

HARPAGON. Bring me a stick – at once!

Enter MASTER JACQUES.

MASTER JACQUES. Now, now now, gentlemen! What *is* all this? What are you thinking about?

CLÉANTE. I'm beyond caring!

MASTER JACQUES. Steady, sir! Steady on!

HARPAGON. Talking to me like that! The impudence!

MASTER JACQUES [*to* HARPAGON]. Now, master – please!

CLÉANTE. I won't budge an inch.

MASTER JACQUES [*to* CLÉANTE]. What! To your father!

HARPAGON. Just let me get at him!

MASTER JACQUES. What! To your son! It would be different if you were talking to me!

HARPAGON. I'll make you the judge between us, Master Jacques, and prove that I'm right.

MASTER JACQUES. I agree. [*To* CLÉANTE] Just stand a bit farther away.

HARPAGON. I am in love with a young lady and mean to marry her, and now this scoundrel here has the impudence to fall in love with her too, and he wants to marry her, although I've told him he can't.

MASTER JACQUES. Oh! That's wrong of him.

HARPAGON. Don't you agree that it's shocking for a son to set up as his father's rival? Isn't he in duty bound, in respect for his father, to refrain from interfering with my intentions?

MASTER JACQUES. Oh yes, you are right, but let me have a word with him. Stay there! [*He goes across stage to* CLÉANTE.]

CLÉANTE. Very well, Since he has chosen you as the judge, I make no objection. It doesn't matter to me who it is, I'm quite willing to submit to your decision, Master Jacques.

MASTER JACQUES. That's very kind of you.

CLÉANTE. I'm in love with a young lady. She returns my affection and receives my offer of love sympathetically. Then my father decides to come along and upset everything by proposing to marry her himself.

MASTER JACQUES. Oh, that's very wrong of him!

CLÉANTE. Should he not be ashamed to be thinking of marriage at his age? Isn't it absurd for him to be falling in love? Wouldn't he do better to leave love-making to younger men, don't you think?

MASTER JACQUES. You are right. He can't really mean it! Just let me have a word with him. [*Goes across to* HARPAGON.] Now look, the lad isn't as bad as you make him out to be. He'll listen to reason. He says he knows the respect he owes to you – that he was carried away in the heat of the moment and that he is willing to do whatever you want, provided you show him more consideration and arrange for him to marry someone to his liking.

HARPAGON. Well then, Master Jacques, you can tell him that, on that understanding, he can count on me absolutely. I leave him free to choose any woman he likes – except Marianne.

MASTER JACQUES. Leave it to me. [*Crosses to* CLÉANTE.] Well now, your father is not so unreasonable as you make him out to be. He has given me to understand that it was your outburst of temper that annoyed him, and all he objects to is your method of going about things. He's ready to grant you anything you ask provided you do it nicely and show him the respect and obedience a son owes to his father.

CLÉANTE. Well then, Master Jacques, you can assure him that if only he will let me have Marianne he'll find me obedience itself and I'll do whatever he wishes in future.

MASTER JACQUES [*to* HARPAGON]. It's all settled. He agrees to everything you said.

HARPAGON. That's splendid!

MASTER JACQUES [*to* CLÉANTE]. Everything's settled. He's satisfied with your promises.

CLÉANTE. Thank Heaven for that!

MASTER JACQUES. Gentlemen! It only remains for you to talk it over together. You are now in complete agreement. You were going to fall out merely because you were misunderstanding each other.

CLÉANTE. My dear Master Jacques, I shall be eternally grateful to you.

MASTER JACQUES. Don't mention it, sir.

HARPAGON. I'm very pleased with you indeed, Master Jacques, and you deserve some reward. [*He feels in his pocket.* MASTER JACQUES *holds out his hand, but* HARPAGON *pulls out his handkerchief and says*] Well, be off. I shan't forget, I assure you.

MASTER JACQUES. Thank you kindly, sir. [*He goes out.*]

CLÉANTE. Father, I ask you to forgive me for having been so angry.

HARPAGON. It doesn't matter.

CLÉANTE. I am very sorry, I assure you.

HARPAGON. And I'm extremely pleased, for my part, to find you so reasonable.

CLÉANTE. It's very generous of you to forgive me so promptly.

HARPAGON. A father can always forgive his children's faults once they remember the duty they owe him.

CLÉANTE. What! Have you forgiven my outrageous behaviour?

HARPAGON. I *must* forgive it now that you show such obedience and respect.

CLÉANTE. I promise you, father, I shall remember your goodness to my dying day.

HARPAGON. And for my part I promise you shall have anything you want from me.

CLÉANTE. Why, father, what more can I ask now that you have given me Marianne?

HARPAGON. What's that?

CLÉANTE. I was saying how grateful I am, father, for what you have done for me. In giving me Marianne you have given me all I could wish for.

HARPAGON. Who said anything about giving you Marianne?

CLÉANTE. Why, you did, father!

HARPAGON. I did?

CLÉANTE. Of course!

HARPAGON. But it's you who promised to give her up.

CLÉANTE. Give her up?

HARPAGON. Yes.

CLÉANTE. Never!

HARPAGON. You've not given her up?

CLÉANTE. On the contrary, I'm more determined than ever to marry her.

HARPAGON. What! Are you starting all over again, you scoundrel!

CLÉANTE. Nothing shall ever make me change my mind.

HARPAGON. I'll see about that, you villain!

CLÉANTE. You can do what you like!

HARPAGON. Clear out of my sight!

CLÉANTE. With the greatest of pleasure.

HARPAGON. I've finished with you!

CLÉANTE. Right! Be finished, then.

HARPAGON. I renounce you!

CLÉANTE. Good!

HARPAGON. I disinherit you!

CLÉANTE. Anything you please.

HARPAGON. And I give you my curse!

CLÉANTE. Keep your gifts to yourself!

Exit HARPAGON.

LA FLÈCHE [*coming from the garden with a strong box*]. Ah
master, here you are, just in the nick of time. Quick! Follow
me!

CLÉANTE. What is it?

LA FLÈCHE. Follow me, I tell you. We are in luck.

CLÉANTE. How d'ye mean?

LA FLÈCHE. Here's just what you are needing.

CLÉANTE. What is it?

LA FLÈCHE. I have had my eye on it all day.

CLÉANTE. But what is it?

LA FLÈCHE. Your father's treasure – I've lifted it!

CLÉANTE. How did you manage it?

LA FLÈCHE. I'll tell you all about it, but let us be off. I can
hear him shouting.

They go.

HARPAGON [*calling 'Stop, thief!' in the garden. He enters hatless*].
Thieves! Robbers! Assassins! Murderers! Justice! Merciful
Heavens! I'm done for! I'm murdered! They've cut my
throat; they've taken my money! Whoever can it be? Where's
he gone to? Where is he now? Where is he hiding? How can
I find him? Which way shall I go? Which way shan't I go? Is
he here? Is he there? Who's that? Stop! [*Catching his own arm*]
Give me my money back, you scoundrel! Ah, it's me! I'm
going out of my mind! I don't know where I am or who
I am or what I'm doing. Oh dear, my dear, darling money,
my beloved, they've taken you away from me and now you
are gone I have lost my strength, my joy and my consolation.
It's all over with me. There's nothing left for me to do in the
world. I can't go on living without you. It's the finish. I
can't bear any more. I'm dying; I'm dead – and buried. Will
nobody bring me to life again by giving me my beloved
money back or telling me who has taken it? Eh? What d'ye
say? There's nobody there! Whoever did it must have
watched his opportunity well and chosen the very moment
I was talking to my blackguard of a son. I must go. I'll
demand justice. I'll have everyone in the house put to the
torture, menservants, maidservants, son, daughter, every-

one – myself included. What a crowd in here! I suspect the whole pack of 'em. They all look to me like the thief. Eh? What are they talking about over there? About the fellow that robbed me? What's that noise up there? Is the thief there? Please, I implore you, tell me if you know anything about him! Isn't he hiding among you? They are all looking at me. Now they are laughing. You'll see, they are all in it, beyond question, all involved in the robbery. Come on! Come quickly! Magistrates, police, provosts, judges, racks, gibbets, hangmen. I'll have everybody hanged, and, if I don't get my money back, I'll hang myself afterwards.

Act Five

HARPAGON, *an* OFFICER *and his* CLERK.

OFFICER. You leave it to me! I know my job, thank the Lord! This isn't the first time I've had a case of theft to investigate. I only wish I'd as many bags of money as I've had people hanged.

HARPAGON. It's to the interest of every magistrate in the country to take hand in this case. If I don't get my money back I'll demand justice on justice itself.

OFFICER. We must go through the proper procedure. How much did you say there was in the box?

HARPAGON. Ten thousand crowns – in cash.

OFFICER. Ten thousand crowns!

HARPAGON. Ten thousand crowns!

OFFICER. A considerable theft.

HARPAGON. No punishment could be bad enough for a crime of this enormity. If it goes unpunished nothing, however sacred, will be safe.

OFFICER. In what denomination of coin was the money?

HARPAGON. In good *louis d'or* and *pistoles* of full weight.

OFFICER. And whom do you suspect of the theft?

HARPAGON. Everybody. Arrest the whole town and the suburbs as well.

OFFICER. If you'll take my advice, it's unwise to alarm people unduly. Let us try to go quietly and collect our evidence, and then – then we can proceed with the full rigour of the law to recover the sum you have lost.

MASTER JACQUES [*calling over his shoulder as he comes on stage*]. I'll be coming back. Cut his throat at once and let them be singeing his feet for me and putting him in boiling water. Then string him up from the rafters.

HARPAGON. Who? The fellow who has stolen my money?

MASTER JACQUES. I was talking about the sucking pig your steward has just sent me. I mean to dress him for you according to my own special recipe.

HARPAGON. We aren't interested in all that. There are other things you have to talk to this gentleman about.

OFFICER. Now, don't be alarmed. I'm not the sort of fellow to get you into trouble. Everything shall be done quietly.

MASTER JACQUES. Is the gentleman one of your supper party?

OFFICER. In a case like this, friend, you must withhold nothing from your master.

MASTER JACQUES. Upon my word, sir, I'll show you all I know. I'll do the best that I can for you.

HARPAGON. We are not worrying about that!

MASTER JACQUES. If I don't give you as good a meal as I could wish, you must blame that steward of yours. He's clipped my wings with his economies.

HARPAGON. You scoundrel! It isn't supper we are concerned with. I want you to tell what you know about the money that has been stolen from me.

MASTER JACQUES. Has somebody stolen your money?

HARPAGON. Yes, you rogue, and I'll have you hanged if you don't give it back.

OFFICER. Good Lord! Don't be so hard on him. I can see by the look of him that he is an honest fellow, and he'll tell you what you want to know without need to put him in jail Now, my lad, if you confess you'll come to no harm and you will get a suitable reward from your master. Someone has taken his money during the day and you must know something about it.

MASTER JACQUES [*aside*]. Here's the very thing for getting my own back on that steward of ours. Ever since he arrived he's been the favourite. They won't listen to anybody but him. Moreover, I haven't forgotten the beating I had a while back.

HARPAGON. What are you muttering about now?

OFFICER. Let him alone. He's getting ready to tell you what you are wanting to know. I wasn't mistaken when I said he was an honest fellow.

MASTER JACQUES. If you want to know, master, I believe that precious steward of yours has done it.

HARPAGON. Valère?

MASTER JACQUES. Yes.

HARPAGON. He who seemed so trustworthy?

MASTER JACQUES. That's the man. I suspect he's the fellow who has robbed you.

HARPAGON. On what grounds do you suspect him?

MASTER JACQUES. On what grounds?

HARPAGON. Yes.

MASTER JACQUES. I suspect him on the grounds – that I suspect him.

OFFICER. But you must indicate what evidence you have.

HARPAGON. Did you see him hanging about the spot where I had put my money?

MASTER JACQUES. Yes, I did that! Where was your money?

HARPAGON. In the garden.

MASTER JACQUES. Exactly. He was hanging about the garden when I saw him. What was your money in?

HARPAGON. In a cash box.

MASTER JACQUES. The very thing! He had a cash box. I saw him with it .

HARPAGON. What sort of a cash box? I can easily tell if it was mine.

MASTER JAQUES. What sort of cash box?

HARPAGON. Yes, yes, yes.

MASTER JACQUES. Well – a sort of – like a cash box.

OFFICER. Yes, of course, but describe it a little so that we can see whether –

MASTER JACQUES. It was a big one.

HARPAGON. Mine was a small one.

MASTER JACQUES. Ay, it was small if you are going by size, but I meant it was big in that it had a big lot of money in it.

OFFICER. What colour was it?

MASTER JACQUES. What colour?

OFFICER. Yes.

MASTER JACQUES. A sort of – what's the word? Can't you help me to describe it?

HARPAGON. Eh?

MASTER JACQUES. It wasn't red, was it?

HARPAGON. No, grey.

MASTER JACQUES. That's it, a greyish red. That's what I meant.

HARPAGON. There's no doubt about it. It's certainly the same one. Write it down, sir, write down his evidence. Oh Lord! Whom can one trust after this? There's no certainty in anything any more. I shall begin to believe that I'm capable of robbing myself.

MASTER JACQUES. Here he comes, master. Whatever you do, don't go and tell him I told you.

Enter VALÈRE.

HARPAGON. Come here! Come and confess to the foulest, most dastardly crime that was ever committed.

VALÈRE. What can I do for you, sir?

HARPAGON. What, you scoundrel! Don't you blush for your crime?

VALÈRE. What crime are you talking about?

HARPAGON. What crime am I talking about! You infamous wretch! As if you didn't know very well what I'm talking about. It's no use your trying to hide it. The secret is out. I've just heard the whole story. To think of your taking advantage of my kindness and getting yourself into my household on purpose to betray me and play a trick like this on me.

VALÈRE. Well, sir, since you know all about it I won't attempt to excuse or deny it.

MASTER JACQUES [*aside*]. So ho. Have I guessed better than I thought?

VALÈRE. I have been meaning to speak to you about it. I was

waiting for a favourable opportunity, but since things have turned out as they have I can only ask you not to be angry, but be good enough to hear what I have to say in justification.

HARPAGON. And what sort of justification can you give, you scoundrelly thief?

VALÈRE. Ah sir, I hardly deserve epithets of that kind. It is true that I have put myself in the wrong with you, but, after all, my fault is a pardonable one.

HARPAGON. Pardonable! A stab in the back! A mortal injury!

VALÈRE. Please don't be angry. When you have heard what I have to say, you'll see that there is less harm done than you think.

HARPAGON. Less harm done than I think. My very heart's blood, you scoundrel!

VALÈRE. On a question of blood, sir, you haven't done badly. My rank is such that I shall not disgrace your blood and there's nothing in all this that I can't make amends for.

HARPAGON. And that's exactly what I intend that you shall do – you shall return what you've stolen from me.

VALÈRE. Your honour shall be fully satisfied, sir.

HARPAGON. There's no question of honour! Tell me, what on earth led you to do such a thing?

VALÈRE. Do you really need to ask?

HARPAGON. Of course I need ask!

VALÈRE. It was that little god who is always forgiven, whatever he makes people do. Love, I mean.

HARPAGON. Love!

VALÈRE. Of course.

HARPAGON. A pretty sort of love! Upon my word! Love of my gold pieces.

VALÈRE. No, sir, it was not your wealth that tempted me, not in the least. That's not what dazzled me! Let me assure you I have no aspirations whatever where your wealth is concerned, provided you let me keep the one treasure I already possess.

HARPAGON. No, indeed! By all the devils in Hell! You shan't keep it. The impudence! Wanting to keep what he's stolen.

VALÈRE. Do you really call it stealing?

HARPAGON. Do I really call it stealing? A treasure like that!

VALÈRE. Yes, a treasure indeed, and beyond question the most precious you have, but not lost to you in becoming mine. On my bended knees I beg you to accord me this most cherished of treasures. Surely you can't refuse your consent.

HARPAGON. I'll do nothing of the sort. What on earth are you talking about?

VALÈRE. We are promised to each other and sworn never to be parted.

HARPAGON. A wonderful promise! A very remarkable compact, I must say!

VALÈRE. Yes, we are bound to one another for ever.

HARPAGON. I'll put a stop to that, I promise you.

VALÈRE. Death alone shall part us.

HARPAGON. He must have my money on the brain!

VALÈRE. I have already told you, sir, that I was not moved to do what I have done by material considerations. My motive was not what you think, but a far nobler one.

HARPAGON. He'll be telling me next that it's sheer Christian charity set him wanting my money. But I'll see to that, and the law shall give me satisfaction on you, you impudent scoundrel.

VALÈRE. Do as you please. I am resigned to bear whatever violence you may resort to, but I do ask you to believe that if any fault has been committed I alone am guilty. Your daughter is in no way to blame.

HARPAGON. I should think not, indeed! It would be a queer thing if my daughter were involved in a crime like this. But I want to be seeing you make restoration. Where's the hiding-place?

VALÈRE. There's no question of restoration or of hiding-place since we have not left the house.

HARPAGON [*aside*]. Oh, my treasure! [*To* VALÈRE] Not left the house, you say?

VALÈRE. No sir.

HARPAGON. Now tell me – you haven't been tampering –

VALÈRE. Never! There you wrong both of us. My love is pure and honourable, and though I am so deeply in love –

HARPAGON [*aside*]. Deeply in love – with my cash box?

VALÈRE. I would die sooner than harbour a single thought unworthy of one so kind and so modest as –

HARPAGON [*aside*]. Modest – my cash box?

VALÈRE. I have asked nothing more than the pleasure of feasting my eyes upon her. Nothing base or unworthy has ever profaned the love which her beauty inspires in me.

HARPAGON [*aside*]. Beauty – my cash box? You might think he was a lover talking of his mistress.

VALÈRE. Dame Claude knows the truth of the matter, sir. She can bear witness.

HARPAGON. Ha, so my servant is in the plot, is she?

VALÈRE. Yes, sir, she was a witness to our vows. Once she found that my intentions were honourable, she helped me to persuade your daughter to give me her promise and accept mine in return.

HARPAGON [*aside*]. Fear of justice must have turned his brain! [*To* VALÈRE] What has my daughter to do with it?

VALÈRE. I am just saying, sir, that I had the greatest difficulty in persuading her to accept my advances.

HARPAGON. Accept your advances? Who?

VALÈRE. Why, your daughter, sir. It was not until yesterday that she gave me her promise to marry me.

HARPAGON. *My* daughter has given her promise to marry *you*?

VALÈRE. Yes, sir – as I gave her mine in return.

HARPAGON. Heavens! Another disaster!

MASTER JACQUES [*to the* OFFICER]. Write it down, mister! Write it all down!

HARPAGON. Trouble on trouble. Misfortune piled on misfortune. Come, sir, do your duty! Draw up the indictment and arrest him as a thief and a seducer as well.

VALÈRE. I have done nothing to deserve such a description. When you know who I am –

Enter ÉLISE, MARIANNE, FROSINE

HARPAGON. Wretched girl! You are unworthy of a father like me. This is how you follow my precepts! You go and fall in love with a scoundrelly thief and promise to marry him without my consent. But you will both find you have made a mistake. [*To* ÉLISE] I'll keep you within four walls in future [*to* VALÈRE] and you shall pay for your audacity on the gallows.

VALÈRE. The question won't be decided by your getting angry. I shall at least be heard before I'm condemned.

HARPAGON. I was wrong when I said the gallows. You shall be broken on the wheel.

ÉLISE [*on her knees to* HARPAGON]. Father, be merciful, I implore you. Do not push your parental rights to the limit. Don't let yourself be carried away in the first flush of anger. Take time to consider what you are doing. Take the trouble to find out a little more about the man you are so incensed against. He is not what he seems. You will be less surprised that I have given him my promise when you learn that you owe it to him that you haven't lost me already. Yes, it was he, father, who saved me from drowning. It is to him you owe your daughter's life and –

HARPAGON. All that amounts to nothing at all. I'd rather he had left you to drown than do what he has done.

ÉLISE. Father, I implore you by your love for me as a father –

HARPAGON. I won't hear any more. Justice must take its course.

MASTER JACQUES [*aside*]. Now you shall pay for that beating you gave me.

FROSINE [*aside*]. Here's a fine kettle of fish.

Enter ANSELME.

ANSELME. What is the trouble, Mr Harpagon? You seem very much upset.

HARPAGON. Ah, Mr Anselme. You see in me the most unlucky of men. All sorts of trouble and difficulty have arisen over the contract you have come to sign. I have suffered deadly blows both to my fortune and my reputation. This treacherous scoundrel here has wormed his way into my household in defiance of every sacred obligation, stolen my money and seduced my daughter.

VALÈRE. Who cares anything about your money that you keep making such a song about?

HARPAGON. They've got themselves engaged to be married – that's an insult to you, Mr Anselme. You must bring an action against him, at your own expense, and get your revenge for his insolence with all the rigour of the law.

ANSELME. I have no intention of forcing anyone to marry me. I make no claim to any affection which is already given elsewhere, but, in so far as your own interests may be involved, you can count on me to support them as my own.

HARPAGON. This gentleman here is a very honest officer who has assured me he'll not fail to do everything his duty requires. [*To the* OFFICER] Charge him with everything he can be charged with and see that you make things black against him.

VALÈRE. I fail to see how loving your daughter can be accounted a crime! As for the punishment you think will be meted out to me for aspiring to her hand, when you know who I am –

HARPAGON. I don't give a rap for your stories. The world is full of self-styled nobility nowadays, impostors who take advantage of their own obscurity to assume the first illustrious name that comes into their heads!

VALÈRE. I should scorn to lay claim to anything that doesn't belong to me, let me tell you. Anyone in Naples can bear witness to my birth and family.

ANSELME. Gently! Mind what you are saying. You are running more risk than you think. You are speaking in the presence of one who knows Naples well and will see through any tale you invent.

VALÈRE [*proudly putting on his hat*]. I have nothing to fear. If you know Naples you know who Don Thomas d'Alburci was.

ANSELME. I knew him well! Few better!

HARPAGON. I care nothing for Don Thomas or Don Martin either! [*He notices two candles burning, and blows one out.*]

ANSELME. Please – let him speak. Let us hear what he has to say.

VALÈRE. I say that he was my father.

ANSELME. *Your* father?

VALÈRE. Yes.

ANSELME. Come now! You are joking. Try a fresh tale and you may do better. You will do yourself no good with this one.

VALÈRE. Take care what you say! This is no tale. I don't make statements that I cannot easily prove.

ANSELME. What! You dare pretend that you are Thomas d'Alburci's son?

VALÈRE. I do, and I will maintain it against all comers.

ANSELME. What astounding effrontery! Let me tell you that the man you refer to was lost at sea more than sixteen years ago with his wife and children while fleeing from the cruel persecutions which accompanied the disorders in Naples, when so many noble families were driven into exile.

VALÈRE. Yes, and let me tell *you* that his son, a boy of seven years of age, was saved from the wreck along with one servant by a Spanish ship, and that it is that son who is now speaking to you. Let me tell you also that the ship's captain took compassion upon me, brought me up as his own son, and that I have followed a career of arms from my earliest years. It is only recently that I learned that my father did not perish as I had always believed. I set out in search of him, and, passing through this town, I met, by a happy chance, my beloved Élise and fell under the spell of her beauty. Such was the effect of my love and her father's intransigence that I decided to take service in his household and send someone else in search of my parents.

ANSELME. But what proof can you offer beyond your own word that this is not just a story built upon some foundation of truth?

VALÈRE. The Spanish captain, a ruby signet ring which belonged to my father, an agate bracelet my mother clasped on my own arm, and lastly, old Pedro himself, who escaped from the shipwreck along with me.

MARIANNE. Now I myself can vouch for the truth of what you have told us. I realize now that you are my brother.

VALÈRE. Can you be my sister?

MARIANNE. Yes. My heart was strangely moved from the very moment you began to speak. My mother – how overjoyed she will be to see you – has recounted our family misfortunes to me a thousand times. Heaven so willed that we too survived that unhappy shipwreck, but we did so at the cost of our liberty. The men who saved my mother and myself from a fragment of wreckage were corsairs. After ten years of slavery we regained our freedom by a stroke of good fortune and returned to Naples. There we found that our possessions had been sold and that there was no news of my father. We took ship thence to Genoa where my mother went to collect the miserable remnants of a despoiled inheritance. Fleeing from the inhumanity of her family she came to these parts, where she has since languished.

ANSELME. Oh Lord! How wonderful are the manifestations of thy power! How true it is that Heaven alone can accomplish miracles! Come to my arms, my children, and mingle your happiness with your father's.

VALÈRE. You are our father?

MARIANNE. It was you my mother so lamented?

ANSELME. Yes, my daughter. Yes, my son. I am Don Thomas d'Alburci. By the mercy of Heaven I was saved from the waves with all the money I had with me. For sixteen years I have believed you all drowned. After many wanderings I was about to seek to renew the consolations of domestic felicity by marriage to a good woman. Uncertain of my safety if I returned to Naples, I renounced my country for ever and, having contrived to dispose of all I had there, I settled down in this place and sought, under the name of Anselme, to forget the misfortunes which the other name had brought upon me.

HARPAGON. Is this your son?

ANSELME. It is.

HARPAGON. Then I shall hold you responsible for paying me the ten thousand crowns he has stolen from me.

ANSELME. Stolen from you?

HARPAGON. Yes, this same fellow.

VALÈRE. Who told you that?

HARPAGON. Master Jacques.

MASTER JACQUES. Oh! You know I've never said a word!

HARPAGON. Oh, yes you did, and the officer here wrote it all down.

VALÈRE. Do you think me capable of such an action?

HARPAGON. Capable or incapable, I want my money back.

Enter CLÉANTE *and* LA FLÈCHE.

CLÉANTE. Don't worry any more, father. Don't accuse anybody. I have news of your money. I come to tell you you can have it all back, provided you let me marry Marianne.

HARPAGON. Where is the money?

CLÉANTE. Don't you worry. It is where I can answer for it. It rests entirely with me. Just say what you want to do. Take your choice. Either give me Marianne or give up your money.

HARPAGON. Is it all there?

CLÉANTE. Every bit. Decide whether you will agree to the marriage and join her mother in giving consent. She has left her daughter free to choose between us: you – or me.

MARIANNE. You are overlooking the fact that my mother's consent is now not sufficient. Heaven has restored my brother to me and my father. You need his consent now.

ANSELME. Heaven has not brought me back to you, dear children, to oppose your own wishes. Mr Harpagon, you must be aware that a young girl is likely to prefer a son to his father. Come then, don't force me to say what I would much rather not. Join me in giving consent to this double marriage.

HARPAGON. I can't decide until I see my cash box again.

CLÉANTE. You shall – safe and sound.

HARPAGON. I have no money for marriage portions.

ANSELME. Well, I have enough for both, so that needn't worry you.

HARPAGON. And you'll undertake to meet the costs of both marriages?

ANSELME. Yes, I agree. Now are you satisfied?

HARPAGON. Provided you buy me new clothes for the wedding.

ANSELME. Agreed. Come, let us go and enjoy the pleasures of this happy day.

OFFICER. Heh! Gentlemen, just a minute, if you don't mind. Who is going to pay for my depositions?

HARPAGON. We want nothing to do with your depositions.

OFFICER. Yes, but I don't intend to work for nothing, not likely!

HARPAGON. There's that fellow there! [*Pointing to* MASTER JACQUES.] Take him and hang him for payment.

MASTER JACQUES. Oh dear! What's a fellow to do! First I'm beaten for telling the truth and now they are going to hang me for telling lies.

ANSELME. Come, Mr Harpagon, we must forgive him his untruths.

HARPAGON. Will you pay the officer, then?

ANSELME. So be it, but let us go at once and share our joy with your mother.

HARPAGON. And let me go and see my beloved cash box again.

THE END

Love's the Best Doctor

L'AMOUR MÉDECIN

*

TO THE READER

(Foreword by Molière)

This play is only a sketch, a mere impromptu, which
the King commissioned for one of the Royal Entertainments. It is the most hurriedly written of all the works
that His Majesty has commanded of me and I am not
exaggerating when I say that it was commissioned,
written, rehearsed, and performed, all within five
days.

It is hardly necessary to remind the reader that, in
such a play, very much depends on performance.
Everyone knows that plays are written to be acted
and this one I commend only to those readers who
can see it in terms of the finished production. Further-
more, one would wish that works of this kind might
always be seen with the embellishments which they
enjoy when performed before His Majesty where they
appear to much greater advantage, and the music of
the incomparable Monsieur Lully, the fine singing,
and the skill of the dancers, lend them a charm without which they would otherwise hardly pass muster.

CHARACTERS IN THE PLAY

SGANARELLE, a merchant
LUCINDE, his daughter
CLITANDRE, her lover
AMINTE, a neighbour
LUCRÈCE, niece to Sganarelle
LISETTE, maid to Lucinde
MR GUILLAUME, an upholsterer
MR JOSSE, a jeweller
DOCTORS TOMÉS, DES-FONANDRÉS,
    MACROTIN, BAHYS, FILERIN
A NOTARY
CHAMPAGNE, valet to Sganarelle

CHARACTERS IN THE BALLETS

CHAMPAGNE, DOCTORS, a quack medicine
    vendor and his attendants
COMEDY, MUSIC, BALLET, LAUGHTER,
    PLEASURES

The scene is Paris, in the house of SGANARELLE

Prologue

COMEDY, MUSIC, BALLET.

COMEDY. Cease then, Oh cease from vain dispute:
  Oh, cease from striving each to take the crown.
  No more each other's claims confute,
  For once a greater glory own.
  Uniting all, all three with one accord engage
  To serve the pleasure of the Great King of the age.
COMEDY, MUSIC, BALLET. Uniting all, all three with one
    accord engage
  To serve the pleasure of the Great King of the age.
MUSIC. From great concerns far weightier than we know
  He stoops betimes to share our pleasures as his own.
BALLET. What greater honour can he show
  Than let us share in his renown.
COMEDY, MUSIC, BALLET. Uniting all, all three with one
    accord engage
  To serve the pleasure of the Great King of the age.

Dance

Scene One

SGANARELLE, AMINTE, LUCRÈCE, MR GUILLAUME,
MR JOSSE.

SGANARELLE. What a strange thing life is! How right was
the ancient philosopher who said that grieving goes with
having and troubles never come singly! I had but one wife
and now she is dead.
MR GUILLAUME. And how many did you wish to have?
SGANARELLE. Guillaume, my friend, she is dead. I feel the
loss deeply. I cannot think of it without tears. Her ways were
not always to my liking: indeed we quarrelled often enough,
but death squares all accounts. She's dead and I weep for her.
If she were alive I suppose we should be quarrelling still. Of

all the children that Heaven vouchsafed me, only one survives and she's the greatest trouble I have. She's in the depths of depression, a dreadful melancholy from which there's no rousing her. And there's no finding the cause. I'm becoming depressed myself and feel a need for advice. You, Lucrèce, are my niece; you, Aminte, are my neighbour; [*to* GUILLAUME *and* JOSSE] you are my friends and fellow tradesmen. Come now, all of you, tell me, please, what I ought to do.

MR JOSSE. Well, I believe that finery and adornment are what girls like most, and if I were you I would buy her a nice set of jewellery – diamonds or rubies, or possibly emeralds – this very day.

MR GUILLAUME. If I were in your place, I should give her a set of tapestries for her room, either in landscape or figure design. They would cheer up the room and her spirits as well.

AMINTE. Well, I wouldn't do any such thing. No, I would marry her off as quickly as possible to that fellow they say wanted her some time ago.

LUCRÈCE. In my opinion marriage wouldn't suit your daughter at all. Her constitution is too delicate. She's not nearly robust enough. No. To expect her to bear children would be to consign her to the next world right away. She's not fit to go out into society, and my advice is to put her into a convent, where she can find distractions more suitable to her disposition.

SGANARELLE. H'm, your suggestions are all, no doubt, admirable, but I suspect they are not quite disinterested. I am sure your advice would be most useful – to yourselves! You are a jeweller, Mr Josse, and your counsel sounds like that of a man who has stocks he would like to unload. Tapestry is your particular line, Mr Guillaume, and no doubt you have some you want to be rid of. As for you, neighbour Aminte, the young man you are in love with has taken a fancy to my daughter, they tell me, so you wouldn't mind seeing her fixed up as someone else's wife. You, my dear niece, know perfectly well I have no intention of letting my daughter marry anyone at all (for which I have my own reasons), but your suggestion that I put her into a convent fits in with that little scheme of yours of becoming my heir. So, ladies and gentle-

men, though your advice is, no doubt, very good, forgive
me if I decide not to take it. Thank you very much. [*They go
out and leave him alone.*] Well, I suppose that's about what
good advice usually amounts to! [*Enter* LUCINDE.] But here
comes my daughter – going out to take the air. She hasn't
noticed me. She is sighing and raising her eyes to Heaven.
[*To* LUCINDE] God bless you, my dear! Good morning! And
how are you? Oh, dear, still as sad and melancholy as ever?
Won't you tell me what's the matter with you? Come along,
open your little heart to your daddy. Don't hide your
thoughts from your father! Don't be frightened! Haven't
you got a kiss for me? Come along! [*Aside*] It infuriates me
to see her in this state. [*To* LUCINDE] Surely you don't want
to see your old father die of grief, do you? Can't you tell me
why you are sad? Just tell me the reason and I promise to do
anything you wish. Tell me the cause of your trouble and I
promise, nay, I swear, that there's nothing I won't do to
please you. Now I can't say more than that, can I? Are you
jealous because one of your friends dresses better than you?
Have you seen some material you would like a dress made
from? No! Is your bedroom not well enough furnished? No!
Would you like some little present – a trinket box, say, from
the Fair of St Lawrence? Is that no use either? You don't
want to study? Shall I get someone to teach you the harpsichord? No use! I suppose you aren't in love, by any chance?
You wouldn't like to get married?

LUCINDE *makes a sign of assent.* Enter LISETTE.

LISETTE. Well, master, so you have been having a talk with
her – have you found out what's the matter?

SGANARELLE. No. The hussy infuriates me.

LISETTE. Let me deal with her, master. I'll sound her a little.

SGANARELLE. No. There's no need to bother. If she wants to
behave like this, the best thing is to leave her alone.

LISETTE. Just let me have a try. She may talk more freely to
me. Well, mistress, aren't you going to say what's the
matter? Are you determined to keep us all worrying? I don't
think you should go on behaving like this. If you are shy of
telling your father, you needn't be frightened of telling me
everything. Come, is there something you want from him?

He has said many a time that there is nothing he won't do to please you. Don't you have all the freedom you want? Would you like to get about more and enjoy yourself? Eh? Has someone annoyed you? Eh? Have you taken a fancy to some young man you would like to marry? Ah, now I understand! So that's what it is! Goodness me! But why make such a fuss? Master, the secret is out, the mystery solved, the problem –

SGANARELLE. Get away, you ungrateful girl. I have no more to say to you. I leave you to your own obstinacy.

LUCINDE. But, father, you asked me to tell you –

SGANARELLE. No! I don't love you any more.

LISETTE. Master, the trouble is –

SGANARELLE. The trouble is she's a hussy who wants to worry her father into his grave.

LUCINDE. No, father, I really want –

SGANARELLE. I had a right to expect a better return for the upbringing I have given you.

LISETTE. But, master –

SGANARELLE. No, I have no more patience with her.

LUCINDE. But, father –

SGANARELLE. No, I care nothing about you.

LISETTE. But –

SGANARELLE. She's a hussy.

LISETTE. But –

SGANARELLE. An ungrateful minx.

LISETTE. But –

SGANARELLE. A slut who won't say what's wrong with her.

LISETTE. It's a husband she wants.

SGANARELLE [*pretending not to hear*]. No. I've washed my hands of her.

LISETTE. A husband!

SGANARELLE. I can't bear her.

LISETTE. A husband!

SGANARELLE. She's no daughter of mine.

LISETTE. A husband!

SGANARELLE. No – I won't hear a word.

LISETTE. A husband!

SGANARELLE. I won't hear a word.

LISETTE. A husband – a husband – A HUSBAND! [*Exit*
SGANARELLE.] It's true enough, there are none so deaf as
those who don't want to hear.

LUCINDE. Well, Lisette, you thought I was wrong to hide the
cause of my trouble and that I had only to tell my father and
he would do all that I wanted. Now you see!

LISETTE. My goodness, what an old scoundrel he is! I must
say I would like to bring him down a peg. But why have you
never confided in me?

LUCINDE. Oh dear! What good would it have done? What use
was there in confiding in anyone? Do you think I didn't foresee all that has happened, that I didn't know what my father
would do? Don't you understand that I was reduced to
despair when he refused the offer that was made for my hand?

LISETTE. What! You don't mean that this stranger who
asked for your hand is the man that you –

LUCINDE. It may be a young girl ought not to show her feelings so openly, but I don't mind confessing to you that if it
rested with me, he's the man I should choose. We have
never even exchanged a word. He has never told me he
loves me, but his looks and behaviour speak for him, and his
offer for my hand seemed so truly the conduct of an honourable man that I could not help falling in love with him – and
now, you see! What is the use of my loving him when my
father is so set against it?

LISETTE. Leave it to me. I might well be offended because
you didn't take me into your confidence but I won't fail you
now, that is, if you are really determined to –

LUCINDE. But what can I do without my father's consent? If
he remains obstinate –

LISETTE. Oh, go on, you mustn't let him have things all his
own way. So long as a girl does nothing to be ashamed of she
has a right to use her wits to get round her father. What
does he expect you to do? Aren't you of an age to be married? Does he think you're made of marble? Come, we must
have one more try. From now on I'll take charge and you
will find I know all the tricks. But here he comes. You go
away and leave things to me.

They go out.

SGANARELLE [*alone*]. It is just as well sometimes not to show how much one really understands. I did well not to let her tell me what she wanted, since I'm not prepared to give in to her. What outrageous conventions a father's expected to conform to! Could anything be more ridiculous than to scrape together a fortune by hard work, to bring up a daughter with every care and tenderness, only to have to give up both fortune and daughter in the end to some fellow one doesn't care a rap for! No, no. I'll have nothing to do with such nonsense. I mean to keep my money to myself and my daughter as well.

LISETTE *runs on stage, pretending not to see* SGANARELLE.

LISETTE. Oh, what a terrible thing! O my poor master, where are you?

SGANARELLE [*aside*]. What's this she's saying?

LISETTE [*running around*] Unhappy father! Whatever will you do when I tell you the news?

SGANARELLE [*aside*]. Whatever can it be now?

LISETTE. My poor mistress.

SGANARELLE. Something dreadful has happened!

LISETTE. Ah!

SGANARELLE [*running after her*]. Lisette!

LISETTE [*running away*]. What a terrible thing!

SGANARELLE. Lisette!

LISETTE. What a misfortune!

SGANARELLE. Lisette!

LISETTE. What a disaster!

SGANARELLE. Lisette!

LISETTE [*stopping*]. Ah, master!

SGANARELLE. What is it?

LISETTE. Master!

SGANARELLE. Whatever has happened?

LISETTE. Your daughter!

SGANARELLE. Ah!

LISETTE. Don't give way like that. There's nothing you can do about it.

SGANARELLE. Tell me quickly.

LISETTE. Your daughter, quite overwhelmed by the terrible things you said when you were angry, went straight up to her room in despair, opened the window overlooking the river –

SGANARELLE. Well? Go on!

LISETTE. She raised her eyes to Heaven and said: 'No, I can't go on living if my father is angry with me. He has disowned me as his daughter, so there's nothing left for it but – death!'

SGANARELLE. And she – threw herself out?

LISETTE. No, master. She quietly closed the window, lay down on her bed, and began weeping bitterly. Suddenly she went pale, and turned up her eyes; her heart stopped beating and she lay still in my arms.

SGANARELLE. Ah, my daughter! So she's dead?

LISETTE. No, master. I shook her and brought her back to herself. But the fit comes on again from time to time and I doubt if she will last the day out.

SGANARELLE. Champagne! Champagne! Champagne!

Enter valet.

SGANARELLE. Quick, send for doctors, lots of them! We can't have too many in a crisis like this. Ah, my daughter! My poor daughter!   *Exit* SGANARELLE.

CHAMPAGNE, *dancing, knocks on doors of the four doctors. They come out and dance ceremoniously with* CHAMPAGNE *before entering the house of* SGANARELLE, *which constitutes the First Interlude.*

Scene Two

SGANARELLE, LISETTE.

LISETTE. What do you want with four doctors, master? Isn't one enough to kill the girl off?

SGANARELLE. Be quiet. Four opinions are better than one.

LISETTE. Can't your daughter be allowed to die without the help of all those fellows?

SGANARELLE. You don't mean to suggest that doctors do people in?

LISETTE. Of course they do. I knew a man who used to maintain that you should never say such and such a person perished of a fever or pleurisy but that he died of four doctors and two apothecaries.

SGANARELLE. Be quiet! We mustn't offend these gentlemen.

LISETTE. Upon my word, master, our cat fell from the house-top into the street a while back and yet he got better. He ate nothing for three days and never moved a muscle. It was lucky for him that there aren't any cat doctors or they would soon have finished him off. They would have purged him and bled him and –

SGANARELLE. Oh, be quiet, I tell you! I never heard such nonsense. Here they come.

LISETTE. Now you will be well edified. They will tell you in Latin that there is something wrong with the girl.

Enter DOCTORS TOMÉS, DES-FONANDRÉS, MACROTIN, BAHYS.

SGANARELLE. Well, gentlemen?

DR TOMÉS. We have examined the patient with every care, and there is no doubt that she is chock full of impurities.

SGANARELLE. My daughter impure!

DR TOMÉS. Hem! I ought to have said that there are many impurities in her system, many corrupted humours.

SGANARELLE. Ah, I understand.

DR TOMÉS. We propose to hold a consultation.

SGANARELLE. Quick, chairs for the gentlemen.

LISETTE [*to* DR TOMÉS]. Ah doctor, so you are one of them, are you?

SGANARELLE. How do you come to know the doctor?

LISETTE. I saw him the other day at your niece's friend's house.

DR TOMÉS. How is her coachman getting on?

LISETTE. Well enough, but he's dead.

DR TOMÉS. Dead?

LISETTE. Yes.

DR TOMÉS. It's impossible!

LISETTE. I don't know whether it's impossible or not, I only know that it's true.

DR TOMÉS. I tell you he can't be dead.

LISETTE. Well, I tell you he is dead – and buried.

DR TOMÉS. You are mistaken.

LISETTE. I saw it myself.

DR TOMÉS. It is quite out of the question. Hippocrates says that such maladies last either fourteen or twenty-one days and it is only six days since he fell ill.

LISETTE. Hippocrates can say what he likes, but the fellow is dead.

SGANARELLE [*to* LISETTE]. Be quiet, you chatterbox, and come out of here. Gentlemen, I implore you to give every attention to your consultation. Although it is not usual to pay in advance – just in case I forget – and to get the thing over – here is – [*He gives money and each one receives it with his own particular gesture. Exit with* LISETTE.]

    The doctors sit down and each in turn gives a little cough.

DR DES-FONANDRÉS. Paris is becoming an awfully big place! Getting about becomes a serious matter as one's practice grows.

DR TOMÉS. Well, you know, I use a mule – a splendid animal for the job. You would hardly believe the distance she covers in a day.

DR DES-FONANDRÉS. I have a wonderful horse. He's simply tireless, is my horse!

DR TOMÉS. Do you know what distance my mule did to-day? I started down by the Arsenal. From the Arsenal I went to the far end of the Faubourg Saint-Germain, from there to the far end of the Marais, from the far end of the Marais to the Porte Saint-Honoré, from the Porte Saint-Honoré to Faubourg Saint-Jacques, from Faubourg Saint-Jacques to the Porte de Richelieu, from the Porte de Richelieu along here, and from here I have to go back to the Place Royale.

DR DES-FONANDRÉS. My horse has done as much as that to-day, and in addition I have been out to see a patient at Ruel.

DR TOMÉS. Well, while we are talking, what is your opinion of the controversy between Dr Théophraste and Dr Artimius? It seems to be dividing the whole faculty into opposite camps.

DR DES-FONANDRÉS. I'm on Artimius's side.

DR TOMÉS. Yes, so am I. Of course his treatment, we know, killed the patient, and Théophraste's ideas might have saved him, but Théophraste was in the wrong all the same. He shouldn't have disputed the diagnosis of a senior colleague. Don't you think so?

DR DES-FONANDRÉS. No doubt about it! Stick to professional etiquette whatever happens.

DR TOMÉS. Yes, I'm all for the rules – except between friends. Only the other day three of us were called in for consultation with a man outside the faculty. I held up the whole business. I wouldn't allow anyone to give an opinion at all unless things were done professionally. Of course the people of the house had to do what they could in the meantime, and the patient went from bad to worse, but I wouldn't give way. The patient died bravely in the course of the argument.

DR DES-FONANDRÉS. It's a very good thing to teach people how to behave and make them aware of their ignorance.

DR TOMÉS. When a man's dead he's dead and that's all it amounts to, but a point of etiquette neglected may seriously prejudice the welfare of the entire medical profession.

Enter SGANARELLE.

SGANARELLE. Gentlemen, my daughter is getting worse. Do tell me quickly what decision you have come to.

DR TOMÉS [*to* DES-FONANDRÉS]. Come, sir.

DR DES-FONANDRÉS. You speak first, if you please.

DR TOMÉS. No, no, you are too kind.

DR DES-FONANDRÉS. I couldn't give my opinion before yours.

DR TOMÉS. Sir – please –

DR DES-FONANDRÉS. Please, sir –

SGANARELLE. Oh, for goodness' sake, gentlemen, cut out the ceremony. Remember the matter is urgent.

They all four speak at once.

{
DR TOMÉS. Your daughter's complaint –
DR DES-FONANDRÉS. In the opinion of these gentelmen –
DR MACROTIN. After much care-ful con–sult–a–tion –
DR BAHYS. To consider –

SGANARELLE. One at a time, if you please.

DR TOMÉS. Sir, we have been discussing your daughter's illness, and my own view is that it arises from overheating of the blood. My advice is therefore – bleeding as early as possible.

DR DES-FONANDRÉS. In my opinion the trouble is a putrefaction of humours caused by a surfeit of er – er – something or other. My view is that she should be given an emetic.

DR TOMÉS. In my opinion an emetic would kill her.

DR DES-FONANDRÉS. On the contrary, I maintain that to bleed her now would be fatal.

DR TOMÉS. You *would* try to be clever!

DR DES-FONANDRÉS. I know what I'm talking about. I can give you points on any professional question.

DR TOMÉS. Don't forget how you cooked that fellow's goose the other day.

DR DES-FONANDRÉS. What about the woman *you* sent to glory only three days ago?

DR TOMÉS [*to* SGANARELLE]. You have my opinion.

DR DES-FONANDRÉS [*to* SGANARELLE]. You know what I think.

DR TOMÉS. If you don't have your daughter bled without delay, you can take it she's done for. [*Exit.*]

DR DES-FONANDRÉS. If you *do* have her bled, she won't last a quarter of an hour. [*Exit.*]

SGANARELLE. Which am I to believe? What's to be done when you get two such different opinions? Gentlemen, I implore you, set my mind at rest, give me an unprejudiced opinion as to which treatment will save my daughter.

DR MACROTIN [*drawling*]. Sir! On these oc–cas–ions one must pro–ceed with cir–cum–spec–tion and do nothing, as one might say, in pre–cip–it–a–tion, for mis–takes thus commit–ted may well, as our Master Hippocrates observes – have dan–ger–ous cons–equences!

DR BAHYS [*in a quick stammering voice*]. Yes, one n.n.needs to be c.c.careful. Th.th.there's no ch.ch.child's play about such c.c.c.cases as th.th.this. And it it's no.no.not an easy m.matter to p.put th.things right if.if.if. you m.m.make a m.m.m.mistake.Experimentump.p.p.p.periculosum,y.you n.need to l.l.look before you l.l.l.leap and weigh th.things w.w.warily, consider the c.c.constitution of the p.p.patient, c.c.cause of the m.m.malady, and the nature of the c.c.c.cure.

SGANARELLE [*aside*]. One's as slow as a funeral, t'other c.c.can't s.s.spit it out fast enough!

DR MACROTIN [*as before*]. But, sir, to come to the point, my diagnosis is that your daughter's illness is chronic and that it may well prove dangerous if nothing is done for her, more especially as the symptoms indicate that a fuliginous and mordicant vapour is inflaming the cerebral membrane. This vapour, which in Greek is called Atmos, is produced by putrescent and persistent conglutinations concentrated in the lower abdomen.

DR BAHYS [*as before*]. These humours are of such long standing and have been inflamed to such malignity that the vapours rise up to the very cerebral region itself.

DR MACROTIN [*as before*]. So much so, that a tremendous purging is essential to loosen, expel, and evacuate the humours. But – as a preliminary I think it wise, if there is no objection, to administer an anodyne, that is to say, some little emollient, emulsive, detergent injection with refreshing juleps and syrups which she can mix in her drinks.

DR BAHYS [*as before*]. Later we can come to purgings and bleedings – repeated as necessary.

DR MACROTIN [*as before*]. All this treatment notwithstanding – it is still possible that your daughter may die, but you will at least have the satisfaction of having done something, and the consolation of knowing that she died according to the rules of the profession.

DR BAHYS [*as before*]. H'm, yes, far better die according to rules than live on in spite of them.

DR MACROTIN. We are giving you our opinion quite unreservedly.

DR BAHYS. As one man to another.

SGANARELLE [*imitating* MACROTIN]. I am most hum–bly grateful to you. [*Imitating* BAHYS.] Th.th.thanks very m.m.much f.f.for the t.t.trouble you have taken.

Exeunt doctors.

SGANARELLE. Now I'm no wiser than I was at the start – but here's an idea! I'll go buy some Orvietan. It's a remedy that has done lots of folk good.

Enter VENDOR *of quack remedies.*

SGANARELLE. Sir, please give me a box of your Orvietan and I will pay you in a moment.

QUACK VENDOR [*singing*]. The wealth of every clime around the ocean

Could it ever pay the value of the remedy I'm selling?
I guarantee a cure, every other one excelling,
A cure for every ill, use it as you will,
As a medicine or lotion.

The itch,
The stitch,
The palsy,
And the gout:
Whatever be
Your troubles,
This cure
Will find 'em out!
I guarantee
A cure to every woman, every man
Who will try but one box of my Orvietan!

The cure for every ill that man is heir to,
And it's nothing but the truth that I'm a-telling.
I guarantee a cure, every other one excelling;
A cure for every ill, use it as you will,
As a medicine or a lotion.

The itch,
The stitch, etc.

SGANARELLE. Sir, I fully believe that all the gold in the world isn't really enough to buy your Orvietan, but here is my shilling. You can take it or not, as you like.

The VENDOR *sings again. Clowns and attendants on the* VENDOR *show their satisfaction in a dance which forms the Second Interlude.*

Scene Three

DR FILERIN, DR TOMÉS, DR DES-FONANDRÉS.

DR FILERIN. Aren't you ashamed, gentlemen, to show so little prudence? Men of your age quarrelling like a lot of hot-

headed boys! Do you not realize how such quarrels damage
our reputation? Isn't it bad enough that educated people see
the contradictions and differences of opinion among our
forerunners and ancient authorities, without exposing again
and to everyone, by our disputes and quarrels, the preten-
sions of our Art? I must say I can't understand the mis-
chievous policy of some of our colleagues. I know only too
well how much all these quarrels have prejudiced our reputations recently. If we are not careful we shall do ourselves
irreparable harm. I am not concerned for myself, because,
thank Heaven, I am now comfortably off. Come rain, come
shine, dead men tell no tales, and I no longer need to rely
on the living. But these disputes do Medicine no good.
Since Heaven has so willed that all down the ages people
should continue to put unquestioning trust in us, let us not
risk disabusing them with these outrageous rivalries. Let us
continue to profit from their gullibility so far as we can.
After all, we aren't the only people who seek to make use of
human frailty. That's the main object of the greater part of
humanity. Everyone endeavours to turn other people's
foibles to his own advantage. Flatterers, for example, try to
exploit men's love of praise by offering them the vain incense
which they crave, and it is an art which brings considerable
rewards – as one sees. Alchemists endeavour to use men's
passion for riches, promising mountains of gold to those
who listen to them. Fortune-tellers by their mendacious pre-
dictions profit from the vanity of credulous minds. But of all
human foibles love of living is the most powerful. And that
is where *we* come in, with our pompous technical jargon
knowing as we do how to take advantage of the veneration
which the fear of death gives to our profession. Let us therefore seek to preserve the high esteem with which human
folly endows us. Let us maintain agreement in the presence
of our patients. Thus we may take to ourselves the credit
when their maladies end happily, and put the blame on nature
when they don't. Let us not, I say, wantonly weaken that
persistent delusion which fortunately provides so many of us
with our daily bread and enables us, from the money of those
we put under sod, to build a noble heritage – for ourselves.

DR TOMÉS. That's all very well, but one's feelings may sometimes be too strong for one.

DR FILERIN. Come, gentlemen, pray put aside all animosities and let us come to an agreement.

DR DES-FONANDRÉS. I'm willing. If he'll agree to my emetic in this case I'll accept whatever diagnosis he likes for the next patient who comes along.

DR FILERIN. What could be more reasonable? You couldn't have anything fairer than that.

DR DES-FONANDRÉS. Agreed, then.

DR FILERIN. Shake hands on it and another time please try to show more discretion.

Enter LISETTE.

LISETTE. Why gentlemen, here you all are and not one of you thinks of avenging the injury which has just been done to the medical profession.

DR TOMÉS. What is it?

LISETTE. An impudent fellow has been poaching on your preserves. Without your leave or prescription he's done a man in by running a sword through his body!

DR TOMÉS. Listen! You are laughing now, but you'll fall into our clutches one of these days.

Exeunt doctors.

LISETTE. When you catch me running to a doctor, I give you full permission to kill me!

Enter CLITANDRE, *dressed as a doctor.*

CLITANDRE. Well, Lisette, what do you think of me now?

LISETTE. Splendid. I have been longing for you to come. I must have been born soft-hearted, for I no sooner see two lovers sighing for each other than I feel sorry for them and have to do what I can to relieve their misery. I have set my heart on freeing Lucinde from her father's tyranny at all costs and handing her over to you. I took a fancy to you from the first. I'm a fair judge of character and I don't think she could have made a better choice. Love leads one to do some queer things and we have worked out a scheme which may answer our purpose. Everything is ready. Fortunately the old man isn't very bright and if we can't manage one way there are plenty of other possibilities of getting what we want. Wait out here until I come for you.

Exit CLITANDRE. Enter SGANARELLE

LISETTE. Master! Cheerful news.

SGANARELLE. What's that?

LISETTE. Cheer up! Oh, do cheer up!

SGANARELLE. Whatever for?

LISETTE. Cheer up, I tell you!

SGANARELLE. Tell me what it's all about and then perhaps I shall be able to cheer up.

LISETTE. No, you must cheer up first. You must do a song and dance.

SGANARELLE. Yes, but what for?

LISETTE. Because I tell you to!

SGANARELLE. Right then, here goes. [*He dances, and sings* La! lera! la! la! lera la!] Oh dear!

LISETTE. Master, your daughter is cured.

SGANARELLE. My daughter is cured!

LISETTE. Yes, I have brought you a doctor, a real doctor this time, one who brings off the most marvellous cures. He despises all other doctors.

SGANARELLE. Where is he?

LISETTE. I'll bring him in.

Exit.

SGANARELLE. We shall see if this one does any better than the others.

LISETTE [*brings in* CLITANDRE *dressed as a doctor*]. Here he is.

SGANARELLE. He has a smooth chin for a doctor.

LISETTE. His skill doesn't depend on his beard. He doesn't work with his chin.

SGANARELLE. Sir, I'm told that you are very skilful in purges and –

CLITANDRE. Sir, my remedies are entirely different from those of other doctors. *They* deal in emetics, bleedings, medicines, injections, but I cure people by words, letters, charms, and talismans.

LISETTE. What did I tell you?

SGANARELLE. This is a great man!

LISETTE. Master, your daughter is here, ready dressed, in her chair. I will bring her in here.

190

SGANARELLE. Yes, do.

CLITANDRE [*taking* SGANARELLE'S *pulse*]. Hm! Your daughter is certainly ill.

SGANARELLE. You mean to say you can tell that from here?

CLITANDRE. Yes, from the sympathy which links father and daughter.

LISETTE [*leading* LUCINDE]. Now, sir, here is a chair near to her. [*To* SGANARELLE] Let us leave them together.

SGANARELLE. But I want to stay here.

LISETTE. What are you thinking of? We must go. A doctor may have a hundred questions to ask which are not fit for a man to hear. [*She draws him aside.*]

CLITANDRE [*in a whisper*]. I'm so happy I hardly know how to begin. When I could only send you messages with my eyes I seemed to have a hundred things to tell you. Now that I am free to speak, as I longed to, I am tongue-tied. I am overwhelmed by my happiness.

LUCINDE. I feel the same. I'm too happy for words.

CLITANDRE. Ah! If only you could feel as I feel and I could measure your love by my own! But am I right in believing that it is to you that I owe this happy idea which gives me the chance of enjoying your company?

LUCINDE. The credit for the idea is not mine, but I welcome it joyfully.

SGANARELLE [*to* LISETTE]. He seems to me to get very close to her.

LISETTE [*to* SGANARELLE]. He is inspecting her physiognomy – examining her face and her features –

CLITANDRE [*to* LUCINDE]. Will you be constant in your love for me?

LUCINDE. Will *you* keep your promises?

CLITANDRE. All my life! I want nothing more than to be yours, and my actions will bear witness to it always.

SGANARELLE [*to* CLITANDRE]. And how is our invalid? She seems a little more cheerful.

CLITANDRE. That is because I have already applied one of the remedies of my art. The mind has great influence over the body, and maladies often have their origin there. For that reason it is my practice to endeavour to cure the mind before dealing with the body. That is why I have been scrutinizing her looks, her features, the lines of her hands, and, thanks to the skill with which I am fortunately endowed, I was able to diagnose that this was a case of illness of the mind, that the trouble arose from a disordered imagination, in short, from a depraved yearning to be married. Of course – nothing could be more ridiculous than such a hankering after marriage.

SGANARELLE [*aside*]. What a clever man!

CLITANDRE. I myself have always had, and always shall have, a horrible aversion to it!

SGANARELLE [*aside*]. What a great doctor!

CLITANDRE. But people who are ill must be humoured. I have detected some signs of mental derangement, and it might have proved dangerous if a remedy had not been applied at once. Therefore I played up to her and told her that I had come to ask permission to marry her. Instantly her expression changed, her colour returned, her eyes lighted up, and, if you will only encourage her in this notion for a few days, you'll see that we shall soon bring her into a much better condition.

SGANARELLE. Very good. I'm willing enough!

CLITANDRE. Later, we can try other remedies with a view to curing her delusions entirely.

SGANARELLE. Excellent! Now, my girl, here is a gentleman who wants to marry you. I have told him that I have no objections.

LUCINDE. Oh, is it possible?

SGANARELLE. Yes.

LUCINDE. You really mean it?

SGANARELLE. Yes, yes.

LUCINDE [*to* CLITANDRE]. You are willing to be my husband?

CLITANDRE. Yes, madam.

LUCINDE. And my father consents?

SGANARELLE. Yes, my dear.

LUCINDE. Oh, how happy I should be if only it were true!

CLITANDRE. There's no doubt about it. I have long loved

you and been longing to marry you. This is my real reason for coming here. To tell the truth, these robes are only a disguise and I have played the doctor to gain access to you and secure what I wanted.

LUCINDE. This is proof of a true affection and I value it deeply.

SGANARELLE [*aside*]. The idiot! The idiot! The idiotic girl!

LUCINDE. Father, you are really willing to give me this gentleman as a husband?

SGANARELLE. Of course. Give me your hand. Give me yours too.

CLITANDRE. But, sir!

SGANARELLE [*choking with laughter*]. No, no. It's to – to put her mind at rest. Join hands, both of you. There now, it's all settled.

CLITANDRE. I give you this ring as a token of my promise. [*Whispers to* SGANARELLE] It is a talisman which cures aberrations of the mind.

LUCINDE. Let us draw up the contract, then, and have everything in order.

CLITANDRE. I want nothing better! [*Whispers to* SGANARELLE] I will have them send up the man who writes my prescriptions and make believe he is a notary.

SGANARELLE. Splendid!

CLITANDRE. Hello, there! Send up the notary who came with me.

LUCINDE. You brought a notary with you?

CLITANDRE. I did.

LUCINDE. How delightful!

SGANARELLE. The idiot! The idiot! The idiotic girl!

Enter the NOTARY. CLITANDRE *whispers to* NOTARY.

SGANARELLE. Now, sir, draw up a marriage contract for these two young people. Write it out at once, please. [*To* LUCINDE] You see, he is drawing up the contract. [*To* NOTARY] I give her twenty thousand pounds on her marriage. Write that down.

LUCINDE. Dear father, how grateful I am.

NOTARY. There, that's finished. It only needs you to sign it.

SGANARELLE. That's quickly written!

CLITANDRE [*to* SGANARELLE]. But sir, at least –

SGANARELLE. No, no, no, I tell you! I know! I know all about it! [*To* NOTARY] Come, give her the pen to sign. [*To* LUCINDE] Come on, sign, sign, sign here! Go on, I'll sign later myself.

LUCINDE. No. I would like to keep the document myself.

SGANARELLE. All right, then. Here goes! [*He signs.*] Now are you happy?

LUCINDE. More so than you could ever imagine!

SGANARELLE. Well, that's splendid. That's splendid.

CLITANDRE. One thing more. I did more than bring a notary. I also had the foresight to bring singers, musicians, and dancers to celebrate the occasion, so that we may all make merry! Fetch them in! I take these people round with me and use them to soothe, with their harmony and dances, the troubles of disturbed minds.

COMEDY, BALLET, MUSIC. Without us, all mankind
Become but low in mind.
'Tis we who, with our lures,
Achieve the greatest cures.

COMEDY. Whoe'er would drive away
The cares of every day,
The troubles that can kill,
The sorrows, grief, and pain,
Should shun the doctor's skill
And turn to us again.

COMEDY, BALLET, MUSIC. Without us, all mankind
Become but low in mind.
'Tis we who, with our lures,
Can work the greatest cures.

    LAUGHTER *and* PLEASURES *dance.* CLITANDRE *leads*
      LUCINDE *offstage.*

SGANARELLE. That's certainly a delightful way of curing people. But where are my daughter and the doctor?

LISETTE. They have gone to consummate the marriage.

SGANARELLE. How do you mean, consummate the marriage?

LISETTE. Upon my word, master, you are caught in your own trap this time. You thought you were doing it all as a joke, but you'll find now it's in earnest.

SGANARELLE. What the devil! [*He tries to run after* CLIT-ANDRE *and* LUCINDE, *but the dancers keep him back.*] Let me go! Let me pass, I tell you! [*The dancers still keep him back. They try to make him dance.*] Oh, confound the whole lot of you!
Dance.

THE END

Don Juan

or

The Statue at the Feast

DOM JUAN

ou

LE FESTIN DE PIERRE

CHARACTERS IN THE PLAY

DON JUAN, son of Don Luis

SGANARELLE, valet to Don Juan

ELVIRA, wife of Don Juan

GUSMAN, squire to Elvira

DON CARLOS⎱ brothers of Elvira
DON ALONSO⎰

DON LUIS, father of Don Juan

FRANCISCO, a poor man

CHARLOTTE⎱ peasant girls
MATHURINE⎰

PETER, a peasant

STATUE OF THE COMMANDER

LA VIOLETTE⎱ servants of Don Juan
RAGOTIN⎰

MR DIMANCHE, a tradesman

LA RAMÉE, a ruffian

Attendants on Don Carlos and Don Alonso

A SPECTRE

The scene is in Sicily

Act One

SGANARELLE [*snuff-box in hand*]. Aristotle and the philo-
sopers can say what they like, but there's nothing to
equal tobacco: it's an honest man's habit, and anyone who
can get on without it doesn't deserve to be living at all: it
not only clears and enlivens the brain, it's conducive to
virtue: a fellow learns from taking it how to comport himself decently. Haven't you noticed how, once a chap starts
taking snuff, he behaves politely to everybody, and what a
pleasure he takes in offering it right and left wherever he
happens to be? He doesn't even wait to be asked or until
folk know that they want it! Which just goes to show how it
makes for honest and decent behaviour in all those who take
it. But enough of that now. Let's come back to what we
were talking about. You were saying, my dear Gusman,
that Dona Elvira was surprised when we went away, and set
out in pursuit of us. She was so much in love with my
master, you said, that nothing would do but she must come
here to look for us. Shall I tell you, between our two selves,
what I think about it? I'm afraid she'll get little return for
her love; her journey here will be useless; and you would
have done just as well to have stopped where you were.

GUSMAN. But what is the reason? Do tell me, Sganarelle, what
makes you take such a gloomy view of the position. Has
your master taken you into his confidence? Has he told you
that his reason for leaving was a cooling off in his feelings
towards us?

SGANARELLE. No, but knowing the lie of the land I have a
fair idea of the way things are going, and I could very nearly
bet that is what is happening without his having said a word.
Of course, I may be wrong, but after all I've had a lot of
experience of this sort of thing.

GUSMAN. You mean to say the explanation of Don Juan's
unexpected departure is that he is unfaithful to Dona
Elvira? You think he could betray her innocent love in this
way?

SGANARELLE. No. It's just that he's still young and he hasn't the heart . . .

GUSMAN. But how could a gentleman do such a vile thing?

SGANARELLE. Ay, ay! A lot of difference that makes, his being a gentleman! I can see *that* stopping him from doing anything he wants to do!

GUSMAN. But surely he is bound by the obligations of holy matrimony.

SGANARELLE. Ah, my dear Gusman, believe me, you still don't understand what sort of man Don Juan is.

GUSMAN. No, I certainly don't if he has really betrayed us like that. I just can't understand how, after showing so much affection, after being so very importunate, after all his declarations of love, vows, sighs, tears, passionate letters, protestations, and promises repeated over and over again; in short, after such an overwhelming display of passion and going to the lengths of invading the holy precincts of a convent to carry off Dona Elvira – I repeat I just cannot understand how, after all that, he could find it in his heart to go back on his word.

SGANARELLE. I understand well enough, and if you knew our friend as I do you'd understand that he finds it easy enough. I am not saying his feelings for Dona Elvira have changed. I can't be sure yet. As you know, I left before he did, on his instruction, and he has said nothing to me since he arrived here, but I will say this much as a warning – *inter nos* – that in my master, Don Juan, you see the biggest scoundrel that ever cumbered the earth, a madman, a cur, a devil, a Turk, a heretic who believes neither in Heaven, Hell, nor werewolf: he lives like an animal, like a swine of an Epicurean, a veritable Sardanapalus, shutting his ears to every Christian remonstrance, and turning to ridicule everything we believe in. You tell me he has married your mistress – believe me, to satisfy his passion he would have gone further than that, he would have married you as well, ay, and her dog and her cat into the bargain! Marriage means nothing to him. It is his usual method of ensnaring women: he marries 'em left and right, maids or married women, ladies or peasants, shy ones and t'other sort – all come alike to him.

If I were to give you the names of all those he has married in
one place and another, the list would take till to-night. That
surprises you! What I'm saying makes you turn pale, but this
is no more than the outline of his character: it would take me
much longer to finish the portrait. Let it suffice that the wrath
of Heaven is bound to overwhelm him one of these days
and that, for my part, I would sooner serve the Devil himself. He's made me witness to so many horrible things that I
wish he was – I don't know where! But a nobleman who has
given himself over to wickedness is a thing to be dreaded. I
am bound to remain with him whether I like it or not: fear
serves me for zeal, makes me restrain my feelings and forces
me often enough to make a show of approving things that
in my heart of hearts I detest. But here he comes – taking a
turn in the palace. Let us separate. But just let me say this – I
have talked to you frankly and in confidence, and I've opened
my mouth pretty freely, but if any word of it were to come
to his ears I should declare you had made it all up.

Exit GUSMAN. *Enter* DON JUAN.

DON JUAN. Who was the man who was talking to you? I
thought he looked very much like our friend Gusman, Dona
Elvira's man.

SGANARELLE. You are not very far wrong.

DON JUAN. Why! Was it he?

SGANARELLE. Gusman himself.

DON JUAN. And since when has he been in the town?

SGANARELLE. Since yesterday evening.

DON JUAN. And what brings him here?

SGANARELLE. I should have thought you would have had a
fair idea of what might be worrying him.

DON JUAN. Our departure, no doubt?

SGANARELLE. The poor fellow is very much upset about it.
He was asking me what the reason was.

DON JUAN. And what reply did you give him?

SGANARELLE. I said that you had told me nothing about it.

DON JUAN. Well then, what do you think about it? What is
your own view of the matter?

SGANARELLE. I think – without wishing to do you injustice –
that you are involved in a new love affair.

DON JUAN. That is what you think, is it?

SGANARELLE. Yes, it is.

DON JUAN. Well, you are quite right. I must confess that someone else has driven all thought of Elvira out of my head.

SGANARELLE. Lord, yes! I know my Don Juan well enough!
I know your fancy's a rover, for ever flitting from one en-
tanglement to another, never content to settle down anywhere.

DON JUAN. And do you not think I am right in behaving as
I do?

SGANARELLE. Well, master . . .

DON JUAN. Go on, speak out!

SGANARELLE. Of course you are right – if you will have it
that way. There's no gainsaying it. But if you'd let me put it
my way – it might be a different matter.

DON JUAN. Well, then, I give you leave to speak freely and say
what you think.

SGANARELLE. Well, then, master, I tell you frankly I don't
like your way of behaving at all. I think it's very wrong to
make love left and right the way that you do.

DON JUAN. What! Would you have a man tie himself up to the
first woman that captured his fancy, renounce the world for
her, and never again look at anyone else? That *is* a fine idea,
I must say, to make a virtue of faithfulness, to bury oneself
for good and all in one single passion and remain blind ever
after to all the other beauties that might catch one's eye! No!
Let fools make a virtue of constancy! All beautiful women
have a right to our love, and the accident of being the first
comer shouldn't rob others of a fair share in our hearts. As
for me, beauty delights me wherever I find it and I freely
surrender myself to its charms. No matter how far I'm committed – the fact that I am in love with one person shall
never make me unjust to the others. I keep an eye for the
merits of all of them and render each one the homage, pay
each one the tribute that nature enjoins. Come what may, I
cannot refuse love to what I find lovable, and so, when a
beautiful face is asking for love, if I had ten thousand hearts
I would freely bestow every one of them. After all, there is
something inexpressibly charming in falling in love and,

surely, the whole pleasure lies in the fact that love isn't lasting. How delightful, how entrancing it is to lay siege with a hundred attentions to a young woman's heart; to see, day by day, how one makes slight advances; to pit one's exaltation, one's sighs and one's tears, against the modest reluctance of a heart unwilling to yield; to surmount, step by step, all the little barriers by which she resists; to overcome her proud scruples and bring her at last to consent. But once one succeeds, what else remains? What more can one wish for? All that delights one in passion is over and one can only sink into a tame and slumbrous affection – until a new love comes along to awaken desire and offer the charm of new conquests. There is no pleasure to compare with the conquest of beauty, and my ambition is that of all the great conquerors who could never find it in them to set bounds to their ambitions, but must go on for ever from conquest to conquest. Nothing can restrain my impetuous desires. I feel it is in me to love the whole world, and like Alexander still wish for new worlds to conquer.

SGANARELLE. Goodness me! How you do reel it off! Anyone would think you had learned it by heart. You talk like a book.

DON JUAN. And what have you to say about it?

SGANARELLE. What I say is – nay, I don't know what to say! You twist things round so that you seem to be in the right, even when you aren't. I did have some good ideas, but you've muddled me up with your talk. Never mind, another time I'll put my arguments down on paper and then I shall be able to deal with you.

DON JUAN. An excellent idea!

SGANARELLE. But, if I might make use of the liberty you've given me, master, I must say I am very much shocked at the life you are leading.

DON JUAN. Indeed! And what sort of life am I leading?

SGANARELLE. Oh! It's a very good life, only – to see you marrying afresh every month or two as you are doing ...

DON JUAN. Well, what could be more agreeable?

SGANARELLE. I admit it may be very agreeable – and very amusing. I wouldn't mind doing the same myself if there were no harm in it, but you know, sir, to trifle like that with a holy sacrament and ...

DON JUAN. Get along with you! That's a matter for Heaven and myself to settle between us without your worrying about it.

SGANARELLE. Upon my word, master, I've always heard tell it was a bad thing to mock at Heaven and that unbelievers came to no good.

DON JUAN. Now then, my dear blockhead, remember what I have told you – I don't like being preached at.

SGANARELLE. I am not referring to you, God forbid! You know what you are doing, you do. If you don't believe in anything, well, you have your own reasons, but there are some silly little fellows who are unbelievers without knowing why; they think it smart to set themselves up as free thinkers. If I had a master like that, I would ask him straight to his face, 'How dare you set yourself up against Heaven as you do? Aren't you afraid to mock at sacred things? What right have you, you little worm, pygmy that you are (I'm talking to the imaginary master), to make a jest of everything that people hold sacred? Do you think because you are a gentleman and wear a fashionable wig, because you have feathers in your hat, and gilt lace on your coat and flame-coloured ribbons (of course, I'm not talking to you) – do you think that you are any the wiser for that, and that you can do as you like and nobody is going to dare to tell you the truth? You take it from me, though I'm only your servant, that sooner or later Heaven punishes the wicked, and those who live evil lives come to bad ends and –'

DON JUAN. Shut up!

SGANARELLE. Why, what's the matter?

DON JUAN. The matter is this. I want you to know that I have fallen in love with a lady and it is her charms that have induced me to come to this town.

SGANARELLE. And aren't you afraid, master, of coming here, where you killed the Commander only six months ago?

DON JUAN. Why should I be afraid? Did I not do the job properly?

SGANARELLE. Oh yes! All fair and proper! He's no cause for complaint!

DON JUAN. Was I not pardoned for that little affair?

SGANARELLE. Yes, but a pardon may not remove the resentment of friends and relations.

DON JUAN. Never mind the disagreeable things that may happen. Let us think of the pleasant ones. The lady I referred to is the most charming creature imaginable. She has just arrived here under the escort of the man she is going to marry. I happened to meet this young couple three or four days before they set out on their journey. I never saw two people so devoted, so completely in love. The manifest tenderness of their mutual affection awakened a like feeling in me. It affected me deeply. My love began in the first place as jealousy. I couldn't bear to see them so happy together; vexation stimulated my desire and I realized what a pleasure it would give me to disturb their mutual understanding and break up an attachment so repugnant to my own susceptibilities, but so far all my efforts have failed and I am driven to my last resort. To-day the future husband intends to take his beloved on the sea and my plans to gratify my passion are laid. Without mentioning it to you I have engaged men and a boat and I expect to carry her off without difficulty.

SGANARELLE. Oh, master!

DON JUAN. What's that?

SGANARELLE. You have done splendidly. You are quite right to do what you are doing. There's nothing in this world like getting what you want.

DON JUAN. Then get ready to come with me. Make yourself responsible for bringing my weapons, so that – Ah! What an inopportune meeting! You rascal! You never told me *she* was here too.

SGANARELLE. Well, master – you never asked me!

DON JUAN. She must be out of her mind not to have changed her clothes and to come to town dressed for the country.

Enter DONA ELVIRA.

DONA ELVIRA. Will you not favour me, Don Juan, with some sign of recognition? Is it too much to hope that you will deign to look at me?

DON JUAN. I confess, madam, that I am surprised. I was not expecting you here.

DONA ELVIRA. Yes, I see that you were not expecting me, and, though you are surprised, it is not in the way that I hoped. Your manner entirely convinces me of what I previously refused to believe. I wonder at my own simplicity, at my soft-hearted reluctance to believe in your duplicity, though you gave me so many proofs of it. Such was my indulgence towards you – no, I confess it now, such was my folly, that I was bent on deceiving myself. I struggled against the evidence of my own eyes, against my own better judgement. In the goodness of my heart I sought excuses for the growing coldness I noticed in you. I invented a thousand reasons to justify your abrupt departure and to acquit you of the faithlessness of which common sense told me you were guilty. The daily warnings of my well-founded suspicions were in vain: I rejected all evidence which counted against you and listened eagerly to a thousand absurd fancies which seemed to indicate that you were not to blame, but your manner just now leaves me no room for doubt, your expression when you first saw me told me more than I ever cared to admit. Nevertheless I should like to hear from your own lips your reasons for leaving me. Speak, Don Juan, I beg you. Let me hear how you will manage to justify yourself.

DON JUAN. Madam, Sganarelle here knows why I came away.

SGANARELLE. Me, master? Excuse me – I know nothing about it.

DONA ELVIRA. Come, speak up Sganarelle. It matters little from whose lips I hear his excuses.

DON JUAN [signing to SGANARELLE to approach]. Come along! Speak to the lady.

SGANARELLE. What d'ye expect me to say?

DONA ELVIRA. Come here, since he will have it so, and explain to me the reasons for so sudden a departure.

DON JUAN. Aren't you going to answer?

SGANARELLE. I can't answer. You're just making a fool of your poor servant.

DON JUAN. Give her an answer, I tell you!

SGANARELLE. Madam –

DONA ELVIRA. Well?

SGANARELLE [*turning to* DON JUAN]. Master –

DON JUAN. If you – [*threatening him*].

SGANARELLE. Madam. We left because of Alexander and the other worlds he still had to conquer. [*To* DON JUAN] That's the best I can do, sir.

DONA ELVIRA. Would you be good enough to elucidate these mysteries, Don Juan?

DON JUAN. To tell the truth, madam –

DONA ELVIRA. Come! For a courtier, a man who must be accustomed to this sort of thing, you do give a poor account of yourself. I am sorry to see you so embarrassed. Why don't you take refuge in a gentlemanly effrontery? Why don't you swear that your feelings for me are unchanged, that you still love me more than all the world, and that nothing but death can part us? Can you not say that business of the most pressing importance forced you to leave without an opportunity of informing me, that you are obliged to remain here for a while against your own wishes, and that if only I will return whence I came I may be assured that you will follow at the earliest possible moment? That you are only too eager to be with me again, and that while you are away from me you suffer the agonies of a body bereft of its soul? Is that not how you should justify yourself instead of letting yourself be put out of countenance as you are?

DON JUAN. Madam, I assure you that I have no gift for dissimulation. I am entirely sincere. I am not going to say that I still have the same feeling for you or that I yearn to be with you again, because the fact is that I came away with the deliberate intention of escaping from you, not for the reasons you imagine, but on grounds of conscience alone. I left because I had come to believe that it would be a sin to live with you longer. My conscience was awakened, madam, and I came to see the error of my ways. I considered how, in order to marry you, I carried you off from the seclusion of a convent, how you yourself broke your vows, and that these are things which God does not forgive. I became a prey to repentance, I came to dread the wrath of Heaven and to realize that our marriage was no more than disguised adultery which must bring down on us a punishment from on high; in short, that I must endeavour to forget you and afford you the opportunity of returning to your former allegiance. Would you oppose so holy a resolution, madam? Would you have me, through loyalty to you, get myself into the bad books of Heaven?

DONA ELVIRA. Ah! Villain. Now I know you for what you are, and, to my misfortune, only when it is too late, when the realization can only bring me to despair! But be assured that your infidelity will not go unpunished, and that the Heaven you mock at will find means to avenge your perfidy to me!

DON JUAN. Ah! Sganarelle, Heaven!

SGANARELLE. Ay, ay, little we care for that! Fellows like us!

DON JUAN. Madam –

DONA ELVIRA. Enough! I will hear no more! Indeed I blame myself for having heard too much already. It is a weakness to allow one's shame to be exposed in this way. In such moments a noble mind should choose its course of action at once. Have no fear that I shall give way to reproaches. No! My anger is not the sort that can find vent in vain words. All its fury is reserved for vengeance. Once again I declare that Heaven will punish you for the wrong you have done me, and if Heaven itself has no terrors for you, then beware, at least, the fury of a woman scorned!

Exit.

SGANARELLE. If he could but feel some remorse.

DON JUAN [*after a moment's reflection*]. Come along, we must consider how to carry out our other little scheme.

SGANARELLE. Ah, what an abominable master I am bound to serve!

Act Two

CHARLOTTE, PETER.

CHARLOTTE. Mercy on us, Peter, 'ee be a-come there just in time, then.

PETER. Lor' lumme, yes. Within a hair's breadth o' bein' a-drownded they was, the pair of 'em.

CHARLOTTE. 'Twould be that there squall this morn'n' 'as capsized 'em?

PETER. Lookee, Lottie. I can tell 'ee just 'ow it did come about. 'Twas me as clapped eyes on 'em first in a manner o' speak'n': first to clap eyes on 'em, I be. Down on the beach we was, Fatty Lucas an' me, a-heav'n' clods at each other for a lark we was. A boy for a bit o' lark'n' be Lucas, an' I bain't for miss'n' it neither. A-lark'n' about we was, the way we do be a-lark'n', when I sees someth'n' afar off like, someth'n' a-bobb'n' up an' down in the water like, as seemed to be a-com'n' t'ards us off an' on. I be a-keep'n' an eye on it when all of a sudden I couldn't see noth'n' no more. 'Luke,' says I, 'I reckon yon's fellers a-swimmin' out there.' 'No, indeed,' says 'e, 'see'n' double 'ee be.' 'Not on thy life,' says I, 'them's fellers out there.' 'Not a bit of it,' says 'e. 'A-dazzled by the sunshine 'ee be!' 'No dazzle about it, will 'ee bet on it?' says I. 'Them's two fellers a-swimm'n' this way,' says I. 'Lumme, no!' says 'e, 'I bet they bain't.' 'Will 'ee 'ave a bob on it?' says I. 'Done!' says 'e, 'and there be my money down.' Now I bain't no fool nor yet I bain't a-fancy'n' things neither, so down goes my money, six pennies and two threepenny diddlers. Blow me! bold as if I'd swallowed a whole pint I was, for I be a real venturesome fellow when I be roused like. But I knows well enough what I be about for all that, mind. 'Ardly be the stakes down when I sees the two men plain as daylight. They starts a-making' signs to us for to come out and fetch 'em in. So I ups with the stakes an' 'Quick, Lucas,' says I, 'they be a-call'n' to us to go out an' help 'em.' 'They bain't going to get no 'elp from me,' says 'e. 'Not arter makin' me lose my money,' says 'e. Well then, to be a-cutt'n' it short, such a to-do I did 'ave for to get 'im to come in the boat along o' me. Then we pulls out to 'em, hauls 'em aboard, takes 'em 'ome to a fire, and they strips themselves naked to dry. By 'n' by in comes two more of 'em that had made shift for themselves. When Mathurine comes in, blow me if one of 'em don't start cast'n' sheep's eyes at 'er, and that be just exac'ly 'ow 't all did befall, Lottie.

CHARLOTTE. Did I 'ear 'ee say that one be better-look'n' than t'others, Peter?

PETER. Ay, that'ld be t'maister. A regular gentleman, 'e be – gold lace on his clothes from head to foot. Even his servants be gentlemen, like. Howsumiver 'e'd have been a-drownded right enough, gentleman or no gentleman, if I 'adn't been there.

CHARLOTTE. Ah! Go on with you!

PETER. Lumme! If 't 'adn't ha' been for us 'is number would ha' been up for certain.

CHARLOTTE. Do 'ee think 'e be still there all nakey body, Peter?

PETER. No, no. We seen 'im dressed again. Lor! – I never seen them sort a-dress'n' afore. What a sight of contraptions them courtiers do be a-wear'n'! I'd be lost in 'em, I would – fair amazed I was at the sight o' 'em. 'Pon my word, Lottie, they'm got hair that bain't fast to their heads! Clap it on last thing of all, they do, like a gurt bonnet of flax. They'm got shirts with sleeves thee and me could get lost in. 'Stead o' breeches they'm got aprons as wide as from here to Christmas! 'Stead o' a doublet they'm got a tiny waistcoat, don't come half down the chest like; 'stead o' neck-bands a great neckerchief wi' four great bows o' linen hang'n' down to their middle like. Then they'm got frills at their waists, like, an' great swathes o' lace round their legs, an' to cap all, such a sight o' ribbons, such a sight o' ribbons as be shameful for to see! There bain't no part of 'em, even their shoes, that don't be a-loaded down with 'em. If they was on me, I'd be a-trip'n' over 'em, I would.

CHARLOTTE. 'Pon my word, Peter, I mun go have a look at that.

PETER. Hark 'ee! Just a minute, Lottie, I got someth'n' more to say to 'ee first.

CHARLOTTE. Oh well, then, but tell me quick what it be.

PETER. Look 'ee, Lottie. I been a want'n' for to open my heart to 'ee as the say'n' is. 'Ee knows how I loves 'ee and we be a-goin' for to marry, but Lord, I bain't no ways satisfied with 'ee, like.

CHARLOTTE. Whatever do 'ee mean by that?

PETER. What do I mean by that? I mean 'ee be a terrible vexation to me.

CHARLOTTE. And how do 'ee make that out?

PETER. Lord 'elp me – I believe 'ee don't love me at all.

CHARLOTTE. Ha ha! Be that all?

PETER. Ay, that be all, an' quite enough too it be.

CHARLOTTE. Lor', Peter, 'ee be always a-tell'n' the same tale.

PETER. Ay! I be a-tell'n' the same tale 'cause it be always the same tale for I to be tell'n'. If it war'n't the same tale I wouldn't be a-tell'n' it!

CHARLOTTE. But what mun I do for 'ee? What do 'ee want?

PETER. Lord help me! I want 'ee to love me.

CHARLOTTE. And don't I a-love 'ee?

PETER. No, that 'ee don't! and yet, don't I do all I can to make 'ee? Don't I buy 'ee – no offence, mind – ribbons from all the pedlars that be a-pass'n' by? Don't I be a-break'n' my neck a-clim'n' after birds' nests for 'ee? Don't I make fiddler play for 'ee on thy birthday? An' for all that I may as well be a bang'n' my head against a wall. Look 'ee now, t'ain't no-ways right nor decent not to love them as do be a-lov'n' us.

CHARLOTTE. But indeed I do love 'ee too.

PETER. An' a pretty way o' lov'n' me, indeed!

CHARLOTTE. How do 'ee want me to love 'ee?

PETER. I want 'ee to love me proper like, same as other folks do be a-lov'n'.

CHARLOTTE. Don't I love 'ee proper like?

PETER. No, that 'ee don't. When a maid do love proper 'tis plain for to be seen – there be a thousand ways of show'n' it for them that do love whole-hearted like. Look 'ee now, that fat Thomasina, she be fair daft about young Robin. She be always around him a-plagu'n' of 'im. She don't never let 'im be: for ever a-play'n' some trick on 'im or a-giv'n' 'im a bump in pass'n' like: only t'other day, when he's a-settin' on a stool, she whips it from under him an' down 'e goes full length on the ground. 'Pon my word, that's the way folk do behave when they do be in love, but 'ee don't never throw me so much as a word like. Same as a block o' wood, 'ee be: a score o' times I might pass along of 'ee and never get a touch or a word out of 'ee. Lor' lumme! 'Tain't good enough! 'ee don't give a fellow no encouragement at all.

CHARLOTTE. An' what do 'ee expect me to do? 'Tis the way I

be made. I can't do no other.

PETER. I don't give a rap for the way 'ee be made. When folk be in love they did ought to show it some ways or other.

CHARLOTTE. Well then, I do love 'ee all I know how. If 'ee bain't satisfied, 'ee mun go love somewheres else.

PETER. Well, now ain't that just what I said! Blow me! – if 'ee loved me proper 'ee couldn't say such things.

CHARLOTTE. Why must 'ee come a-worriting me so?

PETER. Oh lor', I bain't meanin' no harm. I bain't want'n' no more than a bit o' love.

CHARLOTTE. Then why won't 'ee leave me alone and not be always a troubl'n'? Perhaps one o' these days 'twill come over me all of a sudden.

PETER. Give me thy hand on that then, Lottie.

CHARLOTTE. Very well, there 'tis then.

PETER. Promise 'ee'll try for to love me a little bit more.

CHARLOTTE. All as I can do, I will, but love mun come of its own accord. Be this the gentleman, Peter?

PETER. Ay, that be him.

CHARLOTTE. Lor', bain't 'e a pretty man! 'Twould ha' been a shame had he been a-drownded.

PETER. I'll be back again soon. I mun go have a drop for to set me up again after all that I been through.

Enter DON JUAN *and* SGANARELLE.

DON JUAN. Well, Sganarelle, our scheme misfired. That unexpected squall upset both ship and plans, but to tell the truth that little peasant girl I have just left makes up for the mishap. She is so charming that I can almost forget our failure in the other affair. She mustn't slip through my fingers. I think I have already paved the way so that I shan't be kept sighing too long.

SGANARELLE. I must say you astonish me, master. Here we have just escaped from peril of our lives, and, instead of thanking Heaven for its mercy, you are starting all over again, running the risk of its wrath with your usual goings on. These love affairs of yours are disgraceful and dis – Shut up, you fool! You don't know what you are talking about! The master knows what he is doing – get along with you!

DON JUAN [*noticing* CHARLOTTE]. Ha, ha! Where did this one come from, Sganarelle? Did you ever see anything so charming? She's even prettier than the other. Don't you think so?

SGANARELLE. Oh, of course! [*Aside*] Off we go again!

DON JUAN. To what do I owe the pleasure of this charming encounter? Can there really be lovely creatures like you among these wild rocks and trees?

CHARLOTTE. Just as you see, sir.

DON JUAN. Do you belong to this village?

CHARLOTTE. Yes, sir.

DON JUAN. And you live here?

CHARLOTTE. Yes sir.

DON JUAN. And your name is?

CHARLOTTE. Charlotte, at your service, sir.

DON JUAN. What a lovely girl. What fire in her eyes.

CHARLOTTE. You be making me blush, sir.

DON JUAN. But why blush at hearing the truth? What do you say, Sganarelle? Did you ever see anything more delightful? Turn a little, if you please. Ah, what a charming figure! Look up a little, please. What a dear little face! Open your eyes wide. Aren't they beautiful? Now a glimpse of your teeth. Delicious! – and what inviting lips! She is really enchanting. I've never met such a charming girl.

CHARLOTTE. You be pleased to say so, sir, but I don't know whether you are making fun of me or not.

DON JUAN. Making fun of you. Heaven forbid! I am too much in love with you. I do really mean it.

CHARLOTTE. If that is so, I'm much obliged to you, sir.

DON JUAN. Not at all. There's no need to be obliged at anything I'm saying. It's no more than what is due to your beauty.

CHARLOTTE. Fine talk like this be too much for me, sir. I don't know how to answer you.

DON JUAN. Just look at her hands, Sganarelle.

CHARLOTTE. Fie sir! They are as black as I don't know what.

DON JUAN. What are you talking about? They are the loveliest hands in the world. Permit me to kiss them.

CHARLOTTE. Oh, sir! You do me too much honour. If I'd

known it afore, I would have washed them in bran.

DON JUAN. Tell me just one thing, my dear Charlotte – you are not married, by any chance?

CHARLOTTE. No, sir, but I be a-promised to Peter, neighbour Simonetta's lad.

DON JUAN. What! A girl like you marrying a mere peasant! Never! It's a profanation of beauty – you weren't born to live in a village. You are worth something far better. Heaven itself knows it and has sent me here for the very purpose of preventing the marriage and doing justice to your charms. In short, my beautiful Charlotte, I love you with all my heart. You only need say the word and I will take you away from this wretched place and give you the position in the world that you deserve. This declaration no doubt sounds rather sudden, but what of it? It all comes of your being so beautiful, Charlotte. You have made me fall as deeply in love with you in a quarter of an hour as in six months with anyone else.

CHARLOTTE. Truly, sir, when you talk like that I just don't know what to do. I love to hear you talk so and I'd like to believe you, but I've always heard tell as how a maid should never believe fine gentlemen's talk and as how ye all be deceivers as come from the court and only want to lead girls astray.

DON JUAN. I am not that sort of man!

SGANARELLE [aside]. No! Not he!

CHARLOTTE. You see, sir, it's not right for a maid to let herself be led astray. I be only a simple country maid, but I set store by my virtue. I'd die sooner than lose my reputation.

DON JUAN. And do you think I could be so wicked as to deceive a girl like you? Do you think that I could ever be so base as to betray you? No, I could never do such a thing. I love you, Charlotte, truly and honourably, and to show you that I am speaking the truth, let me tell you that I have nothing but marriage in mind. I am ready whenever you wish, and I call my man here to witness my promise.

SGANARELLE. No, no, have no fear! He'll marry you to your heart's content.

DON JUAN. I see that you don't know me yet, Charlotte. You

wrong me when you judge me by other men. There may be scoundrels in the world who make love to girls only to deceive them, but don't include me among their number. Never doubt my word. Surely your beauty should give you confidence. You need fear nothing. Believe me, no one could dream of deceiving a woman like you. As for myself, I declare I would die a thousand deaths rather than harbour the slightest thought of betraying you.

CHARLOTTE. Oh lor'! I don't know whether you are speaking the truth or no, but you have such a way with you I would fain believe you.

DON JUAN. Only put your faith in me. You won't be disappointed. Let me repeat my promise to you once again. Won't you accept my word and consent to be my wife?

CHARLOTTE. Yes, if Auntie agrees.

DON JUAN. Then, Charlotte, since you yourself are willing, give me your hand.

CHARLOTTE. You won't deceive me, sir, will you? It would be a wicked thing to do when you see how I trust you.

DON JUAN. What! Do you still doubt my sincerity? Then I'll swear the most solemn oaths. May Heaven –

CHARLOTTE. Oh lor', please don't swear! I believe you.

DON JUAN. Then give me a little kiss as a pledge of your promise.

CHARLOTTE. Nay sir, wait till we be married and then I will kiss you as much as you like.

DON JUAN. Very well, then, my dear Charlotte, just as you like. Only give me your hand and let me cover it with kisses to show how delighted I am by your –

Enter PETER.

PETER [*interposing between them and pushing* DON JUAN]. Easy, maister, steady on, if ye don't mind – if ye be wax'n' that warm ye'll be a gett'n' 'eartburn.

DON JUAN [*pushing him roughly*]. Where did this lout come from?

PETER. I tell 'ee to keep off – 'ee bain't go'n' to be a-kiss'n' my intended.

DON JUAN [*pushing him again*]. What are you making a fuss about?

PETER. Lumme! Don't 'ee be a-shov'n' folk like that.

CHARLOTTE. Let him be, Peter.

PETER. How do 'ee mean, let 'un be. I bain't nowise for lett'n' 'un be.

DON JUAN. Ah!

PETER. Confound 'ee! Because 'ee be a gen'l'man do 'ee think 'ee can come kiss'n' our women under our very noses? Why can't 'e go kiss 'is own women?

DON JUAN. Heh?

PETER. Heh! [DON JUAN *gives him a box on the ear.*] Lord help us! Don't 'ee be a hitt'n' me. [DON JUAN *gives him another blow.*] Hey! What the ... [*Another blow.*] Lor' lumme! [*Another.*] Hang it! that ain't no way to behave. That ain't no way to repay a feller that's saved 'ee from drown'n'.

CHARLOTTE. Now don't 'ee get mad, Peter.

PETER. I will get mad if I want to and it bain't noways right of 'ee to be a-lett'n' un cajole 'ee so.

CHARLOTTE. Oh, Peter, things bain't the way 'ee be think-ing. This gentleman be a-goin' to marry me and there ain't no call for 'ee to get mad.

PETER. Dang it! Bain't 'ee a-promised to me?

CHARLOTTE. That don't make no matter, Peter. If 'ee do love me 'ee ought to be main glad to see me a-goin' to be a lady.

PETER. Lor' lumme! I'd as soon see 'ee dead as married to another feller.

CHARLOTTE. Go on now, Peter – don't 'ee be a-frett'n'. When I be a fine lady I'll see 'ee don't lose by it. I'll have 'ee bring butter and cheese to the house.

PETER. Criminy! I won't never bring 'ee noth'n', not if 'ee pay twice over, I won't. Be that why 'ee 'ave 'earkened to him? Lumme! If I'd have knowed that I wouldn't never have pulled 'im out o' the water – I'd have fetched 'un one over the 'ead with the oar, I would.

DON JUAN [*threatening to strike him*]. What's that you say?

PETER [*getting behind* CHARLOTTE]. Lumme! I bain't frightened o' nobody –

DON JUAN [*going round after him*]. You wait a minute.

PETER [*dodging round* CHARLOTTE]. I don't care noth'n' for nobody.

DON JUAN [*following him*]. We'll see about that.

PETER [*taking refuge again behind* CHARLOTTE]. I seen many a better man than –

DON JUAN. Hah!

SGANARELLE. Now, master, let the poor beggar alone! It's too bad to knock him about. Listen to me, my lad – get out and don't say another word to him.

PETER [*comes in front of* SGANARELLE *and looks defiantly at* DON JUAN]. I'll say what I want to 'un. I will . . .

DON JUAN. I'll teach you. [*Strikes at* PETER *who ducks and* SGANARELLE *gets the blow.*]

SGANARELLE [*looking at* PETER]. Confound the fool!

DON JUAN. That's what you get for your kindness.

PETER. Lor'! I mun go tell her auntie about these 'ere goings on.

Exit.

DON JUAN. And now I'm going to be the happiest of men. I would not exchange my good fortune for all the world could offer. What pleasures we shall enjoy once you are my wife!

Enter MATHURINE.

SGANARELLE [*seeing* MATHURINE]. Ha, ha!

MATHURINE. What are you doing with Charlotte, sir? You are not a-court'n' her too?

DON JUAN [*to* MATHURINE]. No, on the contrary. It was she was suggesting she would like to be my wife and I was telling her that I was engaged to you.

CHARLOTTE. What does Mathurine want with you?

DON JUAN [*to* CHARLOTTE, *aside*]. She is jealous at seeing me talking to you. She wants me to marry her, but I was telling her that you are the one I want.

MATHURINE. Why – Charlotte – !

DON JUAN [*to* MATHURINE, *aside*]. It's no use trying to talk to her, she's got the idea firmly fixed in her head.

CHARLOTTE. Why, Mathurine!

DON JUAN. It's a waste of time talking to her. You will never make her see sense.

MATHURINE. Can she really –

DON JUAN [*aside to* MATHURINE]. She just won't listen to reason.

CHARLOTTE. I would like to –

DON JUAN [*to* CHARLOTTE *aside*]. She is as obstinate as the very Devil!

MATHURINE. Really –

DON JUAN [*to* MATHURINE *aside*]. Don't say a word to her – she's crazy.

CHARLOTTE. I think I –

DON JUAN [*to* CHARLOTTE *aside*]. No, leave her alone. She's out of her mind.

MATHURINE. No, no, I must speak to her.

CHARLOTTE. I must hear why she –

MATHURINE. What's that?

DON JUAN [*to* MATHURINE, *aside*]. I bet you she tells you I have promised to marry her.

CHARLOTTE. I –

DON JUAN [*to* CHARLOTTE, *aside*]. What do you bet she will make out I have promised to make her my wife?

MATHURINE. Hark 'ee Charlotte! It's not fair to be a-queer'n' other people's pitches.

CHARLOTTE. It's not right of you, Mathurine, to be jealous because the gentleman is talking to me.

MATHURINE. Well, 'twas me the gentleman seen first!

CHARLOTTE. If 'twas you he seen first 'twas me he seen second and 'tis me he's a-promised to marry.

DON JUAN [*aside to* MATHURINE]. There you are! What did I tell you?

MATHURINE. Get away with you, 'tis me, not you, he be a-taking to wife.

DON JUAN [*aside to* CHARLOTTE]. Didn't I just guess as much?

CHARLOTTE. Tell that tale somewhere else – 'tis me he be promised to –

MATHURINE. Ye be trying to fool me – 'tis me he be going to wed.

CHARLOTTE. Well, let him speak for himself. Let him say if I be not in the right.

MATHURINE. Ay, let him say if I don't speak honest truth.

CHARLOTTE. Be it she you have promised to marry, sir?

DON JUAN [*aside to* CHARLOTTE]. Are you trying to tease me?

MATHURINE. Be it true, sir, that you have promised to wed her?

DON JUAN [*aside to* MATHURINE]. How could you believe such a thing!

CHARLOTTE. Hark, how she be stick'n' to it.

DON JUAN [*aside to* CHARLOTTE]. Let her talk as she pleases.

MATHURINE. You are a witness how she will have it 'tis so.

DON JUAN. Let her say what she likes.

CHARLOTTE. No, no. We must know the truth.

MATHURINE. Yes. 'Tis a thing must be settled.

CHARLOTTE. Ay, Mathurine, I'll have this gentleman show 'ee what a young silly 'ee be.

MATHURINE. Ay, Charlotte, I'll have him bring 'ee down a peg.

CHARLOTTE. Please to put an end to the quarrel, sir.

MATHURINE. Please to decide for us, sir.

CHARLOTTE [*to* MATHURINE]. Now 'ee'll soon see!

MATHURINE [*to* CHARLOTTE]. 'Ee'll see, right enough!

CHARLOTTE [*to* DON JUAN]. Tell her how 'tis.

MATHURINE [*to* DON JUAN]. Speak to her now.

DON JUAN [*embarrassed, speaking to both of them*]. What do you want me to say? You both claim that I have promised to marry you, but don't you each know the truth without any need for me to explain? Why make me go over it once more? Surely the one I have really given my promise to can afford to laugh at the other. Why need she worry so long as I keep my promise to her? All the explanations in the world won't get us any further. We must do things, not talk about them. Deeds speak louder than words. There's only one way I can hope to reconcile you. When I do marry, you will see which one I love. [*Aside to* MATHURINE] Let her think what she pleases! [*Aside to* CHARLOTTE] Let her amuse herself with her fancies! [*Aside to* MATHURINE] I adore *you*. [*Aside to* CHARLOTTE] I am devoted to *you*. [*Aside to* MATHURINE] There is no beauty like yours. [*Aside to* CHARLOTTE] Since I have seen you I have no eyes for anyone else. [*To both*] I have some business I must attend to. I will be back in a quarter of an hour [*He goes out.*]

CHARLOTTE. There now, I be the one that he really loves.

MATHURINE. But 'tis me he be a-goin' to marry.

SGANARELLE. My poor girls! I pity your simplicity. I can't bear to see you rushing to your ruin. Take notice of me, both of you. Don't be deceived by his stories, but stay at home in your village.

DON JUAN [*coming back*]. I should very much like to know why Sganarelle isn't following me.

SGANARELLE. My master's a rogue. His only intention is to deceive you as he has deceived many another. He marries any woman he comes across and – [*seeing* DON JUAN] That's not true! You can tell anyone who says so he's a liar! My master doesn't marry every woman he comes across, not a bit of it. He isn't a rogue. He doesn't intend to deceive. He has never deceived a woman in his life. Hold on, here he is. You can ask him yourselves.

DON JUAN [*to himself*]. Yes.

SGANARELLE. Master – there is so much slander in the world, I thought I would take precautions. I was just telling them that if anyone were to come and say anything to your discredit they were not to believe it and they shouldn't hesitate to tell him he was a liar.

DON JUAN. Sganarelle!

SGANARELLE. Yes! The master's a man of honour, you can take my word for that.

DON JUAN. Hum!

SGANARELLE. Such people are just a lot of good-for-nothings.

Enter LA RAMÉE.

LA RAMÉE. Sir, I must warn you that it's not safe for you here.

DON JUAN. What's that?

LA RAMÉE. There are a dozen horsemen coming in search of you. They'll be here any moment. I don't know how they've managed to follow you, but I got the information from a peasant they had been questioning. They gave him your description. You must be quick. The sooner you get out of here the better.

DON JUAN [*to* CHARLOTTE *and* MATHURINE]. I'm called away on urgent business, but remember my promise and be sure that you shall hear from me before to-morrow evening.

[MATHURINE *and* CHARLOTTE *go out.*] Since the odds are against us I must find some stratagem to avert the danger that threatens me. Sganarelle, you had better put on my clothes and I –

SGANARELLE. You can't mean that, master! Would you have me risk being killed in your clothes – it's –

DON JUAN. Come along! Be quick! You should take it as an honour. A servant should be happy to have the privilege of dying for his master.

SGANARELLE. Thank you very much for the honour! Oh Lord, if I must die, grant that I may not die in mistake for somebody else.

Act Three

DON JUAN *dressed for the country and* SGANARELLE *dressed as a doctor.*

SGANARELLE. Upon my word, master, you must admit that I was right. We are properly disguised now. That first idea of yours wouldn't have done at all. This will hide our identity much better than what you wanted to do.

DON JUAN. You certainly look well. I can't imagine where you dug out that ridiculous get-up.

SGANARELLE. They are the robes of some old doctor. I picked them up at a pawnshop. They cost me good money too! But would you believe it, master, I'm already treated with respect because of my clothes? People I meet salute me with deference and some are coming to consult me as a learned man.

DON JUAN. What do you mean.

SGANARELLE. Five or six country people who saw me on the road came to seek my advice about their various ailments.

DON JUAN. And you admitted your ignorance, I suppose?

SGANARELLE. Me? Not likely! I had to maintain the honour of the cloth. I held forth to them about their complaints and gave them each a prescription.

DON JUAN. And what remedies did you prescribe?

SGANARELLE. Upon my word, master, I just took whatever came into my head and gave my prescriptions at random. It would be a joke if they got better and came back to thank me!

DON JUAN. And why not? Why shouldn't you enjoy the same prerogatives as other doctors? They are no more responsible for curing their patients than you are. Their skill is sheer make-believe. All they do is take the credit when things turn out well. You can take advantage of the patient's good luck just as they do, and see your remedies given the credit for whatever chance and the workings of nature achieve.

SGANARELLE. Why, master! Are you a heretic where medicine's concerned too?

DON JUAN. It is one of the greatest errors of mankind.

SGANARELLE. What – you don't believe in senna then, nor in cassia, nor in antimony?

DON JUAN. Why should I believe in them?

SGANARELLE. You are a real unbeliever! But you must have seen what a stir there has been lately about antimony. Its miraculous cures have convinced the most sceptical folk. Only three weeks ago I saw a wonderful case with my own eyes.

DON JUAN. What was that?

SGANARELLE. There was a man who had been a week at death's door. No one knew what to do for him. All remedies were useless. In the end they decided to give him antimony.

DON JUAN. And he got better, eh?

SGANARELLE. Oh, no, he died.

DON JUAN. Remarkably effective, I must say!

SGANARELLE. How d'ye mean? He had been dying a whole week and couldn't manage it, and this stuff finished him off right away. What could you want better than that?

DON JUAN. Oh nothing, of course!

SGANARELLE. Well, supposing we leave medicine, since you have no faith in it, and discuss something else. This get-up gives me confidence and I feel in the mood for arguing with you. You remember I am allowed to argue so long as I don't preach at you.

DON JUAN. Very well, then.

SGANARELLE. I'd like to find out what your ideas are. Do you really not believe in Heaven at all?

DON JUAN. Suppose we leave that alone.

SGANARELLE. That means that you don't. And Hell?

DON JUAN. Eh?

SGANARELLE. No again! And the Devil, may I ask?

DON JUAN. Yes, yes.

SGANARELLE. No more than the rest! And don't you believe in a life after this?

DON JUAN. Ha! Ha! Ha!

SGANARELLE [aside]. This chap will take some converting! [To DON JUAN] Now just tell me this – the Bogy Man – what do you think about him?

DON JUAN. Don't be a fool!

SGANARELLE. Now I can't allow that. There's nothing truer than the Bogy Man. I'd go to the stake for that. A man must believe in something. What *do* you believe?

DON JUAN. What do I believe?

SGANARELLE. Yes.

DON JUAN. I believe that two and two make four, Sganarelle, and that two fours are eight.

SGANARELLE. Now that *is* a fine sort of faith. As far as I can see then, your religion's arithmetic. What queer ideas folk do get into their heads! And, often enough, the more they have studied the less sense they have! Not that I've studied myself, master, not like you have, thank the Lord! Nobody can boast that he ever taught me anything, but with my own common sense and using my own judgement I can see things better than books, and I know very well that this world we see around us didn't spring up of its own accord overnight – like a mushroom! I ask you who made these trees, these rocks, the earth and sky above, or did it all come of its own accord? Take yourself, for example! You exist! Are you a thing of your own making or was it necessary for your father to beget you, and for your mother to bring you into the world? Can you look on all the parts of this machine which make up a man and not wonder at the way one part is fashioned with another, nerves, bones, veins, arteries, lungs, heart, liver, and all the other things which go to – Oh, for goodness' sake do interrupt me! I can't argue if I'm not interrupted. You are keeping quiet on purpose and letting me run on out of sheer mischief.

DON JUAN. I am waiting until you have finished what you are trying to say.

SGANARELLE. What I'm trying to say is that there's something wonderful in man, say what you like, and something that all your learned men can't explain. Isn't it remarkable that here am I with something in my head that can think of a hundred different things in a moment and make my body do whatever it wants; for example, clap my hands, lift my arms, raise my eyes to heaven, bow my head, move my feet, go to the right or the left, forward or backward, turn round – [*In turning round he tumbles over.*]

DON JUAN. Good! And so your argument falls to the ground!

SGANARELLE. Oh, what a fool I am to waste time arguing with you! Believe what you like, then! What does it matter to me if you go to damnation!

DON JUAN. I think we have gone astray in the course of discussion. Give that fellow down there a hail and ask him the way.

SGANARELLE. Hello! You there! Hello! Just a word, friend, if you don't mind.

Enter a poor man.

SGANARELLE. Can you show us the way to the town?

POOR MAN. Just follow this road, gentlemen, and turn to the right when you come to the end of the wood, but I warn you, be on your guard; there have been robbers about here lately.

DON JUAN. I am very grateful to you, friend. Thank you very much.

POOR MAN. Would you care to help me, sir, with a little something?

DON JUAN. So your advice wasn't disinterested!

POOR MAN. I'm a poor man, sir. I have lived alone in this wood for the last ten years. I will pray to Heaven for your good fortune.

DON JUAN. Hm! Pray for a coat to your back and don't worry about other people's affairs.

SGANARELLE. My good man, you don't know my master.

All he believes in is that two and two make four and two
fours are eight.

DON JUAN. How do you employ yourself here in the forest?

POOR MAN. I spend my days in praying for the prosperity of
the good people who show me charity.

DON JUAN. You must live very comfortably then.

POOR MAN. Alas, sir, I live in great penury.

DON JUAN. Surely not? A man who spends his days in prayer
cannot fail to be well provided for.

POOR MAN. Believe me, sir, I often haven't a crust of bread to
eat.

DON JUAN. Strange that you are so ill repaid for your pains!
Well, I'll give you a gold piece here and now if you'll curse
your fate and blaspheme.

POOR MAN. Ah, sir, would you have me commit a sin like that?

DON JUAN. Make up your mind. Do you want to earn a gold
piece or not? There is one here for you provided you swear.
Wait – you must swear.

POOR MAN. Oh, sir!

DON JUAN. You don't get it unless you do.

SGANARELLE. Go on, curse a bit. There isn't any harm in it.

DON JUAN. Hear, take it, I tell you, but you must swear first.

POOR MAN. No, sir, I'd rather starve.

DON JUAN. Very well, then, I give it to you for humanity's
sake. But what's happening over there? One man attacked
by three others. That isn't fair odds. I can't allow that! [*He
runs towards the fight.*]

SGANARELLE. The master's completely mad. Fancy rushing
into danger when he could well avoid it! Upon my word,
though, he has turned the scale! The two of them have put
the three to flight.

Enter DON CARLOS.

DON CARLOS [*sword in hand*]. They have taken to their heels
thanks to your valuable help. Permit me to thank you, sir,
for your noble and –

DON JUAN [*sheathing his sword*]. I have done nothing, sir, that you
would not have done in my place. One is in honour bound
to intervene on such an occasion. The scoundrels' behaviour
was so cowardly that to have kept out would have amounted

to taking their side. But how did you come to fall into their clutches?

DON CARLOS. I happened to become separated from my brother and the rest of our company. I was trying to find them when I encountered these robbers. They killed my horse, and, but for your valour, would have killed me too.

DON JUAN. Are you making towards the town?

DON CARLOS. Yes, but I don't mean to enter it: my brother and I are compelled to stay without because of one of those troublesome affairs which oblige gentlemen to sacrifice themselves and their families to their rigorous code of honour, and must, even at the best, end disastrously, since if one does not lose one's life one must quit the realm. It is, to my way of thinking, an unhappy obligation of a gentleman that he can never be certain, however discreet and honourable his own conduct, that he will not become involved, in observance of the laws of honour, in someone else's unruliness and so find his life, his peace of mind, his property, at the mercy of the first rash fool that takes it into his head to put upon him one of those affronts for which an honourable man must imperil his life.

DON JUAN. We have this satisfaction, that we can make those who wantonly offend us run the same risks and face the same discomforts as we ourselves do. But would it be indiscreet to ask what your own trouble might be?

DON CARLOS. It can hardly remain secret much longer, and once the insult is publicly known we are not in honour bound to keep our shame secret. On the contrary, it rather behoves us to proclaim our desire for vengeance and publish our plans for achieving it. Therefore I need not scruple to tell you, sir, that we are seeking to avenge our sister, who has been seduced and carried off from a convent. The author of this foul crime is a certain Don Juan Tenorio, son of Don Luis of that name. We have been seeking him for several days and followed him this morning on the report of a servant, who told us that he set out on horseback with four or five others and passed along this coast. But all our efforts have been in vain. We have not been able to find what has become of him.

DON JUAN. And do you know him, sir, this Don Juan of whom you speak?

DON CARLOS. I have never seen him myself. I have only my brother's description of him, but one hears little to his credit. He is a man whose life –

DON JUAN. Say no more, sir, if you please. He is, in a way, my friend, and it would not become me to hear him ill spoken of.

DON CARLOS. In consideration for you, sir, I will say nothing at all. The least I can do for you after your having saved my life is to keep silent about him in your presence, for if I did speak of him at all I could say nothing good. But though you are his friend I should hope that you would not condone what he has done, and that you will understand why we seek revenge upon him.

DON JUAN. On the contrary, I am willing to help you and spare you unnecessary trouble. I am a friend of Don Juan. I cannot well be otherwise, but there is no reason why he should offend gentlemen with impunity, and I undertake that he shall give you satisfaction.

DON CARLOS. But what satisfaction can one offer for an outrage of this kind?

DON JUAN. Whatever you can in honour require, and to save you the trouble of seeking Don Juan I undertake to produce him when and where you wish.

DON CARLOS. I should look forward to such a meeting with pleasure, sir, because of the injury I have suffered, but in view of my obligation to you I should hate to have you involved in the affair.

DON JUAN. My connexion with Don Juan is so close that he could hardly fight without my fighting too. Indeed I answer for him as for myself. You need only say when you want him to appear and give you satisfaction.

Enter DON ALONSO *and three followers.*

DON ALONSO. Have the horses watered and bring them along after us. I will go on foot a little. Heavens! What is this? You, brother, with our mortal enemy?

DON CARLOS. Our mortal enemy?

DON JUAN [*withdrawing two or three paces and proudly putting his hand on the hilt of his sword*]. Yes, I am Don Juan. The disparity of numbers shall not make me disown my name.

DON ALONSO. Ah, miscreant! You shall die –

DON CARLOS. Stay, brother! I owe my life to him. Had it not been for his help I should have been killed by robbers.

DON ALONSO. And would you let this consideration stand between us and our revenge? No services received at an enemy's hand could be sufficient to justify such scruple in us. If the obligation is to be measured against the injury, your gratitude is absurd. Honour is more precious than life. What obligation can one owe, then, for one's life, to a man who has already robbed one of honour?

DON CARLOS. I know the distinction a gentleman must make between the two and I do not cease to resent the injury because I remember the obligation. Nevertheless I ask you to let me render back to him what he gave me. I owe him my life. Let me requite him. Let us postpone our vengeance and allow him a few more days to enjoy the fruits of his good deed.

DON ALONSO. No, no. To defer revenge is to risk losing it. The opportunity may never recur. Heaven offers it here and now, and we should take advantage of it. It is no time to think of acting with moderation when honour has received a deadly wound. If you shrink from taking part in the deed you need only withdraw and leave the honour of the sacrifice to me.

DON CARLOS. I beseech you, brother –

DON ALONSO. This talk is superfluous. He must die.

DON CARLOS. Stop! I warn you, brother. I will not permit any attack upon his life. I swear to Heaven I will defend him against anyone who attacks him. I will offer in his defence the life he saved. If you would strike at him, your blows must first fall on me.

DON ALONSO. What! You take our enemy's part against me! So far from sharing my rage at the sight of him, you extend him your sympathy!

DON CARLOS. Brother, our purpose is a legitimate one. Let us show moderation in achieving it. In avenging our honour let us not give way to the unbridled fury which you now betray. Let us master our feelings and show that our valour is free from any element of ferocity, and that reason, not blind range, inspires us. I have no wish to remain indebted to my enemy. I must first of all repay my obligation to him, but our vengeance will not be less but more effective because it is deferred. To have an opportunity and refrain from taking it will make our vengeance appear more just in the eyes of the world.

DON ALONSO. Oh! Strange weakness! What dreadful blindness to endanger the requirements of honour because of a ridiculous notion of some imaginary obligation.

DON CARLOS. No, brother, you need have no concern. If I prove wrong, I shall make amends. I take full responsibility for our honour and I know the obligations it imposes upon us. The day of grace which my sense of gratitude demands for him will only make me the more determined that honour shall be satisfied. Don Juan, you see that I am at pains to repay your boon. You can judge from that what manner of man I am and rest assured that I am not less eager to fulfil obligations of another kind, not less scrupulous in repaying an injury than in returning a benefit. I ask no explanations from you now, but I offer you an opportunity to consider at leisure what decision you must take. You know the enormity of the injury you have done to us: I leave you to judge for yourself what reparation it demands. There are peaceful means of satisfying us and others which are violent and bloody. Whatever choice you make, remember you have promised me satisfaction from Don Juan. Bear that in mind, and remember that henceforward I own no obligations save to honour.

DON JUAN. I have asked nothing of you. I will do for you what I have promised.

DON CARLOS. Let us go, brother: a moment of restraint will not blunt the edge of our resolution.

Exeunt.

DON JUAN. Hello there, Sganarelle!

SGANARELLE. At your service, master.

DON JUAN. So! You scoundrel! You run away when I'm attacked, do you?

SGANARELLE. Pardon me, sir, I was close at hand. I think

these doctor's clothes must have a purgative effect. They are as good as a dose of medicine.

DON JUAN. Confound your impudence! Can't you think of a more decent excuse for your cowardice? Do you know who he is, this fellow whose life I saved?

SGANARELLE. No, I don't know.

DON JUAN. One of Elvira's brothers —

SGANARELLE. One of —

DON JUAN. Yes, and he's a very good fellow. He has behaved well, and I am sorry to have any quarrel with him.

SGANARELLE. You could settle everything easily enough.

DON JUAN. Yes, but my passion for Dona Elvira is spent. The connexion has become irksome. I must have freedom in love, as you know. I cannot resign myself to confining my heart within four walls. I have often told you that my natural propensity is to follow my fancy wherever it may lead. My heart belongs to all womankind. It is theirs to take in turn and keep as long as they can. But what is this noble edifice I see among the trees?

SGANARELLE. Don't you know?

DON JUAN. Indeed I don't.

SGANARELLE. Why! It's the tomb the Commander was having built at the time when you killed him.

DON JUAN. So it is. I didn't know it was here. I have heard wonderful accounts of it and of the statue of the Commander. I should like to have a look at it.

SGANARELLE. Don't go in there, master!

DON JUAN. Why not?

SGANARELLE. It's not the thing, to go calling on a man that you've killed.

DON JUAN. On the contrary, I wish to pay him the courtesy of a visit. He should take it in good part if he's a gentleman. Come! Let us go in.

The tomb opens, revealing a superb mausoleum and the STATUE *of the Commander.*

SGANARELLE. Ah, isn't that beautiful? Beautiful statues, beautiful marble, beautiful pillars. It really is beautiful. What do you say, master?

DON JUAN. I should think that a dead man's ambition could

hardly go further. What is most remarkable to me is that a man who in his lifetime was content with quite a modest dwelling should want to have such a magnificent one for the time when he could no longer have any use for it.

SGANARELLE. This is the statue of the Commander.

DON JUAN. By Jove! Doesn't he look well in his Roman toga!

SGANARELLE. Goodness, master. It's a beautiful piece of work. You would think he was alive and just going to speak. I should be frightened of the way he looks at us if I were alone. I don't think he is at all pleased to see us.

DON JUAN. Well, that's very wrong of him. It's a poor return for the compliment I am paying him. Ask him if he would like to come and sup with me.

SGANARELLE. I should think that is one thing he hasn't any need for.

DON JUAN. Ask him, I tell you!

SGANARELLE. You must be joking! It would be idiotic to talk to a statue.

DON JUAN. Do as I tell you.

SGANARELLE. Your Excellency the Commander! [*Aside*] I'm laughing at my own silliness, but it's my master who's making me do it. Your Excellency! My master, Don Juan, asks if you would do him the honour of coming to sup with him. [*The* STATUE *nods.*] Oh!

DON JUAN. What is it? What's wrong with you? Come on. Speak, will you!

SGANARELLE [*nodding his head as the* STATUE *did*]. The statue –

DON JUAN. Well, what is it? Speak up – you scoundrel!

SGANARELLE. I tell you the statue –

DON JUAN. The statue? Well what about the statue? I'll brain you if you don't speak up.

SGANARELLE. The statue – it nodded its head to me.

DON JUAN. Confound the fellow!

SGANARELLE. It nodded to me, I tell you. It's true! You go talk to him yourself and you'll see. Perhaps –

DON JUAN. Come on – you rascal – come on! I'll show you what a coward you are. Watch me! Would your Excelle the Commander care to take supper with me?

The STATUE *nods again.*

SGANARELLE. I wouldn't have missed that for ten pounds. Well, master?

DON JUAN. Come on. Let us get out of here!

SGANARELLE. So much for your freethinkers who won't believe in anything.

Act Four

SCENE ONE

DON JUAN, SGANARELLE, RAGOTIN.

DON JUAN. Whatever it was, we will leave it at that. It is of no importance. We may have been deceived by a trick of light or overcome by some momentary giddiness which affected our vision.

SGANARELLE. Ah, master, don't attempt to deny what we both saw with our own eyes. Nothing could be more unmistakable than that nod of the head. I haven't the least doubt that Heaven is outraged by your way of life and wrought this miracle to convince you and to restrain you from –

DON JUAN. Listen! If you pester me any more with your idiotic moralizing, if I hear a single word more from you on the matter, I shall send for a whip and have you held down while I flog you within an inch of your life. Do you understand?

SGANARELLE. Completely, sir – absolutely! You've made your meaning quite clear. That's one good thing about you – there's no beating about the bush. You do put things plainly!

DON JUAN. Come along. Get them to prepare my supper as soon as possible. [*To* RAGOTIN] A chair for me, boy.

Enter LA VIOLETTE.

LA VIOLETTE. Sir, there's a tradesman, Mr Dimanche, wants to speak to you.

SGANARELLE. Good! We only needed a creditor to call on us! What business does he think he has, to come asking for money? Why didn't you tell him the master was out?

LA VIOLETTE. I've been telling him that for the last half-hour, but he doesn't believe it. He's sitting there waiting.

SGANARELLE. Let him wait to his heart's content!

DON JUAN. On the contrary. Ask him to come in. It's always bad policy to hide from one's creditors. It's well to pay them with something and I know how to send them away satisfied without giving a farthing.

Enter MR DIMANCHE.

DON JUAN [*very polite*]. Ah! Mr Dimanche! Do come in. I am delighted to see you and I'm most displeased with my servants for not showing you in at once. I had said I would see no one, but that wasn't intended for you. My door should never be shut against you.

MR DIMANCHE. Sir, I am very much obliged to you.

DON JUAN [*to his lackeys*]. Ah, you rascals! I'll teach you to keep Mr Dimanche waiting in the ante-chamber. I'll teach you to know who's who.

MR DIMANCHE. It is of no consequence, sir.

DON JUAN. Fancy saying I was out to Mr Dimanche, and he one of my very best friends!

MR DIMANCHE. Your servant, sir. What I came for was –

DON JUAN. Quick. A seat for Mr Dimanche.

MR DIMANCHE. I'm quite all right as I am, sir.

DON JUAN. Not at all. Not at all. I want you to come and sit near me.

MR DIMANCHE. There is really no need, sir.

DON JUAN. Take this stool away and bring an arm-chair.

MR DIMANCHE. Sir – you can't really mean it –

DON JUAN. No, I know what is due to you. I won't have them make any difference between us.

MR DIMANCHE. Sir!

DON JUAN. Come! be seated.

MR DIMANCHE. There's really no need, sir. There's only one thing I wanted to say to you – I just came to –

DON JUAN. Come and sit here.

MR DIMANCHE. No – I'm quite all right, sir. I just came to –

DON JUAN. No, I won't hear a word unless you sit down.

MR DIMANCHE. As you wish, sir. I just –

DON JUAN. By Jove, Mr Dimanche, you are looking well.

MR DIMANCHE. Yes, sir, at your service. I just came to –

DON JUAN. You are the very picture of health: ruby lips, fresh colour, and a sparkle in your eyes.

MR DIMANCHE. I really wanted to –

DON JUAN. And how is your good lady, Mrs Dimanche?

MR DIMANCHE. She's very well, sir, Heaven be praised!

DON JUAN. What a splendid woman she is!

MR DIMANCHE. She's your humble servant, sir – I just came to –

DON JUAN. And your little girl – Claudine, how is she getting on?

MR DIMANCHE. Very well indeed.

DON JUAN. Such a pretty child. I am really fond of her.

MR DIMANCHE. You are too kind, sir, I just wanted to –

DON JUAN. And little Colin – does he make as much noise as ever with his drum?

MR DIMANCHE. Yes. He's still just the same, sir. I – I –

DON JUAN. And your little dog, Brusquet. Does he still growl as fiercely as ever? Does he still get his teeth into your visitors' legs?

MR DIMANCHE. He's worse than ever, sir. We just can't break him of it.

DON JUAN. Don't be surprised that I want news of all the family. I take a real interest in them.

MR DIMANCHE. We are all very much honoured, sir, I just –

DON JUAN [*offering his hand*]. Give me your hand on it, Mr Dimanche. You really feel you are one of my friends?

MR DIMANCHE. I'm your humble servant, sir.

DON JUAN. Dash it! You know I am genuinely fond of you.

MR DIMANCHE. You do me too much honour – I –

DON JUAN. There's nothing I wouldn't do for you.

MR DIMANCHE. You are too kind, sir . . .

DON JUAN. And for no other reason than the regard I have for you, believe me!

MR DIMANCHE. I've done nothing to deserve such a favour, sir, but –

DON JUAN. Oh come now, Mr Dimanche. Don't stand on ceremony! Won't you stay and have supper with me?

MR DIMANCHE. No, sir. I really must go back at once. I only
came –

DON JUAN [*getting up*]. Quickly, there. A torch for Mr Dimanche. Four or five of you take your muskets and escort him
on his way.

MR DIMANCHE [*rising*]. Sir. There's no need. I shall get along
quite well on my own. But – I just –

    SGANARELLE *quickly takes away the chairs.*

DON JUAN. Come! I insist that you have an escort. I am concerned for your welfare, you know. I'm your humble servant, and, what's more, I'm your debtor –

MR DIMANCHE. Ah, Sir!

DON JUAN. I make no secret of it. I let everyone know it!

MR DIMANCHE. If –

DON JUAN. Would you like me to see you home myself?

MR DIMANCHE. Ah sir – you are joking, sir – I only –

DON JUAN. Well, then, give me your hand. Once again, do
please consider me your friend. There's nothing in the
world I wouldn't do for you. [*Goes out.*]

SGANARELLE. I must say the master's very fond of you.

MR DIMANCHE. So it seems. He shows me such politeness
and civility that I never managed to ask for my money.

SGANARELLE. I assure you everybody here would do anything in the world for you. I only wish something would
happen to you, someone try to beat you up, for example –
you'd see how we should all –

MR DIMANCHE. I don't doubt it, but I wish you would have a
word to him about my money, Sganarelle.

SGANARELLE. Oh don't you worry. He'll pay you, all
right.

MR DIMANCHE. But you yourself, Sganarelle, you owe me
something on your own account.

SGANARELLE. Come, come! Don't let us talk about that.

MR DIMANCHE. Why not – I –

SGANARELLE. Do you think I don't know very well what I
owe you?

MR DIMANCHE. Yes, but –

SGANARELLE. Come then, Mr Dimanche. I shall have to explain to you.

MR DIMANCHE. But my money. . . .

SGANARELLE [*taking his arm*]. Surely you can't be serious?

MR DIMANCHE. I want –

SGANARELLE [*pulling him*]. Eh?

MR DIMANCHE. I mean –

SGANARELLE [*pushing him*]. Oh, nonsense!

MR DIMANCHE. But –

SGANARELLE [*pushing*]. Go on with you!

MR DIMANCHE. But I –

SGANARELLE [*pushing him off the stage*]. Get on with you – I say.

SCENE TWO

DON JUAN, SGANARELLE.

Enter LA VIOLETTE.

LA VIOLETTE. Your father is here, sir.

DON JUAN. Ha! Isn't that nice for me. It only needed that to complete my annoyance.

DON LUIS [*entering*]. I can see that I embarrass you. No doubt you could well do without my coming here. The truth is we are the curse of each other's existence. If you are tired of the sight of me, I am equally weary of your goings-on. Ah! how little we know what we are doing when, instead of being content to leave it to the Lord to decide what is good for us we must needs know better than he does and be importuning him in our blindness for this, that, and the other. Nobody ever wanted a son more than I did, no one ever prayed for one more ardently than I, and now the son for whom I wearied Heaven with my prayers and thought would be my joy and consolation, turns out to be the bane of my life. What am I to think of your accumulation of villainies? What excuse can I offer for them in the eyes of the world? Your never-ending succession of crimes has reduced me to wearying the King's indulgence until I have exhausted the goodwill won by my own services and the credit of my friends. What depths of infamy you have sunk to! Don't you blush to be so little worthy of your birth? What right do you think you have to be proud of it still? What have you ever done to deserve the name of gentleman? Or do you think it is enough to bear the title and the arms of one? What credit is it to be born of noble blood if one lives in infamy? Birth is nothing without virtue, and we have no claim to share in the glory of our ancestors unless we strive to resemble them. The renown which their deeds shed upon us imposes an obligation to be worthy of them, to follow in the paths they marked out for us, and, if we wish to be esteemed true descendants, never to fall short of their virtues. You claim descent from your ancestors in vain. They disown you. Their illustrious deeds reflect no credit upon you. On the contrary, they throw your dishonour into greater relief; their glory is a torch which lights your shame for all the world to see. Finally, you can take it from me that a gentleman who lives an evil life is an offence against nature, a monster, and that virtue is the first title to nobility. For my part, I have more regard for a man's deeds than for the title he can subscribe to his name: I should feel more respect to a labourer's son if he were an honest man than to a prince of the blood who lives the life you do.

DON JUAN. You would talk more comfortably sitting down, sir.

DON LUIS. No, insolent wretch! I will neither sit down nor speak further, for I see that nothing I say makes any impression upon you. But I would have you know, unworthy son that you are, that you have exhausted your father's love by your misdeeds and that I shall find means, and sooner than you think, to set bounds to your evil ways, to anticipate the wrath of Heaven and, in punishing you, wipe out the disgrace of having begotten you.

Exit DON LUIS.

DON JUAN. Ay, well, the sooner you die the better. Every dog has his day, and I have no use for fathers who live as long as their sons. [*Sits down in his arm-chair.*]

SGANARELLE. Ah, master – that was wrong of you!

DON JUAN. Wrong? *I* was wrong?

SGANARELLE. Master –

DON JUAN [*rising*]. *I* was wrong?

SGANARELLE. Yes, master, you were wrong – to let him talk

as he did; you should have pitched him out neck and crop. Did you ever hear such nonsense! Fancy a father coming and remonstrating with his son, calling him to mend his ways and remember what's due to his birth, lead a decent life, and a score of similar absurdities. How could you put up with it – a man like you, who knows the way of the world? I am surprised at your patience. If I'd been in your place, I'd have sent him packing. [*Aside*] Oh cursed subservience! To what depths do you reduce me.

DON JUAN. Will that supper never be ready?

Enter RAGOTIN.

RAGOTIN. There is a veiled lady, sir, wishes to speak to you.

DON JUAN. Who can she be?

SGANARELLE. We must see.

Enter DONA ELVIRA.

DONA ELVIRA. Do not be surprised to see me, Don Juan, at this hour and in this dress. Reasons of great urgency impel me to come to see you, and what I have to tell you will brook no delay. I no longer come in anger – the anger which I recently showed: indeed, you will find me greatly changed from what I was this morning. I am no longer the Dona Elvira who heaped reproaches on you, whose wounded heart could think of nothing but menaces and threats of vengeance. God has purged my soul of my unworthy passion for you, the tumultuous emotions of a sinful relationship, the vain transports of an earthly and a sensual love. There remains in my heart nothing but a love purged of sensuality, a holy tenderness, an affection which is dispassionate, disinterested, concerned now only for your good.

DON JUAN [*to* SGANARELLE]. You weep, I fancy!

SGANARELLE. Forgive me!

DONA ELVIRA. In this pure and perfect love I have come to you for your good, to bring you a warning from Heaven above and to snatch you back from the abyss for which you are heading. Yes, Don Juan, I well know all the irregularities of your life, but God, who has touched my conscience and opened my eyes to my own wrong-doing, has inspired me to seek you out and warn you that your offences have overtaxed his mercy; that his dread anger is about to be loosed upon you and that only immediate repentance can save you now. Perhaps only a single day still stands between you and the most dreadful of all misfortunes. As for myself, I am freed from all earthly ties which bound me to you: I have turned my back, thanks be to Heaven, on all my foolish fancies: I have made up my mind to withdraw from the world and I ask for nothing more than to live long enough to expiate my fault and by strict repentance to earn pardon for my blind attachment to a guilty passion. But in my retirement from the world I should grieve to see one whom I have loved tenderly become an awful example of the justice of Heaven: it would be joy unspeakable for me could I but bring you to avoid the dreadful fate which threatens you. I beg you, Don Juan, as a last favour, grant me this great consolation. Do not deny me your salvation. I implore you with my tears. If you have no consideration for your own well-being, at least let my prayers move you and spare me the horror of seeing you condemned to eternal torment.

SGANARELLE. Poor lady!

DONA ELVIRA. I loved you tenderly. You were dearer to me than all the world; for your sake I forsook my duty and gave you everything. All the recompense I ask is that you should amend your way of life and save yourself from eternal ruin. Save yourself, I beg you, whether for love of yourself or love of me. Once again I implore you with my tears, Don Juan, and, if the tears of one whom you once loved do not suffice, I ask it in the name of whatever is most dear to you.

SGANARELLE [*aside*]. Cruel! Cruel! Tiger-hearted!

DONA ELVIRA. I am going now. That is all I have to say.

DON JUAN. It is late. Stay here to-night. You shall have the best accommodation the house affords.

DONA ELVIRA. No, Don Juan, do not detain me further.

DON JUAN. I assure you it would afford me great pleasure if you would stay.

DONA ELVIRA. No, let us not waste time in unnecessary conversation. Let me go at once. Do not seek to accompany me. Think only of profiting from my message.

Ex it DONA ELVIRA.

DON JUAN. You know, I found I had still some slight feeling

for her – there was something rather pleasant in the novelty of the situation! Her disordered dress, her tenderness, and her tears stirred the last embers of my extinguished passion.

SGANARELLE. So what she said had no effect on you at all?

DON JUAN. Quick, to supper!

SGANARELLE. Very well.

DON JUAN [*sitting at the table*]. All the same, Sganarelle, we shall have to mend our ways.

SGANARELLE. We shall indeed!

DON JUAN. Upon my word, yes! We shall have to mend our ways. Another twenty or thirty years of this present life and then we'll look to ourselves.

SGANARELLE. Oh!

DON JUAN. What have you to say to that?

SGANARELLE. Nothing. Here comes the supper. [*He takes a morsel from one of the dishes which are brought in and puts it in his mouth.*]

DON JUAN. You seem to have something in your cheek. What is it? Speak up! What have you got in your mouth?

SGANARELLE. Nothing.

DON JUAN. Let me see! Good Lord! He has a swelling in his cheek! Quick, something to lance it! The poor fellow can't bear it – the abscess may choke him! Steady! See how ripe it was – ah, you rascal!

SGANARELLE. I only wanted to make sure that the cook hadn't put in too much salt or pepper, master.

DON JUAN. Come along. Sit yourself down there and eat. I need you when you have eaten. You are hungry, it seems.

SGANARELLE [*sitting at table*]. I should think I am, master. I have eaten nothing since morning. Try some of this. It's excellent. [*Servant takes* SGANARELLE'S *plate away as soon as he puts food on it.*] Eh! My plate! My plate! Go easy, please! Goodness me, lad, you are pretty good at dealing out clean plates. As for you, La Violette, you certainly know how to serve wine at the right moment. [*While one lackey is serving* SGANARELLE *with wine the other takes his plate away.*]

DON JUAN. Who can be knocking like that?

SGANARELLE. Who the devil comes disturbing us at meal-time?

DON JUAN. I will at least finish my meal in peace. Let no one come in.

SGANARELLE. Leave it to me. I'll go myself.

DON JUAN. What is it? Who is there?

SGANARELLE. The [*nodding his head as the* STATUE *did*] – it's come!

DON JUAN. Let us go and see. I'll show that nothing can shake me!

SGANARELLE. Poor Sganarelle, where can you hide yourself!
The STATUE *of the Commander comes forward and sits at the table.*

DON JUAN. Come. a chair. Lay a place. Quickly! [*To* SGANARELLE] Come along. Sit down at the table.

SGANARELLE. I've lost my appetite, master.

DON JUAN. Sit down, I tell you. Bring wine. I give you the Commander's health, Sganarelle. Fill his glass, somebody.

SGANARELLE. I'm not thirsty, master.

DON JUAN. Drink, and give us a song to entertain the Commander.

SGANARELLE. I've got a cold, master.

DON JUAN. Never mind that. You others come along and play an accompaniment.

STATUE. Enough, Don Juan. I invite you to come and sup with me to-morrow. Dare you come?

DON JUAN. Yes. I will come – with Sganarelle alone.

SGANARELLE. Thank you very much. I am fasting to-morrow.

DON JUAN [*to* SGANARELLE]. Take this torch.

STATUE. No need for light when Heaven shows the way.

Act Five

DON LUIS, DON JUAN, SGANARELLE.

DON LUIS. What! My son! Has Heaven in its mercy heard my prayers? Is this the truth you are telling me? You are not deluding me with false hopes? Can I really believe in this sudden and surprising conversion?

DON JUAN [*playing the hypocrite*]. Yes, I have turned from the error of my ways. I am a new man since last night; the Lord has wrought a sudden change in me which will astonish everyone. He has touched my heart and removed the scales from my eyes; I look back with horror on the blindness in which I dwelt so long and the wickedness of my past life. When I go over in my mind the tally of my abominable deeds I wonder that Heaven has suffered them so long and not loosed its dreadful vengeance upon me twenty times over. My eyes are open now to the favour and mercy vouchsafed me in withholding the punishment of my crimes. I mean to take advantage of it and offer the world the spectacle of a sudden change in my way of life. Thus I shall make amends for the evil example of my former actions and endeavour to earn pardon for my sins. That is what I intend, and I ask you, sir, to assist me in this design by yourself choosing me a mentor under whose guidance I may safely follow the course I am about to embark upon.

DON LUIS. Ah, my son, how easily can a father's love revive, and filial offences be forgotten at the first word of repentance! What you have told me wipes from my memory every sorrow you have occasioned me. Oh, what overwhelming happiness! I weep for joy, for all my prayers are answered, and I have nothing more to ask of Heaven. Kiss me, my son, and do not falter, I conjure you, in your laudable intentions. I must go at once and take the good news to your mother, share my happiness with her and render thanks to God for the holy purpose he has deigned to inspire you with.

Exit DON LUIS.

SGANARELLE. Ah, master, what a joy it is to see you converted. I have waited for this a long time, and now, thanks be to God, my hopes are realized.

DON JUAN. Confound you! You blockhead!

SGANARELLE. Blockhead! Me?

DON JUAN. Do you mean to say you take my words at their face value? You think that I meant them?

SGANARELLE. Then it isn't – You're not – Oh, what a man! What a man! What a man!

DON JUAN. I have not changed in the least. I'm just the same as I always was.

SGANARELLE. You won't even yield to the miracle of a statue that moves and speaks?

DON JUAN. There is certainly something there that I do not understand, but, whatever it is, it shall neither change my convictions nor shake my courage. When I talked of mending my ways and living an exemplary life it was a calculated hypocrisy, a necessary pretence, which I had to assume for my father's benefit because I need his help, and as a protection against society and the hundred-and-one tiresome things that may happen to me. I take you into my confidence deliberately, Sganarelle, because I like to have one witness to my real feelings and my motives for acting as I do.

SGANARELLE. What! You don't believe in anything, and yet you want to set yourself up as a man of principle!

DON JUAN. And why not? There are plenty of others like me who ply the same trade and use the same mask to deceive the world.

SGANARELLE. What a man! What a man!

DON JUAN. Such conduct carries no stigma nowadays, for hypocrisy is a fashionable vice, and all vices pass for virtues once they become fashionable. The role of a man of principle is the best of all parts to play, for the professional hypocrite enjoys remarkable advantages. Hypocrisy is an art, the practice of which always commands respect, and though people may see through it they dare say nothing against it. All other vices of mankind are exposed to censure and anyone may attack them with impunity. Hypocrisy alone is privileged. It stills the voice of criticism and enjoys a sovereign immunity. Humbug binds together in close fellowship all those who practise it, and whoever attacks one brings down the whole pack upon him. Moreover, men whom one knows to be acting in good faith, men of integrity, are always taken in by the humbugs and caught in their snares, and blindly lend their support to men who only ape their virtues. How many men have I seen contrive to repair the disorders of their youth in this way, making religion a cloak under which they continued to live as wickedly as they pleased! People may be aware of their machinations, they may even recognize them for what they are, but they are not held in less regard on that account. They bow their heads from time to time, heave an occasional sigh of mortification, roll their eyes to Heaven now and again, and that atones, in the eyes of the world, for anything they may do. It is under shelter of this pretence I intend to take refuge and secure my own position. I shall not abandon my pleasures, but I shall be at pains to conceal them and amuse myself with all circumspection. So, if by any chance I am discovered, the whole fraternity will make my cause their own and defend me against every criticism. By this means I shall contrive to do whatever I choose with impunity. I shall set up as a censor of the behaviour of others, condemn everyone, and hold a good opinion of no one, myself alone excepted. Let anyone offend me in however slight a degree, I shall never forgive, but steadfastly nurse an implacable enmity. I shall constitute myself the avenger and servant of the Lord and use that convenient pretext as a means of harassing my enemies. I shall accuse them of impiety and find means to turn loose on them the officious zealots who will raise a public outcry against them without even knowing what it is about, overwhelm them with recriminations and damn them roundly on their own private authority. Thus one may profit from human frailty; thus a wise man may accommodate himself to the vices of the age.

SGANARELLE. Oh Lord! What do I hear? You only needed to turn hypocrite to become the complete villain. This is the final abomination! This is more than I can stand, master. I can keep quiet no longer. You can do what you like to me: beat me, knock me down, kill me, if you like, but I must open my heart to you and tell you what I think, as a faithful servant should. You know, master, the pitcher can go to the well once too often, and, as some writer very truly said – who he was I don't know – men in this world are like the bird on the bough, the bough is part of the tree and whoever holds on to the tree is following sound precepts; sound precepts are better than fine words; the court is the place for fine words; at the court you find courtiers, and courtiers do whatever's the fashion; fashion springs from the imagination and imagination springs from the soul; the soul is what gives us life, and life ends in death; death sets us thinking of Heaven; Heaven is above the earth; the earth's different from the ocean; the ocean's subject to tempests, and tempests are a terror to ships; a ship needs a good pilot and a good pilot needs prudence; young men have no prudence, so the young should be obedient to the old; old men love riches; riches make men rich; the rich aren't poor; poor men know necessity and necessity knows no law. Without law men live like animals, which all goes to prove that you'll be damned to all eternity!

DON JUAN. Fine reasoning, I must say!

SGANARELLE. If you don't admit you are wrong after that, so much the worse for you.

Enter DON CARLOS.

DON CARLOS. This is an opportune meeting, Don Juan. I am glad to be able to speak with you and ask you for your decision here rather than at your own house. You know what my obligation is. I assumed it in your presence. For my own part I admit that I would like to see things settled amicably. I would give anything in the world to induce you to choose that alternative and see you publicly acknowledge my sister as your wife.

DON JUAN [*putting on the hypocritical tone*]. I only wish I could give you that satisfaction, but Heaven itself has set its face against it and inspired me to reform my way of life. Now I am filled with one desire only – to renounce all earthly ties, divest myself forthwith of all vain attachments and henceforward atone by a life of austerity for all the wickedness into which the blindness of youth has led me.

DON CARLOS. But that intention does not run counter to my own suggestion, Don Juan. Lawful marriage is not incompatible with the good intentions heaven has implanted in you.

DON JUAN. Alas, you are mistaken. Your sister has herself taken a like decision. She has decided to retire into a convent. The spirit moved us both at the same time.

DON CARLOS. Her taking the veil does not satisfy us, since it might be imputed to your affront to her and our family. Our honour demands that you acknowledge her as your wife.

DON JUAN. That, I assure you, cannot be. For myself, I could wish for nothing better. Only to-day I sought Heaven's approval for such a course, but after I had prayed I heard a voice that said I should think no more of your sister for I should never find salvation with her.

DON CARLOS. And do you think that you can put us off with these fine excuses, Don Juan?

DON JUAN. I obey the voice of Heaven.

DON CARLOS. Do you expect me to be taken in by this sort of talk?

DON JUAN. Heaven wills it so.

DON CARLOS. You think you can carry off my sister from a convent and then abandon her?

DON JUAN. Such is Heaven's command.

DON CARLOS. And we are to bear this stain on our family honour?

DON JUAN. You must blame Heaven for that.

DON CARLOS. What! Heaven again!

DON JUAN. Heaven so ordains.

DON CARLOS. Enough, Don Juan! I understand you. This is not the place to deal with you, but before long I shall not fail to find you.

DON JUAN. As you please. You know I am no coward and that I can use my sword when need arises. I shall pass directly along the narrow lane that leads to the convent, but I would have you know that if we fight it is by no wish of mine. Heaven forbids me to think of such things. But if you attack me we shall see what will happen.

DON CARLOS. We shall! We shall indeed. [*Exit.*]

SGANARELLE. Master, what on earth are you up to? This is worse than ever. I'd much rather have you as you were before. I have always had hopes for your salvation, but now I begin to despair. Heaven has borne with you till now, but it will never suffer this latest outrage.

DON JUAN. Oh, come now! Heaven isn't as exacting as you think. If every time men –

SGANARELLE. Ah, master [*seeing the* SPECTRE]. It's a warning from Heaven.

DON JUAN. If Heaven wishes to warn me it must speak a little more plainly, if I am to be expected to hear.

Enter a SPECTRE *in the form of a veiled woman.*

Act Five

SPECTRE. Don Juan has but one moment left to profit from the mercy of Heaven: if he repent not now his end is certain.

SGANARELLE. Master, do you hear?

DON JUAN. Who dares speak thus to me? I fancy I know that voice.

SGANARELLE. Ah, master. It's a spirit. I can tell by its walk!

DON JUAN. Spirit, apparition, devil. I will see what it is.

The SPECTRE *changes to Time with a scythe in his hand.*

SGANARELLE. Oh Heavens! Look, master, how its shape changes.

DON JUAN. Nothing can frighten me. I will test with my sword whether it be flesh or spirit.

The SPECTRE *disappears as* DON JUAN *makes to strike it.*

SGANARELLE. Ah, master, yield to these proofs and repent quickly.

DON JUAN. No, come what may it shall never be said that I am the repenting sort. Come, follow me.

Enter the STATUE.

STATUE. You gave me your word yesterday to come and sup with me.

DON JUAN. Yes, where do we go?

STATUE. Give me your hand.

DON JUAN. There.

STATUE. Don Juan, those who persist in their wickedness come to dreadful ends: those who reject Heaven's mercy bring down its wrath.

DON JUAN. Oh God! What is happening to me? Unseen fires consume me. I cannot bear it. My body is aflame – ah ...

Rolls of thunder, flashes of lightning. The earth opens and swallows him up. Flames rise from the pit into which he has vanished.

SGANARELLE. Ah, my wages! My wages! Everybody gets satisfaction from his death: the Heaven he offended, the laws he violated, the girls he seduced, the families he dishonoured, the parents he disgraced, the wives he led astray, the husbands he drove to despair. Every one is satisfied but me! I'm the only unlucky one! After all my years of service the only reward I get is to see my master punished for his impiety with my own eyes and in the most dreadful way possible. My wages, my wages – my wages!

THE END

Notes on the Plays

Notes on the Plays

THE WOULD-BE GENTLEMAN (*Le Bourgeois Gentilhomme*). This comedy-ballet was first performed before the King at the Château of Chambord in 1670.

Tradition has it that the story was suggested by the visit of a Turkish envoy in the previous year. That may well have been so, but, in fact, *turqueries* were the fashion, Molière had already introduced gipsy and Moorish dances into his plays, and the Turkish ceremony differs from them only in its greater elaboration.

As originally performed, the play culminated in a great 'Ballet des Nations' in which dancing was interspersed with songs in Italian, Spanish, and various dialects of France. It lasted for over an hour.

Molière played the part of Jourdain; his wife was Lucile. Lully, wearing a mask, played the part of the Mufti.

THAT SCOUNDREL SCAPIN (*Les Fourberies de Scapin*). The play was first performed at the Palais-Royal in 1671. Scapin, as his name indicates, is a traditional figure of Italian farce. The plot is taken from the *Phormio* of Terence and from various contemporary sources. Molière played Scapin.

THE MISER (*L'Avare*). The play was first performed in 1668 at the Palais-Royal. Molière himself played Harpagon. The plot is culled from a wide range of sources – the *Aulularia* of Plautus, the *Suppositi* of Ariosto, *La Belle Plaideuse* of Boisrobert.

LOVE'S THE BEST DOCTOR (*L'Amour médecin*). Following his disastrous experience with *Le Tartuffe* and the hardly more happy fate of *Dom Juan*, Molière was called upon, at the shortest of notice, to provide an entertainment for the court. The result is LOVE'S THE BEST DOCTOR. Some critics have found in it a harshness which they have regarded as symptomatic of Molière's mood at that time, but it is difficult to see the justification for such a view. His own preface seems to give an adequate estimate of the play. What is new, or developed at length for the first time, is the satire on doctors, which he was to elaborate in *Le Médecin malgré lui* and *Le Malade imaginaire*.

The doctors in the play appear to have represented real people under the pseudo Greek names. Des-Fonandrés, the man-killer, was a well-known physician, Des Fougeraux; Macrotin, the slow of speech, was Guénant, physician to the Queen; Tomés, the blood-letter, was d'Aquin, the King's own physician; Bahys, the barker, was Esprit, physician to the King's brother (in real life he stuttered); Filerin, the quarrelsome, was Yvelin, physician to Madame, the King's sister-in-law. Orvietan, the universal remedy, was a real one first brought from Orvieto and sold by successive Italian quacks in the Place Dauphine.

DON JUAN (*Dom Juan* ou *Le Festin de Pierre*). The story of Don Juan first appears in a play of the Spaniard Tirso de Molina, published in 1632. Two farcical adaptations had been played by French companies, and the Italians had enjoyed great success with yet a third version. Molière may not have known the Spanish original, but he certainly was familiar with the versions played in Paris. His own work combines the tragic elements of the original play and the farcical French variations upon it.

The first performance was at the Palais-Royal in February 1665. Molière played Sganarelle. Cuts were made in the text after the first performance – the greater part of the scene with the poor man was omitted and Sganarelle's last speech was reduced to the first words, 'My wages! My wages!' Taken off after fifteen performances, the play was not printed until 1682 and then in a censored form. The text used for the translation is based on the uncensored copies of the edition of 1682 retained in the official files and a version published in Amsterdam in 1683. It is as near an approach as is now possible to what Molière originally wrote. The theme of the play was so popular that Molière's widow employed Thomas Corneille to provide a version in verse, and it was played in that form until the middle of the nineteenth century.

The sub-title – *Le Festin de Pierre* – is derived from the Spanish original and involves a play on the meaning of *Pierre* or *Piedra*, i.e. stone, but also Peter, the name of the Commander in the original version.

The action of the play is assumed to take place as follows: Act I, A palace, i.e. the public ambulatory or entrance hall; Act II, A sea coast; Act III, A wood near to a town and to the sea; Act IV, A room in the house occupied by Don Juan; Act V, Some place undefined. The Sicilian scene might almost as well be the coasts of Bohemia.

PENGUIN AUDIOBOOKS

A Quality of Writing that Speaks for Itself

Penguin Books has always led the field in quality publishing. Now you can listen at leisure to your favourite books, read to you by familiar voices from radio, stage and screen. Penguin Audiobooks are ideal as gifts, for when you are travelling or simply to enjoy at home. They are produced to an excellent standard, and abridgements are always faithful to the original texts. From thrillers to classic literature, biography to humour, with a wealth of titles in between, Penguin Audiobooks offer you quality, entertainment and the chance to rediscover the pleasure of listening.

You can order Penguin Audiobooks through Penguin Direct by telephoning (0181) 899 4036. The lines are open 24 hours every day. Ask for Penguin Direct, quoting your credit card details.

Published or forthcoming:

Emma by Jane Austen, read by Fiona Shaw

Persuasion by Jane Austen, read by Joanna David

Pride and Prejudice by Jane Austen, read by Geraldine McEwan

The Tenant of Wildfell Hall by Anne Brontë, read by Juliet Stevenson

Jane Eyre by Charlotte Brontë, read by Juliet Stevenson

Villette by Charlotte Brontë, read by Juliet Stevenson

Wuthering Heights by Emily Brontë, read by Juliet Stevenson

The Woman in White by Wilkie Collins, read by Nigel Anthony and Susan Jameson

Heart of Darkness by Joseph Conrad, read by David Threlfall

Tales from the One Thousand and One Nights, read by Souad Faress and Raad Rawi

Moll Flanders by Daniel Defoe, read by Frances Barber

Great Expectations by Charles Dickens, read by Hugh Laurie

Hard Times by Charles Dickens, read by Michael Pennington

Martin Chuzzlewit by Charles Dickens, read by John Wells

The Old Curiosity Shop by Charles Dickens, read by Alec McCowen

READ MORE IN PENGUIN

In every corner of the world, on every subject under the sun, Penguin represents quality and variety – the very best in publishing today.

For complete information about books available from Penguin – including Puffins, Penguin Classics and Arkana – and how to order them, write to us at the appropriate address below. Please note that for copyright reasons the selection of books varies from country to country.

In the United Kingdom: Please write to *Dept. JC, Penguin Books Ltd, FREEPOST, West Drayton, Middlesex UB7 0BR.*

If you have any difficulty in obtaining a title, please send your order with the correct money, plus ten per cent for postage and packaging, to *PO Box No. 11, West Drayton, Middlesex UB7 0BR*

In the United States: Please write to *Consumer Sales, Penguin USA, P.O. Box 999, Dept. 17109, Bergenfield, New Jersey 07621-0120.* VISA and MasterCard holders call 1-800-253-6476 to order all Penguin titles

In Canada: Please write to *Penguin Books Canada Ltd, 10 Alcorn Avenue, Suite 300, Toronto, Ontario M4V 3B2*

In Australia: Please write to *Penguin Books Australia Ltd, P.O. Box 257, Ringwood, Victoria 3134*

In New Zealand: Please write to *Penguin Books (NZ) Ltd, Private Bag 102902, North Shore Mail Centre, Auckland 10*

In India: Please write to *Penguin Books India Pvt Ltd, 706 Eros Apartments, 56 Nehru Place, New Delhi 110 019*

In the Netherlands: Please write to *Penguin Books Netherlands bv, Postbus 3507, NL-1001 AH Amsterdam*

In Germany: Please write to *Penguin Books Deutschland GmbH, Metzlerstrasse 26, 60594 Frankfurt am Main*

In Spain: Please write to *Penguin Books S. A., Bravo Murillo 19, 1° B, 28015 Madrid*

In Italy: Please write to *Penguin Italia s.r.l., Via Felice Casati 20, I–20124 Milano*

In France: Please write to *Penguin France S. A., 17 rue Lejeune, F–31000 Toulouse*

In Japan: Please write to *Penguin Books Japan, Ishikiribashi Building, 2–5–4, Suido, Bunkyo-ku, Tokyo 112*

In Greece: Please write to *Penguin Hellas Ltd, Dimocritou 3, GR–106 71 Athens*

In South Africa: Please write to *Longman Penguin Southern Africa (Pty) Ltd, Private Bag X08, Bertsham 2013*

PENGUIN AUDIOBOOKS

Crime and Punishment by Fyodor Dostoyevsky, read by Alex Jennings

Middlemarch by George Eliot, read by Harriet Walter

Silas Marner by George Eliot, read by Tim Pigott-Smith

The Great Gatsby by F. Scott Fitzgerald, read by Marcus D'Amico

Madame Bovary by Gustave Flaubert, read by Claire Bloom

Jude the Obscure by Thomas Hardy, read by Samuel West

The Return of the Native by Thomas Hardy, read by Steven Pacey

Tess of the D'Urbervilles by Thomas Hardy, read by Eleanor Bron

The Iliad by Homer, read by Derek Jacobi

Dubliners by James Joyce, read by Gerard McSorley

The Dead and Other Stories by James Joyce, read by Gerard McSorley

On the Road by Jack Kerouac, read by David Carradine

Sons and Lovers by D. H. Lawrence, read by Paul Copley

The Fall of the House of Usher by Edgar Allan Poe, read by Andrew Sachs

Wide Sargasso Sea by Jean Rhys, read by Jane Lapotaire and Michael Kitchen

The Little Prince by Antoine de Saint-Exupéry, read by Michael Maloney

Frankenstein by Mary Shelley, read by Richard Pasco

Of Mice and Men by John Steinbeck, read by Gary Sinise

Travels with Charley by John Steinbeck, read by Gary Sinise

The Pearl by John Steinbeck, read by Hector Elizondo

Dr Jekyll and Mr Hyde by Robert Louis Stevenson, read by Jonathan Hyde

Kidnapped by Robert Louis Stevenson, read by Robbie Coltrane

The Age of Innocence by Edith Wharton, read by Kerry Shale

The Buccaneers by Edith Wharton, read by Dana Ivey

Mrs Dalloway by Virginia Woolf, read by Eileen Atkins

READ MORE IN PENGUIN

A CHOICE OF CLASSICS

Honoré de Balzac	**The Black Sheep**
	César Birotteau
	The Chouans
	Cousin Bette
	Eugénie Grandet
	A Harlot High and Low
	Lost Illusions
	A Murky Business
	Old Goriot
	Selected Short Stories
	Ursule Mirouet
	The Wild Ass's Skin
J. A. Brillat-Savarin	**The Physiology of Taste**
Marquis de Custine	**Letters from Russia**
Pierre Corneille	**The Cid/Cinna/The Theatrical Illusion**
Alphonse Daudet	**Letters from My Windmill**
René Descartes	**Discourse on Method and Other**
Denis Diderot	**Writings**
	Jacques the Fatalist
	The Nun
	Rameau's Nephew/D'Alembert's Dream
Gustave Flaubert	**Selected Writings on Art and Literature**
	Bouvard and Pecuchet
	Madame Bovary
	Sentimental Education
	The Temptation of St Anthony
	Three Tales
Victor Hugo	**Les Misérables**
	Notre-Dame of Paris
Laclos	**Les Liaisons Dangereuses**
La Fontaine	**Selected Fables**
Madame de Lafayette	**The Princesse de Clèves**
Lautréamont	**Maldoror and Poems**

READ MORE IN PENGUIN

A CHOICE OF CLASSICS

Molière	**The Misanthrope/The Sicilian/Tartuffe/A Doctor in Spite of Himself/The Imaginary Invalid**
	The Miser/The Would-be Gentleman/That Scoundrel Scapin/Love's the Best Doctor/Don Juan
Michel de Montaigne	**Essays**
Marguerite de Navarre	**The Heptameron**
Blaise Pascal	**Pensées**
	The Provincial Letters
Abbé Prevost	**Manon Lescaut**
Rabelais	**The Histories of Gargantua and Pantagruel**
Racine	**Andromache/Britannicus/Berenice**
	Iphigenia/Phaedra/Athaliah
Arthur Rimbaud	**Collected Poems**
Jean-Jacques Rousseau	**The Confessions**
	A Discourse on Inequality
	Emile
Jacques Saint-Pierre	**Paul and Virginia**
Madame de Sevigné	**Selected Letters**
Stendhal	**Lucien Leuwen**
	Scarlet and Black
	The Charterhouse of Parma
Voltaire	**Candide**
	Letters on England
	Philosophical Dictionary
Emile Zola	**L'Assomoir**
	La Bête Humaine
	The Debacle
	The Earth
	Germinal
	Nana
	Thérèse Raquin

BY THE SAME AUTHOR

The Misanthrope and Other Plays

Translated by John Wood

Molière himself said of *The Misanthrope* 'I cannot improve on it and assuredly never shall' – a verdict which time has confirmed. It is his acknowledged masterpiece, one of the supreme achievements of the European theatre, a play which renews its fascination for each generation. With it in this volume are two works of almost equal reputation – *Tartuffe*, a play with a stirring history which has long enjoyed success in the box office, and *The Imaginary Invalid*, the great comedy of doctors and patients in which Molière turned his own hypochondria and real sufferings to comic account. For good measure there are also included *A Doctor in Spite of Himself*, one of the best known of the farces, and a charming comedy-ballet *The Sicilian*.

The five plays are commended to the general reader, amateurs of the theatre, actors, and producers as classics which still come vividly to life in reading and performance.